Praise for Rebecca Raisin

'I absolutely fell in love with this totally heartwarming tale, written by a booklover for booklovers everywhere! . . . Utterly fabulous – if I could give it more than five stars, I would!' Jaimie Admans, author of *The Beekeeper at Elderflower Grove*

'I always feel like I've been on holiday when I read a Rebecca Raisin book . . . another fantastic read from one of my favourite authors.' Portia MacIntosh, author of *Faking it*

'I enjoyed it so much! . . . This summer's go-to for every bookworm.' Jane Linfoot, author of *The Little Cornish Kitchen*

'The perfect romantic comedy for bookworms and library lovers everywhere!' Annie Lyons, author of *Eudora Honeysett Is Quite Well, Thank You*

'I absolutely did not want this book to end . . . If you love books and libraries and stories about people starting over, you will love *Elodie's Library of Second Chances*.' *The French Village Diaries*

'A gorgeous love letter to libraries . . . There is something so magical about a Rebecca Raisin book; they always have this incredible ability to fill your heart with so much happiness and joy.' *Romance by the Book*

REBECCA RAISIN writes heartwarming romance from her home in sunny Perth, Australia. Her heroines tend to be on the quirky side and her books are usually set in exotic locations so her readers can armchair travel any day of the week. The only downfall about writing about gorgeous heroes who have brains as well as brawn, is falling in love with them – just as well they're fictional. Rebecca aims to write characters you can see yourself being friends with. People with big hearts who care about relationships and believe in true, once-in-a-lifetime love. Her bestselling novel *Rosie's Travelling Tea Shop* has been optioned for film with MRC studios and Frolic Media.

Also by Rebecca Raisin

Christmas at the Gingerbread Café
Chocolate Dreams at the Gingerbread Café
The Bookshop on the Corner
Christmas Wedding at the Gingerbread Café
Secrets at Maple Syrup Farm
The Little Bookshop on the Seine
The Little Antique Shop under the Eiffel Tower
The Little Perfume Shop off the Champs-Élysées
Celebrations and Confetti at Cedarwood Lodge
Brides and Bouquets at Cedarwood Lodge
Midnight and Mistletoe at Cedarwood Lodge
Rosie's Travelling Tea Shop
Aria's Travelling Book Shop
Escape to Honeysuckle Hall
Flora's Travelling Christmas Shop
Elodie's Library of Second Chances
The Little Venice Bookshop

Summer at the Santorini Bookshop

REBECCA RAISIN

ONE PLACE. MANY STORIES

HQ
An imprint of HarperCollins*Publishers* Ltd
1 London Bridge Street
London SE1 9GF

www.harpercollins.co.uk

HarperCollins*Publishers*
Macken House, 39/40 Mayor Street Upper,
Dublin 1 D01 C9W8

This paperback edition 2024

24 25 26 27 28 LBC 5 4 3 2 1
First published in Great Britain by
HQ, an imprint of HarperCollins*Publishers* Ltd 2024

ISBN (UK): 9780008559397
ISBN (US): 9780008670115

Printed and bound in the United States

Joan and Zorba Radis.
For those magical Fremantle days where anything seemed
possible and there was always an adventure on the
horizon. Those times are forever in my heart.

Chapter 1

It's impossible to mistake the bark of new CEO Hank Johnson of Hollywood Films. He doesn't so much talk as snarl, or (if you're particularly unlucky) snaps and spits like he's some kind of military man ordering his lackadaisical troops about. My cubicle is on the other side of the foyer to his office, and I swear the floor vibrates in time with the less than politically correct recriminations he's been bellowing at staff since his arrival yesterday.

I'm not going to lie, I'm quaking in my boots. Confrontation is not my thing, especially when I'm facing a six-foot, bald-headed sweary pants who doesn't seem to care that this sort of behaviour went out in the Noughties.

We have rights, dammit. But I'm not going to be the one to tell him.

This is Hollywood. AKA Holly*weird*. A universe unto itself.

A year ago, I landed the perfect job as a book scout; a feat really that I – quiet achiever – managed to get myself hired in Tinseltown after a decade in various publishing houses back in NYC.

Here, I spend most days reading manuscripts in the hopes I'll find the perfect romantic comedy to adapt into film. It's a bibliophile's dream but, as always, it's the people peopling around me that take the shine off.

1

There are so many big personalities in showbiz; it's intense for someone who prefers the comfort of the written word to, say, actual conversations with living, breathing humans. But I am passionate about finding those hidden gems: the books that don't shout the loudest, yet have the most beautiful message and a story worth sharing, so I persist.

Work was going swimmingly until my fabulously old-school Hollywood boss Gene announced he'd up and sold the business.

Enter stage left: Hank.

A potty-mouthed pedant who spent his first day telling us all how useless we are and that big, devastating changes are coming our way. Yikes. For someone who suffers with anxiety and is socially awkward at the best of times, this kind of remonstrating has been enough to send me into a tailspin. My inner critic is already quite proficient at negative self-talk, so he really doesn't need to admonish me further.

Are we useless though? Am *I* useless? This has been running in a loop in my mind since yesterday. It doesn't take much for me to sink into this kind of self-doubt and get stuck there. The only thing that pulls me out of such funks is reading. Nose in a book, the real world slips away and, best of all, I get to call it work.

'EVA!'

The internal walls shake at the same rate my hands do. Penelope, one of his personal assistants pokes her head in my door, her expression fraught. 'That's you, Evie. He's calling you.'

'Right.' Of course, I knew it was me, but at times of high stress, I shut off and pretend to be invisible. I'm guessing this coping mechanism won't work with Hank Johnson.

Penelope darts a worried glance over her shoulder as if Hank might pop up behind her. 'He wants to see you in his office, like five minutes ago.'

'Coming, coming.' I shuffle my proposals together, not quite sure what to have at hand.

'Don't worry about all that. Just hurry!' Penelope says.

I shuffle, half-run and try not to let fear show on my face. It doesn't help when everyone shoots me looks of abject pity. Do they know something I don't? I feel an overwhelming sense of impending doom, which might be my anxiety or a premonition of what's to come. Hard to tell.

At the shiny double doors, I take a moment to compose myself. Tuck an always stray hair behind my ear and—

'Where the hell is she?'

Heart galloping, I knock. 'Sir, Mr Johnson, it's me, Evie. Hi!' Tentatively, I peek around the door.

'I don't have all day, Eva! Get in here and shut the door!'

A headache looms from all his thundering but I duly enter and sit in the chair in front of his vast desk, clasping my shaky hands together so he doesn't clock my nervousness.

'Right so, let me see here.' He dons specs as he reads a sheet of paper. 'Book scout, eh? One of three hired by Hollywood Films.'

'Yes, sir, I—'

Hank holds a meaty palm in the air that implies I should stop talking. That's fine by me.

'OK, so you've been here a year. Relocated from New York. Already have two films in development. Romantic comedies.' And with that he drops the piece of paper as if it's downright offended him. 'Well, as you can imagine, Eva . . .'

'It's Evie.'

'Don't interrupt.'

What century have I astro-travelled to?

He leans back on his chair with a creak and places his hands across the wide expanse of his generous belly. 'We're taking a more streamlined approach now that I'm at the helm. Romantic comedies, yeah they've had their time, but that time has been and gone. We're going to focus on superhero films – that's where the money is. As of now, your position is redundant, Eva.'

My mouth falls open. This can't be happening! 'Redundant?

Sir, it's just that we've seen the profitability of romantic comedies and bringing those . . .'

'This isn't up for debate.'

I float inside myself wondering how I can convince him that I love this job, and I work hard at it. I muster all my courage to fight for those stories that I believe in. 'Mr Johnson, I understand that you're making this decision based on numbers alone, but if you'll allow me to present you a proposal I've been . . .'

'No need. It's been decided.'

I eye the stapler on his desk and have a brief fantasy about fastening his lips together so I can finish at least one bloody sentence, but common sense prevails. 'These stories *matter*! Sure, superhero films will be blockbusters at the box office, but romance isn't dead, sir. Far from it! Every single romcom Hollywood Films has developed has been profitable.'

'Clear your desk and leave your security pass.' Spittle flies from his mouth.

Just like that? 'Ah, before I go . . . the redundancy, does it come with some kind of fiscal remuneration?' At least that might keep the wolf from the door for a bit while I internally combust over the loss of my dream job.

'*You're* redundant. It's not a redun*dancy*. Words matter. You of all people should know that.'

'But that's not—'

With that, Penelope reappears, face pinched. 'It's OK,' she whispers as she pulls me, in my now semi-catatonic state, out of the office and deposits me back in my teeny cubicle.

Eyes glazed I say, 'I'm fired?'

'Redundant.'

That bloody word! It's so hurtful, as if my skills are so basic that my job just went ahead and dried itself up, *poof*, gone!

'Is he firing everyone?'

With a slight shake of the head, she says, 'So far just you.'

'Right.'

4

'But it's only mid-morning. I'm sure lots of us will be sent packing soon enough.'

'It's a small comfort, Pen.' I will myself to *think*. Is there any way I can salvage this job, even if horrible Hank is running the place? I feel protective towards the manuscripts that sit patiently on my desk and in my inbox. I'm their voice. What happens to them now?

Penelope gives me a hopeful smile. 'You're better off, seriously. Can you imagine working for this brute? There's not enough cabernet sauvignon in all of Napa to handle this kind of stress.' The industry, as it's known, really is not for the faint of heart.

I expel a breath. 'This was going to be the making of me. Gene said so! He promised me that if I picked up and moved from my safe little literary bubble in New York to the bright lights of Hollywood, my career would grow exponentially.' Gene and I met when I edited his memoir. It went on to be a worldwide bestseller with readers who were keen to peek behind the curtain of Hollywood. He claimed I had an eye for a compelling tale and soon after offered me the book scout position.

'Gene sold the place, Evie. We can't sit here lamenting his choice.'

'Can't we?' I'm very good at lamenting. In fact, I can sit on this for days, weeks and not get over it. I can obsess over it until it steals into my dreams, wondering where it all went so wrong.

Penelope gives me a maternal smile. 'I'll be sad to see you go, Evie. You're the best book scout we've ever had. Two films are already in development because of you!' She gives me an encouraging smile. 'You'll find a better job than this! You just need to get out there and network a bit.' Networking, such a buzz word in this biz. 'Flash that dazzling smile of yours. Light up a room.'

I can't quite imagine myself lighting up a room, I'm a *lot* more low-wattage than that. In fact, at work functions I field requests for drinks as if they assume I'm the waitstaff. Penelope says it's because I slink rather than saunter. I hover awkwardly whereas my colleagues make entrances worthy of the red carpet. Is this why I'm the scapegoat today? They have to cut expenditure, so they're clearing the decks with the quiet ones they assume won't make a fuss?

'I'll stick with fictional people thanks. Isn't my job about finding books to develop into film? Why do "people" have to come into the equation at all?' Therein lies the root of all my problems. Peopling.

She sighs and pats my shoulder. 'It's the way of the world, dear. What will you do now?'

'That's the million-dollar question.' Penelope gives me a warm hug, which I allow since I'm now redundant and at an all-time low.

After I pack my belongings, I consider how to frame this in a text to my mom. My all-star sister never finds herself entrenched in disasters like this. Posy is an ambitious singer/actress and well-known Broadway celeb. Will Mom secretly compare me to her and find me lacking? Gah. I can't catch a break no matter what I do. In the end I go for a succinct message because crying at work would catch attention I'd rather not have.

Hey, Mom. I'm no longer a romance book scout at Hollywood Films. E xoxo

As I'm carting my lucky bamboo (perhaps I didn't talk to it enough?) from the building my phone pings.

Darling, sorry to hear this! I'm working away on a case but I'll be home tomorrow. We can video-chat then. Chin up. Love Mom xoxo

I'll drown my sorrows with an espresso Frappuccino that will keep me awake all night so I can count the ways I've failed. And when Mom's home tomorrow I'll video-call my support team; that's what I'll do. Mom'll smother me in love and sympathy knowing this is just a blip . . . and Posy will highlight my flaws and tell me just where I went wrong.

6

Chapter 2

The next day a grainy orangey blur appears on screen, like the surface of Venus. Mom's holding the phone to her ear even though it's a video call. Honestly, the woman never learns. Still, I press on and tell them the latest in the Chronicles of Evie.

'Fired!' my sister Posy screeches. 'Did you pretend to be invisible again? I've told you a billion times they assume that you're *shirking* when you behave like that.'

Talk about exaggeration. 'A *billion* times, Posy? Be real.'

So, I've found it hard to assimilate in new environments. Mostly because I don't like the whole talking around the watercooler thing. I avoid people, which in a work setting can be misconstrued. *You're not a team player, Evie.* Why can't I work in a team of one? It's a lot more efficient for starters.

'Mom, hold the phone in front of your face for crying out loud. If you can't see us, we can't see you!' Posy admonishes from behind her laptop. We've clashed since childhood because Posy is bossy and opinionated, but I don't take it personally; she's just one of those larger-than-life types, whereas I'd much rather hide in the shadows.

I gather my wits. How best to explain this latest rejection? 'Well, I wasn't *exactly* fired, I was . . .'

7

'Oh, *there* you are!' Mom says, just like she does every video call, as if seeing us on screen is a marvel she will never quite get used to.

'Hi, Mom,' I give her a little wave. 'As I was . . .'

'There could be a silver lining to this dismissal,' Posy rushes on, cutting my sentence short. 'Evie can help with the Gran fiasco! We can have feet on the ground in Santorini and find out what's *really* going on with that crazy woman!'

Santorini?

'I told you, I wasn't fired! I was made redundant. It's different!' Honestly, are they even listening? 'And Gran is not crazy. She's a . . . free spirit.'

They ignore me and continue talking over the top of each other as if I'm not even there. Usually that suits me just fine, but not today when I need some good old-fashioned comforting. They ramble on about the many times wayward Gran has got herself in a pickle and how *this* time she's gone too far. What have I missed? It's true, I've been avoiding the family group chats, but only because there are books that need reading and it is, *was*, my job. And my family is dramatic, to say the least – there's always some conspiracy that needs solving and I find it a tad monotonous.

'STOP!' I yell, drawing wide eyes from them. I'm not a yeller. 'What Gran fiasco are you talking about? I thought she was cruising the Greek isles?'

Mom heaves a sigh. 'She was. Until she stepped off the ship in Santorini a month ago, fell in love with a local, *married* him and took over the running of his business, or some silly thing.'

'Gran got married? Again!' I count back in my mind. Is this husband eight or nine? The last one, Henry, went missing off a boat under suspicious circumstances. Before him was Zhang Chen, a wealthy investor and ice-climbing aficionado. He met his untimely death taking a selfie and fell backwards into a crevasse because his belay wasn't clipped in. We were all relieved when

Gran gave up ice climbing after that. Terribly dangerous, especially at her advanced age.

'Yep married. Husband number nine! And . . .' Posy does jazz hands '. . . Gran also got arrested!' Her eyes twinkle with the scandal of it all. 'But not on the same day.'

I gasp. 'What! Arrested for what?' Did they find Henry at the bottom of the South China Sea?

Mom scrubs her face as if the memory pains her. Gran sure is a wild one. 'Early this morning she got arrested for disturbing the peace but got let off with a warning. *Allegedly* she had a disagreement with the landlord, and you know Gran. Why speak if she can *yell* to get her point across? Now they've put restraining orders on each other, so how they'll manage to do business is beyond me . . .'

'You have to rescue her from herself, Evie. She's in a foreign country. God knows who she's married or what's really going on,' Posy pleads. 'I know you think Gran is this sassy, vivacious powerhouse but, in reality, she's going a bit doolally. You need to make her see sense and bring her home.'

I scoff. 'This is Gran we're talking about! There's no chance of me convincing her if she doesn't want to come.'

Mom presses an eye up close to the screen, which is downright terrifying. 'Use your wiles.'

'What wiles?' Posy says. 'Evie isn't exactly the persuading sort. She'll probably be there a week before she works up the courage to announce her arrival.'

I roll my eyes. 'So? Unlike you Posy, not all of us like to be the centre of attention.'

I belong to a family of overachieving extroverts. Just once I'd have liked to succeed, the way they all do effortlessly. Posy is on Broadway and has the ego to match. My dad is a famous divorce lawyer who handles high-profile celebrity splits. And Mom's supposed to be semi-retired, but we'll be prying a yellow legal pad out of her cold dead hands before she gives up litigating. Her firm is her life.

'Right, you don't like being the centre of attention, so with that in mind, you're going to have to be *fierce* with a capital F when you get to the island. Convince Gran to stop messing about,' Posy says. 'We don't want her having another altercation with this landlord guy. A Greek jail is no joke.'

So much for being smothered in love and sympathy over the loss of my dream job. I don't have time to rescue Gran, who I know will most certainly not *need* any rescuing, unless it's from her own family. I need to find another job and fast. Zero-bed apartments in LA do not come cheap. And book scout jobs are almost impossible to find. Yet now I'm being forced on a mercy mission. This is so typical of my family and our dynamic.

'I can't go to Santorini. I have a life here, you know.' OK that's a lie but I'm working on it (if that includes reading about fictional people with complex relationship woes). 'Gran's a formidable woman. I don't get why you insist on intruding into her life like this.'

'Please. I'll pay for your flight. It's the least I can do,' Mom says. 'Gran's too old to be running around a sun-drenched bookshop, pandering to tourists. You know what her knees are like.'

Wait, what? 'A bookshop?'

'Keep up, Evie!' Posy says, exasperation in her voice. 'Gran's new husband has a little bookshop perched on some cliff, which she's apparently spent the last month renovating. Picture her up on a ladder painting. She's one step away from a fall that will break her hip – or worse, her head! Although, I suppose it could knock some sense into that melon of hers . . .'

Well, well, well. Perhaps I could relinquish my frightfully expensive zero-bed apartment lease and stay with Gran for a bit. There could be worse places to cool my heels than a sun-drenched clifftop bookshop on a Greek island while I figure out what to do about my job prospects. 'Book me a ticket then, Mom. I'll go and see what all the fuss is about.'

Chapter 3

I arrive in Santorini having lost all track of time, head fuzzy from the last-minute scramble of packing up my LA life and getting on a plane in the next breath. I'm a knot of anxiety, but I'm hoping that'll ease when I see my gran in the flesh.

Suitcase in hand, I spot a driver holding a sign bearing my name – Mom to the rescue, planning my journey with military precision. Handy when you're not the most adventurous traveller, like myself.

Once it's obvious I don't speak Greek, he motions for me to follow him. We find the car and get going. There's no time to check out the view because we move like the speed of light and everything is a supersonic blur.

The driver doesn't say much, which is probably a good thing because I'm white-knuckled as he takes each bend as if he's a rally car driver, all the while gazing at the azure of the sea and not the road itself. I picture my imminent death, kamikazeing into the deep blue as the car explodes, because my demise wouldn't be cinematic without a fireball of some sort. And if I'm to die young, it better be bloody spectacular.

We pass a sign announcing the upcoming Megalochori traditional village. At least that's what I hope it says as we hurtle past.

What I've learned from my very hasty research into Gran's latest choice of abode is that Megalochori is located on the south-west side of the island, about seven kilometres from Fira, the capital of Santorini. It's a winemaking region, which might come in handy after this car ride of doom.

What feels like a lifetime later, he pulls to a stop, gravel crunching and dust rising. No matter that I'm wearing white jeans, I grab my suitcase and launch myself at the volcanic-y soil, never happier to see ground beneath my feet than I am right this moment.

'Thank you, Aphrodite! Persephone! Artemis! All the goddesses. I'M ALIVE!' The tension leaves my body with a whoosh. It's not often you have a second chance at life and arriving here not dead is a huge adrenaline rush after that nail-biter of a ride.

Without so much as a goodbye, the driver is up on two wheels as he burns rubber on his way back to wherever nightmares are made.

Standing up, I pat myself down, thrilled that every appendage is where it's meant to be. My self-analysis is interrupted by a chorus of two very animated voices. Their heated argument sounds incongruous in a place where the rocky cliffs fall away to the breathtaking blue of the Aegean Sea.

I walk towards the noise, recognising Gran's strident voice shouting Greek words like bullets. Since when did Gran learn another language? She is a woman of many talents, that's for sure. The wily fox probably picked it up easily over the last month or so.

By a blinding-white building, I spot her, dressed fabulously in a colourful caftan, wearing a full face of make-up and blingy OTT jewellery. She's flamboyant, like a bird of paradise, which is why everyone flocks to her.

Inexplicably, the younger guy standing opposite her doesn't seem to be under her spell. Curious. In fact, he looks downright irritated from the way he's gesticulating and scrubbing his face as if she's pushed his very last button.

A thought hits. *Please don't let that be her husband and this is some sort of lover's tiff!* He's got to be my age, or a touch older, and it would be grossly unfair if this eighty-three-year-old is pulling the likes of him when I can't even get my fictional book boyfriends to commit.

Gran takes control of the conversation again and goes ballistic. I'm no expert on the language of Greece but part of me wonders if she's partaking in a bit of coinage. Are they in fact words, or just an angry mix of letters set to bamboozle him? Did I mention she can be crafty when she wants to be? Still, she's my gran and I must protect her at all costs. Posy's advice springs to mind: *Be fierce with a capital F.*

While confrontation is not my thing, I've been sent on a mission, and I am nothing if not a steadfast comrade. You want fierce, you've got fierce, even if my knees knock while doing so. But just how to convey this to Mr Scrub-his-face when I don't speak the language?

Look ferocious? Make a growling sound! A two-handed chest-push. No, it would be just my luck he'd fall off the cliff and land in a bloody mess, appendages akimbo and then we'd have to hide the body. Not worth the hassle.

I go for the storming-over, hands-on-hips angle. '*Excuse me! How dare you speak to this little old lady in such a manner. You should be ashamed of yourself!*'

He turns to me; confusion slips over his features before he breaks into a slow smile. Did he not translate my meaning from the velocity of that delivery? I widen my baby blues and channel a fierceness from within, but it doesn't quite surface. He's sort of disarming what with his Greek god looks and soulful seductive eyes. If he is Gran's husband, she has really hit the jackpot, the lucky thing.

Honestly, all her husbands have been stunners. Well, except my own granddad, husband numero uno, who had the unfortunate luck of being born with a face that looked like he'd had an

13

altercation with a pot of hot soup. According to Gran he was a squat, square man with nary a happy bone in his body. I can't say for sure since I never met him myself. Tragically, he died young, after a mix-up with some antifreeze.

'Evie! What on earth—' Gran says, her face softening as she takes me in for a hug. 'I take it the Fun Police heard about the arrest and they've sent you to do their bidding?'

'That they did,' I confirm. 'They know about the whole abandoning the cruise ship thing. The quickie marriage. Something about you up a ladder and a broken hip, the list goes on. Coincidentally, I was made redundant – so here I am!'

Gran gives my shoulders a squeeze. 'I'm sorry about your job, darling, but I'm not sorry that you're here.'

The Greek god clears his throat, probably in readiness to start yelling again. I'd almost forgotten about him. He hasn't even apologised to her yet.

'Give me a minute here with Georgios, who is intent on stealing my newly married glow.'

'Georgios is your . . . ?'

'My landlord Yannis' grandson. He's been sent in lieu of Yannis since we're now forbidden to cross paths after the whole disturbing the peace debacle. Georgios is delivering a message from Yannis, who claims I've made his life a roller skate. Can you even believe that?'

'No, what does that mean?'

She waves me away. 'Oh, Greek people have the most amazing expressions. It's akin to saying I've made his life hell. And apparently, I've "broken his nerves", AKA irritated him. Anyway, take your things and follow the pebbled pathway. You'll see a little Cycladic guest villa out the back. Settle in and I'll be right along.'

'OK.' I give Georgios the side-eye, not sure I can trust him around my gran. Yeah sure, she's not a shrinking violet, but you never know what a person's blood pressure is doing and Gran

14

isn't exactly a spring chicken. 'If you're sure—' I make a thumb at the guy '—he's not going to start bothering you again.'

He lets out a long sigh as if I'm testing his patience. 'I'm simply passing on a message from my grandfather,' he says in perfect English. American-accented English. Interesting! 'Honestly, I'd rather be anywhere but here, so if we can just sort out the issue, I'll be on my way.' He turns back to Gran and speaks in rapid-fire Greek, to which she shakes her head.

It's sort of entrancing watching him slip between the two languages effortlessly. Why is Gran not using English? Perhaps she's trying to fit in, be respectful learning the local language. There's something about the guy that is so familiar and I can't quite put my finger on it. Ah! Got it. Georgios is the epitome of tall, dark and handsome, with his symmetrical, sun-kissed features and athletic physique.

I've magicked up the perfect male lead for a romantic comedy. I must be missing my job. I *know* I'm missing my job. And how can I not think of swoony heroes when I've got this specimen standing in a power pose with a stunning blue backdrop, the salty sea breeze tickling my skin. It's the same sort of prickling sensation I get when I discover a book ripe for development. A sort of heady wooziness that screams: *This is the one!*

But that sort of thought process is strictly for fiction-land, and this is reality, so I give him one last glare for good measure, so he understands we will not be bullied. Instead of returning such a look, which is the way these things are supposed to go, he smiles, his eyes twinkling with mirth. Is he trying to wind me up? An intimidation tactic? Whatever his angle is, I must do my best to appear unruffled when I'm really rather ruffled by him.

'Georgios. I'm going to unpack my things but just so you know, I happen to have exceptional hearing and first-hand experience at making things *disappear*, if you get my drift.' OK, I don't but that does sound rather menacing and that's the character arc I'm going for.

He gives me an infuriating grin that could be construed as a touch maniacal. Maybe he's not romcom material after all. More likely to be the hot spy who double-crosses his hot spy girlfriend even though she really loves him, despite it being unwise to do so. She soon learns the hard way when her parachute doesn't open . . .

Georgios has the audacity to salute me, which *is* rather spy-like. I must keep my wits about me here in sunny Santorini.

I kiss Gran's pillowy cheek and stride off, concentrating on pulling my shoulders back so I look like I have the strength to heft a dead weight without breaking a sweat. I must admit I feel a buzz at how well I faced up to such a confrontation. Posy would be proud.

I fetch my suitcase and find the guest villa. It's gorgeous; dome-shaped with curved walls like it grew right out of the volcanic earth itself. It's independent from the main house with a stunning view of the sea. I unpack my things and plan to take a quick shower to wash the long journey from my skin.

When I see my reflection in the bathroom mirror, I groan. My nose is blackened from kissing the volcanic earth. That's why Georgios was grinning like a mad fool! Why would Gran not have mentioned it? Urgh. But what does it matter? It's not as though I care about Georgios. Here's hoping he won't continue to darken our door after I made my intentions abundantly clear.

I'm desperate to seek out the bookshop, but with the intensity of packing up my apartment and then rushing to catch trains, planes, and automobiles, life fatigue has caught up with me. Each passing minute slows my synapses down as sleep beckons.

On the bedside table is a card with a Wi-Fi code. I plonk on the bed and punch the numbers into my phone. It only takes point four of a second to realise my mistake as my message alerts go haywire. The Fun Police want an update. I skim their many texts and flick to the latest one from Mom.

16

Did you arrive at Gran's? I can't get hold of you or your driver. If you're safely ensconced, why the heck haven't you called? If not, I'm sorry and I'll do my best to find you if you've been taken! How is Gran? Talked any sense into her yet? Mom xoxo

Gran never did say what her confrontation with Georgios was about. Curiouser.

I'm alive and well, no thanks to the driver who thinks moving at the speed of light is too slow. Alas, I'm still kicking and so is Gran. Have seen her in the flesh and she's as fabulous as ever. Just settling in now with major jet lag. Life lag. Gran is happy and healthy. Evie xoxo

There's no point worrying Mom and the gang about Georgios' visit until I have some more details. Once I've had Gran's explanation, I can decide what to feed back to the family. They behave a little theatrically when it comes to Gran's adventures. The woman subscribes to a lifestyle that is so outrageous and carefree that part of me wonders if they're trying to clip her wings because she doesn't fit into the same mould as them.

With a fortifying breath, I go outside to see Gran heading towards me, her face pinched. 'What was all that about?' I ask. 'Why is that family picking on a defenceless little woman like you?'

'Defenceless!' At that she cackles like a witch, making her seem the very opposite of defenceless. 'They've increased the rent after the renovations and I'm refusing to pay – that's all, darling. I guess with me being fresh off the cruise ship, they think I'm an easy target.'

The no-good money grabbers! I'm outraged. 'They're trying to increase your rent after *you* paid and did all the renovations? How is that fair after you've improved their property?'

She throws up her hands. 'Don't you worry, darling. I won't let them extort me. They've picked the wrong coffin dodger.

17

If they think they're getting an extra euro out of me they're sorely mistaken.'

I shake my head. 'Where's your paramour then?'

'Konstantine.' She sighs. 'Well, it's a long story. Let me get you an ouzo and we can chat.'

I climb under the covers while I wait for Gran to return. I give myself an imaginary pat on the back for surviving the chaos of the last twenty-fours, *sans* panic attack, or pills – progress.

Chapter 4

The next morning, I'm up bright and early, refreshed after a long sleep. I go to the main villa and call out for Gran, but there's no sign of her or Konstantine. Last night we didn't have the intended big chat because I fell asleep and she must've left me to it, having pulled the blanket up to my chin and switched the light off.

Gran's abode is cool and immaculately decorated in maximalist style. Just like her, it's colourful and homely, with all sorts of weird and wacky items on display. She's not here so I head back outside to find the bookshop. Perhaps she's getting a head start on the workday? I hope there's coffee at hand. I'd could murder a cup and breakfast wouldn't go astray either.

The door to the bookshop is unlocked and creaks a welcome as I push it open. Inside is deliciously cool as I step on blue mosaic tiles. The walls are a bumblebee yellow and contrast nicely against the white stone archways that separate each room. Fuchsia pink bougainvillea creeps through open windows, as if trying to escape the heat outside.

The showstopper is the books themselves. Gran has them arranged in colour blocks, like a rainbow from red, orange, yellow, green, blue, indigo to violet. The bold, bright visual is complemented by the view of the never-ending sea outside. Cane peacock-style chairs with textured throw rugs are dotted around the space, just waiting for a reader to visit. There's a spearmint green and white striped hammock swaying the breeze by a window, whispering my name.

A step down leads to a beautiful, faded teal door with an intricate wrought-iron gate that is so delicate it almost looks like lace. I try to open it, but it's locked.

'Darling! I've found you at last,' Gran says, making me jump in fright.

'You scared the bejesus out of me.' I turn to find her dolled up in a shimmery white dress that sparkles in the sunlight. She's wearing pair of cat-eye-shaped sunglasses and a wide-brimmed hat.

'Sorry, darling. I'm just back from my morning walk to Caldera beach.' She pulls off her hat. 'I've got to see a man about a dog so you're going to have to run the bookshop today. The code for the till is 1111. The fridge in my place is fully stocked so help yourself. Have fun, darling, and we'll catch up for sunset cocktails this evening, OK? You're a gem.'

The stop-out goes to leave, but I grab her elbow before she can escape. 'Wait, wait, wait. You have to see a man about a dog? Where's Konstantine? Can't he run this place?'

Panic mode is activated.

'No, he's away at the moment. I have a lot on my plate right now, and there's some finessing that needs to be done. Mind the fort. I'll be back in a jiffy.'

My anxiety ratches up a notch – peopling is one thing, peopling in a foreign language is quite another. 'Gran, wait! I don't speak a word of Greek.'

'Use a translate app.' She rolls her eyes. 'Really, Evie, don't be such a pill. I've got a lot to do, and I'm counting on you to help me out. I promise I'll tell you everything later.' When she lays the guilt trip on thick, I know it's a con.

'Tell me now.' I fold my arms and give her the mother of all stare-downs.

Gran checks her watch and sighs. 'Fine. But you're not to tell your mother about any of this. Deal?'

'As long as it's not illegal.'

I'm met with silence.

'Gran?'

'Of course not!'

Hmm. Doesn't ring true but I let it go. How much trouble could an eighty-three-year-old get up to anyway?

'I'm having a few issues is all, but nothing I need help with. And I don't want the entire *precinct* of the Fun Police arriving to escort me back to safer shores, so you have to keep everything on the quiet.'

'If Mom finds out —' and she's better at investigation than the FBI so there's every chance she will '—then I'll have some explaining to do about why I covered for you. You know she's sent me here for intel.'

'Darling, you have to learn how to manage your mother better. It's your only real downfall.'

'True. It's the way she patiently probes into every little detail and does all those long pauses that a person rushes to fill . . . it's intimidating.'

'A carefully crafted skill she's honed over the years. So, the quick version is: my landlord Yannis has rented the property, including the bookshop and a bar, to my husband Konstantine for years. The seedy drinks area drew a few locals who'd guzzle cheap beer and gamble over card games. The bookshop never did well because Konstantine had given up on it. When we got married, I decided I'd revamp it.'

Gran and her pet projects. They have led to many escapades around the world and always reinvigorate her. 'Go on,' I say as she plonks herself on a stool.

'After the renovations, we reopened the bookshop, having stocked it with new books, in English and Greek, but it was still quiet. The unsightly bar fizzled out and the poker players moved on.

21

That area also needed a facelift, a new direction. A unique idea that would draw people here.'

'Makes sense.'

'This village is a little off the beaten track, which is a crying shame because the view is incomparable. And then it struck me like a bolt of lightning!' She covers her mouth at her gaff. 'Oh, dear. God rest his soul. Ludwig was . . .' Her words peter off as she grapples with her memories.

Gran's sixth husband Ludwig left this mortal coil after being struck by lightning. The man was so incinerated they couldn't even use his teeth to positively identify the body. Investigators closed the case, deeming it a tragic case of wrong place, wrong time.

'. . . a real numbskull.'

I gasp.

'I know, I know. One shouldn't speak ill of the dead, but he dodged the Grim Reaper so many times, I wasn't surprised when it finally found him. Ludwig had all manner of near misses, from that episode with the faulty brakes to the scuba-diving debacle. Don't forget the close call with the helicopter rotor blades that took his ear clean off. I mean, the list goes on . . .'

'None of that came up at the inquest.'

Her eyebrows pull together. 'What inquest, darling?' Gran waves away the reminiscences of husband number six. 'Forget it, he's in a better place.'

'Yeah, I suppose so.' Poor Gran couldn't have predicted a lightning strike or she'd never have sent him into the forest to forage for mushrooms.

'I've got this place all set up to be an exclusive club of sorts . . .' She waggles a devious brow. 'Patrons can pay for membership and can use the facilities and engage with other like-minded people. I'm waiting on some tradespeople to finish a few things and then we're good to go and can have a launch party.'

Oh no, not this again! 'Is this code for sex parties?' I'm on high alert. It's a sex den. A red room. A bondage boudoir. No wonder

22

Gran doesn't want Mom to find out – she'd be scandalised. *I'm* scandalised.

'For goodness' sake, Evie, it's not a kink-fest or whatever risqué thing you're conjuring in that head of yours. That was *one* time back in the Seventies. Two times, if I count that . . . oh never mind. You weren't even born then so I don't know why you're still so shocked about it.'

I blush to the roots of my hair and wish I could teleport myself away. Gran shakes her head as if I'm a prude.

'I'm more into monogamy – that's all.'

'Really. Evie, you're so sensible at times, it kills me.'

'Thanks?' Honestly, she's such a handful.

'Behind these pretty doors, is a literary wonderland called Epeolatry, which means the worship of words. A night-time library, if you will, that will offer literary cocktails and smooth jazz and a veritable treasure trove of reading material from the classics to modern day. Let me show you.'

We go from the bright kaleidoscope of colour, to the drama of a dark academia aesthetic. The space resembles a Gothic library of yesteryear with its mahogany shelves, stacked with hardback books. There are dark leather sofas and emerald-green velvet armchairs with gold gilding.

Draped ruched curtains hide the sunlight, giving the room a moody, mysterious air. It's decadent and luxe. Stone busts sit on plinths, and I bend to read the gold plaques, announcing the names of famous Greek authors. There are small nooks, that lead to hallways full of intrigue. Ornate chandeliers lend the room a warm, filmy illumination. The décor is stunning, as if every detail has been assiduously thought out. There's a bar area, with plush stools lined up neatly in a row.

'Gran, this is incredible. It's like stepping back in time, visiting another era.' The decadent jazz era of the roaring Twenties.

'Isn't it? I spent a bomb to achieve this vision and that's why I need more time to prove its worth.'

'Is this why Yannis wants to put the rent up?' Is that even allowed?

She fiddles with her jangly earrings, a subtle tell she does when she's gearing up to lie. How did I not pick up on this sooner? Blame the jet lag. The life lag that caught up with me on my arrival.

I wait her out, wondering which way she'll go. Truth or bald-faced lie. 'I presume so.' She blushes and gives a loose shrug. 'Yannis thinks I'm rolling in dough, but as you can imagine this level of intricacy does not come cheap. And *everything* doubles in price when you live on an island and need deliveries from the mainland.'

A sinking feeling hits. 'Gran, did you invest your life savings in this place? Or did your husband fund it?'

She drops her gaze. *Oh no.* My mother is going to go nuclear if she hears about this. It's Gran's money though, so she has every right to spend it how she likes. Well, I suppose it's technically the culmination of her bequeathments and life insurance policies from eight husbands, but that's never come up in conversation, which is probably for the best. God rest their souls.

'What's really going on, Gran? Why are Yannis and his grandson Georgios breathing down your neck? Don't give me that claptrap about increasing the rent. I don't buy it.'

She drops the poor little old lady routine just like that. 'OK, OK fine. I lied. The issue is I haven't *exactly* paid the rent. There's no money left. I've tried to explain to them that I need a few months to get back on my feet fiscally and I'll pay them back with interest. But will they have it? No!'

I let out a long sigh. 'This isn't like you. How did you not budget correctly for renovations and your rent?' Gran is as savvy as they come with her finances. This is a mistake she wouldn't usually make.

Is Posy right and Gran is becoming more forgetful? My heart seizes at the thought.

Gran's face falls. 'I did budget, but things got out of hand and before I knew it, it was all gone.'

'Where's your husband in all of this?' A terrible thought hits. 'Is he dead? *Already*?'

She scoffs. 'Why would he be dead, for crying out loud!'

'Well, historically speaking . . .'

'He's on an oil rig. OK? Money's been tight, so we felt that a steady income would help tide us over.'

'An oil rig? How old is he?'

'Seventy.'

I stare her down.

'Sixty.'

I cock my head.

'OK, he's fifty, a very *mature* fifty.'

Really, I shouldn't be surprised. 'Right.' How am I supposed to navigate this mess? Mom will be expecting an intelligence report and I'll have to word it just so, giving breadcrumbs but not the whole loaf.

'They won't throw you into jail for not paying rent, will they?'

Her gaze shifts about the place as if she isn't quite sure how to answer. 'Yannis has threatened that. Says he went to school with the chief of the Hellenic Police or some other nonsense. But I can smell a bluff a mile away.'

I cover my face with my hands. 'What if it's not a bluff? What then?'

'Don't worry, I've got a new plan! One that will buy me some time and get them off my back. Tell you over cocktails.' She air-kisses me and goes to leave.

None of this is good. Just how much money did Gran sink into this place? How much does fancy furniture cost? Maybe it all went on books. Yeah sure, Epeolatry is a haven for literary lovers, but Gran always leaves herself a monetary safety net in case she gets into a bind.

By the door, Gran turns back. 'Oh and a word of warning,

if Georgios appears, be on high alert. Don't let him snoop around. He's likely to take my cherishables as collateral.'

'How am I supposed to fend him off? Should I kick him out?' Knowing my luck *I'll* end up in a Greek jail.

'No, darling! Kill him with kindness.' She gives me a fluttery wave as she shuts the door behind her. How can she be so calm? Will the launch of Epeolatry be enough to keep the wolf from the door? I toy with what to message Mom to keep her off my back.

The bookshop Bibliotherapy is a wonder. Library bar Epeolatry, to launch soon, is a showstopper. Gran's got a few money quibbles, what with the bookshop being on the quiet side of the village, but she's got a new plan that she's going to wow me with later. Husband Konstantine is away working, so that's one less thing to worry about. Gran seems to be enjoying island life, despite a few rocky patches. Evie.

What a muddle this all is, but Gran seems unperturbed, so I let it go for now.

What does a girl have to do to get some food around here . . .

Chapter 5

As usual, the universe provides, but never in the way I want. No sooner has my belly rumbled in protest than he doth appear. The Greek god, holding none other than a fragrant-smelling box of just-baked goodness.

My mouth waters in anticipation, but I cannot, and I will not, yield to the likes of him. I remember Gran's warning to be on high alert, but my resolve crumbles with every step closer he takes. Blame the hunger pangs and Gran's speedy exit this morning. Here I'd been expecting us to breakfast under the soft morning sun with the sea lapping gently in the distance while she caught me up on what exactly has unfolded since she stepped off the cruise ship. Alas, she's MIA, I'm starving, and here *he* is.

'Sorry we got off to a bad start yesterday.' Georgios gives me a warm smile that belies his traitorous heart. I've seen these ploys in romance novels a million times. Does he think this kind of sultry smile will work? Well not on my watch. He's probably scoping the place out for valuables he can sell to recoup their rent money. I can't exactly blame the guy, but I will because Gran told me to.

I pretend to be completely uninterested in him and flip the page of my book, not able to take in a single word with him looming so close and me being so hungry and all.

He lifts the lid and it's all I can do not to jump up and snatch the box from him. The sweet scent of cinnamon and syrup perfumes the balmy air. I must not give in to temptation.

'My grandmother made fresh *loukoumades* especially for you and Floretta this morning. We're sorry things got fraught these last few days.'

I raise a brow and give him a slow once-over, regally like cats do, thus proving I'm completely unimpressed, when I'm anything but. My stomach has a mind of its own and is telling me to dive right in, morals be damned! 'And does your grandmother know that you berated a little old lady over a few euros?' Look at me go, playing the part of indifferent heroine! Does that make him the hero? *This isn't fiction, Evie!*

'Well, it's not exactly . . .'

I hold up a hand. 'Gran told me everything so you can save it. Leave the loukoumades. I won't reject a gift your grandmother has clearly made with love.' If only Posy could see me now! Even she would have to begrudgingly agree that I am a force to be reckoned with.

Georgios hands over the box. 'Wait,' he says and dashes outside to his car.

Time waits for no one, and these bite-sized balls of joy are still warm. I pop one in my mouth, and yes they are what dreams are made of. Pillowy-soft inside, crispy and sweet on the outside. Georgios comes back with two takeout coffees. Got to give the guy credit – he really has put some effort in. If only I could be stronger and send him on his way with an icy glare, and a taut moue. Alas, my body craves nutrients, so here we are.

'Do you like Greek coffee?' he asks as he passes me a cup.

'Is it decaf?'

Georgios shakes his head.

'Then yes.' I take a sip. It's stronger than coffee back home, thicker like it hasn't been filtered. It's a turbo-charged version and I for one, dig it. I can't help feeling a little like he's wooing me.

And that is a problem because I sense it's a devious ploy to get me on-side. The likes of him do not usually woo the likes of me. This isn't some plain Jane, ugly duckling excuse – it's that we're different. Him with his designer sunglasses, massive ego and the way he expects I'll fall at his fancy-leather-moccasin-encased feet. And me, a full-fledged member of Romancelandia who can recognise a plot a mile away.

I remind myself I'm supposed to be 'killing him with kindness' whilst remaining on guard. Really, I don't mind gazing at him over breakfast, while I figure out what his angle is.

'It's quiet.' He motions to the bookshop.

Not one customer so far, but it's early and I presume tourists soon run on island time, their rhythms becoming languid as they settle into summery holidays.

'Exactly. So why don't you and your family give Gran a breather to get this place going and you'll soon have your money paid back, with interest.' All this chit-chat is hard when the loukoumades are begging to be inhaled. I take a delicate bite as I wait for his reply.

He considers it. 'I understand, things have been really tough for her . . .'

'I wouldn't go quite that far. Gran tackles projects like this all the time. OK, yes she gets arrested fairly often, hence the need to move a lot, *or* skedaddle back to her home base in Brooklyn, but that's not the point. The point is, when she has a vision, she brings it to fruition. This little Santorini village is lucky to have her and I know you don't see that yet, but you will. I have every faith she'll put this quiet spot on the map.' Hopefully not for another murder probe, but I keep that to myself.

Georgios frowns, as if he doesn't quite believe me. I get that. He doesn't know Gran and the many feats she's achieved in her remarkable life. 'It's only that my grandfather has bills to pay. Floretta can't expect him to hold off indefinitely and now her husband is gone too. What if this place never gets going? Then what?'

How to convince him that Gran *never* fails. 'You'll have to take my word for it. She has a magic touch when it comes to business. And yes, this predicament isn't ideal, and very out of character for her . . .'

He cuts me off. 'Floretta shouldn't have completed the renovations if she can't pay the bills.'

I can't really argue with that. Why *did* she sink everything into this place without any thought of her rent? 'I'll be sure to pass that on. Now if you don't mind, I've got books that need reading.'

With a shake of the head, he lopes out, taking the box of Greek donuts with him. The monster! I try to sink back into a memoir, *My Family and Other Animals* by Gerald Durrell, but something niggles at me, making it impossible to absorb the printed words on the page. Georgios said: *She can't pay her bills. Plural.*

Was it a figure of speech, or does she owe a lot of people money? As they say in the biz, the math ain't math-ing. Gran isn't the type to rack up debt all over town. She's squeaky clean in that respect. I'll ask her at sunset.

As predicted, customers trickle in as the day heats up, some only to escape the bite of the sun, others to peruse the books on display. I manage to avoid most of them by hiding behind the counter. An elderly man wanders in, smoking a cigar whilst he picks up books and puts them down in different sections, mixing up the colour order Gran has fastidiously kept neat. It's a crime that the pristine new books are clouded in his second-hand smoke! This is going to mean human contact, quite possibly a confrontation. In any other scenario I'd avoid him altogether, but I must be a voice for these precious books who cannot speak for themselves. Gah. 'Excuse me, sir?'

He rakes up a brow. So not one for small talk then? Perhaps he doesn't understand English. I really should have downloaded a translation app like Gran suggested.

'Would you mind smoking your cigar outside?' I mime him puffing away and then point outside.

'Outside?' he says with a scowl. OK, he does understand. My mistake.

'Yes, outside.' I give him a winning smile to convey that I am not judging him just because he's choosing to fill his lungs with a toxic substance. Live and let live is my motto.

He gives me the evil eye and stomps off, muttering all the while. Golly, customer service is a minefield.

Later that day, I'm about to close the bookshop up when my phone rings, startling me.

Incoming group video from The Precinct.

'Mom, look into the screen,' I say when I'm met with the vision of a squished dangly earring.

Mom sighs. 'Why can't we use our voices the old-fashioned way?'

'We can, but you don't get the same nuance from voice chats as you do with face to face,' Posy says, '*If* you're looking at the caller's face and not their inner ear, that is.'

'You do overdramatise, Posy. Now, about your text, Evie. I don't like the sound of *any* of this. The husband is where?'

I have to play this right and give Gran the chance to fix things herself. 'Konstantine is working on an oil rig.'

'An *oil* rig?' Mom shakes her head. 'So this man she's known for a month marries her then takes off? That doesn't make any sense.'

'The renovations exceeded their budget, so he's gone offshore to bring in a salary.'

'OK, I can understand she's gone all out decorating – it's Gran; she doesn't do things on the cheap – but I don't see how he can just up and leave her like that.'

I roll my eyes. 'It's not like he's run away. He's working to help them stay afloat.'

'Her savings though; you can't tell me she's gone through all her money? It's impossible.'

31

'Really, none of us know where Gran stands financially. And why would we? It's not our concern if she's happy and healthy – which she is.'

Mom lets out a long sigh as if I'm testing her patience. 'Darling her import-export business has done surprisingly well over the years. The woman has a knack for finding the next big thing. She squirrels a lot of those funds away, and now she's got money quibbles? No. This smells fishy.'

'Yeah, it's fishy all right.' Posy nods. 'Got to hand it to Gran, she's got the nous when it comes to the import-export side of things. It's the rest of her life that's a disaster.'

I bristle. 'It's anything but, Posy. She happens to live authentically, unlike *some people*.'

Posy gasps. 'Are you referring to me?'

'If the shoe fits.'

'Well at least I—'

'Now, now, let's not start all this,' Mom says, having refereed us too many times to count. 'Can we focus on the issue at hand, please? You might think everything is hunky-dory, Evie, but if Gran's having money woes, then we need to figure out why.'

'Do we though? She's a grown woman. Can't she figure it out herself? Maybe her money is tied up in investments, who knows, but it's not our place to pry if she doesn't want us to.'

Mom pinches the bridge of her nose.

'She's a *million* years old,' Posy says, her voice high. 'She's gone and got herself married for the ninth time, Evie. Ninth. Her husband is missing and she's having money troubles. Wake up! I mean, is this guy even *real*? She's probably lost it all in crypto or something zany.'

'Why would she make him up?' Honestly, my family love a good conspiracy.

'I'm with Posy,' Mom says. 'Something is off. I'm going to investigate this end.'

32

If Mom goes snooping, Gran's secrets won't be safe. Mom's like a dog with a bone when there's a mystery to be solved.

'I wish you wouldn't,' I say, exasperation leaching from every syllable.

'Keep an eye on her, Evie. She's up to something.'

Just what planet are they living on?

Chapter 6

The day wears on and still no sign of Gran. I take a moment to gaze outside the arched windows. In the distance is an array of white, domed houses with blue roofs, stacked one atop the other all the way up the cliff face, all vying for a view of the deep blue sea. It's picture-perfect like a postcard. So beautiful it almost doesn't feel real. I turn back to the bookshop, which in comparison is a riot of colour.

Colour blocking is in vogue with bookworms, but it really does work well with the blue sea as a backdrop. Tomes stand out, as if showing off their spines in the hopes of being chosen by the next sandy-footed tourist.

I peruse the collection of stock. Gran's got all sorts from romance to Goth-fic, sci-fi and the classics. There's travelogues and memoirs, and she's highlighted Greek authors and stories set in Greece.

While customers are sporadic, I scroll employment websites. There are a couple of book scout jobs at small indie studios, not romance-centric but maybe I can change that if I get the position. I apply just in case. My CV is current, so the application process doesn't take long. I use Penelope the PA from Hollywood films as a character reference and shoot her a text to warn her that she may have to wax lyrical when it comes to endorsing my bubbly, sparkly personality. I'm not going to allow the whole interview panic mode to set in but seriously why can't we interview by a series of emails since it's a literary job and all? Surely my grasp on the English language would be better expressed that way. Still, no one tends to go this route, and how imprudent is that when a huge chunk of my role is composing emails to wordsmiths?

'Darling! How did you go, did you enjoy being in charge?' Gran sashays in, the sun behind her giving her a halo like the angel she is not. God, I love her.

'Absolutely not.' I explain about the dishevelled elderly guy with a fat cigar stuck to his lip, breathing toxic fumes all over the books.

'Ooh, that's Zorba. Owns a pig farm. Don't let him worry you, darling. He's bored and likes to visit and mix up the colours of the books now that his son has taken over the day-to-day running of the farm.'

Gran leads me outside, where I'm surprised to see a bunch of scruffy dogs, slumbering in the heat of the day. She really did go and see a man about a dog(s)?

'*Six* dogs, Gran? Why?'

Hands on hips, she says, 'A chum of mine told me about them. These are the lost and broken mangy mutts that nobody wants. This old fella Zeus here.' She points to a huge grey-faced dog who opens a rheumy eye and then promptly shuts it again. 'Has been at the kennel for three years. *Three years!* I couldn't have that. I went to adopt him, and then one thing led to another and they all came home with me. No animal deserves to be starved of love and here they will have an abundance of it.'

While Gran can be shrewd in all her dealings, she's a softie at heart.

A tan fluffball runs over to me and sinks his weight into my legs as if he weighs nothing, nearly bowling me over with his excitement despite his small size. 'Who is this gorgeous pooch?'

'That loveable ball of fuzz is Sir Spud.'

'He's a cutie pie. What are the rest of their names?' I give Sir Spud's head a pat and my hand comes away dirty but I can't resist picking him up for cuddles. He has the cutest little face and is eager to be held.

'The little tyke is Pee Wee. And Lily is the shy skittish white one. Houdini is the slinky dog who can escape the inescapable, and Pork Chop . . .' She points to a brindle-coloured pooch who lets off a backfire so loud I briefly lose the ability to hear.

'Was that . . . ?' My words taper off as a noxious smell removes all my other senses.

What seems like minutes later I recover, coughing and spluttering.

'Golly,' Gran says, her eyes glistening with unshed tears. 'That was downright atomic. They did warn me that Pork Chop here is a bit of a deviant getting into bins and eating all manner of unsavoury things. I guess it's having an effect on his . . . gastro-intestinal tract.'

'You guess? Wow. OK. We need to change his diet, stat.'

Gran throws her head back and laughs. 'We'll get them ship-shape; don't you worry. And they'll need a good rub-a-dub, darling. Would you mind?'

I go to protest until I think of all the ways Gran might be injured bathing six mangy mutts of various sizes. If she indeed broke her hip under my watch, I'd be in all kinds of trouble with my mom and Posy would never let me hear the end of it. 'You're pushing it.'

'I know.' She giggles. 'But first let's have that drink and I'll tell you my plan.'

I'm sent off to make ouzotini cocktails – an entire jug of – with a warning not to skimp on the ouzo, vodka or peach schnapps. 'And don't forget to swizzle with a cinnamon stick and finish with a squeeze of fresh lime.' When I return Gran is reclining in a sun lounger, stroking Zeus who gazes at her adoringly. Gran takes the proffered drink and smacks her lips. 'Not enough ouzo but you're getting there.'

I take a sip and cough. 'There's enough ouzo in there to knock down an elephant!' Houdini dashes under my chair. I go to pat him as he comes out the other side to find he's vanished. Where did he go? I bend to make sure I'm not mistaken but there's no sign of him. Either he's fast or he really can make himself disappear.

'Pish-posh. Is this going on the literary cocktail list, and if so, what do we name it?'

'Hmm.' I consider it. Gran's been 'researching' AKA imbibing all sorts of concoctions for Epeolatry's cocktail menu but wants only the most delicious to make the cut. 'Let's name this one the Nora Roberts. An author who can write any genre and succeed, just like this cocktail with its varying flavours.'

'Scribble that down then, darling. Otherwise, I'm likely to forget.' There's no chance she'll forget, she's got a mind like a steel trap, but I play along and type the note into my phone. It's more likely that I'll forget, so I've been compiling notes of all of Gran's plans for the place in the hopes I can help her get some sort of system together in case I have to up sticks and go when a bright shiny new book scout job comes along. It will be a wrench to leave her, no matter how much I yearn to develop romance novels into film.

'So let's hear this plan that you're certain will keep Yannis and Georgios off your back. Mom and Posy have already been on the phone asking all sorts of questions.'

'Let me guess, they think Konstantine isn't real?'

I double blink. 'Erm.'

'As transparent as always those two.'

'So how bad is it, Gran? These money troubles? I take it it's not just your rent that you're behind with?'

'It's not super great, but conversely it's also not the worst predicament I've ever been in either. I owe some of the tradespeople for the renovation work. But it was a stroke of genius, the way I handled Yannis and the whole restraining order thing, so he cannot visit and harangue me.'

My eyebrows shoot up. 'You got yourself arrested on purpose?' Houdini reappears, licking the back of my leg, and is gone again, but I'm too shocked by Gran's explanation to ponder his magical abilities.

Her eyes twinkle with mischievousness. 'Yes! What fun! However I *didn't* know his grandson Georgios would be visiting from America, which has thrown a bit of a spanner in the works. Alas, there's an easy fix for the likes of him.' She lets out a throaty chuckle that implies she's up to no good.

Inexplicably my mind goes to the many accidents that may befall a person around Santorini. Those cliffs, they're a killer.

Gran continues, 'You're going to woo Georgios. The man is going to be putty in your hands, Evie. And that will buy me some time for the problem-solving I've got to do.' She claps hard as if giving herself a round of applause for coming up with such a daring plan. I'm all for celebrating wins but this, *these* are the mutterings of a mad person. 'I do love a good challenge and I'm in the thick of one here. Keeps one's soul alive, darling!'

So she's not joking? 'Hang on – what? Are you suggesting that your bright idea to save this place is to pimp me out? Absolutely no way!' I'm not sure if the alcohol in the ouzotini lulled me into a false sense of security but I did not see that coming. And I really should have. Nothing is ever simple in my family.

'Oh please. Pimp you out! What do you take me for? All you have to do is *fake*-date the guy, darling. A few walks along the beach. A candlelit dinner or two. Some alone time under the magnificent starry Santorini sky. It's the only way I can think to keep them sweet until I sort all my troubles out. Unless you have a better idea?'

'I mean, you could easily borrow money from Mom. There's one idea.'

Her eyes go hard. 'Over my cold dead body. I'd never hear the end of it. If she finds out that I'm having money troubles she'll start rummaging around in my affairs – oh who am I kidding, she probably already is!'

38

Yikes!

'Posy then?' She has more money than sense but who am I to judge?

Gran scoffs. 'Lend money from my precious granddaughter? That's a low I will not stoop to.' Shy skittish Lily slinks in and out between Gran's ankles before taking up position under the shade of her chair, her fearful gaze darting this way and that as if she's not quite sure about her new home.

'Yet, you'd allow your other *precious* granddaughter to fake-date a guy because you're too proud to ask for a loan from family?'

She chugs back the rest of her cocktail and holds the glass out for another. 'Yes, that's exactly right, Evie. This whole scenario would be *fake*, therefore, I'm hardly the flesh peddler you're making me out to be. And come on, it would be fun, would it not?'

I'm aghast. I have no words. There are so many problems with this scenario I don't even know where to begin. And I rue the fact that I'm the financially poor grandchild who doesn't have enough dough to bail out my wild Gran. What are the chances? Now I'm left with this outrageous proposition. 'You know this is my worst nightmare. Plus, he's really not my type.'

'I have every faith in you. Do it for your dear old Gran, darling?' The helpless little old lady persona comes back into play.

I cock my head. She knows that gets to me every time, dammit. While it's glaringly obvious it's a farce, a ploy, a put-on, it's hard to ignore. 'It won't work.'

'Why?'

Zeus bounds over and throws himself in my lap as if he believes he's a lapdog and not a large breed. For a moment we teeter backwards on the chair before I right it. He stinks to high heaven, and I bet I'll have a battle on my hands trying to bathe the cheeky mutt. I gently ease him to the ground and pat his matted fur. 'Because he's the epitome of a Greek god, and I'm . . . me.'

She frowns. 'What's that supposed to mean?'

'*Gran.* I'm not the flirty, giggly, hair-flicking, oozes-confidence type that I suspect Georgios is used to.'

'Which is why you're perfect, Evie. Not just for this mission, but for whoever the lucky man is who steals your heart. You *don't* fit in; you stand out because you don't pretend to be anything other than you. A beautiful bookworm sprite, who only allows special people into her world.'

Gran's always been this way with me. Shoring me up, heaping me with praise for not changing the real me when everyone else is always trying to. Telling me that my lack of social skills are *not* a lack, they're a superpower. Over the years it's given me the confidence to remain true to myself and stand firm when I need to. Or lie if the situation calls for it so I can avoid peopling in a more socially acceptable, polite way. However, Gran still expects me to fake-date a guy, so I can't let her win that easily. 'You're trying to soften me up so I'll accept your ludicrous mission.'

Fluffball Sir Spud barks as if agreeing with me.

Gran trains her vivid blue-eyed gaze on me. There's so much vibrancy to her that time never dulls. I love her with every fibre of my being, even though she's untameable and wild with it.

'Will buttering up work? Because if so let me count the ways I love you. And if that's a no-go, may I remind you how many times I lied to your mother on your behalf when I knew you were the culprit. Who doesn't love a bit of blackmail, eh? Let's see, there was that time you skipped a week of school because you were under a cloud of suspicion over the emptying of the Olympic-sized swimming pool prank.' She does an intimidation stare-down worthy of my mother. 'You did it, didn't you?'

I bite down on my lip. Is there any point lying now? Zeus trains his suspicious eyes on me with an almost human gaze, as if he's expecting me to fess up too. Soon all the dogs are staring at me in the same way, as if they're waiting out the truth. I can't lie under this kind of scrutiny! '*Fine.* Yeah, I did it. It's one thing to wear swimwear at the beach, quite another at school with a bunch of hormonal boys making lewd comments. The CCTV cameras were switched off that night, so they didn't have enough evidence to catch the perpetrator.'

'Lucky. But they still suspected you?'

'Not lucky. I disabled the poolside CCTV. But what I didn't stop to consider were the cameras in the car park. The principal narrowed it down to five suspects, but she couldn't prove for sure who it was.' Pee Wee comes bounding over with a chew toy in his mouth, which he promptly dumps in my lap, as though now I've told the truth we can become friends.

'A near miss.'

'I was more careful the following year.'

'The broken leg?'

'Yeah, fake.'

Gran laughs. 'How glorious. And your mother never suspected?'

'No, I paid Posy to lie about witnessing the tumble off my bike and a faux hospital visit. I'd made a cast myself weeks before that I could slip in and out of.' And boy did Posy make me pay, she insisted on double what I offered her, but I figured it was worth it. Plus, she'd been forced to keep my secret because she'd been part of the ruse.

'Genuis.'

'School swimming should be illegal.'

'Well, my darling, as I see it, you're quite suitable for a bit of hijinks. You've been pulling these scams your whole life.'

'Only to avoid situations I feel uncomfortable in. You know, like fake-dating, for example.' Really what choice do we have if she won't loan money from anyone?

Hand on her chest, she leans back on the sun lounger. 'Why . . . I don't feel so good suddenly. It might be my heart.'

I narrow my eyes, having seen this scenario being acted out one too many times in the past. 'That might work with Mom, but it won't with me.'

'What?'

41

'The fragile old lady bit. Against my better judgement, I'll accept your mission, only if you *promise* me, you won't tell Mom about any of my priors. The less she knows the better.' Golly, if my mom knew half the pranks I've pulled she'd enforce some kind of backbreaking community work, so I learned my lesson or something. It doesn't bear thinking about.

'My lips are sealed, darling. As if I'd ever spill your secrets, as juicy as they are.'

'They were all done in the name of self-preservation, Gran.'

'Yes, darling, but you really must learn to always be unpredictable and cover your tracks. Always, I repeat, *always* have an alibi.'

I raise a brow. 'Speaking from experience?'

She stares me down. 'I have no idea what you're talking about.'

All this alibi talk reminds me of Gran's husband number five. Jimmy from Australia who suffered horrifically in a rare dropbear attack. Gran had been miles away, crewing in the Sydney to Hobart yacht race so she couldn't have been involved. And it's not like she could have orchestrated a drop bear to fatally attack the guy. They're wild animals! For some reason, the detective from Australia had been extremely suspicious of Gran, but her alibi was rock solid. Another case of a man in power trying to intimidate a defenceless woman.

'So, darling. How are you going to engender your first date with the hunky Georgios? Who knows, you might actually fall in love with the guy and I'll get to keep you on my island.'

'Urgh, I hardly think so. Hollyweird calls, remember? I'm determined to find myself another book scout job, by using all the connections I don't have.'

'I know people in the movie biz. I could easily make a few calls once you've completed your Santorini mission.'

I shake my head. 'Thanks, Gran, but I'd prefer to do it on my own merits.'

'Sure, I respect that.'

'Where will I find Georgios? And how do I even try and chat the guy up?' Even the thought of such a thing is enough to make me want to curl up in the foetal position. But I must do this for my beloved Gran, who despite her adoration of me, will go through with blackmail if she has to. There are some secrets from the past that are best left buried.

Gran holds her glass out for a top-up. The woman can sure put it away. 'Georgios is always at Kamari Beach, hence the stunning tan on that stunning body. As for chatting him up, you read romance novels every day. Just follow the script.'

A meet-cute . . . ? 'Gah. Are you hearing all of this, Sir Spud?' I say, bending to him as he lies supine, tongue lolling to one side, scratching his back on the grass. 'What have I got myself into?'

Chapter 7

A couple of days later I don't what resembles a Hazmat suit and plonk on some goggles and gloves. My first bathing attempt of the pooches did not go well. This time I'm prepared to battle the gang of six. They might think they have the upper hand, but they do not. Not today. Not when I have very informative dog-wrangling advice from TikTok on my side. Despite appearing utterly ridiculous, I wind plastic wrap around my forehead and lather it with lashings of peanut butter.

Outside, the dogs bark not recognising me in my waterproof disguise. 'It's me!' I say holding some dog treats in my gloved hand. All of them bar Lily approach me. Ruled by their stomachs. Gotcha!

'Who is up first then? I'm looking at you, Pee Wee.' They give me blank stares, which I now know from experience means they know exactly what's going on. The gang of six are as canny as Gran and it seems fitting she'd rescued this motley group who are as clever as she is. But not today. I will win this battle!

I grab Pee Wee, who barks and shows his teeth. 'Be nice, Pee Wee.' I place him gently in the outside tub full of frothy luke-warm water. I duck my head so he can lick the peanut butter while I soap him up but instead, he turns his nose up as if it's below him. Huh. TikTok experts advised this was a sure-fire way to distract dogs when you bathe them.

Still, he is so little he's easy to scrub, even though he thrashes about dramatically like I'm trying my best to drown him. I ease him out and dry him off with a towel, but he soon escapes and shakes out his fur, scurrying straight off to the nearest patch of volcanic earth to tumble in. 'You little . . .'

It's of no matter. I replenish the tub with fresh water and give the other dogs a bath. The peanut butter works a treat. That only leaves me with Houdini who thinks he's in charge. I give my foe a beady-eyed stare that says: *you won't mess with me. Not today, Satan.* Houdini holds my stare, not backing down as I smother more peanut butter on the plastic wrap on my forehead. I'm sweating. I'm not sure if it's from being covered in plastic or the physical nature of this mission. 'Come on, boy! Do you want another treat?' He inches slowly towards me, a flinty look in his eye that suggests he's not going to make this easy.

I drop to my knees and lean down so he can smell the peanut butter. As I go to grab him, he somehow loosens the plastic wrap and is off with it, leaving a trail of slimy peanut butter across my forehead. How? That dog has superhuman abilities! I chase him this way and that, yelling for him to stop. 'Houdini! You stink worse than a garbage can. Now get over here right this minute!'

Soon the other dogs join in, jumping in front of him when I get close. Their defence is on point and I can't begrudge them that, but I do because this is taking a lot longer than it needs to. I change tack and pretend to walk away. I sense he's slinking up on me because that's what he does. Just as I'm about to turn and snatch him up, there's a twang of the gate unlatching. Good, Gran can help me wrestle him into the bath.

'Gran . . .' Oh God no. Why, universe? Why do you disrespect me so? Just when I resemble a space man with a peanut butter forehead, he appears. It's almost like fate wants me to appear deranged. My only option is to roll with it. 'Georgios, welcome.'

I'm meant to woo this guy so somehow I have to make this look . . . sexy? Is that even possible? I throw a hand on my hip and pop it. That should do it. 'Don't mind me, I'm just bathing the dogs.' I give him a sweet toothy smile that implies all is well and I'm a woman of many talents.

'In a space suit and goggles?'

'The canines are covered in a smell that will outlast human civilisation. This attire is necessary, trust me.'

'Right.' He appears unseduced. *Glaringly* unseduced if his frown is anything to go by. I pout, puffing my lips. What the bloody hell do heroines actually do that I can mimic? The batting of lashes won't work with goggles on.

'What's all over your forehead?' His mouth twists as if he's tasted something sour. Hmm, my hip popping must need more work but what else is there?

'It's peanut butter.'

He laughs, but it's more of a strangled sound than one of pure joy. His gaze darts about as if he's looking for an escape route. 'Why?'

'I'm having a little trouble convincing Houdini to bathe. He's quite the nimble sort. TikTok suggested this as a distraction method. It worked for the other dogs.' How dare he make me explain myself like this! As if he doubts my method. My *sound* method.

'I see.' He rubs his chin as his lips quiver, either with held-in laughter or outright fear. Hard to tell. I get that a lot. 'Could you not have layered peanut butter along the edge of the tub itself?'

Damn it. *Thanks for nothing, TikTok.* 'Do you always saunter in with solutions *after* the fact?' I bristle. No one likes a smarty-pants.

He grins as if I've said something funny. Does he not understand that I just cut him to the quick? 'I saunter?'

'That's what you took from that sentence?' Oh the ego on him! It's to be expected but still.

He fans out his hands in apology as if he's expecting to be forgiven for being self-absorbed. Just how am I supposed to woo him when he's clearly in the midst of the greatest love affair of his life. *With himself.*

'Sorry. I just thought I had more of a lope than a saunter.'

Is that some fake sort of humble? 'What, like a horse?'

At that real laugher bubbles from his lips. Even his laugh is attractive, which is irritating. 'Wouldn't that be more of a canter?'

I roll my eyes and hope he can see the gesture even though my goggles appear to be fogging up. 'Are you always so contrary?'

He presses his lips together as if biting back yet another unnecessary retort that will only prolong this tedious conversation. How am I supposed to fake-date this guy? We'll be back and forth forever arguing about semantics. It's one way to pass the time, I guess.

'Sorry,' he repeats.

'As well you should be.'

'OK, well I'll pop back later when you're not so . . . indisposed.'

He gives me a wave and is out the gate before I can think to ask what his visit was in aid of. And, I mentally face-palm, wasn't I supposed to ask him on a date? Sow the seeds of a faux romance? Well, it's not exactly my fault he came out all guns blazing.

I blow out a breath and turn to find Houdini having the time of his life in the tub, splashing and gambolling as if he hasn't spent the last hour avoiding it. I'm sure he winks at me. Can dogs wink?

After showering and changing into non-plastic attire I call Penelope. 'Hey, Evie! How is sunny Santorini?'

'Hot.'

'You lucky thing!'

'Ah – yeah. So Pen, just calling quickly since you didn't answer my texts or emails . . .'

'You know I'm more of a phone person,' she cries. There are two types in this world. Phone people and email people. I will never understand why anyone would choose to chat rather than type. It blows my tiny mind but, hey ho, here we are.

'Right. Did anyone reach out to you regarding my references?'

She yells to someone in the background. 'Sorry, it's chaos here. Hank has hired a slew of new staff and let's just say, they all need babysitting.'

'He *hired* people? Wasn't he cutting costs? Focusing only on superhero movies?' The betrayal hits my solar plexus like a punch.

With a lowered voice she says, 'Yeah he did that too. And then replaced them with these bigwigs that he stole from rival studios. I can't see it lasting. The testosterone in here is so thick you could cut it with a knife. There's already been one disagreement over parking spaces that ended in a punch-up! I can't wait to leave, to be honest.'

'Where will you go?' Penelope has been with Hollywood Films for decades. If she goes, they'd be losing part of the glue that holds the place together.

'Anywhere. I'll put feelers out soon. And as for your references, Lighthouse Studios called and I gave you a glowing review. They said they'd get in touch with you soon.'

'Really? Thanks, Pen.'

'You're welcome.'

'Phoebe!' A voice thunders in the background.

'The moron *still* doesn't know my name or he mispronounces it on purpose. I better go, Evie. But keep in touch.'

'Will do and good luck, Pen. I hope it all works out.'

I fire up my laptop and check my application for Lighthouse Studios only to find the position has been filled. So close. I don't take it personally but resolve to widen my search parameters. For a moment I ponder who in my small network I can reach out to that won't make me break out in nervous hives. Phil, the executive producer working on the two romcoms I signed might know of a position. As far as EPs go he seemed amiable enough. An attention-to-details man, which I admire, rather than a blustery bellower like Hank. While Phil doesn't own a studio, he's been in the industry for ages and might be able to point me in the right direction.

I draft an email and hit send, hoping he's not a phone person too. In the meantime, I hit the job websites again, searching for that unicorn I know is out there if I look hard enough.

Chapter 8

What Gran didn't mention was that a trip to the beach is only possible by use of transport, as the swimming beaches are on the other side of the island. There's no way I'm driving on these Santorini roads, so she suggested I try her bicycle.

A few days later, after many beach visits, I *finally* spot Georgios suntanning on the shore. I'm not big on fitness and these daily rides to 'bump' into him have been a little onerous when he's been missing in action. This morning, his eyes are closed as he lies on his back, a book open in his hand as if he fell asleep reading.

He's wearing itty-bitty bather briefs that leave nothing to the imagination. I take a moment to catch my breath – whoa. His every muscle catches the sunlight. Such precise definition suggests the man spends a lot of time working out. Is he one of those guys who ogles himself in the mirror at the gym as he pumps weights? I could never love a man like that, and then I brighten as I remember I don't have to. I'm simply buying time for Gran and this is a ruse of the highest order. Still, it's nerve-racking.

What if the muscle mountain rejects me on sight? The only muscle definition I have is from lifting hardbacks. What is he preparing for, the apocalypse? And I don't exactly worship the sun as much as try and hide from it. After all, it's not cool to cook for looks no matter how attractive a tan is, but I guess Georgios didn't get the memo. As I survey the other beachgoers, I see that most of the women wear barely-there bikinis and have sculptured bodies. A few lusty wenches frolic close to Georgios to try and catch his eye. How blatant!

Anxiety gnaws at me as I take a few more tentative steps towards him. The thought of Gran being tossed in jail for failing to pay her bills is the only thing that stops me spinning on my heel, sprinting away screaming. That, and the fact my quads are still smarting from the ride here and sprinting seems like far too much effort.

I pause again, comparing myself to the bronzed beauties around me. They don't seem to have bottoms on their bikinis, as in their actual bottoms are on display. Is this a new thing? Personally, I feel like I have far too few clothes on for my taste. I'm wearing boy-leg bathers, a long-sleeved swimming costume and a voluminous sarong over the top. My legs haven't seen the sunshine in years and are so white they're almost translucent. What can I say? I didn't exactly delve into the LA beach scene as much as actively avoid it, and I was kind of hoping to replicate that here too.

Sartorial choices aside, more pressing is just how to facilitate this faux romance so he says yes and it helps Gran get out of a spot of bother . . .

In fiction there are always archetypes. The huntress, the siren, the maiden, the coquette, and so on. Which would work best? More importantly: which could I pull off?

The siren, a Marilyn-esque persona will definitely get his attention. I cast my mind to all the Marilyn films I've seen. She's always slightly breathy, peers through her lashes, coy smile. How hard can it be?

Red lipstick would have been ideal but I'm too far in the process to turn back now.

As I step closer my shadow falls across his face, stealing the sunshine from his tough, toned bod. He opens his eyes and frowns.

'Oh, hell-oo, you,' I say, breathlessly. 'Do you come here o-often?' I flutter my lashes, wishing I'd at least swiped some mascara on them.

He bolts upright. 'Do you need help? Is it asthma?'

Asthma? 'What?'

'Your voice, it sounds like you can't catch your breath. Are you OK? Did you jog here?'

Jog here? What does he take me for! Concern is etched on his features. Doesn't the fool know what *breathy* sounds like? I don a coy smile and flutter my lashes yet again. 'Beauu-tiful day.'

His face scrunches with worry. 'Shall I call Floretta?'

Oh for crying out loud! I drop the act. Clearly my lack of preparation is hindering this archetype. I'm not sure where to go from here. I'm not exactly well versed on the art of seduction, in real life at least. Why couldn't I have swiped a bit of make-up on? It surely would have helped him join the dots of me to Marilyn. Put it down to yet another rookie error by me. You live and learn.

'Evie,' he says. 'Should I call her? You could be suffering from sunstroke, dehydration . . .'

'That won't be necessary.' The man makes me feel slightly unhinged and by the worry written all over his face, he recognises that. 'Mind if I sit down for a moment?'

'Of course. But . . . aren't you my sworn enemy?'

I bristle but manage to hide it. 'I've forgiven you for taking back the gift of loukoumades, if that's what you mean?' Who *does* that? What kind of family are they? After a little old lady for some rent money, and he reneges on a dessert offering too. Not to mention all his dog-bathing blustering.

That grin of his is back. 'Sorry, that *was* rude of me. It's only that I find this whole situation so frustrating. For the first time in years I've taken a sabbatical from work and came back to visit, only to be embroiled in this drama. I've never met two people as headstrong as my grandfather and Floretta. It's crazy.'

52

That, I do understand. My bookshop vacay has also been snatched away on this ridiculous mission. Perhaps that's a way in with him?

We can trauma-bond.

'I feel the same. I've been sent here by my overbearing family to make sure Gran is OK. They always coddle and underestimate her, not seeing the formidable woman she really is. Although I suppose their worries *are* valid, in this instance, since she hasn't paid the rent and all.'

And she owes money to tradespeople in town, but I keep that to myself. I figure Gran wouldn't want me to go behind her back and let that slip. 'What are you taking a sabbatical from?' I ask.

He picks up the book, a Lucy Strike mafia romantic suspense. Interesting choice. It's a genre-bender, in that it's got a bit of everything: drama, thriller, romance and a killer plot. Killer as in everyone usually dies, *even* the killer.

'I'm in publishing. Editorial. Or *was*, I should say. There was a scandal with one of our authors. I said my piece about why he needed to go, and I'm no longer gainfully employed. You?'

'Book scout. Recently made redundant because superhero movies are more important than romcoms, *allegedly*.'

We size each other up. Gran never mentioned he worked in publishing. And he's jobless too for a skirmish that doesn't seem to be of his making. I'm dying to know what the scandal with the author was about, but I'm not the prying kind. Not when I can use Google and save having to outright ask.

I feel a frisson . . . of something. Maybe this fake-dating farce will be a little more fun than first expected. Anyone who enjoys the shape of words is good in my book. I get lost in a daydream staring at him. The new improved idea of him, that is. Perhaps I can look past his overt hotness?

Eventually he says, 'Floretta is a real character. She's only been in Santorini a short time and yet her name is on everyone's lips.'

'That's Gran. The life and soul of the party. I do hope Yannis

53

will give her some time to get her finances in order. They might become friends – you never know.'

Georgios shoots me a look that conveys he doesn't think friendship between them is on the cards, but he doesn't know Gran very well. She can turn up the charm when she needs to. We lapse into silence. I wish I could fall back on my witty repartee, but I lack that particular social skill as well. My stomach clenches. I have to ask him on a date but how does one go about such things? Just blurt it out or wait for a lead-in to it?

'Would you like to have dinner Friday night? We could start with sunset cocktails at the beach bar?' he says. 'I'd love to hear more about your work as a book scout.'

I'm stunned silent. A real-life guy just asked me to dinner and cocktails. I'm not exactly an expert on non-fictional men. My past relationships have tended to be short-lived mainly because they talked too much and too often, or they had some huge flaw I couldn't get past, like saying romance novels are formulaic and predictable, thus implying not of any literary note or some other such nonsense. No one needs to live with that sort of narrow-minded negativity.

But this is one for the books. He asked me out and not the other way around . . . ! All the tension I'm holding tight evaporates.

I've left my answer too long and struggle to kick my brain into gear. 'I could eat.' Can't look too hard in his direction to study him because it's like looking directly into the sun. This kind of intensity is exhausting.

He laughs as he stands and shakes the sand out of his towel, and I will my gaze to remain on his face and not on his sparsely covered sexy bits. 'OK, great. Meet you at the beach bar Friday night at sunset?'

'Actually . . .' I have a quick internal debate before deciding to trust my instincts. 'Why don't you meet me at the bookshop and I'll show you the new and improved bar. It's really special.' Epeolatry's literary appeal might just be thing that convinces him to tell his grandfather to back off.

He tilts his head. 'Sounds intriguing. I'll be there. Until then, Evie.' He does that cool-guy chin lift nod thing and saunters off, and I wasn't expecting anything less. Men with bodies like that do a lot of sauntering. He must know he's not the kind who lopes, or canters for that matter. I remind myself to be on guard. It could all be some massive trick to get information or something. I'm not a conspiracist like Posy but it pays to be careful.

I can't hide my grin as I watch him go, towel slung over his shoulder, his book in hand. I, Evie, socially awkward hot mess, wangled a dinner invite with a hot Greek guy and also managed to have a semi-successful conversation despite the fact he is wearing one small piece of fabric over his nether regions. A guy who also happens to be my arch-nemesis because my gran is having a war with his family and blood is thicker than water and all that.

From my long and distinguished past experience with romance novels, it's clear to me the fake-date trope always, always leads to the unlikely duo falling in mad passionate love; however, this is *real* life and I won't be lulled by his charm. That's only for fiction. Still, I'm not sure why my heart is beating a rhumba. Probably the thrill of deception. That and the fact Gran's livelihood hangs in the balance of this whole circus.

My legs wobble slightly as I head home. I haven't seen a man that exposed in a good year. OK two. Fine. Three. But that's only because I've been focusing on my career. I rush back to my bike as quickly as my out-of-breath body will take me. Why is walking on sand so arduous? I've got the long ride back to the villa to contend with when my legs are already having trouble holding me up. But the excitement of it all is enough to propel me along.

Back at the villa, I'm a sweaty mess from the long journey up and down hills. I find Gran and recount my not-so-chance meeting with Georgios and am rewarded with a long exhalation and her megawatt smile. 'That really takes the pressure off, darling. If you can keep them sweet, I can get the business up and running and profitable. We just might be able to drag Konstantine home.'

For the briefest moment her eyes pool with sadness. Gran must really miss her new beau.

Our chat is interrupted as Pork Chop bounds over with a huge bone in his mouth. A very meaty bone that to my untrained eye looks rather human. Could it be . . . Yannis, the landlord, come to a grizzly end after an altercation with the gang of six, who were protecting their queen?

'Pork Chop!' Gran calls. 'That was supposed to be dinner, you little minx!' Bile rises in my throat. Dinner? Surely not . . .

Gran proceeds to wrestle Pork Chop, eventually jumping up dusty but triumphant, bone held aloft like the Statue of Liberty torch. I'm frozen to the spot when she swings a glance at me. 'What is it, darling? You're decidedly green around the gills.'

I point a shaky finger to the bone. 'Where did . . . *that* come from?'

'This?' She holds the fleshy bone aloft. 'Zorba's pig farm.' She narrows her eyes at me. 'Why, where did you think it came from?'

I don't know how to answer that.

'Did you think it was *human*?'

I gulp.

Before I can answer she doubles over laughing, leg of indeterminate species dangling by her side, chortling so hard I worry she might stop breathing. Pork Chop takes this moment to gnaw on it again, teeth flashing. It's an alarming sight. I feel like I'm smack bang in the middle of a true crime re-enactment for some reason.

After an eternity, Gran composes herself and wiggles what's left of the appendage from Pork Chop's tiny razor-sharp teeth. 'Oh you're killing me, Evie. If I wanted to hide a body I most certainly wouldn't eat it! That would take forever and really, it's not very palatable. Sixteen pigs can eat a dead man in eight minutes. Or so I've heard. That would be a far more effective way to get rid of a pest.'

'Uh . . . huh.' As of right now all pork products are off the menu. And there will be no innocent tour of said pig farm either.

Who knows what's really going on there. A man who messes up the colour order of books for fun is clearly someone with a troubled soul.

'So,' Gran says, dumping the bone on the sink before washing her hands. 'You'll be around for dinner tonight?'

I give her a long look. 'Where else would I be? A nightclub?'

Gran twerks – at least that's what I presume the movement is supposed to resemble. 'A nightclub with that sexy Georgios. What's not to like?'

'The noise, the dark, the people. Over-eighties women dancing like they're Beyoncé – you know, the usual.'

'Moi? I'm dropping it like it's hot.'

'Please don't.'

'OK, I *am* a little puffed. These days it's such a long way down and then to get back up requires a lot of muscle power.' Sweat beads her brow. Next minute she'll put her back out and the Fun Police will be enraged when I explain it was a simple booty-poppin' accident. 'So no plans for this evening?' There's disappointment on her face as if I'm letting her down by being the perfect non-wayward grandchild. Gran moves at a faster pace than me. If she were the poor lamb fake-dating Georgios, they'd have moved in together already.

'I have a date with my book boyfriend, and it's not like we can eat . . . *that* now.'

'It's OK. You go relax for a bit. Later I'll throw together a meze plate: olives, dips and the like. We can sit under the trellis and enjoy the sea breeze.'

Vegetables sound good right about now and forevermore. 'Perfect.'

My phone beeps with a text.

'Off you go, darling. We all know who it'll be.'

I scoff. 'It could be any number of people, I'll have you know. It could be a job offer. A secret admirer. An ex-flame.'

'It could be. However, we both know it's my busybody daughter

57

who surely has better things to worry about than me.' Gran picks up the meaty appendage again and jabs it in the air to emphasise her point. 'Remember our little deal, darling.' She grins and walks away, Pork Chop jumping wildly beside her trying to get his prize back. I lean against the kitchen bench to check my message and manage to step in a small puddle. Has one of the dogs upended their water bowl again? I find some paper towels and tidy it up before I go back to my phone.

Darling, you've been very quiet. How's it all going there? Mom xoxo

Hmm, I'd been expecting more of an inquisition. Perhaps she's learning to leave well enough alone?

Nothing to report. Gran seems happy and relaxed and enjoying the slow pace of island life. Will call soon. Love you, Evie xoxo

The next morning, a man rushes in and spits Greek words at me. I'm so used to his visits now, that I'm not perturbed. He doesn't have the patience for me to use my translation app. Instead we use charades in order for him to get his point across, which actually takes far longer than the app would but it's also a lot more fun. He gestures outside to where his donkey is tied up.

Even this doesn't faze me anymore. Yeah, sure a donkey at a bookshop; I've seen worse. I get the feeling it's more like his pet than a farm animal. Zeus loves the donkey visits and I often catch them nose to nose as if they're communicating without sound. Today the man gesticulates wildly at the animal and performs charades that I can't translate no matter how hard I try. He points to me, and then outside.

'Ah, the donkey needs water? *Aqua?*' I mime myself drinking water from a bottle.

'*So latrevo.*' I make a mental note to remember how to say water in Greek.

I hold up a finger, telling him to wait. I find one of the dogs drinking bowls and take it outside to the donkey, refilling it with water from the hose.

The man's wrinkled face creases with a smile. We've had a number of these performances and I'm slowly but surely able to understand what he's after. While the donkey drinks with Zeus supervising, the man wanders into the bookshop and peruses a table with a small selection of second-hand books. I wish I knew what he was looking for. I'm determined to crack the code.

I take stock of him, yet again. He seems to be drawn towards books about animals. Perhaps, like Zorba the pig farmer, he also has a plot of grazing land? I take a few books from the shelves and show him. He shakes his head no. With an apologetic raise of the hands, he's gone for another day.

While I'm pondering what books he might like that I can have ready for his next visit, another customer arrives, widening her arms as she enters like she just won first place in a running race. 'The gods have answered my prayers! This used to be a very sad excuse for a bookshop and now look at it! A riot of colour, of words, the sweet smell of new novels. I vow to spend my summer days in here expanding my mind. And also, because my mother is driving me crazy but what can you do? She's been ill so I must bite my tongue and be a good dutiful Greek daughter. But my oversized suitcases are fit to burst with the big guilt trip she's sending me on. Mothers, eh?'

'Tell me about it.' I laugh at her description. 'Our moms sound freakishly similar.'

'Is your mother Greek?'

'No.'

She twists her mouth. 'Then you're probably on easy street, but we won't do that whole competition thing because everyone has their own journey and I'm not big on comparison woe.'

'Right.' I don't quite know what to do with this starburst of a person. She's effusive but in a very relatable way. 'Comparison is the thief of all joy.'

She slaps a hand down on the counter. 'Yes! You get it! I *knew* you'd get it. You've got a certain vibe, an energy about you that screams a quiet intelligence. You're not one to parade your superior brain power but it lies just below the surface nevertheless.'

Is this the part where I tell her that quote is something I once read on a coffee mug? 'Why thanks but . . .'

'No buts. You just are. Deal with it.'

'Umm OK.'

She holds out a hand to shake. 'I'm Roxy, short for Aphroxia.'

'I'm Evie. Short for Evie.'

'You look like an Evie – of course you do. Tell me, Evie, what's your favourite book?'

'I can narrow it down to top ten at best.'

'We're going to be great friends.'

'Let's swap book recs.'

'Deal.'

There's something about Roxy that puts me at ease. I'm not usually a fan of friendships, having no desire to be remonstrated with when I turn down yet another invitation to leave my abode, but for a moment, I open to the idea of making it happen.

Gran and I are finalising the wording for the literary cocktail menu for Epeolatry. I play around with a design and sit typing them up ready to be printed. Gran informs me her friend Athena from the Squashed Olive, a nearby café, has agreed to do the catering for the launch. I'm only half-listening as I drop and drag design elements, giving the menu a roaring Twenties Gatsby vibe using black and gold.

'You've missed your calling,' Gran says peering over my shoulder.

'This site makes it easy. And look . . .' I save the menu project before clicking out of it and going back to the home page '. . . we can make bookmarks, posters, flyers, all sorts of marketing material. Literary coasters for the cocktails, membership cards all with the same aesthetic.'

'Clever.'

'That I am.'

I jot notes about projects to complete on the site when a lanky bow-legged teenager walks in box in hand. 'Evie?' he asks.

'That's me.'

'Delivery from Georgios.'

The tanned teenager hands over the box and lopes back outside. Teenagers lope; Greek gods do not. I'll have to educate Georgios on this fact when I see him next. From the scent alone, I already know what is secreted inside the pretty box. What a glorious man Georgios is, righting his very big wrong. Food – it's my love language. There's a note that reads: *I'm looking forward to Friday. Can't wait to get to know you better. Love Georgios.*

Love? What is he playing at? Could be just a figure of speech, but the more I contemplate the whole Georgios scenario the more it bamboozles me. I'm probably overthinking it.

My work email signature says: *Lukewarm regards* because I want to set the tone for my professional life. So for Georgios to sign off with 'love' is quite presumptive, but that might just be the introvert in me who tends to take words on their literary merit.

Gran flips the box open. 'Ooh, loukoumades. His grandmother is famous for them.'

'Well, these are *redemption* loukoumades.' I explain his visit and how the evil beast took them back with him.

She surveys my face. 'And he's learned the error of his ways . . . *interesting.*'

'Is it? Or does he simply understand I'm ruled by my stomach?'

'Hmm, could the man be enchanted by our Evie?' She waggles her brow excessively in case I haven't picked up what's she's getting at.

I scoff. 'Oh please.' Gran lives in fantasyland when it comes to me and men.

'You know what they say, darling, Greek food is the best in the world. And Greek men, well they have the biggest . . .'

'Bookshelves?' I slap a hand over her mouth, sensing whatever the words are that finish that sentence are going to be tawdry. 'Shush. You'll put me off my loukoumades.'

While we're eating the syrupy Greek donuts a thirty-something woman wanders in, sunglasses atop her head. She stands out firstly because she's the first customer we've had in hours and secondly because she's wearing a fitted dress that seems almost formal and business-like compared to the beachwear most customers prefer. There's an impatient air to her, as she picks up non-fiction books and throws them down with a frustrated sigh. I'm a tad offended on behalf of the hardbacks. I mean, do they *really* need to be thrown down like that? Yeah, they might be inanimate and all but still, it's a respect thing.

'G-o-d,' she says disdain heavy in those three little letters.

Gran gives me a nudge. 'Looks like she needs a hand. Off you go.'

'She's a prickly pear and quite clearly going to be rude and dismissive and send me into a tailspin about how I am lacking in some form or another.'

Bad energy rolls off the haughty woman in waves. The word *disgruntled* comes to mind. I really don't like customer service at the best of times, more so when it's obvious she's going to act hostile just because she can. Gah.

'She's a prickly pear with *money*,' Gran whispers. 'And if she hurts your feelings, she'll suffer for it – mark my words.'

Yikes. I approach the customer with the knowledge we need any sales we can get.

'Welcome to Bibliotherapy. Can I help you find anything?' I try not to scare her with my rigor-mortis smile. When people intimidate me, like she does with all her unsatisfied sighing as if the very tomes themselves have ruined her day, I can't get my lip muscles to relax into a proper smile, so I appear somewhat crazed. Like I've got lockjaw.

She gives me a slow once-over, her subtle grimace implying she finds me lacking in some way. What a shocker. 'I'm in need of some coffee table books.'

'We have plenty of pictorials. Were you after English or Greek?'

'English, obviously.'

'OK.' I'm going to come back in the next life as a customer. 'And what theme were you after? Travel, art, history . . . fashion?' I lead her to a display of oversized hardbacks. Her high heels click-clack on the mosaic tiles as she follows behind me.

'I don't care what they're about, they just have to be visually pleasing.'

Internally, I reel. She doesn't *care* about what's inside the books?! They're simply props, never to be opened, pored over. Read and appreciated. Argh, my heart.

However, she's the customer, and customers are always right even when they're wrong. Right? My job here is to sell books and make money for Gran. I keep my feelings to myself and will my lips to relax into a warm smile.

'OK, I'd suggest a mix of these.' I pull out a book about flower-infused cocktails, in pastel pink. To match that I choose a book about Chanel fashion through the ages in a creamy peach and then an art book with a white and gold spine. 'Sitting together as a trio they . . .'

'Fine. Wrap them.'

Wrap them, *please.* Just as I'm muttering internally about horrible customers Zeus wanders in and sticks his nose under her skirt. She jumps with a scream. 'Sorry. He really shouldn't have done that without your consent.'

'Consent? He's a dog!'

'Yes, but he's a very clever dog and even though he's old he's proving quite capable when it comes to training him not to look up ladies' skirts. But he has his bad days.' He does it again. 'Obviously, like all of us, he's a work in progress.'

She holds her skirt tight against her side. 'Surely it's against health and safety to have a big dirty dog like that mooching around sticking his nose where it most certainly does not belong?'

Dirty dog? I take offence after my efforts washing him. His fur is fluffy and clean. 'He's employed to ward off thieves.' It's the best I can come up with as this woman is intimidating the reason right out of my brain.

'Now I've heard everything. Can you move a little faster? I've got places to be.'

'Sure.' She's definitely not going on the Bibliotherapy Christmas card list. Zeus sits beside Gran, and I'm not sure if I imagine it or not but he seems to be grinning. Did he behave like that on purpose to usher the woman out faster? Wonders will never cease.

Gran pastes on a bright smile that's as fake as the woman's tan. 'We're holding a launch party soon for our exclusive club: Epeolatry. Strictly invitation only. Would you like to join as a member?'

'What kind of club is it?'

'A night-time library.'

'Oh God no, who has time for reading? Bores me to tears. Even if it is exclusive, it sounds decidedly dull.'

As I wrap her beautiful artistic coffee table books in tissue paper, I damn near bite my own lip off to stop a retort that would surely get us gossiped about around the island. And because confronting her would be terrifying. No. Instead I mutter about her silently in my mind, and I win the argument too.

Gran says. 'Totally understand – not everyone can afford to be a member. Times are tough these days what with the skyrocketing price of living.'

'Excuse me?' She glares at Gran so hard I'm almost certain she's going to spontaneously combust. 'Are you implying I can't afford to join?'

'Not many can, darling. It's *that* exclusive. A literary hideout for book lovers, you know. Very low-key, very chill. Very prestigious.'

'Sign me up.' She flicks her credit card at me. 'And my husband too.'

I smother a grin and ask her to fill out her details on a sign-up form so I can add them to the database. 'You'll get your membership cards in the mail soon and we'll send you an invite to the launch.'

'Fine.'

When she leaves with her bundle of books, I face Gran. 'That wasn't very nice.'

'Neither was she. But isn't Zeus a good boy!' She gives him a pat under the chin.

'What were you thinking? Now she's a member and we'll have to put up with her.'

Gran chews her lip before saying, 'Doubt we'll ever see her again. It's just sales, Evie. Everyone has their pressure point and hers is obviously trying to fit in by impressing people with her lavish tastes. Let's think of it as a donation to the greater good of literature.'

My jaw drops. 'You cunning fox.'

Gran sits on a stool behind the counter, shuffling paperwork that needs to be inputted into the accounts program. 'That's me. Now, how is our mailing list going?'

I join her behind the counter and bring it up on screen. Just how is Gran going to manage all of this when I'm gone? There's a lot to be done in terms of working in the bookshop, Epeolatry and the time-consuming behind-the-scenes stuff, like stock purchasing and promotion and marketing. She's going to need staff, but I guess, first things first. Rent money.

Like clockwork, every day at two o'clock an elderly man wearing a waistcoat and holding a guitar comes in, a worried expression on his face. In thick Greek he speaks, and just like always,

I remind him I don't speak the language. He nods and says in stilted English, 'Helena, not here?'

'No, I haven't seen her. Sorry.'

The more often he stops to ask, the more curious I become. Just who is Helena? Is he intending on serenading her with a guitar song? Did she run away from him? What's the story?

'What does she look like?' I say, but he's already retreating, probably off to the next place to enquire about Helena's whereabouts. I really must ask Gran who he is and whether Helena is a figment of his imagination.

My phone beeps with an alert. It's an email from Phil the executive producer working on the two romance novels in development at Hollywood Films. Hallelujah, he's not a phone person either. I quickly open it and speed-read.

Dear Evie,

It's lovely to hear from you. I'm sorry things didn't work out at Hollywood Films but I'm not surprised. Hank's been around the block a bit and has a reputation for replacing staff with his own circle of friends. You could reach out to Olympus Media. They're on the hunt for documentary ideas based on memoirs, adventure stories that kind of thing. I know you prefer romance but it might lead to other things. Email Val and tell him I sent you. Until then, I'll keep my ear to the ground. Good luck.

Phil

I shoot off a reply and thank him for the tip and for recommending me and assure him I'll contact Val from Olympus Media. It's not my ideal role, but like Phil said it could be a stepping stone. The industry can be so closed off, almost impenetrable at times, that it feels like once the door closes I'll be locked out forever so at this stage any book scout position is better than none.

Once that's done I send Val an email highlighting my history with Hollywood Films, the two romantic comedies in production with Phil as EP and a brief history about my time in publishing. If I have to binge Olympus documentaries to get a feel for what they produce then I'm happy to do that.

I google Olympus Media. They're all about high-adrenaline extreme sports, like ice climbing, base jumping and free soloing. Yikes, my heart rate is erratic just picturing those daredevils partaking in such an activity. But I could eke out those memoirs, those travelogues in the hunt for their next documentary star. It might actually be fun since I don't actually have to do any of the pursuits, I just have to read about them.

Sir Spud trots over to the desk, sniffing the shelves for treats. I scoop him into my arms. There's nothing quite like a cuddle from a fluffball like Spud. He gives in to it and lolls in my embrace, gazing at me with trusting eyes. 'Who's a good boy?'

Sir Spud kicks his legs in answer and I laugh.

'What's so funny?' Roxy traipses in. Today her black hair is windblown and wild like she's been at the beach. We've been texting back and forth about our favourite romance tropes. I've given Roxy the friendship seal of approval because A: She texts rather than calls. B: She adores romance novels (I'm willing to overlook her predilection for true crime stories). C: She's quirky and funny.

'Sir Spud seems so human sometimes. Like he knows exactly what I'm on about.' I take a treat from the box and give it to him.

'You don't think it's good old-fashioned bribery? He acts adorable and you give him a treat.'

I shoot her a questioning glance. 'Are you suggesting Sir Spud is playing me?' I hold him up and stare into his honey-coloured eyes. 'Are you hearing this, Spudly?!'

She folds her arms across her chest. 'I'm suggesting exactly that.'

'He's ruled by his stomach but he works for it. Watch this.' When there's downtime in the bookshop, I've trained Sir Spud who is a fast learner. I place him on the mat. 'Sit.' The furry canine duly sits. 'Drop.' He lies flat, staring up at me. 'Play dead.' He rolls over, closes his eyes with a groan before letting his tongue flop out the side of his mouth.

Roxy hoots. 'Wow! How did you teach him that?'

'I had to demonstrate a fair bit. He's destined for great things, this pooch, eh?' What I don't tell Roxy is that a few customers wandered in and caught me acting like a dog, lying on my back, legs and arms folded and my own tongue hanging out of my mouth. I'd had my eyes closed tight playing dead to show Sir Spud what was expected of him. Rookie mistake. I did try and explain myself away, but the customers only spoke Greek so it was quite the conundrum. They left before I could dust myself off and open my translate app. I only hope word doesn't get around that there's a crazy woman in the bookshop pretending to be a dog.

I give Sir Spud a treat and he's up and out the door with a bark.

'He's a clever boy.' Roxy points to a stack of boxes. 'What's all this?'

'New stock! Gran's order of summer romance novels arrived. Want to help me price and shelve them?'

'I'd love nothing more.'

We open the boxes of pretty pastel-coloured books and get to work when a young couple wander in. They speak Greek so I get my phone and open the translate app in case I need it. 'Oh my God,' Roxy whispers. 'He's spoiling her for her birthday.'

'Buying her a book?'

'Even better. He's doing a five-minute book challenge!'

I glance at the couple. She's hugging him around the hips, gazing adoringly at him while he fiddles with his phone, reading something aloud to the girl. 'What's that?'

'He's going to set a timer and she has three minutes to famil-iarise herself with the bookshop and then two minutes to go on a book-buying spree. The rules are: she has to be able to hold them all in her arms. She can't buy a book she's already read.

If she finds a romance novel set in Santorini she gets another minute added to the timer. If she drops one, she loses it. If she finds one with her first name on the cover – either author or in the title – she gets to put the books she's holding on the counter and start the challenge over, essentially doubling her time.'

My mouth falls open. 'Is he the best boyfriend in the whole wide world?'

Roxy nods. 'He really is.'

'What's her name I wonder?'

Roxy speaks to them and translates for me. 'Her name is Alyssa.'

I squeal. We have a range of Alyssa Cole books in the romance section but because everything is in colour order, not alphabetical, she'll have to hunt for them. I don't give away the secret but I hope she spots them within her first three-minute perusal of the shop.

Roxy chats to them. 'He's filming it for her BookTok account.'

Gran wanders in with Zeus by her side. We tell her what's going and her face breaks into a wide smile.

'What fun!' She turns to the birthday girl and speaks in clunky Greek. Alyssa lets out a squeal mirroring my own. I turn to Roxy for an explanation.

'Gran said she'll get them ten per cent off the total.'

'Aww, that's sweet!'

We stand behind the counter so we're not in Alyssa's way. Her boyfriend starts the timer and Alyssa goes straight to the romance section to check out the books on offer. I'm holding my breath, hoping she'll find the Alyssa Cole books so she can double her time. Alyssa puts a finger to the spine of certain books as if anointing them, reminding herself where they are on the shelf. For three minutes she familiarises herself with the layout of Bibliotherapy and tracks back and forth chatting away to the camera as her boyfriend films.

Roxy laughs behind her hand. 'She's telling him she's counting her steps, working out the quickest route around the shop so she doesn't double back and lose time.'

It's the sweetest thing ever, watching them film, having so much fun, pointing out books she's been dreaming of buying for months. Alyssa has a handle on all the new releases and books made famous by TikTok.

The boyfriend turns and speaks to Roxy.

'It's time!' Roxy says, clapping her hands.

He brings his girlfriend back to the entrance of the shop and does what I presume is a countdown. With a screech she's off and running with Zeus trailing close behind. The big dog doesn't seem to understand what's going on and barks as he chases her around the shop, darting in front of her almost tripping her over.

'He says the dog is great – he's slowing her down,' Roxy says and laughs. Zeus finally seems to get the idea that's she's book shopping, so begins to nose titles for her.

'Aww, Zeus has his own recommended reads,' Gran says. 'What great taste he has. Who doesn't love a romcom with an accidental female serial killer?'

'Gran, don't get any ideas.' She *definitely* doesn't need a cheat sheet.

A minute later Alyssa's arms are full, and she still has two whole minutes on the clock. She walks slowly, filling the gap between her elbow and the tall stack of books resting on her palm. She spots the Alyssa Cole book at the end of her time. 'Yay, she found one with her name! The clock starts again!' The boyfriend does a faux eye-roll but it's evident he's happy she gets to start over again and potentially double her stack of books. Alyssa places her original armful of romance novels on the counter, readying herself for the timer to start again for the second round.

Time races away. We're cheering for her and telling her she can fit more in her arms if she's careful. There's no way she can see over the stack of books, so she cranes her head to the left and reaches out slowly to pick up more tomes and fit them somewhere like she's playing a game of Jenga. Before long she's got another armful of colourful romcoms and a couple of books on long-distance running.

I point to the odd ones out and Roxy says, 'She got them for him.'

'Young love. Is there anything sweeter?' Gran muses.

The timer goes and we clap. 'I so want to do that!' I say.

'Same!' Roxy says.

The couple wrap up their filming for BookTok. We ring up their purchases and Gran gives them a nice discount. Roxy chats away with the couple and then translates for me. 'Alyssa says thank you so much. It's the best birthday, ever!'

They wander out hand in hand, with him carrying her books for her like the perfect gentleman.

'He's a keeper – I can always tell,' Gran says.

I manage not to recoil in surprise what with her history of husbands and all. 'How can you tell, Gran?'

'When you've been married as often as me you get to know a thing or two.'

My gran, so wise.

'How often have you been married?' Roxy pipes up.

'Nine times, and if my beloveds hadn't met their grizzly ends prematurely then who knows what the future would have held?'

'They died?' Roxy asks, eyes twinkling with what . . . awe?

'Yes. Tragically.'

'*All* of them?'

'Well, Konstantine is still of this world.'

'There's still time,' Roxy says laughing.

Gran cocks her head and stares at her, as if only just now realising there's a stranger in our midst. 'I like the cut of your jib.'

Roxy holds out a hand to shake. 'Thanks, I like yours too. I'm Roxy. Bookworm, sweet-romance reader, desperate to find love, specifically with a guy I'm not distantly related to.'

Gran takes her hand. 'Floretta, book nymph, spicy romance reader, desperate to make this place a success.'

I smile. Roxy is one of *us*. I love the way true bookworms support their local bookshops, knowing how sacrosanct they are. How important their survival is. Gran and Roxy are going to get along just fine.

Chapter 9

Gran and I are in the outdoor area of Bibliotherapy on Thursday morning, adding finishing touches to make it a comfortable space for customers to read and enjoy the sea view. Gran's stacked a table with second-hand tomes whose pages flutter in the breeze as if waving. I find a book titled: *How to Raise Happy Sheep*. I smile, sensing this is the kind of book Donkey Man will enjoy. I put it aside, ready for his visit later in the day.

'Weren't we lucky getting all these book babies so cheap?' She gazes at them lovingly as if they truly are as special as newborn babies.

'Cheap? You mean free!' An expat stopped by and donated her collection of books because she'd fallen in love with an Italian man and was off to live *la dolce vita* in Umbria.

Gran fans herself with one of the books. 'Sort of free. I gave her some money for them. It didn't seem fair otherwise. And now look, we've got a whole new outdoor area that will appeal to customers.'

It's just like Gran to do that so the expat had at least a nominal amount to start her new book collection in Umbria. 'We need a name for this area,' I say. 'To distinguish between inside and outside and new and second-hand books.' We do have a small table inside with second-hand books but they're mainly guide-books and memoirs about Greece.

Gran taps her chin, thinking pose 101. 'Muses?'

'Ooh I like it.'

'Named for the Greek goddesses of literature. While I love all of our shiny new books, I do love these weather-beaten, dusty tomes, the vanilla perfume of old book scent.'

I pick up a book and sniff it. The aroma of time, yellowed parchment, inky words and wandering minds. 'Muses is the perfect name, to sit out here with a well-loved novel and read and *muse*.'

'I'll ask Zorba to make me a sign. He's handy like that.'

Gran helps me string up a hammock under the shade of two cypress trees. Sun loungers sit awaiting readers to soak up the view.

Who wouldn't want to relax here and read all day with the gentle sound of waves lapping in the distance, salty air on your skin? I open a few beach umbrellas for those who want to hide their bodies from the bite of the Santorini sun.

'Darling, there's a box behind the counter with some other pretties I purchased. Can you get it for me?'

I go back inside and relish the cool before hefting the box back outside onto the table near Gran. I open it to reveal a bunch of luxe cushions.

'They're for the sun loungers,' she says. 'Flax linen – only the best for our book lovers.'

'They're gorgeous, Gran.' I run a palm over the expensive material. Gran really does have outstanding taste in décor.

Her cheeks colour. 'In hindsight I should have paid the rent first, but I got caught up in the thrill of this renovation.' She sits on the edge of a sun lounger and continues to fan her face with a book while she reflects on it all. 'My whole life I've always been on the move, one project after another, one husband to follow the next. Going back and forth from my Brooklyn base when I had a pang of homesickness and a need to reconnect with you all. This time feels . . . *final* somehow. As if I've found the place I'm going to settle in for as many years as I've got left. All practicalities slipped my mind. If it's my last hurrah, I want it to be beautiful. I want to leave a literary legacy – a wonderland for fiction fanatics, book sniffers, those who judge a book by its cover, plot-twist afficionados. People like us, Evie.'

I swallow a lump in my throat. Now it makes sense; the lack of following a budget, the muddle of money woes. Gran's not planning on leaving this island. Her words have an inevitability to them, as if she's predicting the end of her life. The pang of hearing it hurts deep in my heart, producing a sharp visceral pain.

A world without my gran will be a dark, dull place indeed. It doesn't bear thinking about. 'What a wonderful place to call your forever home.' Not final, I won't say the words out loud.

She leans over to pat Lily. 'That's why I got these old pooches. They've been around the block many times too, and they deserve to live out their days in comfort.' Gran lifts Lily into her lap. 'Their twilight years will be their best – I'll make sure of it.'

This revelation cements the fact that I have to make it work with Georgios so Gran can live here peacefully in her sun-drenched literary paradise. Even if I have to play the part of a woman who has her life together, a woman who dates hot, buff beach bods all the time. I'm going to have to fake it until I make it. I do feel guilty about lying to Georgios, but if I keep things casual it should be fine. I'll take things so slow he'll probably die of boredom, but it needs to be this way, so no one gets hurt feelings.

Zeus lightens the mood when he bounds over and attempts to steal the cushion from my hands, as if we're competing in a wrestling match. 'Hey! That's not for you!' We battle in a tug-of-war, where he wins, the varmint. He does victorious circles around me, as if parading his prize.

'It's not a game, Zeus!' I give up and stroke his fluffy ears, unable to be stern with him for one single minute. Out of all six pooches, he and Sir Spud are the most affectionate. Zeus doesn't think twice about jumping into your lap, even though he must weigh a good forty kilos. The big dog is of no determinate breed, like the rest of them. They're a bit of this and that, as most stray island dogs seem to be. I do feel for him with all his fluff in this heat, but he doesn't seem to mind it.

'Now,' I say bending to his level, gently prying the cushion from his slobbery mouth. 'I'm going to place this cushion on here for customers, and you're not to touch it! Understand? Then I'm going to unpack these books and you're not to pee on them!' We've learned the hard way that if the dogs are outside, the rules don't seem to apply, so I try to protect the book babies from the fur babies.

He gives me the puppy dog eyes, and it's all I can do not to throw him the cushion and be done with it. But Gran has forked out a lot for the red and white striped linen covers, which are a little too fancy for a dog toy.

Mere moments after I've I placed the cushion on the sun lounger, Zeus snatches it and dashes off to the cool of the bookshop, looking behind once to see if I'm chasing him.

'Darling, you ever think that he might not understand because he's a Greek dog?'

'And . . . ?'

'He can't translate your English words!'

'Ooh!' I laugh at the thought the Greek fuzzball has no idea what I'm saying. I hadn't even considered such a notion. 'I'll have to learn Greek commands.' Sir Spud understands just fine but maybe that's because we use a charade system, although I've promised myself not to do that anymore, at least not in the bookshop.

Lily soon sprints out with the cushion, giving Zeus a run for his money, even though she's a half the size of Zeus. I snatch her up with the cushion. 'Hurrah!' She wiggles against my chest and yaps to be put down. I throw the cushion to Gran and give Lily a soft kiss on the head. I'm not sure where's she's been but she's still skittish around humans, so we're doing our best to shower her with love in small doses.

I place Lily down and she runs to safety underneath the sun lounger, barking at Zeus.

Gran gives me a sweet smile and leans against the wall that separates us from the long drop of the rocky cliff face. 'I had an idea for the pups.'

'This motley crew?' They're clearly not pedigree. You can see the scars and scrapes they've had living on the streets and in shelters. It's those imperfections that make them so loveable. Wherever they've been and whatever they've endured is over now. They're safe, and well fed; some are medicated. They're clean and happy, albeit Lily is still wary and rightfully so. Trust takes time.

'Yes this ragtag bunch. What about if we Rent-A-Dog to readers?'

'You'd let strangers take them home?' My heart lurches at the thought.

'No, no way! I mean here. This outdoor area. Customers can pay a small fee, nominal really, and that money can go to the other rescue dogs. There are new pooches at the shelter every single week. We could use the funds to help with their vet bills because sadly we can't adopt them all, as much as I'd love to. The Rent-A-Dog initiative may encourage customers to come and visit the bookshop, but more importantly, it gives the fur babies someone to cuddle with. Show them that humans are kind and loving. Customers can walk them and stop and take in the spectacular views. These fur babies have been starved of affection. This way, they'll have it in droves. We'll be here supervising, so it's not as if it's any different to them wandering around.'

Whenever Gran has settled into a new place, she always has a sense of community and finds a way in which to help out. In Nairobi it was clean drinking water for remote villages. In Timor, she sourced school supplies and uniforms for children.

Her impact might be considered small but she leaves an indelible mark, wherever she goes. 'It's a great idea! Shall I take some portraits of our superstars and share them on your social media accounts, highlighting the Rent-A-Dog initiative?'

'My . . . social media?'

I tilt my head. 'Don't you have that all set up for the biz?'

'Well, no. I had that run-in with the Zuckerberg guy and since then . . .' She peters off.

Does she mean the CEO of Facebook? 'What run-in?'

'Oh a small misunderstanding about a data breach. A teeny-tiny little hacking incident. This was way back when his company was in its infancy.'

I double blink. 'A data breach by whom?'

'By whom? Have a listen to yourself. By me – who else?'

I suppose I've always lumped Gran in the over-eighties group who didn't grow up with technology at their fingertips, and thus aren't all that familiar with it. But a data breach, a teeny-tiny little hacking incident? 'Do I even want to know?'

'Probably not. They have fancy lawyers. Luckily so do I. Your mother has come in handy too many times to count, but don't tell her I said that. All's I'm saying is, if you'd like to set up social media that's great. Just don't use my name.'

'Riiiight.' I'm not even surprised. OK. I'm a little surprised. But I shouldn't be. And damn it, I'm intrigued. 'So you hacked into Facebook. Why?'

Gran lets out a long sigh, like I'm testing her patience. 'You remember Vlad?'

'Husband number four hailed from Russia? Died in a plane crash?'

'That's the one. Apparently he was involved with a billionaire Russian oligarch, whose name I won't mention for your safety. Vlad helped him move his money into offshore tax havens for a small fee.'

'Let me guess, they moved the funds to the Cayman Islands?'

'How positively Nineties, darling. No, they moved it all to Liechtenstein. Anyway, Vlad was happily working for them and then one day, boom.' She clicks her fingers. 'He goes missing.'

I gasp. 'They *killed* him because he knew too much?'

'What?' Her eyebrows knit. 'No, darling. Why would they? He did their dirty work and the man was just as crooked as them. They adored the scheming rule-breaker.'

I frown, confused. 'So, what happened then? And why did you need to hack into a social network?'

Lily leaves the comfort of the sun lounger and sprints to Gran, doing figure of eights around her ankles before settling beside Gran's chair. 'There were rumours floating around that Vlad was getting a little too close to a certain ballerina. I mean of all the *clichés*. Can you even imagine?'

'Wait, what? You thought Vlad was cheating?'

Gran heaves a frustrated sigh as if the retelling of this memory is still a sore point. 'A woman always has to protect her interests, and I can't have a husband who I don't trust. Hence I had to poke around and see what I could find.'

'Hence the small hacking incident.'

'Right.'

'And what did you find?'

'A vast array of concerning information and, therefore, I booked him a one-way flight over the Bermuda triangle.'

I gasp. 'On purpose?'

'What do you mean on purpose? He had to get from A to B, didn't he? It wasn't my fault the plane went missing. Navigational error is my best guess. Alas, the poor man hasn't been seen since. Sad.'

'Yeah.' I don't remember much about Vlad, as he was always away on work trips and when he returned he didn't smile much. I always thought there was something a little odd about him.

We're interrupted by a woman holding takeaway cups. 'Coffee has arrived,' Gran says. 'This is Athena, who owns the Squashed

Olive Café down the lane. It offers the most gorgeous range of Greek specialities, including *tomatokeftedes*, a tomato fritter dish that will blow your socks off. The lovely lass brings me a cup of Joe every Friday and we have a bit of a gossip.'

'Nice to meet you, Evie.'

'You too.' Athena is about mid-fifties and wears a bright floral sundress and yellow sandals.

We take a seat at one of the outdoor tables and invariably Zeus tries to sit in her lap. I shoo him away before finding his chew toy and throwing it onto his outside bed. Gran disappears before returning with Pee Wee in one arm and a book for Athena, something racy by the look of it. Trust Gran! I keep my mouth shut because I'll just get another lecture about being a prude and that the human body is made to be enjoyed until my complexion will be *tomatokeftedes* red and I'll be racing up the hills no matter how steep and arduous the ascent. Gran sits and little Pee Wee cracks one eye open as if to remind Gran to rock him like a baby, which she promptly does.

'Are you planning on staying in Santorini long-term, Evie?'

I swallow a mouthful of coffee so strong it stops my ability to form thought. Once the headrush abates I say, 'Umm, just for the summer. I've got work to get back to.'

'Ah, a career woman! Where do you work?'

Dammit. 'Well, I'm currently unemployed due to no fault of my own, but I plan to change that.'

Confusion dashes across her features. 'I see,' she says, clearly not seeing. We lapse into silence. A regular occurrence when people chat with me.

It doesn't take long for Athena to launch into local gossip. By the sounds of it, there's a lot happening on this so-called quiet side of the island from an argument over whose tomatoes are the sweetest (Athena's) to a teenage bust-up over a missing smartwatch. Once that situation had been resolved another cropped up. Nethra gave Xenia the evil eye, also known as *mati*, although it can't be unequivocally proven. This has divided the small village with those who say Xenia deserved it and those who disagree.

I breathe a sigh of relief that I don't need to contribute and relax into my chair, pulling out my phone to check if there are any replies to my job applications or a reply from documentary filmmaker Val from Olympus Media. Zilch. My inbox is empty. A feat I would have celebrated back in LA. I slip my phone away, determined not to let the lack of response get me down. These things take time; they're busy people. Gran needs me, so it's really a blessing in disguise. Or that's what I tell myself.

When I catch Athena say the name Konstantine, I flick my gaze back to the duo as she drops her voice to a whisper. 'I'm sorry to be the one to tell you, but word around town is he was seen flashing large amounts of cash at the Corfu Casino last night.'

Gran laughs it off but her energy changes; her shoulders stiffen. 'Not possible, darling. I spoke to him on the satellite phone and he was definitely on the oil rig last night.'

'They seemed so certain, is all.' Athena raises her palms.

'Who's "they"?'

Athena blushes. 'Maria.'

Gran's eyebrows shoot up. 'Maria, my landlord Yannis' wife – *that* Maria?'

With a small cough, Athena agrees, 'Yes, that Maria.'

'Loukoumades Maria?' Surely not! She made those Greek donuts with love. I tasted it in every bite. A person who makes delicious food like that cannot be a gossiper, surely?

'They're spreading these scurrilous rumours in the hopes of further tarnishing my reputation. Of all the dirty tricks. I'm not sure what they hope to achieve except to keep people away from my business, which further hurts *their* cause.'

Could it be true?

Outwardly Gran appears cool as a cucumber, but if you know her as well I do, you can see the set of her jaw, the slight pitch change in her voice that tells me there's more to this than there first seems. I'd never question Gran in front of a friend, but I plan to do just that when her guest leaves.

'Sorry, you're right. It couldn't be him – I should have told them straight.' Athena plays with a loose thread on her dress.

'You don't need to fight my battles, darling. Don't give it a second thought.'

The conversation moves to happier subjects before Athena takes her leave. As soon as she's gone I zone in on Gran. 'Was it him at the casino?'

'Don't you start!'

'It was, wasn't it?'

'It's not as simple as all that, Evie. And I really can't get into it right now.'

'*Gran.*'

She lets out a sigh. 'If you really want to help, darling, then come up a launch plan for Epeolatry. Funds, or the lack thereof, is one of the biggest hurdles I'm facing right now. The membership fees will tide us over until I figure out phase two of my plan.'

Phase two. Oh God. 'That's it? You're not going to enlighten me about what's really going on?'

'It's complicated.'

I huff and puff like the big bad wolf, knowing it won't matter an iota to Gran. She's a vault when she wants to be. 'Fine. But it's going to be increasingly hard to keep the Fun Police away. You know what Mom's like – she will find out.'

'Lie, darling. As we've discovered, you're good at it when you want to be.' Dammit, she's got me there.

'Fine. I'll come up with a launch plan but you have to promise to enlighten me soon.'

She waves me away, looking distractedly to the deep blue sea. 'Sure, sure. Look after the shop, will you? I've got some errands to run.'

'Now? But . . .'

'Yeah, now. Why?'

'The first fake date is in a few hours. I'm showing him Epeolatry, and I wanted to discuss with you in slow, painful detail every worry that springs to mind.'

Using her compact mirror, Gran reapplies bright fuchsia gloss and smacks her lips together. 'Oh, darling, how I've missed your neuroses. Lily is a wonderful listener.' She bends down and scoops up the little dog.

Before I can protest her lack of support, Gran thrusts wise-faced Lily into my arms. 'Tell her everything.' And she dashes off, her energy as always astounding me.

With a sigh, I tickle Lily's belly as I ponder where Gran is rushing to this time. Lily lets out a wide yawn that sounds more feline than canine.

I've got the whole fake-date fiasco to contend with and need a solid hour or two to panic about it, but luckily for me I've got Lily to confide in.

'So, Lily the main issue is . . .' I glance at the small pooch in my arms. Her eyes are closed tight and she softly snores. Just what does a girl have to do to get a fake romance pep talk around here? There's no time to internally quail and rue my choices, as a family of three walk in to peruse the shelves. 'Hello,' I greet them. 'Welcome to Bibliotherapy.'

Their little boy, a child of about ten or so, creeps close to peek at a snoozing Lily. 'He's so cute!' Hurrah, he speaks English, albeit with a Greek accent. I really must learn some conversational Greek so I don't come across as rude.

'She. Her name is Lily. Did you know you can Rent-A-Dog here?' I go on to explain the initiative and his eyes light up.

'Now?' he asks, his voice awed.

'If your mom and dad have time, I don't see why not.'

'Sure,' his mom says, tucking a tendril of his hair back. 'Just make sure you're gentle with them.'

I take the boy to outdoor area. 'This is Zeus, he will try and jump in your lap, so be careful. He doesn't understand how big he is. He loves ear rubs. This little cutie is Pork Chop who has a slight problem with . . .'

The dog lets off a sound that would wake the dead.

'Oh!' The boy giggles. 'Pork Chop, what have you been *eating*?!'

His giggles are contagious, and inexplicably he doesn't seem to mind the eye-watering noxiousness that follows in Pork Chop's wake. 'Yeah, that's the thing, he's very naughty and breaks into bins, the pantry and can craftily open the fridge, like some kind of dog burglar who eats all manner of things he shouldn't. Hence his digestive upset.'

'Wow, he's clever.' Pork Chop runs around the boy's legs, tooting a tune as he circles him. I leave them to it, his laughter following me. Inside. I go see if his parents need any help finding a book. They quiz me about the Rent-A-Dog initiative and are so taken with the idea they leave a donation for the dogs at the rescue centre.

Turns out I can people just fine when it comes to children. Dogs. And bookworms. It's the rest of society I have trouble with. The couple give me a smile, so I relax my shoulders and fall into my default personality. Bibliophile. I give them some bookmarks to go with their purchases and tell them they're welcome to lounge in Muses as long as they want.

I'm on a bookshop high when Roxy comes in and leans on the counter. I step in yet another mysterious little puddle. Before I can determine what it is, Roxy says, 'Do you get many men in here?' There's a certain charm about her with her Princess Leia braids and short denim overalls. A sort of punky, edgy fashion style. If I wore that outfit I'd probably resemble an out-of-work house painter.

'Umm . . . ?'

'Good-looking, obviously.'

'Good-looking men? Why?'

'I'm done with dating apps, done with beach bars and tour-ists who only want holiday flings. I need a real man, one with substance. A man who *devours* books. A man who goes to the beach to read, not to gawk at other women. Like the guy the other day who organised the bookshop challenge for his girlfriend. I want the dreamy kind you find in romance novels.'

'That's quite the shopping list. Does such a man exist?' Georgios' supine body, lolling on a towel at the beach, romantic suspense novel in hand, springs to mind. Is he the perfect man?

'Surely. The type of guy who gifts you a book bouquet, just because.'

My body tenses. 'What's a book bouquet?' If it's flowers made from pages of a book I'm going to have to make my feelings known. Destroying a precious book for the sake of art is a crime and I'll have to speak up for those innocent tomes that will never be read again. Bookselling is rife with this kind of desecration.

Just yesterday I had a customer ask for a hardback that he planned to cut a hole inside to hide an engagement ring – now that's romantic, yes, but that book will forever be ruined, *murdered*, for the sake of love. A crime of passion. *Just no*. I had to send him on his way with a little white lie that our hardbacks were for display purposes only and a stern talking-to about books having feelings too even if they are inanimate. I'm sure Gran would have understood, had she been here.

Roxy reels back. I enjoy her dramatics – she'd fit right in with my family. She's familiar in that way. It makes me feel safe around her. Like I can trust her. I know I won't be the butt of her jokes when I'm not around – that kind of thing. 'You don't *know* what a book bouquet is and you're in the business of selling books?'

'I'm new to retail.'

'Oh, right.' With a nod, she says, 'It's a curated selection of books that are displayed wrapped in a bouquet like flowers.'

I breathe out a sigh of relief, clutching my heart. No books shall die! 'Who wouldn't love being presented with a bouquet of books! Perhaps I can make some for the shop?' Instead of buying one book, customers would be tempted to buy a bundle.

They'd be a great idea for birthday presents, Valentine's Day, holidays and celebrations.

'You should. You can add other touches, like bookmarks, book tabs for annotation, book lights, the list is endless.'

I jot the ideas down. 'We've got some gorgeous library card notebooks; they'd suit a bouquet of books set in a library.'

'Yes! Let's have a coffee and we can come up with book bouquet themes. But first, back to my question, what's the chances of me finding a man to fall in love with here? What's the ratio of men to women, roughly?'

Roxy is just the right amount of oddball for my tastes. 'Sadly, the ratio is about seventy–thirty. And out of that thirty, twenty of them are husbands and fathers. So that leaves ten per cent who are *possibly* unattached. A few of those are elderly Greek men, a retired pig farmer who likes messing up the colours of the books, a guitarist who pops in every morning to ask if I've seen Helena, and an elderly gent who wears a waistcoat and ties up his donkey out front while he orders me about in Greek.'

'What does he say?'

'No idea. I don't speak Greek.'

She laughs and shakes her head. 'So what do you do for him?'

'We use charades to communicate. So far, I've fetched coffee for him, water for the donkey, yesterday I gave him a second-hand book about how to raise happy sheep in New Zealand.'

'Why?'

'I couldn't find one with donkeys.'

'You're a riot.'

'OK.'

'And the guitarist, has he found Helena?'

'I think Helena might be dead.'

'Oh God.'

'Yeah. Either that or she left him.'

'Well.' Roxy pulls a stool from behind the counter as if she's been here a thousand times. 'Those percentages don't bode well for me, but I'm an eternal optimist and willing to wait *the one* out. What better place to kill time than somewhere as wonderous as this?'

'We're going to need a big pot of coffee then. You watch the shop, and I'll make the drinks.' I go to Gran's villa and pull out olives, Santorini's best tomatoes (if you're asking Athena), pickled vegetables, hummus and pitta bread, assembling a meze plate, smiling all the while. This summery paradise has really put a spring in my step.

Like always, Gran has made magic happen in this little forgotten village perched high on a cliff. Bookworms can usually sniff out a book lover's paradise within a twenty-kilometre range, and slowly but surely they're finding Bibliotherapy. If we can hold out long enough to recoup her costs and the rent – if we can just keep our heads above water long enough not to drown, this might just be the sort of haven that Gran's dreamed about for so long. Not just for her enjoyment, but for all the word nerds who also need a place to belong. A place they can bury themselves in books alone or share the joy with other bibliophiles.

If Roxy is anything to go by, we are going to have quite the eclectic mix and I just hope time allows us a grace period to achieve such a thing.

Chapter 10

It's fake-date time and there's nothing left to do except ruminate on all the ways I can make a fool of myself. Starting with: my choice of attire. I'm kicking myself that I didn't ask Roxy's advice, but in retrospect then she would have quizzed me about the guy and it's best if I keep this quiet for now in case I mess it all up. And the way the outfit choices are going, it's highly likely.

So far I've tried a floral number – too chirpy. A black sheath – too funereal. Denim cut-offs – just no. I'm about to cancel the whole damn thing, when I find a simple white linen dress with a woven plaited belt. Perfect.

Hair and make-up done, I slip into some strappy leather sandals, and survey myself in the mirror. The Santorini sun has given my cheeks some colour, and I look a little brighter than usual. Could it be this place agrees with me? There's something about island life that makes even a homebody like me want to go outside and explore, soak up the sun and watch the waves roll in, utterly mesmerised at how a place can be so breathtaking.

I head to Gran's villa to find some jewellery. At her dressing table, I spy a range of pretty perfume bottles. I choose one and spritz it on my pulse points. It's a wild evocative scent of spiced rum, cedar and citrus. She really is a woman of the world, Gran. Even her perfumes are exotic, like she is. I go through her jewellery box and find wooden bangles that suit. I dig around to see if there are any matching earrings, before realising that might be reaching into 'trying too hard' territory. Just as I'm about to close the lid, I spot a balled-up piece of paper.

I shouldn't read it. It's probably nothing. A receipt. A shopping list. The plumber's phone number.

My curiosity gets the better of me and I quickly unfold it. *Your husband isn't to be trusted.*

What does that mean? Is he having an affair with another woman? The woman he was seen with in Corfu? Let's face it, the age gap is a concern, and the fact that Gran does not like a cheater. Any number of accidents may befall such a person.

My heart is racing at my duplicity. Gran wouldn't care I was borrowing her things, but she wouldn't like me snooping. I'm hoping it's not more complicated, like her luck has run out with the many detectives investigating one of her dearly departed husbands, including the most recent, Konstantine, who with every growing day I'm concerned is no longer earthside.

There's no time to ponder it all – Georgios will be here soon.

The bracelets jingle-jangle as I close her bedroom door and scurry off to the bookshop to meet my fake date. My stomach tries to revolt, until I remind myself this is all pretend, therefore I don't have a thing to worry about.

'Evie,' he says, leaning against the cool of the stone wall. 'You look beautiful.'

'I . . . will accept that.' Oh God. I'm not good with compliments. And strange situations like the one I find myself in now. Why did I think meeting here was a good idea?

He shades his eyes from the sun that is slowly sinking into the horizon.

'Come in, come in.' I open the door and lead him through Epeolatry.

I watch his expression as he takes it all in. As with my very first visit to the library, awe is evident on every line and plane of his face.

'Wow.' The air is ripe with the earthy scent of leather-bound books. The perfume of libraries, and antiquarian bookshops. A heady, enveloping musk that provokes comfort for those who recognise it.

'That about sums it up.' I laugh. Unsure of how to proceed. Alcohol? Numb the senses – what could go wrong? A memory forms of my last first date. I drank for liquid courage and ended up expounding on the many vagaries of first-date etiquette on which we had vastly different ideals, culminating in me drinking alone, telling the bartender how hard it is to find a hero like the ones in a romance novel.

In the end, after a spot of karaoke atop the bar, bellowing the lyrics to 'I Want to Know What Love Is' I made my way home. The next day my impromptu singalong went viral on a stranger's TikTok and I vowed to remain sober on all future dates. I mean, how is it legal they can film a person like that when I didn't grant permission? I'd have sued their butts off, but the thought of my family seeing the video ruled that out. Posy would never let me forget such a thing. Thank God she's not a TikToker. So, no cocktails for me.

Books, focus on the books.

'How did Floretta even come up with this idea?' Georgios has love written all over him, like he's fallen for Epeolatry. Any man who worships words is good in my eyes, and I just might be able to pull off this plot if we share this one great passion – literature.

'Gran's always been a lover of words, the rhythm, the shape of them. I got my love of reading from her. Whenever she'd return to home base in Brooklyn from one of her jaunts around the world, we'd read together. She'd point out the melody of a certain sentence, how the pulse of letters gave a word its own heartbeat. I'd never heard of such a thing before. It made my storybooks mythical, magical, *alive* almost. And I was hooked from those early fairy tales.'

He takes a stool at the bar, his expression contemplative. He's only half here, half in the land where stories are conjured. Where words matter. And the order they arrive in.

I go behind the bar to fix us a drink, allowing Georgios time to soak up the atmosphere. I read the literary cocktail menu and choose the Sophocles for my date. Who doesn't love a bit of Greek tragedy in their tipple? For myself I make the Maya Angelou, which is a little more subdued, being a mocktail. Even though I'm tempted to imbibe alongside him, I must keep my wits about me and in situations like this, alcohol just doesn't help. Next minute I'll be telling Georgios every thought that flutters through my intoxicated mind.

I pass him the cocktail, and he thanks me, reeling back when he takes his first sip. I'm used to mixing these at Gran's level, which is more alcohol less mixer.

'Too strong?'

He coughs. 'No, it's great. A little fire down the gullet never hurt anyone.'

'It's the Sophocles – it's supposed to be dramatic. Would you like me to show you around?'

'Sure.'

We leave our drinks on the bar and he follows me. I point out rare book collections that Gran has magicked up, safely tucked behind temperature-controlled glass to keep them pristine in the hot Greek climate.

'They're magnificent. So, are they just for display purposes?'

'Not exactly.'

He gives me a questioning look. 'What is this place, Evie? It's more than just a bar; it's too special a place for beachgoers.'

'Far too special. It's a night-time library bar named Epeolatry, which means the worship of words. Gran's big idea is to have a launch party with all the bells and whistles. Patrons will have to pay for membership – yearly, monthly, or weekly – to fit in with locals and holidaymakers. It's an exclusive club for bibliophiles, where they can read rare books, listen to live jazz and consume literary cocktails, use the space for events. Let me show you some more.'

I take him down the hallway of intrigue. Works of art adorn the walls. Between them are open archways that lead to small rooms, furnished in the same aesthetic, bookshelves lining the back walls. 'These spaces are set up for book clubs, or author events. Intimate gatherings between friends. Engagement parties. Marriage proposals. Anything goes. Heavy velvet drapes can be pulled across for privacy. Each room has a theme: romance, poetry, history, the classics.'

Georgios goes to the shelves and plucks out a book. 'Where did she get them all?'

'They're all from her personal library. A collection she's amassed over her lifetime. It's so special to me that she's willing to share her cherishables with like-minded souls who understand the value of such a thing.'

And this is an indicator to me that Gran is deadly serious about Santorini. Never in all of her travels, has she shipped her beloveds over. Part of me is happy she's surrounded by her books, but the other part is forlorn that Gran isn't keeping her rent-controlled apartment in Brooklyn, New York. It's been her base as long as I can remember and we'd had many an adventure together when she returned from an overseas jaunt (and possibly another deceased husband) to immerse herself in the Big Apple for a bit until the next place beckoned.

We won't link arms and go for pizza at Lombardi's where Gran'll reminisce about her first visit there back in the Sixties. There'll be no more roller skating at Rockefeller Center where Gran will hitch arms with whichever hottie takes her fancy as she plays the old lady card to flirt and get up close and personal. There'll be no more sneaking into art gallery exhibitions to guzzle free champagne and act haughty, as if we're collectors lamenting our conflict about how the daubs of *red* make us feel. While Gran making this place her full-time home feels bittersweet, I'm also happy I got to have so many madcap escapades with her.

Maybe she'll visit from time to time, but it won't be the same as when I sleep at her condo, and we spend all night watching romcoms, eating our bodyweight in caramel popcorn and chocolate chip cookies and rating the heroes on a one-to-ten scale – me for their moral code and Gran on their looks alone.

New memories will be made here in Santorini, if we can get things on an even keel quick enough.

'Why didn't you show me this place before, Evie? It changes everything. Now I understand how Floretta's spent so much money renovating and why she's protecting it so fiercely. I'll have to convince my grandfather.' With that his face twists as if he's pained.

'What's that look?'

Either it's some bad news concerning his grandfather's motivations, or else I've accidentally poisoned him with the Sophocles literary cocktail. Accidental mix-ups with poison are much more common than you think.

Gran's third husband, Riku Shenjuku, went to bed after a lovely anniversary dinner with Gran at a sashimi restaurant in Tokyo, only to wake up dead six hours later. It's believed his simple serving of puffer fish wasn't prepared properly and he ingested the toxin tetrodotoxin. Gran was in bits over it, but luckily hadn't shared the dish because she doesn't eat seafood. Well, she didn't that night at least.

'I overheard my grandfather talking with a friend, and he said if the rent wasn't paid soon then he'll look at selling the property. He's tired of worrying about it, and at his age, he said he'd prefer to have the money in the bank rather than chasing tenants over unpaid rent.'

'Oh no! He can't sell this place, not after all the money she's invested in renovating it. This is a disaster.' *God why am I poor!*

'I mean . . . he almost got arrested for disturbing the peace. It shook him up a little. He's been a law-abiding citizen his whole life.'

I swallow a guilty lump in my throat, knowing that farce was orchestrated by Gran to keep him at arm's length. Had she considered it might push him too far the opposite way? She usually plans for every scenario.

'I wish I could say the same for Gran, but she's been arrested on at least eleven occasions for being a public nuisance and that's just the times I know about. Can't we level the blame directly at her and assure him he's still a good man, and selling is *never* the answer with property investment?' My voice rises as panic sets in. 'Would it make a difference if she showed him Epeolatry?' The situation is suddenly desperate and again I'm bamboozled about how Gran landed in this predicament.

With a shrug, he says, 'I doubt it. It's supposed to be my early inheritance, but he's holding off until I get married. All the other grandkids have been gifted theirs.'

'Well tell him you'll take it as is! Just like this!'

He gives me a sad smile. 'It comes with a lot of rules though, Evie. And marriage is one of them. It's so old-fashioned, but that's the way he thinks.'

'OK, so that's out for the foreseeable.' I love my gran but getting fake-married to the guy to keep the bookshop doesn't sit well with me. 'If we can increase bookshop sales and get this place up and running, perhaps we can persuade him not to do anything hasty.'

We stare at each other as the sun bursts on the horizon in an orange cloud. Even the colours are brighter here, more vivid. 'I'm sure you and Floretta can do it. While it's quieter on this side there's still a bunch of tourists and day trippers. It's about exposure, informing them that this place exists and is the perfect stop to get their beach reads sorted. And Epeolatry,' he says, wistful note in his voice. 'Who wouldn't want to spend an evening or two here? It comes down to spreading the word so they can find you.'

He's right. We've probably had hundreds of missed opportunities simply because people aren't aware that on the top of the cliff is a veritable treasure trove of novels just waiting to find their owner.

'The launch has to be *big*. The name Epeolatry must be on everyone's lips, so when a tourist asks they can be directed here. That's going to be the indicator of whether or not all of this is viable. The only problem is, I'm not much of a party person so in terms of organising it, I'm not sure where to start.'

What I omit is the fact I routinely avoid all parties, as a matter of course. I've had every debilitating tummy bug you can imagine. Suffered through Covid eleven-seven times. Three broken wrists and two broken legs. Shingles. A small apartment fire. A couple of dead Tamagotchis. Three kidnappings and one severe book hangover.

That's just in the last year or two, thus I'm not experienced with what is expected at parties, especially happening ones that need to be the talk of the town. Do people even say happening parties anymore? No clue.

'OK, I can help you plan the launch if you like? I've been involved with a lot of publicity campaigns through the years.'

I bet he's always the life of the party too. 'That would be amazing! Do you think we can have one of those banners that say: *Please leave by ten*?'

He goes to speak then stops himself.

'*Joking!* That was a joke! Unless you think we could? In which case I'm all for it.'

This time, laughter barrels out of him like machine-gun fire. When he's composed he says, 'All we have to do is make sure no "for sale" sign gets pitched out front before Floretta can achieve her goals here.'

I come crashing back to reality with a thud. The stakes are even higher with the impending threat of Yannis washing his hands of the property. It can't happen.

I'll have to really up the romance with Georgios. Surely his grandfather wouldn't dream of selling if he thought Georgios and I were madly in love? Even though it's strictly against my first-date principles and a wild leap out of my comfort zone, more of a long jump really, I throw myself at Georgios and smack my lips against his. He tastes sweet, like grenadine from the cocktail.

It's chaste, as far as kisses go – closed lips is my limit at this point – but a thrill races the length of me at my derring-do. A warmth spreads when he drops his hand to my hip and pulls me tight against him. A moment later, I pull my lips from his. We're both wide-eyed and breathing heavily. He double blinks. I smile, a little robotically, but it's the best I can do under the circumstances. I've just broken one of my own cardinal first-date rules and I feel a sort of wanton abandon. Like I could even perhaps attempt an open-lip kiss, but then I talk myself down. That would be a step too far.

My heart skids against my ribs, a great *kathunka-thunka* as if I've just committed a crime rather than innocently kissed a major hottie. Is it the ruse that makes my body react in such a way, or the fact that he's delectable? Ah no – it's breaking my own rules. Even my mind is muddled and I'm confusing myself when it's quite plain that . . . I lose track of my thought as he gives me those bedroom eyes, a sensual loaded gaze that I'd once presumed was a simple descriptor for works of fiction. Just what is going on here? The man looks like he's ready to pull me into his arms and kiss the life out of me. Possibly with an open mouth, and that might lead to God knows what else. It's too fast. Too soon! What if I return the passion in some chaotic, fevered way? It cannot happen like this.

'Ah, sorry . . .' *I need a good excuse.* 'Can't do dinner, Georgios. The thing is . . . I – uh, left a pot on the stove.' What?! 'And it's probably boiling over and doing untold damage. The last thing we need is this place to burn down, amirite?' Perfect! The old pot-on-the-stove trick, it never fails.

I grimace-smile to imply that if I didn't have this boiling pot *dramedy* to contend with, I'd be perfectly at ease with him throwing me that lusty-eyed gaze. I'm expecting him to be understanding, but instead he gives me that same small smile as if he's amused. Why would a potential fire hazard be humorous for crying out loud? There's no time to stick around and ask, as I'm still in reaching distance and my heart is thudding away with no care that I'll need it to keep beating yet for another good fifty years or so. I do what I do best.

I run.

Until I hit the bookshop where it's more a slow jog, and then finally more of a walk. Blame the excessive beating of my heart. I can barely catch my breath, as blood must be pooling around the organ to keep me alive when I need it to circle around my entire body. Yikes. What is happening to me? I'm light-headed. Woozy.

Inside my villa, I flop on the bed to allow my body time to get itself back on track and resume its regular functioning. As far as first dates go, I'm not sure it was a success, but it wasn't a total disaster either. Was it?

I groan. I literally ran away from the guy when I was supposed to be wooing him! Wooing him as if my life depended on it. What if he changes his mind about me now? I may have done an unimaginable amount of damage. How to fix it?

I'll text him! I'll explain. This is salvageable.

Sorry about my abrupt exit . . .

Really, I'll have to stick with the pot excuse otherwise he'll think I'm unstable. Maybe he already does? I'll gloss over it – pretend everything is as it should be. I delete the sentence and start the message again.

Crisis averted. No pots were harmed in the making of this text. Today was fun. Hope to do it again. Evie.

Chapter 11

Behind the counter my phone buzzes. When I see it's a group chat from home, I leave Gran to it in the bookshop and head to my villa.

'Hey, Mom. Posy.'

'Gran's bank statement arrived yesterday.' Mom moves her face close to the camera and lowers her voice as if about to disclose classified information. 'Even though it's *technically* a felony, I opened it.'

'No "technically" about it,' Posy says. 'Mail fraud.'

'Mail theft, if you want to be pedantic about it.' Mom rolls her eyes. 'Anyway, the point is, Gran is up to her eyeballs in debt; her funds are in arrears. *Arrears!* How can that be?'

Oh no! I knew she'd find out eventually; I just didn't think it would be in such a simple way. Why oh why did Gran not redirect her mail if she's trying to hide her budget blowout from Mom? Amateur move that she's usually too clever to make.

'Renovations don't come cheap,' I say. 'If you saw this place, you'd understand. The cost of having things shipped to an island is exorbitant. She just needs to recoup some money, that's all. I'll send you some better photos of what she's done and you'll see.'

'Photos are all well and good but those funds were supposed to last her retirement.'

'Like you, Gran will never retire. She's invested in Santorini, Mom. This place is magical, truly beautiful and it's where she wants to stay long-term.'

'Why did she go all out like this? Every last penny is gone. It's not like her.'

'Maybe Gran's moved the money to another bank account?' Posy says. 'God, I hope she's not mixed up with the mafia again.'

Mom lets out a groan. 'That's all we need. They said they wouldn't be so forgiving next time.' Gran got embroiled in a scheme with some slot machines and made a packet. Unfortunately, she kind of cut out the other investor, a mafia hood, claiming that Billy the Knuckle didn't uphold his side of the deal. Mom got involved and made some of their legal troubles disappear and Gran kept all her fingers. We learned the hard way, you can't cross mafioso even if they deserve it.

'Do *not* tell her that I opened her mail.'

Posy smirks. 'Gran wasn't born yesterday. You can bet your bottom dollar she suspects you'll hire a forensic accountant to go over everything.'

Mom blushes. 'And what's wrong with that?'

'You don't exactly have her permission,' Posy says. 'I'm guessing she moved the money so you can't track her spending. And she'll probably call the cops on you, to slow your investigations down.'

Mom shudders. 'She'd get a lot of enjoyment out of that too. Seeing me cuffed and led away like one of my clients. It doesn't bear thinking about! Promise me you'll keep this under wraps for now, but watch her like a hawk, Evie.'

My mind wanders to the note I found in Gran's bedroom saying her husband wasn't to be trusted. After the first fake-date fiasco I'd almost forgotten about it. I don't dare breathe a word about it to Mom and Posy, but I'll prod Gran for some answers. It might be connected to this latest problem.

'I don't want her to rack up anymore debt.'

Posy scoffs, but we make a promise to Mom to keep our traps shut before we ring off.

I head back to the bookshop, head buzzing with it all. If I told Gran Mom opened her mail she probably *would* call the cops just for fun. Would she also assume I was snooping when I found the balled-up note? 'Mom's suspicious.'

I take a swig of water, my mouth dry from the adrenaline that's pumping with all these secrets.

'Can never leave well enough alone, that woman. I'd never have imagined my own daughter to be such a snoop. It's the lawyer in her. Bet she's going through my bank statements like some forensic accountant.'

I choke on the mouthful of water.

'Don't bother covering for her. I know exactly what she's like. The woman has never understood my lifestyle, expecting me to settle down still, at the ripe old age of eighty-three.' This *isn't* the right time to bring up the note I found. Gran'll think we're all conspiring against her.

'Umm, OK.' I think back to the call and the issues Gran's been entangled in previously. 'Are there any mafioso in Santorini?'

'Mafioso, no why?' There's a hint of challenge in her eyes, like she's ready for round two with them. Gran didn't take kindly to Mom's interfering into the whole slot-machine stunt very well. She insisted that if they did cut off her pinkies, her new moniker would've been something like Floretta Four Fingers, garnering her lot of street cred, because she'd lived to tell the tale where so many have not.

'Just checking.'

'All you have to do is keep Georgios sweet and I'll handle the rest.'

'That's *all*,' I say with a smile. I don't dare tell her about the threat of Yannis selling. Gran doesn't need any more on her plate right now. Just how much pressure can one woman handle, even if that woman is my formidable gran? All I have to do is keep

Georgios sweet – but so far he hasn't responded to my text from the previous day after I did a first-date runner. Have I already ruined our fake relationship?

I dilly-dally with the idea of texting him again, but it feels like that would be heading into Stage Four Clinger territory. No, isn't it best to remain aloof? Let him chase me and all that? But what if it's over before it's even begun?

Golly, there's no rule book for this kind of thing. Who knew fake-dating would be as angst-ridden as real dating?

We get an influx of customers. I peek outside and see a tour bus where a seemingly never-ending stream of tourists are alighting. This is a very good sign! I dash behind the counter and help Gran serve. We chat to our newest customers who tell us they're from Guangzhou in China and are doing day trips around the Greek islands.

They're happy and bubbly – the perfect kind of customer. That is, until they ask to take photos with me. Why me? 'You're so pretty!'

'Umm, OK.' I'm not much of a compliment-taking/photo person, but they seem so friendly and genuinely excited about the idea, that I agree.

Houdini takes this moment to leap into the air and photo bomb. The customer screeches with laughter when she views the screen and holds it out for me to see.

Houdini looks like he's base jumping. His jowls have rippled outwards with the momentum of his leap, his eyes are crazy wide but it's the devilish grin on his face that is hilarious. I go to pat him for taking such a funny photo but of course, *poof*, he's disappeared. I'm sure he was once a circus dog, or something.

The tourists continue to take pictures around the bookshop and with the canines, who all put on a show, except for Lily who dashes outside to Gran's villa to hide.

I'm helping a young couple find walking guides for greater Greece when Roxy comes in with Houdini in her arms. 'You will never guess where he was.'

'Where?'

'The roof of your villa!'

I reel back. 'But . . . how? How did he get up there and how on earth did he find his footing?' The roof is a dome shape. I can't see how he'd find any traction without tumbling off.

Roxy shakes her head, her eyes wild as if she can't believe it either. 'Scared the life out of me. I called him down and he leapt into my arms and we both fell to the grass. He's got daredevil blood in him!'

'He does!' Houdini seems to like living life on the edge like some kind of stunt dog.

The queue of book buyers grows as we chat. 'I'll help,' Roxy says, putting down Houdini with a stern warning that he's to keep his paws firmly planted on the earth.

Chapter 12

A few days later, Gran and I are stacking the shelves at Muses with more second-hand books for the Rent-A-Dog initiative when Georgios arrives. 'Good morning,' he says.

Oh God, he's quite disarming in the sunlight. 'Hi.' I focus all my attention on lining the books up symmetrically. Anything to not stare directly at him. I'm not sure how I feel about the radio silence between us. And now he's here in the flesh.

'You look beautiful today, Evie.'

I admit I might have acted rashly by running, but I'm a little rusty with romance and I'd been caught up in the plot, the moment, the headiness of a man in my orbit. At least that's what I'm telling myself.

'Umm.' I narrow my eyes. I won't mention the fact he didn't reply to my text and left me worrying for days on end. I'm better than that. 'Why didn't you reply to my text?' *Damn it.*

He's probably judging me for kissing on the first date. I know I would.

'Sorry, I went swimming with my phone.'

'What – you couldn't find a friend to go with?'

He double blinks and then laughs. 'She was busy working.'

Does he mean me? 'Right.'

103

'I replaced my waterlogged phone and here I am.' It could be my woeful dating history and my general distrust of men and/ or people but there's a niggle. Is it just that I'm used to having a diabolical love life and am reverting to type, or could it be he needed a few days to decide whether he wanted any part of the Chronicles of Evie? And that's OK, isn't it? For someone who likes to be invisible, chaos seems to find me in the most unlikely places. And what does it matter since this is not real? Golly, I really have to remember that I'm doing this for Gran and no other reason.

'Well, thanks for explaining.' Words fail me in my time of need. How is that fair? He's just a lot to take in. If this were a movie, I'd drop something and we'd both go to pick it up and, surprise, we'd bump heads thus giving us a moment to stare deeply into each other's eyes and realise with a start – Cupid has struck. Sadly this isn't a movie. Instead, these lengthy awkward pauses give me the impetus to run again but I really don't think I can get away with doing that twice.

'Look at you both!' Gran approaches, having no doubt seen my vacillating. 'Such a fine-looking couple, if I may say so myself. A perfect match!'

Oh God. Maybe *he'll* do a runner this time?

'I agree,' he says with a shy smile. *What?!* 'I'm a lucky man.' Eh? He barely knows me! I'm asleep and this is all a dream. As subtly as possible I pinch myself. Nope, it appears this is real.

What if he were to genuinely fall in love with me? Next minute I'll be fake-marrying the guy and having fake babies because I'm too polite to tell him the truth. We'll live in a fake house, that I fake-decorate with bookshelves lining every wall. We'll adopt fake dogs with fake names.

I suffer a rush of the blood to the head – what have I gotten myself into?!

'Would you like a glass of *visináda*?' Gran asks, giving him a saccharine smile. She sure can turn on the charm when she needs to, while I ponder what my fake children will be named. Little Odysseus and . . . *No, Evie. Stop!*

'Sure, but I was going to ask if you could spare Evie for a few hours.'

'Of course!' Gran says before I can open my mouth to protest. 'Evie would love a break from the bookshop. Poor thing hasn't seen much of our beautiful island since she arrived.' With ice clinking in the jug, Gran pours Georgios a glass of the sweet cherry drink that is popular in Greece and hands it over. He takes a deep sip and nods his approval. 'In fact, Evie can have a few days . . .'

'It's OK,' I butt in. 'I'm here to help you, Gran. Besides, the tiler is coming to finish the bathrooms in Epeolatry this afternoon. And the painter is doing those touch-ups.' Someone has to keep an eye on the books. What if they pick them up with a dusty hand? Spill paint near them? And it's hot today. I'll need to fetch them some icy cold drinks.

My former bravado has been dashed by how relaxed Georgios is, as if none of this is a huge deal. He and Gran act like they're best pals, and he doesn't seem to care that I ran from our first date with the old pot-on-the-stove the trick. Perhaps my little white lies are terribly convincing?

'We'll only be a few hours,' Georgios says, with a ravishing smile. Just how does that work so naturally? It's something about the symmetry of his features, the way light reflects from his dark eyes and those pearly whites of his. If only there was smile school for those of us who can't quite get their facial muscles to behave.

'Perfect!' Gran says. 'There's no rush. I can let the tradespeople in.'

The tradespeople! I don't know how to broach it in front of Georgios, but I signal to Gran with my eyes, hoping she translates my meaning. The trades expect to be paid and I fear there's not enough in the coffers. 'It's just . . .'

Gran shakes her hand as if implying there's no problem. 'It's fine, darling. I've got it sorted. Off you go.'

105

'I'll wait in the car for you, Evie. Bring a swimming costume and towel. Have a good day, Floretta.' Oh good, he expects me to wear almost nothing. This is what happens when you break your set-in-stone first-date rules.

'You too, darling man.' She makes puppy dog eyes at him before he leaves.

'*Darling man*. Gran! What are you playing at?'

She shoots me a sly smile. 'He's clearly smitten with you, and like a knucklehead you're completely oblivious to it. I'm helping things along.'

'Last time you saw each other there was a screaming match, and now he's *darling man!*'

She giggles like a schoolgirl. I fight against the upward tilt of my own lips. It's either laugh or scream and boy oh boy is this pendulum *intense*. 'He'd make great-looking babies.'

'Oh my God.' She's past rational thought. It's no use while she's back in fantasyland, imagining Georgios' future babies. Just like I'd been a moment ago with little Odysseus. Has he hypnotised us or something? Best to stick to practical matters. 'But the trades, Gran. They're expecting to be paid today.'

'Let me worry about that.' She massages the wrinkle between my brows. 'Relax, Evie. Go and let your hair down. Have some fun with that ravishing man. Do something I'd do! I've got a lovely bikini inside that's never fit me, but it'll fit your stunning curves. Why don't you wear it? A little white number.'

'A bikini? That's leaving myself open to all sorts of clothing malfunctions and it's not very sun smart. No thank you.' I give her a glare for good measure as I go inside to change, before grabbing my bag and a hat. 'Call me if you need me.'

'I won't.'

I find Georgios in his car, the air-con blasting. How well do we even know this guy? He could be kidnapping me, in lieu of rent money. Holding me in exchange for euros that we don't have.

An awkward silence sits between us, as I strap on my seatbelt.

Has Gran considered this might all be a ploy? My mind races as fast as his car takes the hilly bends. Does no one drive the speed limit here?

'Are you going a little fast, perhaps?' Georgios is a New Yorker, so more likely to walk or use public transport rather than drive. Just how much experience does he have with these winding roads that have a great big pool of water on one side?

'Sorry,' he says. 'I'll slow down. To be honest, I try and get around these bends as fast as possible because the thought of going over the edge freaks me out.'

'So you go *faster*?'

'Gets it over quicker.'

'But you might lose control quicker.'

'You don't trust me?'

'I don't know you, Georgios. Not really. And when it comes to your driving prowess, the jury is still out. I'm not sure your method is sound.'

He laughs. 'I like your honesty.'

I tend to drop truth bombs when I fear for my life. Not only do I have to contend with the car skidding off into the sea, but also the fact he might be taking me prisoner. There's a lot to worry about.

We drive on, albeit at a slower pace. 'Any luck with the job hunt?' he asks.

'Not yet. I've reached out to my contacts and applied for various roles but it's a slow process.' There's been no word from documentary maker Val, from Olympus Media, which I take as a positive. It's not a no. In the interim I've applied for anything within the field of book scouting, casting that net far and wide.

The roads even out and to my great delight, we veer away from the cliffs and on to flat land.

We pass through populated towns and come to a port.

By my great powers of deduction, I guess we're doing some kind of water activity. A boat. A jet ski. Snorkelling? If this is a way to make Gran pay up quicker, I will move heaven and earth to get those funds. Sports aren't my thing; water sports are the work of the devil. All that activity whilst trying not to drown and expected to do so wearing itty-bitty swimwear. Nope.

He parks the car and runs around to open my door. The man clearly does read the occasional romcom because his romance game is strong. 'Shall we go?'

'Umm. I'm not really a strong swimmer.' Probably because I avoided school swimming lessons my entire life, heck you could even say I orchestrated such things, which in retrospect seems quite dangerous when you're surrounded by water in Santorini. It's *everywhere.*

'Don't worry. I'll be right beside you. You'll mostly be above the water, once you get the hang of flyboarding.'

Whatever that is, I don't like the sound of it. How can we be above the water? As god-like as he is, he's not Jesus. I trudge glumly behind him, my feet heavy, as if I'm being led to my death, and who knows, I just might be. He points to a group frolicking in the water and all the breath leaves my body in a whoosh.

'What fresh hell is that?'

These toned, tanned, demigods with athletic physiques, have some kind of jetpacks strapped to their feet that propel them from the water, to around seventy foot into the air. They're literally flying above the water from great heights.

'Flyboarding. I've always wanted to try it.'

'It's up there on the dumb ways to die list, and I should know, since I've seen a lot of avoidable death in my short life.'

He holds a hand to his stomach and laughs, as if I've said something hilarious when I'm being one hundred per cent serious. Does he not get that? The man seems to think I use sarcasm for humour when I clearly do not. 'Evie, you kill me.'

'It could be arranged.'

He throws his head back again, laughter bubbling out of him. My frown deepens. It's like we're having two different conversations. Just what am I missing here? What the hell is so funny? When he manages to compose himself, he puts a hand to the small of my back and pushes me towards this terrible idea.

When he gets to the ticket booth I shrink in on myself and go invisible; at least that's what I hope happens. I hope I turn around and see him frantically searching for me. But no such luck as he speaks to the woman and then turns and locks eyes with me. 'What size shoe are you?'

Can I play the Cinderella card and say if he doesn't know then it's not going to happen? As I stall to answer a queue forms behind us. 'There's so many people waiting; perhaps I'll just watch.'

'I'd love to do this together.' His expression is so earnest that I forget for a moment why I'm delaying. I tell him my damn shoe size.

Before I can give my panic time to manifest into a great big ball of terror, we're being led to a seat and instructed in English how to work the flyboards and what to do in the event of an emergency. Oh God. I'm going to die alone in a body of water and Gran will feel so bad for forcing me to go with Georgios. She'll probably faint and finally break that hip of hers.

Once we're suited and booted and strapped with life vests, we're taken into the water. It's surprisingly warm. 'You go first, and I'll follow you,' Georgios says.

'No way, you go first.'

'OK, but what if you need help?'

'I'll scream.'

'Umm OK.'

Like the penultimate gym junkie, he takes off without a hitch and flies high into the sky. From this angle it looks so far away. I hope I can hover just above the water, an inch maybe two. The instructions are a muddle as I try to remember the process and send myself catapulting into the sky. This is not the inch or two I'd been aiming for. I let out the mother of all bloodcurdling screams, simultaneously exhilarated and terrified. The swell of the sea looks like a rippled blanket beneath me. Eventually my scream fades as I pull in a breath of pure sweet, sweet oxygen before I start my descent.

When I hit the water, Georgios is there grinning. 'What do you think?'

'Let's do it again!' I've never felt a rush like it before, a weightlessness, a freedom. It might be obvious to some that I'm not one of those adrenaline junkies, so this is a bit of a surprise. Together we shoot upwards and somehow manage to synchronise our timing to be side by side. He reaches out a hand and I brush my fingers against his, feeling a zap that could be love, lust, or quite possibly an electric shock from all the currents flowing through my body at such a great height. There's no time to overthink it, as we lock eyes and share a laugh at our bravery, flying high like some kind of human jets.

When we hit the water again, I manage to land almost on top of him. 'Sorry,' I say. 'Have to practise my dismount. Is it a dismount? Or just a free fall?' I'm not quite sure which leg belongs to who, but it seems like mine might be the ones around his waist. There's all that water in the way, so I pretend not to notice and enjoy the sensation. Who knew Evie Davenport could be this brave soul? Not only have I flung myself into almost another galaxy, I've landed on his erogenous zone and I'm not even freaking out. OK, I'm freaking out a little bit but I'm playing it cool. Only because my heart literally cannot beat any faster without some kind of internal explosion, so I'm really just trying to keep my body from malfunctioning.

'Whatever it's called you did it perfectly.' He pulls me close, our faces an inch apart as droplets of water catch the light and run in rivulets down the smooth surface of his skin. It's mesmerising. I resist the urge to trace the pattern with a fingertip. When I gaze back at him, he's staring so intently with a look I can only describe as longing, a sweet sexy smile on his lips. Yikes. It's enough to make the hammering of my heart go into overdrive. The only solution

I have to stop the intensity of such a moment is to bridge the small distance between us and kiss him. His lips are wet and soft and I melt into the moment. All rational thought . . . evaporates. Just when I think I might die, I hear a smattering of Greek words volleyed in our direction. He pulls away, apology written on his features. 'They're yelling at us to bring the gear back.'

Oh my God. There's a crowd of people waiting to use the equipment and here we are making out in the water like it's a private hotel room or something. It's not like me to forget my surroundings. It's especially not like me to smooch in public with an audience. My cheeks colour as Georgios motions to them that we're heading back to shore. He takes my hand as we drift back and I don't feel so seen, I don't feel foolish, I just feel alive with all the possibilities before me. What a day!

After our time flyboarding is up, Georgios says, 'One more adventure to be had.' We get back into the car and drive back towards Gran's side of the island. When we arrive, he points to a dock and we find a boat called *Lady Kriller*. 'Keep hold of my hand and I'll lead you across the gangway.'

'We're going sailing?' That seems so sedate compared to flyboarding, but I check just in case because if he suggests scuba diving with gigantic octopuses or a creature equally as terrifying then I'm going to fake my own death to avoid it.

'Yes, around the Santorini caldera and I've organised canapés and champagne. If you're up for it we can finish with a swim in the sea.'

A swim? Will an octopus wrap itself around me, or worse a shark? There's a lot of water, a lot of *deep* water. Who knows what lurks beneath? At least with the jetpacks I had half a chance to zoom away. 'What's the shark kill count around these parts?'

'No shark attacks that I'm aware of. I can always swim further from the boat so in the unlikely event of a shark swimming casually by, it'll go for me first.' That same grin is back, like he's enjoying humouring me. Do regular people not ask these kinds of questions, and just throw themselves into these activities with no care for life and limb? He's even suggesting himself as shark bait. It's sweet and all but has he never watched *Jaws*?

'You'd do that for me?'

'Sure, why not? You said you're not a strong swimmer, so we can stay close to the boat.'

I don't know why I'm so touched by the idea. Maybe it's because I really am scared of sharks and every organism that hides in the deep blue waiting to pounce on unsuspecting frolickers. 'Come on, Evie.' He helps me on to the boat while I'm still smiling like a loon.

We're met onboard by a crew of three. They welcome us with a glass of champagne and motion for us to relax on the deck outside. We take a seat under the canopy that provides some delicious shade from the glare of the Aegean Sea.

'This is gorgeous,' I say taking a sip of chilled champagne that goes down well after the earlier shenanigans. All that adrenaline being pumped around sure does leave a person parched.

The crew pull in the ropes and we set off. 'I've always wanted to sail around the caldera, but I never had the time. When I've visited it's always been a week at most, and I used that time visiting extended family. It's fun to explore Santorini like a tourist.'

'What is the caldera?'

'It's the view you see from Floretta's villa.' He sips his champagne and lies sprawled on the daybed beside me. 'It's a volcanic crater, now a giant lagoon surrounded by cliffs. Calderas are formed after volcanic eruptions. It's amazing to me that something so spectacular can come from a natural disaster.'

I try not to panic. 'There's the possibility that a volcano might erupt?' They don't mention that in the guidebooks, do they!

He shades his face with a hand. 'It's dormant.'

'Uh-huh.' For how long?

'It's got a fascinating history actually. During the second millennium BC it erupted and sunk the western part of the island. Some people believe the tidal waves it created caused the destruction of the Minoan civilisation; other theories say that Thira had been the capital of Atlantis, the lost civilisation, but that's up for debate.'

'Wow. I need to brush up on my Greek history. It *is* fascinating.' Miraculously Georgios has distracted me from worrying about volcanic eruptions and replaced that with imagining the lost civilisation of Atlantis. 'I bet Gran's got plenty of books on the subject.' I plan to hunt out a couple of Greek history books when I get back to Bibliotherapy.

A staff member wearing aviator sunglasses approaches with a tray of food in hand and describes the feast that awaits us. 'We have *kolokithokeftedes:* fried zucchini balls, *tiropitakia:* mini feta filo triangles and *marides tiganites:* crispy whitebait with a drizzle of lemon juice.' He also places down a bowl of fresh Greek salad with plump kalamata olives that look different to ones from home. Fuller and fatter as if they've soaked up all the juices of their garlicky, oily marinade.

'Thank you,' I say, as another crew member brings napkins and cutlery. My mouth waters in anticipation. 'What to try first?' I say, placing a napkin over my lap.

'Try the tiropitakia while it's warm.' He lifts a feta triangle to my lips and I take a delicate bite, trying not to munch his fingers in the process. The gesture is strangely intimate and I'm glad I'm eating so I don't try and fill the silence with inane chatter to cover my nerves. The crispy tangy triangle is delicious.

'Another bite?' he says and I nod.

I've never had a man gently feed me like this before. It feels wildly romantic as he takes every care to save me from filo crumbs, holding a napkin under his hands as he brings the treat to my lips again and again.

Georgios must know about love languages and that I'm ruled by my love of food. Not in a gluttonous way, well not always, but that there's an art form in making dishes with love and respect for the produce, for the person who will eat those creations and appreciate the care that went into creating every bite. I love that food can tell a story, share a history of a place, a culture. Its climate.

I want to thank him in return so I pick up a plump olive and pop it in his mouth. My fingertip brushes against the softness of his lip. It feels sensual somehow. I glance away, not sure what it means or if this is just what people do here when sharing luscious morsels of food.

We continue feeding each other as if it's the most natural thing in the world. We delight over the flavours, the freshness, our luck at sharing such an adventure on the water, washed down with fancy champagne, the sun on our faces.

When we get to the caldera, it's almost an afterthought. I'm so consumed by him I feel a bit like I'm upside down. It's stunning – a marvel – but so is he. It's as though we've both peeled back a superficial layer of ourselves today, and exposed the white heat of what lies beneath. Either that or it's some kind of sunstroke.

After our adventure, I feel more at ease with him. I suppose facing your fears really puts things into perspective. 'We should do more Santorini sightseeing.' I'm supposed to be wooing the man, after all, and it turns out I'm enjoying it. A little too much.

'I'd love to,' he says.

Later that afternoon we return to Bibliotherapy. I'm sleepy after so much sunshine when I'm met with the cool shade of the bookshop. Gran's helping a few customers and waves me away, implying she doesn't need any help. It's only because Georgios is beside me, otherwise she'd usually leave for cocktails with her friends at this hour, but I keep that little nugget to myself. The sun has a bite and has left its mark on my cheeks. Blame the amount of fun we were having.

I turn to the Grecian god himself and say, 'Do you want to head outside to Muses? I'll get some drinks sorted and we can brainstorm for the launch party?' Usually, I have a finite limit for peopling but so far Georgios hasn't hit that threshold. And

114

he seems keen to help with the launch party ideas, even though my brain feels mushy from the day. From him.

'Sure,' he says, 'I'll borrow a notebook and pen from Floretta and meet you outside.'

'There's a pen thief. Long story but I have a stash inside a book box, cleverly disguised as *War and Peace* under the counter.'

'I'm not even going to ask.'

'Smart.'

When I return with a jug of lemon water and glasses I find Georgios surrounded by the pups all vying for his attention, including skittish Lily. Well, there's one for the books. Even canines flock to him like he's the second coming. The man must have some strong pheromones or something. It's another tick in the box for Georgios because dogs can sense good and bad when it comes to humans. If their antics today are anything to go by, they *adore* him.

Zeus pulls rank and jumps into his lap. Georgios lets out an 'Oomph'. Houdini appears and then just as quickly disappears. 'Where did that dog go?' he asks, darting his head around to search for him. 'I'm sure he had a wallet in his mouth.'

'A wallet?' Part of me wants to ignore Houdini's antics because he has the ability to make me feel like a heart attack is imminent, but for his own safety I narrow my eyes and crane my neck. Dammit. 'Houdini, get down this SECOND!' I'm sure he's smirking at me from his perch on the blue domed roof of Bibliotherapy with what looks to be a wallet in his chops. He's got some ninja stealth skills being able to bound so high and so fast without a sound.

'How did he . . . ?' Georgios gazes up at the cheeky mutt who in one fell swoop lunges towards me. I let out a scream and get ready to catch him but at the last minute he pivots and lands gracefully on a sun lounger, spitting the wallet to the ground.

My heart hammers at his death-defying stunt. 'You naughty . . .' He's gone. We're left with only the imprint of his paws on the cushion. 'Is this yours?' I ask Georgios.

'Yes, how did he get it out of my pocket?'

'No idea.'

I pour two glasses of water to rehydrate; after all that glorious champagne, and we toss around ideas before deciding to keep the party relatively simple so Epeolatry itself will be the focus. I jot down notes about marketing materials I can whip up and what we'll put in gift bags for guests: bookmarks, a notebook, personalised Epeolatry pens. A library card pencil case. Small things that bookworms will use with our branding. I expect Georgios to raise a brow at the suggestion of spending money that could be used for the rent arrears, but he must understand we've got to spend money to make money, so I plough on.

'Now to the important part. Aside from members who've already joined who shall we invite?' I ask. While Georgios doesn't live in Santorini full-time, he still knows almost all of the locals from spending his formative years here.

He puts on a thinking face, a sort of duck lips that looks adorable. 'You definitely want to invite the local mayor and her husband. Mayor Andino is heavily invested in literature and the arts and will be a real asset going forward.'

'That sounds promising.'

'Also, you've got the billionaire beach bums; they're bound to make a splash sharing Epeolatry pictures online.'

'Billionaire beach bums . . . who are *they*?' Have I come across them in on my bike rides to the sea? I'm slightly jealous that they can buy their body weight in books and spend all day reading under a beach umbrella with nary a monetary care in the world.

'The brat pack. Super-wealthy twenty-somethings who live on trust funds and follow the sun on their luxury yachts. One Instagram post from them and Epeolatry's reputation will be made.'

'Ooh imagine! Let's hope a few of them are bookworms. OK who are they and where will I send their invites?'

Georgios gives me a handful of names. 'Probably best to find out who their publicists are and email them the invites directly.'

'They have publicists?'

'They have everything!'

I shake my head. 'Well as long as they read, I'll allow it.'

He laughs. 'Let's hope.'

In the end, our invite list is a few pages long and I can't help but feel this is going to work. Who wouldn't be intrigued by a night-time library?

As I put down the notebook, our hands brush and a charge runs through me. Georgios leans in to kiss me. I can smell the citrus scent of lemon on his breath. Our lips touch and I quickly pull away.

'I don't want to rush into anything,' I say, with a wonky smile. OK, I might be telling a small fib. For some strange reason I want nothing more than to pull him to me and kiss the life out of him. But I'm sure that goes against all the fake-dating rules in the handbook, if there was such a thing. Gran is inside and there's customers milling about and it just seems too forward to be smooching for all the world to see. Well, *again*.

'Of course,' he says, like a perfect gentleman. 'Let's take things slow. I've had such a great day with you, Evie.'

Chapter 13

A few days later, Gran relieves my shift at Bibliotherapy, waving me away distractedly as she chats to someone on her phone in an agitated manner. Gran's always lived her life on hyperdrive but lately her demeanour has been a little less sparkly. Could be the heat. It bears down during the day and saps a person's strength.

It's obvious Gran wants me to skedaddle by the way she keeps pointing to me and then the direction of my villa, so I save my invitation design progress on my laptop. I can't wait to show her when she's less distracted. The invites resemble vintage library borrowing cards like you'd find in the back of library books before the advent of computers. I know she'll get a kick out of them, but not while she's in this mood, so I make an exaggerated bow and hightail it.

New husband Konstantine is still MIA. From what I gather Gran doesn't have much contact with him. Could be that he's in the middle of an ocean somewhere and the satellite phone is unreliable, or it could be the guy is a dud of a husband – hard to tell right now. If Gran doesn't want to confide in me, there's not much I can do until she's ready to share her story. One thing I respect is that Gran will always fess up when the time is right. Mom's been strangely quiet, which is ominous in itself. She probably *has* hired a forensic accountant and will know before I do if something is amiss.

I go to my villa and flop on the bed. No sooner have I angled the blinds to block out the bright sunlight than her name doth appear on my phone – I have to remember not to summon my mother just by using the power of my mind.

'Hello, Mom. No Posy today? To what honour do I owe this brief reprieve?' It's like looking into the eye of a storm. I shudder to think what the hell is going on with Mom's inner ear.

'Darling! Don't be mean. You know your sister loves you very much. It's not her fault she got a bad dose of the sarcasm gene. Blame your father.'

Her face finally appears on screen. 'There you are!'

'Here I am!'

I flutter my fingers. How can my eighty-three-year-old grandmother understand how to hack into Facebook and my legal eagle mother can't understand how a video call works?

Mom does the whole squint one eyeball up to the camera thing. Yikes, I can see why she's good at interrogation. 'Have you found out any more about this husband of hers? From what I can gather, he's a bit of a mooch. Do we know if he's really working?'

'I can only take Gran's word for it.' I'm reminded of the note I found in Gran's jewellery box: *Your husband isn't to be trusted.* I can't exactly mention that to Il Capitano of the Fun Police though. And I don't want to admit to Gran I found the balled-up paper, in case she thinks I've been snooping, but it does give me pause.

Are we trying to save a sinking ship with no help on the horizon?

'And has any of this salary of his arrived?'

Gran hasn't mentioned any salary and the figures are still squarely in the red. 'I'll see what I can find out.'

'Do that. And look for any mail there, any identifiers on this guy. Social security numbers, or anything I can run a trace on him with.'

'Umm.' I'm not going to do that.

'Have you been listening in on her phone conversations?'

'No?' But maybe I should, even if I keep the information to myself. It might give me a lead on just what is going on here.

'Evie!' she says exasperated. 'Listen in, and report back. You do want to help your ailing grandmother, don't you?'

'I am helping.'

'Well that's remains to be seen. Did you talk to . . .'

'Mom, stop. This isn't a cross-examination. I'm not going to do any of those things.'

'You will too.'

'I will not.'

'Don't make me come over there, young lady.'

I bite down on my lip to stop from laughing, until I realise she might very well follow through on that threat and then we'll really be in trouble. Mom will arrive wearing one of those headlamps strapped to her head and have her magnifying glass at the ready as she searches for Gran's secrets.

'OK, OK. I'll do my best to listen in a bit harder on any phone conversations and see if there's anything lying around that points the way to whatever it is you're trying to unearth,' I lie.

'Thank you, darling. I'm only doing this because I care.'

'Sure, I get that. So how're things in New York?' I'm surprised to find I don't miss the bustling city, the bright lights. The *speed* of American life.

Mom launches into a spiel about how Posy is being frightful now rehearsals have started for her latest Broadway show. I groan just thinking about it.

'She puts the D into diva when the spotlight is on her,' I say.

'Between us, she's not as confident as she appears. This is a coping mechanism. A way to take control when she feels out of control.'

I arch a brow. 'You think Posy lacks confidence?' I can't keep the doubt from my voice. Posy is the most confident person I've ever met. She certainly never gets confused for a waitress and I'd hazard a guess that most of her fans believe she lights up a room with her high-wattage starry eyes.

'Of course, darling! It's scary, what she does. Going up in front of those big crowds and playing a part. Don't you know she suffers from terrible stage fright?'

'Posy, my *sister* Posy?'

'Yes, your sister Posy. Why are you so surprised?'

'Because it doesn't ring true. Posy's so self-assured, so in control.'

Mom laughs. 'That's what she *wants* you to think. It's all smoke and mirrors. That's how she fools herself – to be able to switch off and get up there and transform into another person. You're not so different the both of you, you know.'

'Erm.' Not once has it occurred to me that Posy suffered with stage fright. It's a huge revelation; to do her job each and every night she has face up to those fears or at least compartmentalise them to be able to sing and dance and transform into the char-acter she's playing. 'Huh. I never knew that.' Is Posy more like me than I first thought but can just fake it better? It gives me hope. Maybe I'm just a late bloomer?

'Well, I suppose she'd be insufferable if we openly talked about it, so let's keep it our little secret. And keep me informed about what's happening there. I wish the old woman would see sense and come back to New York, but she's always been contrary.'

'She's not contrary, just free-spirited, but I'll keep you updated.' While Gran confided in me that Santorini is going to be her last home, is it really my place to tell Mom that? She'll freak out. Use it as an excuse to Gran-nap her back to NYC. I remind myself to tread gently as Mom's heart is in the right place, only she doesn't understand Gran's motivations just yet.

'I *promise* you, Gran's happy here. Who wouldn't be living on an island as bright and beautiful as Santorini?'

Mom sighs. 'It's so far away from us, Evie. What if she needs medical help? What if she goes missing one day on her morning

121

walk? We won't know if she fell, was pushed, or was taken. We don't know anyone there. Her place is *here*, with us.'

My mom is obsessed with us being taken, which means now I'm also obsessed with the idea. I can't even go for a walk without wondering if today is the day. A therapist would have a field day with my family.

'What's brought this sudden worry on?' Gran's spent her whole life flitting about the globe, and while Mom's always been concerned for her wayward mother, she's never been this insistent on Gran returning home. And trust me, Gran has managed to get herself into some major scrapes before. Let's just say none of us feel safe travelling to Colombia after the bust-up she had with that tomato crop farmer. Turns out they *weren't* crops of tomatoes Gran was hiking through, but how was she to know? Innocent little eighty-year-olds don't know much about botany.

'She's turning eighty-four soon, Evie. There's going to come a time when she'll need day-to-day help and I don't trust her to ask for it.'

Posy's constant exclamations over Gran losing her marbles must have gotten to Mom. 'I'm here now, and I can tell you she's as energetic and full of life as ever. Having a bookshop has always been a dream of hers, so why don't we let nature takes its course? Fine, you don't trust her to ask for help, but it's not like we're never going to visit her again. We can take it in turns spending time here and keeping an eye out that way. She's already made a nice group of friends who you can call if you're worried. She's fiercely independent and that's *never* going to change.' They talk about Gran as if she's got one foot in the grave!

Mom sniffles. That's the thing about my family. We argue, bicker, bait each other, but there's a deep abiding love there, no matter how much we push and prod for a reaction. I hadn't understood until now that Mom's need for control is a protective instinct. I'd presumed it was her wanting to be the puppet master, pulling the marionette strings, keeping us all in line.

'You're probably right, Evie. It's pains me, is all. I'd love her to be here, around the corner so I can visit after a long day, where she will accuse me of being a workaholic and tell me I'm hopeless at mixing martinis. That I need to stop frowning the way I do or the wind will change and I'll have a face like a stuck pig. You know, all those ways in which she shows me that she loves me, in not so many words?'

I laugh. I've heard Gran say those very sentiments to Mom on so many occasions. 'Just what *does* a stuck pig look like?' I could visit the pig farm, but for safety reasons I'd rather not.

'Who knows!'

After chatting a few more minutes, I promise to l keep her in the loop and we say our goodbyes. Once we hang up, I open up the email app on my phone to see if I've had any progress on the job front. There's an email from documentary maker Val. I manage my expectations by giving myself a pep talk. If it's a no, it wasn't meant to be. But if it's a yes, then I'll celebrate.

Evie,
    Sorry, the position has been filled. We'll keep your details in case anything else comes up.
    Best,
    Val

Val gets top marks for a concise email. But for once, I didn't want an abrupt response. It's OK; it wasn't the role for me. But I'm bummed that I didn't even get to the interview stage. It shows how quickly book scout jobs get snapped up.

Who else can I contact? Yet again I rue the fact I'm not a sauntering peopler who collects business cards and stashes them away like they're precious diamonds. You live and learn.

The only other person I can think of is Gene. But he's retired. Really, I should leave the man in peace. At his going-away party (which I attended because I actually like the guy and thus faced my fears and attended, spending most of the night fetching drinks for people I don't know) his wife Betsy reminded us all in no uncertain terms he was out of the biz for good and to leave him well enough alone. She said she'd been competing with his first love her whole marriage – the film world – and now it was her turn.

So, dare I contact him and possibly face Betsy's wrath? Probably not. That sounds like the kind of thing that could backfire and lead to a messy confrontation. Instead I scroll the job ads and find an editorial position with a big five. Do I want to go back into publishing? I have the sense that if I do, I'll never find my way back to being a book scout and I'm not ready to give up that dream just yet. Instead, I click back on Val's email and send a reply thanking him for his consideration and then I do the unthinkable. I ask if he knows of any book scout jobs going or anyone I could contact, offering to 'jump on a call' with him, them, anyone.

Everyone in Hollyweird is always 'jumping on a call', which is a nightmare of epic proportions for me, but at this stage I'm willing to try, even though we could just as successfully jump on an email.

That done, I head back to Gran in the bookshop whose specs rest on the bridge of her nose while she enters invoices into the computer. 'There's always another bill to pay.'

I dither with asking her who she was talking to, but she doesn't seem in the mood for my probing into her life. I sit beside Gran, picking up the stack of mail she's opened and flick through them. Some have big red overdue stamps that scream in protest on the paper. 'What do we start with first? Rent, trades or these? We do have a small income coming from the bookshop, already. I've been tallying the sales and we are seeing small increases day by day, but the invoices keep coming. Set-up costs are high, but I figure we're almost there in terms of stock and renovations. All we've got to factor in now are the launch party costs.

'These invoices first, otherwise we won't be able to replenish stock once we've sold it. Then trades, then rent. I'm sure with you wooing Georgios that will buy us some time on that front.'

'What else can I do to help, Gran?'

She leans over and gives my hand a pat. 'You're already helping me so much, Evie. If we can get the invites done for the Epeolatry launch that means we're one step closer to hosting the launch of the century in Santorini.'

'Sure. They're almost done; they only need a final polish. Georgios is coming by again tomorrow. We've got our invite list done and once the invitations are finished we'll get them sent. That'll free us up to work on a marketing plan to help spread the word.'

'Georgios is coming over again soon? Just like that? I knew he'd fall for you. Who wouldn't?' She's completely overlooked the party prep and moved straight to Georgios. She's incorrigible when it comes to men!

'Well, it's early days, and obviously it's not real.' I don't dare tell her about our stolen kisses. She'll make a huge deal about that and then I'd have to tell her Yannis is thinking of selling, hence why I've upped the ante and broken my own set-in-stone dating rules.

A woman of her vintage does not need that sort of stress. And truthfully, I'm confused about it all. Why does my soul feel deliciously ignited when our lips touch? I'm supposed to be faking this, not having real-life *feelings*. It's confusing, and I put it down to the fact I'm behaving so out of character. It's almost like I'm being swept up in my own lies and muddling the truth. 'We're mainly bonding over books and this place. He's a word nerd too.'

'I know, darling. I follow him on Goodreads. Eclectic taste, which is always good in my eyes. Shame about him getting fired.'

Ooh trust Gran to have the juicy gossip. 'What happened? What was the scandal about?' Lily dawdles in and sits on the rug at Gran's feet.

'Adam Flynn. Thriller writer and mentor to debut authors.'

125

'Wow, I've heard about this. He was the author who stole his wife's work and passed it off as his own?'

'That's him. Not only his wife's Izzie's work either. He "restructured" a first draft of a submission and claimed it was his.. By chance Georgios also happened to have read the unpublished author's work as part of a project to find underrepresented voices and recognised it when Adam Flynn passed it off as his own.'

'But how . . . ? Did Adam Flynn presume the unpublished author wouldn't notice when his own book was a global bestseller with someone else's name on it?'

Gran shakes her head. 'Word is that Adam had been desperate. Izzie had finally left him so he couldn't persuade her to write his books anymore. If Georgios hadn't spoken up with his suspicions, it makes you wonder if Adam would have gotten away with it. Who would listen to an unpublished author claiming a global juggernaut had stolen this work?'

My eyebrows are up somewhere near my hairline. 'So it was Georgios who blew the whistle and started the whole investigation?'

'Yes. And he paid the price for it, even though he did the right thing.'

'Surely good legal counsel can get his job back?' You can't grow up around lawyers and not think litigation at every hurdle, especially in this instance when it's such a huge wrong.

'Yes, but from what Yannis told me, the whole sorry saga took the shine off publishing for Georgios. The fact that Adam built his reputation off the back of Izzie's writing really got him down, and the idea that a select few knew about it and kept quiet made it so much worse.'

So Gran and Yannis were on friendly terms once upon a time? 'Yeah, wow, why couldn't they just publish under Izzie's name?'

Gran shrugs. 'Maybe once upon a time Izzie was happy with the deal? She wrote the masterpieces, and he got the credit and did all the publicity tours. Who knows? But obviously their marriage turned sour and the truth came out.'

'Golly, what a shambles. There are times when I consider if I should leave the world of words and get into the import-export business myself. It's a dog-eat-dog world out there in Literati-land, Gran.' And when you're more of a behind-the-scenes person like me, it can be downright anxiety-inducing.

'Literati-land is for schmucks, you're from Romancelandia, a far more friendly province. You're a words person and you always will be. So is Georgios. This is a hurdle that you're both facing. Him for speaking up and you for taking a chance chasing your dream job even though it meant stepping out of your safe literary bubble. Don't give up, darling. There's no quit in you, not when it comes to your passion for unearthing those beautiful books whose stories need to be shared on the silver screen.'

Gran's right. I'm having a wobble, that's all. Really, it's to be expected. Book scout jobs are rare, so patience is key. Perhaps I *could* put feelers out with Gene if nothing eventuates with the slightly desperate email I sent back to Val.

I'll give it a bit of time. Gene's probably sunning himself in the Florida Keys like he promised at the going-away party. He's a powerhouse like Gran. I never expected he'd retire – the movie biz seemed too ingrained in him. I bet he misses it.

'I'd love to have my old job back, focusing on romance novels. Who doesn't love love?'

'You'll find the perfect job, darling. The universe has great plans for you. For now though, help out your old gran by taking over the entirety of the Epeolatry launch. Parties used to be my thing – maybe it's the sun zapping me, or the fact that Konstantine is away – but I can't summon the strength. I know I promised you I'd help but you've got Georgios on-side so that makes me feel a little better leaving it all on your shoulders.'

This is a concern. Nothing usually stops Gran if there's a party to be organised. Maybe her age really is finally starting to slow her down like Posy keeps suggesting. Or maybe it's something to do with the note I found and Gran is dealing with some kind of fallout. As I go to ask her about it, she rubs her temples as if she's got a headache and the words dry on my tongue. 'Leave it to me. Why don't you go and have a rest?' The heat bears down, warming the whitewashed walls and fighting with the air conditioning for supreme power. I hate to think of the energy bills from cranking it all day for the sake of customers.

Gran removes her pink specs and lets them dangle on a gold chain above her decolletage. 'A nap is in order. Why not? Where's Zeus?' At the sound of his name, he comes bounding in, knocking a display table of Greek cookbooks, sending a couple of them flying. I launch myself around the counter, arms stretched to try and catch them before they hit the ground. I manage to get close before they hit but only because I slip and do an ungainly version of the splits, which for the record, I'm not trained to do. There's a snap like a rubber band, which I can only guess is some kind of ligament of mine. The cookbooks land just past me with a splat. 'Dammit. I hope they're not damaged.'

'How on earth did you twist into a pretzel like that, darling? Who knew you were so flexible!'

'Uh. That's the thing. I'm not flexible. Push me over would you?'

I'm stuck, my muscles frozen in a place they've never been before. 'Push you. Where?'

'Sideways so my legs are airborne.'

'Oh, Evie.' She giggles. 'You really do breathe life into an old woman!' Gran gives me an almighty push as if I'm cemented into the floor and I let out a gurgle of shock.

'Gran!'

She's no help, what with being doubled over with laughter and all. Despite the pain radiating throughout my body I'm glad to see a smile back on Gran's face.

When I right myself the room spins. 'Golly, Gran! A gentle nudge would have sufficed.' Zeus licks my face, and barks directly into my ear as if to make sure I'm compos mentis. I give him a pat. 'Thanks, Zeus.' While I'm floor-side, I pick up the books and inspect them for dented corners. Surprisingly they're still in pristine condition.

Once Gran is composed she wipes at her eyes. 'I wish I'd filmed that. We could have our own BookTok account: *Love and other accidents that happen in a bookshop*.' Zeus barks again and stands at Gran's feet. 'He agrees.' They've formed a close bond. It's so sweet to see. Even at night Zeus guards Gran, sitting at the foot of her bed, like a sentry.

'That would be just my luck. Going viral twice on TikTok for all the wrong reasons. Let me show you the last time I became internet famous.' I take my phone and find the video. It's ingrained in my mind, so finding the link is straightforward. I press play and cringe as my off-key voice belts out the lyrics to 'I Want to Know What Love Is' and, worse, I have this scrunched-up expression on my face that suggests I *really* want to know. I'm doing the arms out in supplication thing, until I make one hand into a fist, which I use as a god damn air microphone. I shudder at the memory of drunken me atop the bar, making quite the spectacle of myself.

Gran's mesmerised by the performance. Either that or she's gone catatonic in efforts to drown out the caterwauling of my voice. Yikes it's bad.

'You could be a star, Evie! You're naturally hilarious.'

'But that's the thing, isn't it? I wasn't trying to be hilarious. It's a clear case of lovelorn but it just didn't translate. Bad dates and blueberry martinis should be outlawed.'

'I mean it, you look amazing, you've got the world at your feet.'

I wrinkle my brow. 'That's me, the next TikTok sensation. Gran, your love for me is admirable, but you really are misguided.'

She laughs and gives me a peck on the cheek. 'Never! The world needs to share in the Chronicles of Evie but I'll let it go for now. What are all these puddles I keep stepping in?'

'Tiny little ones!' I've found them in the most unusual of places too.

'Who knows. Anyway, darling, I'm off.'

129

After Gran wanders away, I head outside and check the dogs have plenty of water in their bowls. They laze under the shade of a row of cypress trees, their bellies full from breakfast, their energy depleted by the sunshine and their long morning walks.

A woman wearing yoga attire wanders in, water bottle in hand. 'Hi,' she says, with a British accent. 'I've come to rent a dog and read a guidebook.'

'Wonderful. May I ask how you heard about the Rent-A-Dog initiative?' It'll be helpful to know going forward what's working for Gran in terms of building clientele and spreading the word that the bookshop exists. It's not a place they'd stumble on naturally being on the top of the cliff.

'I had a cocktail at the beach bar last evening and saw a flyer about it. I love the idea, especially that the funds help care for them and the other dogs at the rescue centre. I'm a dog lover; people eh, not so much.' Gran's been handing out flyers on her morning walks and they seem to be doing the trick.

'I can relate.' The British customer pays a few euros to rent Houdini. The issue with that being Houdini will ghost her before she can blink. The tourist is demure, quiet, and I recognise the signs of another like-minded introvert who just wants to snuggle with a dog and read in peace.

I check she has everything she needs, including offering her the shade of a beach umbrella, which she accepts. Sure enough Houdini is long gone as soon as she's fed him his treats. Luckily Sir Spud is around and runs to his new buddy. The cuddly fluff-ball soon has the woman playing fetch with a rope toy, which he only relinquishes when she relaxes back into the sun lounger. He plays dead and that gets a laugh from her. Once again, he's charmed the socks off his latest fan.

I doubt she's going to get much of the guidebook read but she seems to delight in Sir Spud, so I leave them to it and head back into the cool of the bookshop to find a couple of people perusing the book tables.

While sales aren't exactly record-breaking, we are getting a lot more foot traffic from social media posts and word of mouth.

Guitar Guy comes in and asks for Helena. I could set my watch by him: two o'clock on the dot. Instead of telling him I haven't seen Helena, I ask him what she looks like and motion for him to sit down. His English is almost non-existent and I kick myself I haven't learned even the most basic of the Greek language yet. I pull up my translation app but he shakes his head no and haltingly he says, 'What you *mean*, what she look like?'

Why does everyone prefer charades around here? 'Does she have brown hair, brown eyes? A dimple in her cheek, that sort of thing.' I point to my own hair, eyes and cheeks but he stares back at me like I've lost my marbles.

'I come back.'

Is he offended I asked what her physical attributes were? Is that not the done thing here? But how else will I know if it's Helena visiting the bookshop if I have no clue what she looks like? It's a riddle for another day. I get back to work.

Keeping the colour order is time-intensive. While it looks great, customers don't seem to place them back where they got them from so I'm constantly switching them to their rightful place.

I dust the tops of the books and sweep the floor. Once I've caught up, I brainstorm new ways we can advertise the upcoming launch. Just how will we spread the news far and wide, and more importantly get members to pay a joining fee? Perhaps we need a guest speaker, an author of repute that would be a major draw-card for members. I think of all the literary connections I didn't maintain – but I bet Georgios has a whole bunch up his sleeve.

To be frank, I'm enjoying spending time with Georgios. He doesn't seem to mind if we're doing activities, plotting the launch or loafing about in Bibliotherapy. Part of me wants to accept that he's just a good guy and genuinely interested in me, but the broken part of me that enjoys a bit of self-sabotage questions it. Can he really be trusted? There's times he just appears a bit too good to be true. I can't confide in Gran. She'll march me outside, stick a martini in my hand and tell me to stop doubting myself. But still, that niggle is always just below the surface. And worse is, what if he is as good as he makes out? I'm fooling the guy. And he will hate me for it. The guilt I feel about the whole sorry scenario is real.

Chapter 14

Roxy sashays in and brings her buzzy energy into the bookshop. 'Hello, you,' she says. 'Any potentials on the horizon?'

I'm in the middle of unpacking a stack of new books. For someone with money problems Gran sure seems to get a lot of deliveries. I assume lengthy freight delays are the issue, what with being on an island, so they're arriving later than intended.

'I take it you mean future husbands?'

'You can read me like a book. A valuable asset in a bookseller.'

I laugh. There's something so fun about Roxy. She's easy-going and energetic and I've leaned into friendship with her, which has come so naturally, it feels almost like it's been orchestrated. It's nice to have a friend like her who I can reach out to by text when I'm at a loose end. 'Sadly, I haven't seen any future-husband material, but we are having a launch party soon for the night-time library, and I'd love to invite you. There could be any number of singletons just ripe for the plucking.'

'Singletons, yes please. And what is this night-time library you speak of?' Her eyes light up and she leans forward as if I'm about to tell her the secrets of the universe.

I share our plans and explain we're still in the midst of organising the event itself. 'Ooh, I have to become a member!'

I take the sign-up form from under the desk and hand it over. 'There's a membership fee and for that you have exclusive use to everything in there. But for you, we shall waive said fee because you're always helping out here.'

'No! I'm not helping out, I'm hanging out! It's a bargain price too if I meet Mr Right. I'm practically related to everyone on this island, so the dating pool is more of a pond really. I'm stuck here now, so I need to make the best of it and find that veritable needle in a haystack shaped like a buff, bronzed bookworm of a man. Pen?'

I go to my book box and take a pen out for Roxy. She fills in the form and hands it over.

'Help me with the new display on Santorini,' I say. A huge percentage of our customers are tourists who often stop by for books about local attractions and activities. A display table by the entrance full of guidebooks and travelogues with covers featuring the ubiquitous Santorini backdrop is sure to draw them in.

'Sure,' she says.

'Where were you before you came back home?' I take an armful of books to the display table and plonk them down before heading to the local travel section to select some more. Roxy holds out her arms to cradle the books I select.

'That one about Santorini wine tours is good,' she says. I read the blurb – it's exactly the kind of guide tourists are searching for, complete with a maps highlighting the winery trail and sights to stop and visit along the way. I pop a couple of copies into the pile Roxy holds. 'I was in Athens, doing PR and marketing for a major fashion brand. My mom got sick, so I came back to Santorini to help care for her.'

Roxy has touched on her mom's illness before. I didn't ask her any details then because it felt wrong to pry into a virtual stranger's life. 'I'm sorry to hear your mom hasn't been well. Is she doing better now?' I kneel to the bottom shelf where there are a couple of books about the best spots to scuba dive in Santorini.

134

'Much better. And I'm resolved to stay here for good. Having this scare, the possibility of losing my mom, really put things into perspective, you know? As much as we squabble, I love her to pieces and I feel like my place is here again, even if finding a man to love who isn't a distant cousin is no small feat. Mom reminds me every day that my baby clock is ticking like a time bomb. Greek mothers – you've got no idea.'

I laugh. Roxy's got a way of lightening the heaviest of subjects. However upbeat she is, it must've been a worrying time for the family. 'I'm glad to hear she's doing well now. I bet she's happy you're staying.'

'She is. But even she knows the husband prospects around here are dire. You're OK – you're not related to any of them. You'll have the pick of the bunch.'

Do I tell her about Georgios? Isn't that what girlfriends do – share those intimate details about love and life? But what if he's a distant cousin of Roxy's and I accidentally blurt out a secret and she finds out it's all fake? My name would be mud and Gran's too. Better to hold off for now. Once again that same guilt creeps up on me. 'I wish I could but I'm at capacity with book boyfriends right now.'

She lets out a sputtery laugh. 'You really do have the perfect life.'

This isn't my real life though, is it? 'This is sort of an enforced limbo. I was made redundant from my job and sent here to spy on Gran by my interfering family. I'm only staying until I find another book scout job.'

'What's a book scout?'

'I read romance novels that can be developed into film adaptations. I worked for Hollywood Films before they pivoted into superhero movies, making my position untenable.' Gah. It still hurts.

'Wow, there's a job for that?'

'Right? I was in editorial before that. Book scouting – that is something else. I finally felt like I'd found my place in the world.

Feet on my desk, nose pressed in a book, just me and the words on the page as I imagined them being spoken on the big screen. Heady stuff.'

'You're my hero.'

'I'm a redundant book scout though.'

'It's only a blip. Soon you'll be back in La La Land doing what you love . . .'

I smile at her encouragement.

An idea springs to mind. 'Roxy why don't you do some free-lance work for us?' I gulp. What does that sort of thing cost? Surely we'd recoup those fees with the customers she'd bring in? 'I'm not exactly great with marketing. In fact I'd say I'm terrible at it. I'm not even sure where to begin aside from the obvious, and the Epeolatry launch really needs to be a showstopper for us to make this place a viable business.'

'I'd love to help! I can get the word out there with magazines, newspapers, digital and hardcopy. Set up radio interviews. I'd be happy to do it gratis; seriously it would give me something to do and fire up those parts of my brain that have gone to sleep since I got back.'

While I'm thrilled with the offer, the thought of being inter-viewed on radio is enough to send me into a tailspin. I'd freeze, I'd croak, I'd make a mockery of the whole thing by being me. 'Umm . . .'

I must look green around the gills because Roxy picks up on it. 'What is it? Oh. You don't like the limelight, do you?'

'It's not that I don't like it, more that I actively despise it.'

She lets out a loud snort-laugh. 'I get it. I can speak for you, if you want? I'd love to dip my hand back in. Perhaps I can build up my own part-time PR and marketing company here in Santorini. I could use the launch as a way of testing my connections and you can have my skills for free. What do you say?'

'I'd say yes, all your help will be gratefully accepted. But not for free. We can't allow that.'

136

'OK.' She taps her chin and then snaps her fingers. 'How about I get lifetime membership to Epeolatry?'

I give her a wide smile. 'Done. Gran will really appreciate this, Roxy. And we can also sort some form of payment for your help.'

'Nah, it's the least I can do if I'm going to mooch around here all summer.'

I take her on a tour of Epeolatry, which she is suitably blown away by.

Later that evening there's a text from Georgios.

Meet at the beach noon tomorrow?

Never in my wildest dreams did I think I'd become a regular beachgoer. Georgios makes it fun. Fun enough I can get over the lack of clothing, the crowds, the heat and the intensity of being social.

Should be OK. I'll check Gran can cover the bookshop and let you know.

Who am I kidding? All I'd have to do is mention his name and she'll be throwing barely-there bikinis in my direction. Still, she has been rather aloof of late as if she's weighed down by heavy thoughts. It could be the business, but I suspect it's more than that.

Under the guise of asking about time off for the beach jaunt tomorrow, I sneak into her villa and snoop around. Specifically searching for any more notes that mention her new husband. I dart into her room and check the same jewellery box, but there's nothing to be found. I don't have the courage to broach it with her until I have some more information. So far there's nothing concrete to go on. In the kitchen I check the drawers but again come up empty.

Am I buying into another of Mom and Posy's conspiracies? As I search the rest of the villa, I contemplate it all. It's the wording on the note I found that bothers me most. Why isn't he to be trusted? And who wrote it? My search is fruitless so I resolve to keep a closer eye on Gran . . .

Chapter 15

After yet another epic cycle, I chain up my bike and I head to the shore to meet Georgios. I spot him on the sidelines chatting to a group of people who toss a frisbee back and forth. Since we've been catching up, I notice slight changes in him, like he's adjusting to island time, the rhythms and the pace of Santorini. I too, feel like I'm taking a deep breath here, and behaving in a more relaxed manner, as the real-life rush of big-city living recedes.

As I get closer, I note he has a book tucked under one arm. It makes me smile. I've got one in my tote in case I arrived before him. Who wants to be kept waiting without the company of a good book?

It's fun to watch him interact as if he knows these people well. Like Roxy, maybe he's distantly related to half the island too. I love the fact they have this solid base where they can return, where it seems like nothing ever changes except the faces of tourists.

When Georgios clocks me he waves hello and jogs over. All he needs is one of those orange life preservers and he could be in a *Baywatch* trailer. The theme music plays in my mind and I hope to God that ear worm won't last all day.

'Evie.' He pecks my cheek; the scent of his peppery cologne mingles with the salty air.

'Hi, Georgios, you look happy today.'

'I am, I think.'

'You think?'

He kicks the sand with a toe. 'My publisher issued a formal apology. While it's a formality, it should stop tongues wagging that I was under some cloud of suspicion about the impromptu firing.'

While I'm thrilled he's had this sort of exoneration, part of me deflates at the idea that he might pack his suitcase and catch the next plane out of here and return to his job. Where would that leave Gran? Our fake relationship would end, just as quickly as my real ones do. Disappointing but strangely consistent with real life. 'Wow. Will you go back to your job?'

He shakes his head. 'Not in a million years. It wasn't handled well and I became the scapegoat. Forgivable but not forgettable.'

I exhale the angst and spontaneously jump-hug him. I've never jump-hugged anyone before, so it takes us both by surprise. I land in his arms, with one leg sort of wrapped around his knee, the other up near his neck. All this cycling is really doing wonders for my flexibility. But it's still ungainly and awkward and I don't quite know how to extricate myself.

Do I pretend this is the norm for a jump-hug and continue trying to climb him like a tree or give up and suffer my fate like the fool I am? I decide to go for it, and bring both legs to his hips and pray he catches them. He does! He puts a hand under my rump and brings me in tight. His poor novel falls to the sand. Once there, I die of mortification. Firstly: because our sexy bits are basically touching with only the thinnest fabric between us and secondly: WHAT THE HELL WAS I THINKING? What on earth compelled me to partake in such an exercise?

His lips are a mere breath away from mine, and it's like I'm possessed by some kind of lusty devil because I feel the urge to kiss him again. As I'm dithering he takes the lead and kisses me. I'm so shocked I go to protest and accidentally find myself in an open-lip kiss. And boy can the guy kiss! I melt into his arms and the sensation, and figure since this isn't real I may as well enjoy it, even though we are constantly breaking my dating rules: when kissing is permitted and just what type of kiss. Spoiler alert: open-mouth kissing is either one month, or eleven dates, depending on what comes first. These rules have been made mathematically, with previous ex-date statistics factored in. FOR VERY GOOD REASON.

When I think I'm going to die from lack of oxygen, panicking and perhaps this strange lust that Evie 2.0 is forcing upon me, the kiss ends. What is going on with me? We stare deeply into each other's eyes, and I look for clues that this is a dare, or he's pranking me – anything to explain this strange set of circumstances – but find nothing except a sort dazed look that reflects my own. How can a fake kiss be so . . . potent? It's probably because we've done things out of my specific order. Rushing ahead like this is bound to cause this sort of feeling of unrestrained lust.

It's time to abort mission! I edge my way down his body, which turns out to be a mistake as I can feel lumps and bumps and I do not want to picture just what those are. I will my muscles to relax as Georgios shifts position and lifts me from his body and places me on to the soft sand.

I smooth down my hair, which is wild and woolly as if I've just been flung around a bed or something. That's sort of what it feels like and I colour, thinking that every single person on this beach may just have witnessed whatever the hell that was. I'm not a PDA person, which I expect doesn't surprise anyone, yet here I am again making a spectacle of myself.

'Would you like to have some lunch? Get out of the sun for a bit?' he asks, picking up his fallen book simply as if my world did not just tip upside down while I'm hanging on by my nails and sheer adrenaline alone.

'Lunch. Yes.'

I'm hot from the sun and the whirring of my brain. I'm like a computer that needs to be restarted again so the electrical impulses going haywire have a moment's rest.

There's a group of teenagers cavorting at the beach. A young girl waves and takes her phone, snapping a picture of us.

I'm slightly alarmed at the intrusion when Georgios says, 'That's my cousin.'

'Why would she take a photo of us like that?' I only hope my jump-hug wasn't filmed. Going viral once on TikTok is plenty for this lifetime. And I can't even blame alcohol, dammit.

'The thing is . . .'

He motions to a black-pebbled road as we head away from the beach and zigzag up small laneways. It should be obvious that Santorini is hilly from the often-shared pictures of the iconic whitewashed buildings with blue roofs stacked up the side of a cliff, but I guess I never really considered I'd be walking up and down those very steep slopes every day. I'm beginning to understand why visitors wear minimal clothes. It's too hot to wear layers.

We meander up slowly; I take a moment to catch my breath and turn back to the stunning vista as I wait for Georgios' explanation about his cousin.

Georgios lifts a hand to shade his eyes from the glare of the sun. 'She'll be posting it to the family group chat with a line saying something like: *I saw Georgios in the flesh with a living, breathing woman!*'

I cock my head and try to make sense of this information. 'Do you not date when you're here or something? Is it because you're related to everyone and you dating pool is more like a pond?' I use Roxy's rather apt description of the dilemma.

He laughs. 'I have a lot of cousins, yes. But it's not that. I haven't had the busiest of love lives.' He shrugs as if it can't be helped. 'My family want me to find a nice girl, settle down. My grandfather especially. He has visions of me moving back to Santorini, having a million babies – you know the drill. The group chat is often about me turning thirty soon and *still* being single. Like I'm faulty, or defective or something.'

Georgios defective? Those two words just don't belong together

142

but I laugh at the fact they have a family group chat and Georgios' singledom is the bone of contention, just like my family group chat, where I'm usually the topic of the day, unless Gran steps up and gives me a break.

Still, it strikes me as odd that he doesn't have a busy love life. He's as hot as they come and seems to always be surrounded by women, so why hasn't he been snapped up? It must be by choice. Or more worryingly he *is* defective – like maybe he dog-ears the pages of books! Or reads the end of a book first like some sort of sociopath.

I narrow my eyes, on full alert. 'Why *haven't* you found your person? Is it that you want your freedom, and don't like the idea of being tied down? Or is it a character flaw of yours that has women you date running off into the sunset?' Oh my God do I even want to know? Imagine if I found out he doesn't like reading Nora Roberts books!

'A character flaw?' He grins. 'Like what? What would make Evie Davenport run off into the sunset?'

My brain is having problems switching gears. 'Me? Uh. If you cracked the spine on a book? And if you insisted on attending nightclubs to dance. If your favourite pastime is watching sports in a massive stadium. If your idea of fun is . . .'

He holds up a hand to stop me. Probably best as my list is long. 'I'd never crack the spine on a book – that's as bad as cracking the spine on a person. Nightclubs, no – too noisy, too dark. Sports – not for me, unless I'm doing them.'

'OK, good. And what about you, Georgios? What character flaws are a no-go?'

'If you dog-eared a book, there would be no hope.'

I grin. Is he reading my mind? 'Not a chance. So really, why are you single?'

He shrugs. 'I haven't found the right person. I'm not into dating apps, and those kinds of things. But I'm open to love . . .' He leaves the words hanging. Am I supposed to declare my love?

My intentions? But if they're not real, then wouldn't that be needlessly cruel? Are my feelings real? That's an even more terrifying prospect. Someone needs to unplug me and press reset, because I'm about as confused as a person can get right now.

'Apps are the worst,' I eventually manage. I toy with whether to share my past history with them and figure why not? 'I tried a dating app a few years back, and soon understood it was purely a way to hook up for those who don't follow dating rules, *at all*. The men I met weren't searching for a long-term commitment; hell they weren't even prepared to commit an entire evening. A word of warning: Netflix and chill does *not* involve TV and popcorn. Let's just say that particular man was soon evicted from my apartment with some harsh words and a spritz of pepper spray to the eyeballs.' I stay well away from online introductions after that dud of a date.

He laughs, although I'm not sure why. I'd been forbidden to bring my pepper spray here on the plane but I've got the next best thing. Fly spray. Needs must and all that. Mom's constant threats I'll be taken are always front and centre of my mind and Georgios might be a cutie-patootie but that doesn't mean he's not secretly a body snatcher. It's best to be prepared for every eventuality.

'I don't go near dating apps either, so I've found it difficult to find that special someone. I guess I'm a little shy when it comes to love. Every passing year my family up the pressure, in case I forget that I'm still resolutely single. They say I'm not active enough in the dating world. The only thing I'm actively looking for is a new job.' He runs a hand through his hair, a gesture he does whenever he talks about work. While outwardly he seems calm, resigned to the fact he lost his job, it's clear it still bothers him.

Then it dawns on me, he said the only thing he's been actively looking for is a new job! What the hell am I in this scenario? A . . . way to pass the time? *Gasp!* A holiday fling? For the record,

I don't do one-night stands and I definitely don't do holiday flings. I'm only interested in long-term commitments; otherwise, as they say back home, *fuggetaboutit.*

I'm about to give him a piece of my mind when I remember my mission. Oh. I can't berate the man for stringing me along when I am stringing him along. *Damn it!* It'd be a little hypocritical of me to be offended since none of this is real, but for some reason what he's shared stings a little.

While I've been busy having an internal debate he's been staring at me, probably waiting for a response. I rack my mind to recall what the hell he said. Ah, got it. Work dramas. Unemployment.

I rearrange my expression to one of genuine concern. 'Gran filled me in on what happened. You did the right thing, you know. Speaking up is never easy, especially when it's you against a behemoth of an author.' Even though you're stringing me along like a row of fairy lights, you monster! OK, perhaps I'm still a little offended. I remind myself I am also stringing him along. And if I asked him outright if he's the commitment type then I'd be a monster participating in this *fiction* I've become embroiled in.

He shrugs. 'Doesn't feel that way since I'm the one who got ousted.'

'Yeah, that was really unfair.' Life *is* unfair, Georgios! Gah, what's gotten into me? I need water. A seat. A nap. Something. 'What will happen to the author Adam What's-his-face now?'

'I'm not privy to the plan. I assume they'll quietly cancel his contract and hope it goes away. He's claiming all sorts of things, threatening to sue them, his wife . . . trying his best to come out smelling like roses. And the scary thing is, he just might.'

Anger riles me. The situation is grossly unfair for Georgios but he's handling it remarkably well. 'How is that even possible?'

'You'd be surprised at what people will do to make a scandal of this size go away. And Adam is as charismatic as they come, which has served him well. If only he'd kept his wife sweet, he'd have gotten away with this forever.'

'Why didn't you fight for your job? After all, you did nothing wrong.' I'm genuinely curious. He doesn't seem the sort to back away from standing up for himself when he already did the scariest thing by outing Adam's crimes.

'Their first instinct was to protect him at all costs. Not me. I don't want to work for a company that doesn't have my best interests at heart.'

'That's a good point. How could you ever trust them again?'

'Exactly. I couldn't.'

'So where are you looking? The big-five publishers? Something more bespoke?'

He dips his head as we walk along a narrow road in a humbler part of Santorini. Cows graze in open fields; there are fewer cars as the road thins more to a rural path. It's really quite charming how he has these moments of nervousness. But is it all part of his plan, to stay single at all costs? 'Actually, I had this crazy idea. It could be desperation talking.'

Somehow I can't see Georgios being the desperate kind. He's too measured, too methodical for that. 'What's your idea?'

'What if I start my own publishing house?'

Georgios reads a broad range of literature, so I presume he'd publish an eclectic range of books if he had his own company. 'I love that idea. Why not? You obviously have plenty of connections in the industry. Just how would you go about developing such a business?'

'I'd start off small; have a few quality authors. Really champion those in my stable. Focus on looking after the authors I have rather than trying to scale up too quickly. It might be a pipe dream . . . I'd have to figure out how to fund it. I have savings but a lot of them are tied up in investments so I'll have to speak to my financial adviser and work out what the best way forward is.'

We come to a quaint little family-owned taverna called Attica and are greeted effusively by the owners. They offer us a seat outside under a big blue umbrella. Olives are plonked on the table as they chat in rapid-fire Greek to Georgios. While they catch up I ponder his business idea.

Chapter 16

While the family from Attica fuss and fawn over Georgios like a long-lost son, I pretend to read the menu while my mind whirls. There's a very simple solution that would fund his publishing dreams. Georgios can tell his grandfather to sell and take his early inheritance like the rest of his siblings have done. So why hasn't he? Is his grandfather really that strict that he'd expect him to be married first? Isn't that a bit of an antiquated way to live? But Yannis has mentioned that it might be easier to sell the property – if Georgios asked him to fund his business venture surely he'd do it. Who wouldn't invest in their grandson's dream? And that would be disastrous for Gran.

Beachgoers are ant size from our perch high up on the hill. When the Attica family finish catching up with Georgios, they leave us with offers of the freshest specials of the day, to which we happily agree. No need for a menu after all.

I train my gaze back on Georgios. 'What about your inheritance? Surely that's a way to fund your dreams. Would your grandfather agree?' What if they really do sell out from under Gran? Yet another problem that will take a giant miracle to solve.

A teenage girl with long curly hair brings us a bottle of sparkling water, all the while staring at Georgios like he's her dream

148

man come to life. I hide a smile, wondering if I also wear that same lovestruck look in his presence. It should be illegal for a man to be so blithely unaware he's setting hearts on fire everywhere he goes.

When she goes, tripping over her own feet, I turn back to him. 'Wouldn't you tell your grandfather your publishing plans and see if he could help with the financial side of things?' I hate to put the thought in his head but it's only fair, and better if we know it's a real possibility before Gran sinks any further funds into a lost cause.

He lifts a palm to acknowledge the idea. 'I'd prefer to do it on my own. If I rely on my family for money, then where does it end? It would feel then like I had investors rather than running my own show.'

I give him a nod, struck once again by his morals. What remains unsaid is the fact that it would also put Gran out of business and she'd lose the money she spent on renovations. It's highly unlikely a new owner would be as lenient about unpaid rent as Yannis has been. 'I get it. And I really believe you can do it. Find those precious gems in the slush pile and make them shine.'

'My concern is . . .'

The teenage daughter returns, plates in hand. 'This is *fava me koukia* and *spanakopita*,' she says placing the food down. You definitely eat with your eyes in Greece. Every plate is a work of art.

We thank her and Georgios explains the dishes. 'This one is smashed fava beans with lemon and fennel and this one is spinach and feta in filo pastry.'

'Delicious. So you were saying?' I take a hefty scoop of smashed fava beans and reach for a slice of pita bread, glad he's not offering to feed me in front of the family.

'Will the gamble pay off? Or is this some kind of middle-aged panic. A publishing pipe dream?'

'You're hardly middle-aged! It's not a pipe dream, it's an achievable dream. You have plenty of experience to pull it off. These days you don't even need an office space, right? You could work anywhere and make it happen. Keep your overheads down and focus on what matters: the words. You have plenty of connections.'

He nods, acknowledging that. 'Ten years in publishing. I started as an assistant who fetched coffees, before moving to the lofty heights of fetching lunch, and slowly paid my dues until I worked up to editorial director. I've been involved in every facet of the business, in one way or another. I'll crunch some numbers and see if it's viable. But that's sort of where I'm headed. What about you? Any callbacks on those job applications?'

I sigh. 'A documentary job I applied for is filled so I sent a rather desperate email asking the recruiter if he knew of anyone else I could contact, but so far no reply. I'm considering contacting Gene who originally hired me for Hollywood Films, but I'm not sure. He's living it up in Florida and I don't want to intrude.'

Georgios plates a spoonful of the smashed fava beans. 'I'm sure one phone call won't hurt.'

'I'm more of an email person.'

'Even better then. Why not email? If he's busy he won't reply, so as I see it you haven't got anything to lose.'

'You're right. And as far as bosses go he was the best. The thing is, his wife Betsy practically outlawed any contact with movie biz people. Other than that, I might have to go back to New York and beg for my previous editorial job back. It's not that I didn't enjoy it – I love editing – it's that they were big on the whole team-player aspect. And don't even get me started on all those Friday morning meetings that could have been emails.'

He laughs, a velvety sound that produces a rash of goose bumps along my skin. Like, seriously? Even his laugh is golden. There's times like this when he's so interested and supportive that part of me forgets this is meant to be fake. The truth tickles the tip of my tongue and I want so badly to admit I'm fake-dating him so we can start fresh for real, but the sensible side of my brain kicks in and reminds of my gran and what she stands to lose. 'Email Gene and give it time.'

'Yeah. My dreams have sprouted wings and I *really* want to be a book scout, but it's proving hard yet not impossible. I'm considering other options rather than focusing on only romance and that's OK as it could lead to other opportunities. You're right, it's a waiting game and I'm lucky enough to be able to stay here and keep busy in the bookshop.'

'Your gran needs you right now too.'

I smile like I always do when I think of Gran. 'I love staying with her. The timing has been ideal in that respect.' That reminds me of the other job that needs doing. 'What are the chances we could draw on some of your literary connections to find a guest speaker for the launch of Epeolatry? Reclusive writer graces us with their presence, makes a big splash and library bar and memberships go nuts.'

He places another filo parcel onto my plate. The man really is thoughtful when it comes to sharing food. Or maybe he's a feeder? I'll be in a food coma, lethargic and dreamy while he does whatever it is body snatchers do. He brings me back to the now by saying, 'Love it. But name a reclusive writer? Who've you got in mind?'

I conjure images but no authors spring to mind. 'Someone broody and mysterious.'

'So we're after the drama of a J. D. Salinger-esque novelist?'

I try to cut my filo pastry into bite-size pieces so I'm not covered in crumbs. 'Yes! A literary great who hasn't been seen in society for the last fifty years or so?'

As he considers it, he tilts his head. 'Is there such a thing these days when it's crucial writers are engaged with their readers? They're across social media. They attend festivals, host writing workshops and . . .'

I roll my eyes. 'You're killing the vibe, Georgios.'

He grins, that same smile that lights up his face, as if I have truly made him happy on the inside. 'Sorry. You're right, we do need a drawcard, a person who usually shuns the limelight . . .'

We pause when another dish arrives. '*Melitzanes Santorini.*' A white eggplant dish with tomatoes, herbs and kefalotyri cheese. It would be easy being vegetarian in Greece with the way they transform humble vegetables into hearty, wholesome dishes. I take a bite. The white eggplant is much sweeter than the purple eggplant from home.

'Why don't we go for a writer who *loves* the limelight?' I ask, the practical side kicking in.

'Anyone spring to mind?' He dabs at the corner of his mouth with a napkin.

'The writers whose books I chose to be developed into film live so far away, I doubt they could rearrange their schedules in time.'

'Yeah, the last-minute nature of this is going to be an issue.'

I consider the options. 'Who's big right now, but not too big that they'd never consider such a thing? Besides, we're not exactly rolling in cash to woo them with. Gah, I can't think of a writer who'd attend just for kicks. Won't they expect the red-carpet treatment? An attendance fee? Possibly legions of screaming, adoring fans? We can't offer any of that – not really.'

He clicks his fingers. 'What about Lucy Strike? She likes meeting her fans, old and new.'

Lucy Strike has quite the reputation for being a seductress. 'I've read a few of her books. I especially enjoyed her mafia series. What an eye-opener. Really rang true.' And I should know, being caught up in Gran's Cosa Nostra catastrophe. I'm sure Lucy has ties to the oldest family in the world – that or she's done some epic jailhouse interviews with a snitch who would then most likely be . . . exterminated.

'Yeah, they're fun, fast-paced reads.'

'The publishing grapevine is always hot with gossip about the flirtatious author, sometimes I wonder if it overshadows her writing.' There I've said it.

'Lucy is a huge flirt but it's part of her public persona; it's all smoke and mirrors. I *could* ask her about attending as guest speaker,' he says with the lift of a shoulder.

'You know her personally?' Could he be one of her previous conquests?

He takes a sip of water. 'Yep, she's one of my authors. *Was*, I guess. She jumped ship from Bennett Press to us with her last book. Lucy springs to mind because she lives in Palermo, Italy. Not too far for the launch if we can promise her a night to remember.'

Urgh, she's probably in love with the gorgeous fool and will spend the night draped over him like a blanket. *Actually, no* she can't, because he's in a committed faux relationship with me. It's time we had the boundaries talk.

'Sure, sounds great. Let's get her on board. Just one thing . . .'

Another course comes and with it the salty scent of seafood distracting me for a moment. Octopus tentacle, nope. Fried calamari, yes.

'You don't want any octopus?' He asks, sensing my hesitation, probably because I can't look at the octopus without screwing up my face.

'No thanks. I always have this feeling that their suckers will suction on inside my body and need to be surgically removed. I'll happily eat the calamari though.'

'Umm, I've never heard of anyone having that problem before.' Georgios waits with his fork poised patiently while I try the calamari, which tastes fresher than any seafood I've had before. I never want to leave this magical island.

'Because they're probably dead.' It could happen and likely it has. 'Best to be wary of anything with a built-in suction cup.'

'Good advice. I'll eat this though because I don't want to offend the Attica family.'

'It's your life.' He sure likes living on the edge. He better be careful because one day he might just fall off. 'So, I'm just thinking out loud here: do we have rules when it comes to flirting with others, or say, if another person makes certain . . . advances towards us, we'd have to politely decline, right? I'm not saying we're like *exclusive*, or anything, I mean what even is this? A holiday fling?' NO. 'A brief dalliance?' GOD NO. 'Erm, a . . . ?'

'Lucy making advances do you mean?'

My mouth resembles a puffer fish, as I work hard to bring it in line. 'What? No, just in general. A man could also make a move on me, you know. I've been a party to seduction before . . .' *What!* Oh God, when I get nervous I revert to historical-romance speak. Blame the editorial life.

'I don't doubt that, Evie. I'm sure you've got men falling at your feet. Sorry, I didn't mean it to sound otherwise. It's just we were discussing the possibility of Lucy visiting so I *presumed* that's what you were alluding to. Silly of me.'

'Right.' Men falling at my feet – hah! Even book boyfriends play hard to get, the monsters. The atmosphere changes. I should have kept my mouth shut. Why would I try and define this, whatever it is, SINCE IT'S FAKE. Do I want to make my life harder? What if the poor fool falls in mad, chaotic love with me? I mean, there's a small chance. Some men find hot messes alluring.

'Shall I email her and ask if she'll help out at the launch?'

How deftly he deflects my actual question. Interesting. Methinks the man does not want to broach even the idea of being tied down, not for a moment.

Bloody Lucy. I recall her author photo. Another lusty woman with come-hither eyes and a body that would probably suit the bottomless bikinis that beachgoers favour here. 'Yes, if we can get her here, it would be quite the coup.' My tone is stiff but I can't help it. It's almost like a rejection, him not bothering to answer my question about defining 'us'. The brush-off feels real somehow, and I can't understand why it stings. 'Email her, I guess.'

Next he's going to tell me she owes him a favour. A favour she'll probably want to repay tangled between the sheets. Romance authors, you cannot trust them one bit.

'She owes me a favour.'

I can't hold in an eye-roll. I bet she does! I fold my arms defensively. 'So . . . ?'

'So she'll probably say yes.'

'A word of warning. Romance authors are always on the hunt for . . . *experiences*, of a sexual nature, shall we say? You know, for their . . .' I make air quotes '. . . *"writing"*. Just be on guard. Having a grip on the English language is one thing but acting out scenes for their next book – *One Night in Santorini with My Hot Editor* – is quite another.'

His face scrunches in such a way, I don't know if he's about to laugh or scream. Eventually he composes himself after a battle with expressing whatever emotion had him in its grip. 'Noted. I'll be very careful. I don't want to be a party to that. Not ever.'

Poor naïve fool. Just how many of his authors have already taken advantage of him in the name of research?

I sigh. 'Send the email then.'

Chapter 17

The next day, Roxy breezes in, her skin pink from the sun. 'Why the long face?' She props herself on the stool near the counter. Pee Wee sidles up for some love, which is duly handed out in the form of a neck scratch.

'Ooh, where to start. Georgios is inviting Lucy Strike to the launch . . .'

'LUCY STRIKE!'

'I gather you've heard of her?'

'Have I heard of her? Whoa, she's a BookTok sensation. Everyone wants a piece of her. It'd be quite a feat if she says yes.' Her eyes shine with excitement. Golly *everyone* loves Lucy. 'Is it confirmed? Because if so, I can get a lot of exposure for Epeolatry if she's the guest speaker.'

'Not confirmed yet. But Georgios seems to think he has enough sway to convince her. He edited her latest novel.'

'This is amazing!' Roxy goes behind the counter and hunts around for a notebook and pen. 'Why are there never any pens?'

'Pen lady takes them.'

'Pen lady?'

'Yes, yet another weird and wonderful character. She visits a few times a week and asks for rare books that I presume she

156

knows we don't have. Still, I humour her, and pretend to search for whatever tome she's after. While I'm hunting high and low she fills up her pockets with mints and pens. I mean, it's not ideal but I figure maybe she needs the sugar hit.'

'But why the pens?'

'I don't know. Gran says it's better than her stealing the books so we turn a blind eye.' Even my cleverly disguised *War and Peace* book box has been raided. Pen lady sure is fast.

'The life of a bookseller: never a dull moment. OK, so no pens.' Roxy takes her phone from her pocket and types up some notes. 'Can you let me know as soon as Lucy has confirmed and I'll get onto my contacts to spread the word. With her name attached I can aim for some bigger publications and mainstream radio stations.'

'Sure, sure. She'll probably be a massive diva about it and we won't hear back until the very last minute.' My phone pings with a message, which I duly ignore.

Not today, Satan.

'Was that your phone?' Roxy asks.

'It's OK, I'll check it later.'

'Check it now! I'll wait.' I don't want to because I've got a sneaking suspicion who the message refers to.

I hold in a sigh and open the text:

Lucy has confirmed! She's so excited to be the guest of honour at the launch. She did have one stipulation, that it be black tie. Love Georgios

'Don't leave me in suspense! Who is it?'

Begrudgingly, I hand Roxy the phone. Once she's read the message she lets out an ear-piercing shriek. 'Fabulous! Santorini is going to be *inundated* with people wanting to meet her. This is a marketing dream.'

I try to arrange my face into a smile but it's inexplicably frozen up and feels like more of a grimace. 'It's. Super. But . . . isn't she a *bit* of a prima donna, asking for black tie. I mean . . .' Who is Lucy to start making rules?

'Yes, she's exactly that and rightly so! I'd be a prima donna if I were her too. Black tie is a great idea. Much better for publicity photos. Actually.' She types another note into her phone. 'We need to hire a photographer. We can later share publicity pics online and possibly even sell to some gossip mags, but we'll need someone of note to take snaps.'

'That would be great but sadly there's no money for such a thing, Roxy.'

She holds up a finger. 'It's OK, leave it with me. I'll see if I can find someone to do it in exchange for the scoop and a cut of the profit if we manage to sell to a celebrity gossip site, or whatever.'

'Good plan.'

We go back and forth and make a note of what else needs to be done and who Roxy will contact in the media. It's sweet to see her in her element, buzzing with ideas and reignited with her passion for PR and marketing.

'Wait a minute.' Roxy suddenly stops dead. 'He said *Love Georgios* in his text. *Love?* That's a bit much for a platonic friendship. What's going on there?' She folds her arms and gives me one of those fess-up stares.

I blush to the roots of my hair. The whole Georgios thing has never come up in conversation with us. I prefer to keep my love life private and my fake love life even more so, since then there's less chance our devious plan will be found out. Especially considering all of the family connections on the island. But how to explain this?

'Don't tell me you've found *the one* in a bookshop! I knew it – didn't I say it would happen? My theory proved correct! I guess I need to commit to spending a greater chunk of time here if I want to be shot through the heart by Cupid's arrow next.'

Do I break it to her that it's not real? I can't be that person who thwarts another's ideals! 'Shot through the heart sounds needlessly vicious.'

158

She lifts a shoulder. It's a metaphoric arrow. And don't try and weasel out of telling me the full story. Are you and Georgios a couple?'

'Umm, it's early days.'

'Early days and he signed off: *Love Georgios!* Who is this Greek god? Tell me everything.'

Yikes, her excitement is palpable. I debate with what to say, just how far down the rabbit hole I'm prepared to go. All this lying is *intense*.

While I'm still grappling with how to answer, Roxy peppers me with questions. 'Have you kissed? Is he the best kisser you've ever had?'

'Well . . .'

She gasps. 'Sex?'

'No, thank you.' Golly that escalated fast.

'No.' She cackles like a witch. 'Oh my God, Evie! I meant, have you and *Georgios* had sex already?'

'Ooh, right.' I need to answer or she's going to continue showering me with questions, but inside my gut twists at my duplicity. 'We've kissed. And as far as kissing goes, he's gold-medal standard.' I stop for a moment, remembering the jump-hug debacle. But yes, the kiss was sweet and saucy. I'd felt possessed, as if someone else was in control of my body but I can't tell Roxy that. She'll think I'm insane. 'And as for sex. It's far too early for all of that.'

'Is it though?'

'Much too early.' I'm not going to explain my dating rules, but let's just say there's a lengthy wait for that sort of commitment. Hence the lack of any of the between-the-sheets sort of shenanigans lately. It appears most men work to a much quicker timeline. If they don't want to wait that's fine, but I'll know they are not the right person for me.

'Right, right, I see. You're taking things slow. I respect that. So I've seen the glossies – each month Lucy has a new man on her arm, the lucky thing. Do you think Georgios and Lucy were an item when they worked together or was it purely platonic?'

'That's a hell of a segue, Roxy.'

Lucy Strike manages to pop her beautiful head into almost every conversation. Surely Georgios would have mentioned it if they'd had fling? And if they did, does it matter? My head says no but my traitorous heart screams in protest. 'Oh my God! Do you think he suggested Lucy attend as the guest of honour just to get her on the island? To get close to her again?!' Is this all some devious con and I'm suddenly cast in role of gooseberry?' Is he secretly in love with her? Why can't I be one of those confident types who never worry about worst-case-scenario situations like this?

'Why are you speaking so fast?'

I pull my hair at the temples. 'Stress! How will I ever compete with the likes of Lucy Strike?'

Roxy scoffs. 'What do you mean compete with her? You're gorgeous, Evie! Yeah sure, Lucy is all saucy siren, purring-voiced, voluptuous, pin-up, bedroom-eyed, sex bomb, but you're girl-next-door cute! Like, have a look at yourself!'

I take a moment to unpack her protestations and still come up blank. 'Thanks? But . . . does girl-next-door cute really cut it if we're side by side?' How does one compare themselves to a sex bomb for crying out loud?

There's no stopping Roxy – she's off and away glassy-eyed, dreaming about celebrity authors with glamorous lives. 'Can you imagine the legion of fans she's got trailing after her? Men with their tongues hanging out, drooling as she sashays past? Who could be *bothered* with all of that? And then there's you, perched on this cliff, living your best bookworm life. Your days are spent talking books, allowing your pens to be pinched, being bossed around by Donkey Man, assuaging Guitar Guy's fear for poor old Helena, and biting your tongue when Pig Farmer upsets the colour order of the books. I mean, I know which life appeals more, and it's not Lucy's.'

'True, true. But this life is temporary. Soon enough I'll go back to my real life, my book scout job.'

'Have you heard back from anyone?'

'Not in the affirmative.' Should I be worried?

'Well, until then we've got you here and I for one am going to make the most of it.'

I give her a warm smile. I haven't had many close friends in my life and certainly none as real as Roxy. Santorini will hold a special place in my heart when it does come time to leave. 'Thanks, Roxy.'

'Welcome. Back to the business at hand.' She surveys the counter. 'I'll need my own desk. And my own pens. Keep the coffee coming while I call my network and tell them we have one of the biggest literary stars coming to our little island.'

I can't help but laugh. But it's true, Roxy will need her own space to work and have privacy to make calls. There's plenty of rooms in Epeolatry – we can rope off one of the rooms for her exclusive use. 'I'm back to fetching the coffee, am I?'

'You don't want to make the phone calls do you?'

'God no.'

We set Roxy up in her own little hideaway in Epeolatry with pens galore. I dash off to make enough coffee to keep her going, and once again I find Gran on the phone acting squirrely, talking in hushed tones, a frown marring her usually happy face. When she sees me she goes to her room and shuts the door. Curious. Why this sudden need to have private conversations? Gran's always been loud and proud, not giving a damn who hears what. Is there more going on with Georgios' family, or is this to do with her husband? I take the coffee back to Roxy and dither with whether to confide in her. Confide what, that's the question.

'Do you know Konstantine, Roxy?'

She shuffles her papers. How did she amass so much already? 'Yes, I used to shop here but the spoils were not plentiful – let's put it that way. The only romances the guy had were Mills and Boon circa 1970.'

'Is he a nice guy?' The note is still bothering me. He's not to be trusted in what way?

She taps a pen against her chin. 'I guess. A silver fox sort but there was always this aloofness to him, as if he was only partly here. You know what I mean?'

That's Gran. Always going for the ones who need fixing. 'Would you say he was trustworthy?'

Roxy cocks her head. 'What's this about then?'

'Nothing, nothing. Just curious is all. He's away working and I get to wondering how their new marriage is coping with the separation so early on, is all.'

With narrowed eyes she says, 'You think he's left her?'

'No! Nothing of the sort. Just thinking out loud.'

'Well, I'm sure he's dying to come back to his blushing bride. Floretta is a catch, no two ways about it. Whether he's trustworthy or not, I have no idea. He better be! His mother would kill him if he did the wrong thing and ruined their family name. I've said it before, you do not mess around where Greek mothers are concerned.'

I laugh, buoyed by the fact fear of his mother would at least make him stop and think before doing anything he might regret. I shelve the worry for another time. Maybe the note is from a local gossip. I've seen this happen time and again when Athena visits and catches us up on all the village drama.

I leave Roxy to it and return to the bookshop. There's a man standing in the entrance wearing an anxious expression on his face, so I give him a wide smile and say hello. I understand anxiety and want to make sure he knows he's welcome here.

'There's a problem.' His voice has a Greek inflection.

'Oh?'

He points to the hem of his trousers that are discoloured as if they've been wet. I'm not sure how his trousers are my concern

162

but I'm always willing to help with a wardrobe malfunction. 'Would you like a paper towel?'

He glares at me. 'You dog accosted me and did this!'

'*Accosted you!* Which one?' All of our pooches are sweet-natured, if a bit cheeky. I can't imagine any of them being aggressive.

'That one!' He points to teeny tiny Pee Wee and it suddenly makes sense. The damp books in Muses, the little puddles I find in the strangest places. And now this guy's wet trouser hem.

Pee Wee is not named for his size but rather his bladder issues! Wait until I tell Gran I've solved the puddle mystery.

The man's cheeks are pink with anger. And I get it. No one wants to be peed on by a rescue mutt the size of a small cat, but still, accosted is a strong word and quite offensive to Pee Wee's happy disposition. 'You're suggesting this infinitesimal animal *accosted* you? How?'

'It came right up to me and cocked its leg and did *this*!'

Another day, another bookshop confrontation. No one mentions this side of retail. 'Well that's not exactly accosting you, is it? And to be fair, your trousers are beige. I presume little Pee Wee got you mixed up with a tree. I'm sorry but it happens.' Pee Wee snarls in his direction. How odd!

'That's it? You're sorry?' The man's eyes darken and I can't help but feel I'm missing something here.

I'm dumbfounded. What else can I be? '*Very* sorry?'

Pee Wee doesn't like the man's tone and snaps at him, baring his small teeth, which glint in the sunlight. I've never seen Pee Wee act hostile before. It makes me question why. He bites the man's dry trouser leg and tries to pull him from the entrance back into the middle of the bookshop. 'Pee Wee! What are you . . . ?' I drop to Pee Wee's level and try to loosen his fangs from the trousers but he's latched on tight and won't let go. Has our smallest dog really attacked this man? From his behaviour it certainly seems possible.

I look up, ready to apologise again and then I spot his hidden bounty. Books are tucked down into his trousers, his shirt just covering them. Oh Lord. This is going to be intense. My very first shoplifter caught by none other than Pee Wee the Wonder Dog. How does one navigate this sort of crisis? Calmly. With a level head.

'PUT THOSE BOOKS BACK RIGHT NOW OR YOU'RE GOING FOR A TRIP TO THE PIG FARM AND, SPOILER ALERT, YOU WON'T BE COMING OUT AGAIN!'

The shoplifter's eyes go wide with fear and he lets out a pig-like squeal, hastily pulling books from his trousers, his socks and places I'd rather not think about. I'm incensed for those poor tomes, being snatched in such a way.

Pee Wee goes berserk and the other dogs come running at the sound. They form a semi-circle around me and growl at the guy who sports the reddened face of someone ruing their life choices. 'What's your name?' I hiss.

'I'm no one.'

'You'll be no one soon if you don't answer my question! Sixteen pigs can eat a dead body in eight minutes, and you might wonder how I know such things but it's best you don't!' Oh I wish Posy could see me now!

'It's Vinnie, V-Vince.'

'Well Vinnie Vince, I don't want to ever see you around here again.'

'You won't. I promise.'

'And if I do, I'll find your Greek mom and tell her what you did!'

He holds his hands up in surrender, his expression pained. 'Please don't! Not that! I'd rather go to the pig farm!'

'Don't steal. It's not nice.'

With that he sprints off into the distance wailing about pigs and moms.

Gran appears behind me. 'What are they barking at?'

'Pee Wee caught his very first shoplifter, Vinnie Vince. And it turns out Pee Wee is named not for his diminutive size but because he pees on people.'

'Ah, Pee Wee the puddle maker! That's one mystery solved. Who is Vinnie Vince?'

I shrug. 'He won't be back. I threatened to tell his mom.' I don't mention the pig farm as it's best if Gran doesn't suspect I know what really happens there. It could be innocent but I'd rather not find out.

Gran smirks. 'Look at you go, Evie! All Greek men are terrified of disappointing their mothers.' Gran picks up Pee Wee. 'And our smallest security guard has earned a treat, have you not?'

The other dogs trail after Gran and I pick up the fallen books, checking them for damage.

Once I've sanitised them I leave them to air behind the counter. I take some deep breaths, willing my heart rate to slow. Golly, being a bookseller requires a range of skills I've never even contemplated. It's quiet so I find my laptop to check my job prospects. There's a reply from Val. Adrenaline is still coursing through my veins as I open it.

Hey Evie,

I appreciate the hustle in you. Not sure if it will help but we're looking for a PA with movie biz experience who'll work on location with our producer. Might be a nice change for you? Let me know in a week or so as we're about to advertise the role.

Val

Oomph. I consider it. It's a great opportunity and could lead to other roles in the industry. Working on location is a dream most people would kill for. But, I remind myself, I'm not most people. It would include a lot of peopling in far-flung places. Am I being too fussy if I turn down this great offer? I decide to mull it over for a few days.

Chapter 18

By Tuesday my nerves ratchet up a notch because there's still so much to be done for what Roxy is calling Santorini's bookworm party of the century. Lucy Strike arrives on Saturday and we have the launch of Epeolatry on Sunday evening.

I'm in Bibliotherapy making bookmarks with bloody Lucy Strike's glamour-puss author photo on it. She's wearing a rather low-cut dress, with her bosoms on display. It's her brand: sex-bomb scribe, I guess. Does Georgios like this kind of look? It's not how I'd market myself, but if you've got it, flaunt it and all that jazz.

Could this be jealously on my part? I can't imagine wearing such a number but does that mean it's wrong for her? No. Even though I subscribe to the policy live and let live, I have limits. It's probably her energy I'm not vibing with. She's most likely a horrible person, with airs and graces. A diva. A diva who I'll have to run around after, making sure her every whim is catered for. You'd be surprised just how bratty celebrity authors can be. They expect the red-carpet treatment and treat us minions as if we're a slightly distasteful but necessary evil in their superstar world. That kind of thing is rife in Hollywood, so I steel myself for it.

Anything for Gran, right? With relish I cut a hole in the top to thread a ribbon through and because I'm a perfectionist, the dead centre of the bookmark just so happens to be her face. Symmetry matters and we can't have the hole off centre.

Shy Lily pitter-patters over, sensing my edginess. It must be the heat, the heaviness of the humidity making me overthink things. Lucy Strike might be a gregarious sweet woman who I'll instantly bond with. It's not like I have a real claim to Georgios, seeing as though it's fake on my part.

'Hello, princess.' I lift Lily into my arms and give her ears a scratch. She replies in kind with a quick lick on my hand. Progress. A few weeks ago Lily wouldn't leave the safety of the underside of the sun lounger and now she will allow cuddles from women and children. Men she's still dubious of. Probably sensible.

Look at the man mess I'm in. Enjoying time with Georgios far too much, living this wild and wanton existence that is so out of character for me. Perhaps that's why I'm so confused: this Santorini me isn't the real me. It's the holiday version. Georgios is probably feeling the same way, without work to tie him down, without the pressures of our real lives, we've transformed into these happy-go-lucky beachgoers. I can lose hours watching him read when we loll on the shore. Before I know it, I'm lost in a daydream picturing us book shopping together or reading manuscripts in search of the next big thing – him for publishing, me for adaptation.

When Georgios is enraptured with a story, his face softens and he does this crooked smile as if he can't quite believe he's been whisked away by words again. The same words he reads every day, but in an order so magical they almost make time stop. That's how I translate the expression anyway and it's downright addictive. I too, am constantly surprised by beautiful prose, and characters with open hearts and huge flaws who draw me in and don't let go.

My phone beeps, so I shuffle Lily to one arm and swipe open the message.

Mom's on the warpath. She's got some kind of proof that husband #9 is not on an oil rig. Gran's not answering her calls. Get Gran to call her, otherwise there's a good chance you'll have another guest at the villa. Posy xoxo

This is not good. Not good at all. What is Gran playing at ignoring Mom's calls? If he's not on the oil rig then where the heck is he?

And where is Gran? I note the time. She should have been here hours ago to take over. I ease Lily on to the peacock chair and give her a chew toy to play with before I walk over to Gran's villa. She's lying down on the sofa with a flannel on her forehead, protector Zeus standing guard at her feet.

'Gran, are you OK?' She's always so vital, so energetic, seeing her horizontal like this is alarming.

'Yes, darling, I'm fine. You'd think after eighty-three years on the planet I'd learn my lesson. Alas, I have not.'

'What does that mean?' Do I tell her about Posy's text message that Mom's suspicious Konstantine is not on the oil rig? Will that push Gran off the edge, as she's so obviously in a fragile state right now?

While I'm pondering where Konstantine could be and whether Gran knows, a seagull flies past the window and lands on the edge of a bird bath. A bird bath that Gran had incorporated into an aggregate cement path poured just a few days ago. At the time I'd been surprised that she deemed a concrete path crucial when she can't afford her rent, but I'd been busy and let the thought slide.

The more I look at the new path, the more it seems unnecessary being laid smack bang in the middle of the garden. Could it be the final resting . . . No. The heat and the fake-dating dilemma are getting to me. But what lesson is Gran talking about – remorse? Guilt? Regret?

She heaves a sigh. '*Alcohol. It's the work of the devil, that's what.*'

I shake my head as relief floods me. What was I *thinking*?! Having dark doubts about my own darling Gran for crying out loud! Look at her sitting there, flannel atop her head; she's the very picture of innocence. I mentally slap my own forehead for having such traitorous thoughts.

'Seriously, you've got a *hangover*? Didn't you go to bed after dinner last night?' It certainly appeared that way as we gathered our plates from the terrace and tidied the kitchen and went our separate ways, discussing briefly what book we were both heading in to read. Sure, she'd had a few cocktails but she wasn't inebriated.

That same shifty look returns and she dips her head. 'I did go to bed and snuggled with my book but then I got a call from a friend inviting me for a quick digestif, a small tipple of *mastiha*. I should know by now that you can never have just the one. It goes down too well, too fast. And innocent victims like me are then numbed to the dangers of consuming too much. Dastardly drink!'

I can no longer fight the urge to face-palm. 'Gran! We've got a hundred problems and you're drinking until the small hours? Who is this so-called friend who's leading you into temptation like this?'

'Oh don't you start, Evie. You sound too much like your mother at times. Life is for living. I was catching up with Zorba, the old man who mixes up the colours of the books for fun.'

The retired pig farmer. I'll never understand the woman. 'Well speaking of my mother, Posy says Mom's on the warpath because she's got proof Konstantine is not on an oil rig and you're not answering her calls to explain.'

'Oh God.' She groans and replaces the flannel. 'She's on her way here, isn't she?'

'She will be if you don't sort it out. Where is Konstantine, Gran, if he's not on the oil rig? Did he steal your money? Is that what this is all about? I borrowed some jewellery when I went on my first fake date and I wasn't snooping but I found a note that said something like: *Your husband isn't to be trusted.*'

169

She groans. 'It's all these meddlesome, gossipmongers who are putting their nose in where it isn't wanted that are causing all these extra problems.'

'What? Who wrote the note?'

'I'm guessing loukoumades Maria.'

I gasp. 'Georgios' grandmother. Why?'

'Because she saw Konstantine at the casino in Corfu. And she figured if we couldn't afford the rent then he shouldn't be able to afford to gamble.'

'So you're admitting he *was* at the casino?'

'He was.'

'And . . . you're OK with that?'

'Yes, darling. Look, I've made a few mistakes along the way, but life is a gamble, is it not?'

'I don't like the sound of this. Tell me you didn't send him to a casino to bet it all on black?' It's something she'd do, risk it all in the hope Lady Luck would come through.

'No, *of course* not. I always bet on red and that's exactly what he did on my express orders.'

I slap my head. 'Gran, *seriously*! You thought that roulette was the answer to your money problems? And how did that go?'

She pulls a face. 'Not well. Turns out we should have bet black. We'll know for next time.'

I exhale a long breath. 'You never learn.'

'Isn't it fabulous? Anyway, poor old Kon lost the remaining funds, got spotted by nosy Maria in the process, snuck back to the rig late and got fired.'

If I was a sweary pants I'd let out a string of expletives but I'm not so instead I mutter and mumble about responsibilities and her being old enough to know better, knowing full well my mumbled meanderings are falling on deaf ears.

I remember Athena's visit and her warnings that Konstantine was spotted at a casino with a *lady* on his arm. 'Who was the woman he was spotted with?'

She rolls her eyes. 'An Uber driver, well that's what I told *him* anyway.'

'Told him? Who was she really?' God, the plot thickens.

Gran swats the air as if my questions are pesky flies. 'A pal looking after my best interests. I've learned a thing or two when it comes to marriage. It's best not to be too trusting. I'd given him a hefty dose of cash, and I wanted to make sure my instructions were followed. *Always* have a witness, Evie.'

I scrub my face so hard I'm sure my freckles come off. 'Gran, why would you waste your money like that? Urgh. And now he's unemployed and where . . . ?'

'Don't panic, darling. Golly you're reverting to type. Kon has since found work on another oil rig. Obviously the timing hasn't been great, and all those weeks he spent looking for another job means he wasn't earning anything but it won't be long now; maybe another month and we'll have a steady income from him again.'

'Another *month*!' I'd expected his salary would be arriving any day and that would be part one of the rent payment arrears. 'I could cheerfully strangle . . .'

'Save your strength for more important matters. Your mother. Call her and tell her I'm fine. Hubby nine has switched jobs and everything is A-OK.'

'Can't *you* call her? She's not going to believe a word I say. She'll get all huffy and puffy and talk over the top of me like she always does.'

Gran lets out a sound that's half-shriek half-sigh. 'Golly, you'd think I'd be able to live my life unmolested, but no. I've got the entire District of Fun Police all set to barge in and create more problems. Ring your mother, *darling*, and put her off. Tell her I've taken a tumble and broken that hip she's so obsessed with. Oh no, tell her I fell off the roof and now I've got amnesia! And that I get very agitated when I don't recognise my own family. And the doctor, no, no the *trauma* specialist advises against family visits for the near future. Yes, say all that. Do you want me to write it down for you? But you can't read it robotically, it has to sound natural.'

'Amnesia, Gran? She's never going to buy that.' I scoff at the thought.

'Fine. I'll text her. The pounding in my head is too loud for a phone call with your mother right now.'

Chapter 19

Later that afternoon, pig farmer Zorba wanders into Gran's villa looking fresh as a daisy. He doesn't seem to be suffering from the effects of the poison they downed last night like she is.

'Why do you look so healthy?' Gran asks.

'It's my Greek constitution.' He pats his belly and pulls at his suspender straps. He's a bit of a contradiction wearing a white linen shirt and suspenders coupled with farm-worn denim jeans and plastic boots.

'You're far too cheerful and my granddaughter says you're a bad influence.'

He grins as if he's pleased. I don't bring up his very worst trait of mixing up the colour order of the books, but I really want to. 'Gran,' I say. 'I'm supposed to meet Georgios and Roxy at the vineyard. I'm already running late but you're in no fit state to run the bookshop. Shall I reschedule with them and leave you to rest?'

'Don't be silly. It's nothing a glass of Crazy Donkey can't fix.'

'Do I even want to know?'

'A crisp cold beer, a bit of hair of the dog.'

'What?'

Zorba turns to me. 'It's a well-known beer made by the Santorini

Brewing Company. It's a local secret that it cures hangovers. Helps with hydration, you see.'

'Sounds legit. Why have a blood stream, Gran, when you can have an alcohol stream?'

'That's the most sensible thing I've heard you say since you arrived. Now scoot. Zorba can drive you to meet your friends and then he can return with said miracle hangover cure. I'll sit on a sun lounger in Muses and let the customers come to me.'

There's not point arguing with her. I won't win. 'OK, thanks.' I get my things and give Gran a kiss on the cheek. 'Eat something too, won't you?'

'Zorba would you bring me back a gyros too? Extra garlic sauce.'

He touches the side of his nose. 'That's the second hangover cure. But you have to have extra garlic sauce or it doesn't work.'

Just how many hangovers have these two shared? 'Call me if you—'

'I won't. Go and have fun.' Zeus barks a goodbye.

We go to Zorba's dusty farm truck that is so rusted out I'm amazed the panels are still attached. It's so decrepit that I'm hesitant it'll make the distance to the winery. Still, there's one positive. I bet it can't go very fast, otherwise the panels would surely blow away in the wind. He starts it up and I'm surprised to find it thrums and purrs like it's got a powerful motor under the hood.

Seatbelt fastened we take off, and I clutch the dash. Why does everyone drive like it's the apocalypse and we're being chased by brain-eating zombies? What the hell is the rush when every other facet of life here is lived so achingly slowly?

I'm meant to be meeting Roxy and Georgios for a team meeting at Santorini Vineyard. But will I make it there alive? I call out for Zorba to slow down but the words are snatched away by the wind that blows through the many rust holes in the cab of the truck. I'm going to die next to a retired pig farmer who may or may not feed dead people to his pigs. There's a certain Guy Ritchie aspect to it all, and I envision Posy playing the part of me in a daytime movie. She'd get a kick out of it too, she would. She'd overplay all my quirks until she was a caricature version of the real me. Still, it would mean I'd live on, if only in film.

And then I picture my beloved Gran, flannel atop her head waiting patiently for gyros and a bottle of Crazy Donkey, only to find Hellenic Police at her door, sharing the terrible news that not only is her hangover not going to be cured, she's also lost her late-night drinking buddy, and her favourite granddaughter has met the same fate as her eight or possibly nine husbands and is waiting for her in the afterlife.

No, she couldn't stand that sort of shock. Not at her age. 'Zorba, I don't want to die!'

'Eh?'

'I DON'T WANT TO DIE!'

'I no understand.' He lifts both palms off the steering wheel. That crafty so-and-so. It's now evident why he and Gran are as thick as thieves! Now, he suddenly doesn't understand English either?

'Would you mind steering the vehicle with your actual hands?' I gulp back the acidic taste of fear as he drives using only his knees. His *knees* while he combs his windblown hair back with his fingers.

Just when I'm about to give in to my fate we arrive at the vineyard. I open to door and the handle comes clean off in my hand. Never mind. There's no chance in hell I'll ever be a passenger in Zorba's vehicle again.

'Umm. Thanks for the lift.' I want to berate him for scaring me silly but good manners have been engrained in me. My legs shake like a newborn foal's as I make my way to find my friends who reserved an outside table.

As my sandalled feet hit the volcanic ground I connect once more to this earth and my heart resumes its usual rhythm. It's a stunning winery overlooking a jaw-dropping view of the caldera and the never-ending blue of the sea.

We booked wine tasting in the hopes we can stock their wines at Epeolatry in the future. The village of Megalochori is known for its vineyards, which are famous for producing Vinsanto, a sweet style of wine. Roxy is big on collaborations and has schooled me in the art of networking like this. Highlighting how beneficial it can be for business. It requires a fair amount of peopling, but needs must and all that.

Georgios and Roxy are sitting at a table snacking on olives, chatting away as if they've known each other forever yet this is the first time they've met in person.

Roxy wears oversized spectacles, a white shirt and a beige knee-length skirt, as if she's a serious businesswoman, albeit with a penchant for ostentatious eyewear. In comparison Georgios is dressed in casual beachwear, his rippling muscles evident under the thin fabric.

'Hello, hello.' I take a seat.

Georgios leans over and pecks me on the cheek. Roxy gives me an exaggerated wink.

'Sorry, I'm late. Gran's . . . not feeling well.'

'Is she OK?' Georgios asks, concern in his voice while Roxy pours me a glass of wine.

'Self-inflicted. At almost eighty-four she still hasn't learned to say no to late-night drinks.'

Roxy shakes her head. 'She's iconic.'

'She's definitely not boring. Never fear, she'll be cured soon enough with a bit of hair of the dog—'

'A bottle of Crazy Donkey and a gyros with extra garlic,' they say in unison provoking laughter.

'It really is a Santorini hangover cure?'

'Sure is,' Roxy says. 'Never fails.'

'Everyone knows it to be true,' Georgios says with a grin.

'So,' Roxy launches straight in. 'We were chatting about Lucy and the order of events for the launch. We need an emcee, and I'm guessing you don't want to be that person?'

'You guess correctly.' I bite into an olive that tastes of rosemary.

'OK, then I'm happy to do that. Probably best if I know exactly what I'm dealing with when it comes to the talent.' She zeroes in on Georgios.

'What do you need to know about her?' I ask.

There's a devilish glint in her eyes. 'Our main man Georgios is probably best answering this question since he's got history with Lucy. So . . .' Roxy takes a notebook and pen from her handbag and adjusts her supersized glasses that engulf most of her face; just like always they suit her. 'Would you say your relationship with Lucy was more of the . . . platonic kind?'

His lips twitch. 'Excuse me?'

She holds her notebook to her chest and gives him a 'be straight with me' look. 'From an emcee perspective, I need to be kept abreast of any potential hiccoughs that may arise. Forewarned is forearmed and all of that.'

I hide a smile. She's so transparent, but I'd like to know the answer myself so I keep my lips pressed firmly together while Georgios squirms. What if he's not the kiss-and-tell type?

'We don't have all day, Georgios. There's wine that needs drinking. Don't be shy – you're among friends.'

The poor guy shakes his head as if he can't quite believe he's having to explain himself like this. There must be more to it because he really is stalling. I have to use all my powers of relaxing the mind and my facial muscles so I don't appear so obviously interested. And why should I care about his past? So what if we've shared a few illicit kisses. Big deal.

'There's nothing between us of a personal nature, never has been and never will be. I edited her latest book.'

'And?'

'And what?'

'Can you tell us a bit about that process? Who signed her, did she visit the office, was there a party, a book launch . . .'

He scrubs his face. 'Lucy's agent reached out and said she wanted to move on and would we be interested in reading her next novel. We were. There was a bidding war for it, and we came out trumps. She became one of my authors.'

'At whose request?' Roxy asks quick as a flash.

He shrugs. 'It was an organic thing. I was most senior and Lucy's sales speak for themselves.'

'Lucy specifically asked for *you*, didn't she?' Roxy probes, pulling her sunglasses down the bridge of her nose.

'Her agent did, yeah. We've worked together for years. Lucy came to the office to sign the contract; they put on a party so we could take photos and promote our new acquisition. A year later we hosted a book launch but that was handled by the marketing team. Anything else?'

I pipe up, 'Why were you reading one of her backlist books?' Is he obsessed with her saucy writing? For a killer thriller writer she sure likes writing about sex.

'Because she gifted it to me before I left.'

I pretend to be completely uninterested. I am uninterested.

Roxy taps the pen on her chin and reads her notebook. 'Look, this might come across as too personal but it's better if we know ahead of time so we can do our best to protect you. Lucy has a reputation for seducing every man who locks eyes with her. She's known to be a love 'em and leave 'em type. This is a safe circle, a vault. Nothing you say leaves this table. *Did* Lucy proposition you?'

He laughs. 'She flirted with me, but that's it. But like I told Evie, that's kind of her author persona. It comes across more as an act, like she's on show and selling her brand if that makes sense? Our business relationship always remained professional. Now, has the inquisition finished? Can we discuss the actual launch party and taste the wine? I'm personally going to need a bucket rather than a glass.' He shakes his T-shirt collar as if he's sweating under the spotlight.

Roxy stares at him long and hard as though she's deciding whether she can trust him or not. 'I suppose we can leave it there. But let the record show we brought this to your attention and we'll be right there with you on the night if you need us to step in.'

'Um. Thanks?'

I bite down on a smile. Poor Georgios, he's a good sport.

We spent the next few hours discussing marketing and promotion, and I'm blown away by how far and wide Roxy has managed to spread the word. Having a big name like Lucy Strike has proved invaluable. The wine goes down too well and soon we're laughing and joking and have made a deal with the winemaker to stock their wines in Epeolatry.

Chapter 20

By Wednesday I'm in panic mode about how quickly the launch is creeping up when Georgios arrives at Bibliotherapy to go over our guest list. Worryingly, we haven't had many confirm. 'Is it an island thing?' I ask. 'People are in holiday mode and they don't want to commit in case a better offer comes along?' Truthfully, I'd expected RSVPs to pile up because we landed Lucy Strike as a guest speaker, but that doesn't seem to be the case.

He rubs at the stubble on his chin. Over the last few days, he hasn't shaved and it gives him a less manicured air, more beach bum than cover model and it suits him. 'Could be that.'

'Or maybe we're being too elusive with our invite?' I ask.

I reread the text:

You're cordially invited to the grand launch of Epeolatry. A hidden library bar high up on the Santorini cliffs. It's a place to read first editions and second-hand treasures sourced over a lifetime from around the globe. Sip a literary cocktail while being lulled by soft smooth jazz. Become a member of this exclusive club and use the facilities to read, to ponder, or even to pursue your own literary ambitions. Our guest on the night is bestselling, award-winning author

Lucy Strike, who'll spend time with our members and share her publishing story – how she went from living paycheque to paycheque to become the global phenomenon she is today, selling over five million copies of her books, which have been translated into twenty languages and optioned for film and TV.

Epeolatry is more than a bar, it's a lifestyle. A sanctuary for bibliophiles. A night-time library for those who worship words.

'Too vague?' I ask. 'We don't mention pricing, or what exactly they get for their membership investment.'

'I wouldn't panic. Vague is good,' Georgios says. 'I've contacted family and friends who live locally and literary types who are just a short flight away. We'll get an influx at the end, don't worry.'

But I'm top of the class at worrying! I wring my hands. 'If it flops it will be *so* embarrassing, especially now that Lucy has confirmed. Can you imagine her sashaying into an empty room?' This is why I prefer the comfort of the written word to social events. There's always so much angst involved. Added to that is the fear that this won't save Gran and it'll all have been for nothing, after she trusted me to make this a success.

He takes my hand and gives it a squeeze. 'It's going to be OK, Evie. Lucy's a huge drawcard. Roxy has done wonders in getting the event publicised. Even my sister called me from New York and asked if I was going and my sibling is one of those busy important types who doesn't call if she can email.'

'I like her already.'

He grins. 'We might not have confirmed numbers yet, but I bet they'll be queuing to get in. How about we run geo-targeted ads on social media and push the fact that RSVP is required to avoid missing out.'

'Good idea. We can also offer a one-time discount to those who join as library members before the event.'

'Now you're talking.' Georgios is always so calm and moderated and has the ability to stop me spiralling into a panic when I'm living largely outside of my comfort zone.

'Also, Gran's hired a local jazz quartet who are well known around these parts so we can share that news across socials too.'

Before we move down the list Roxy appears. 'Hello, lovebirds,' she says. Today she wears denim cut-offs and a tie-dyed tee that shows off her midriff. Times like this I wonder if my own style needs a bit of an overhaul. I'm a creature of habit though and I affectionately call my style bookworm chic, which consists of comfortable clothing that allows a person to stretch out into any reading pose and not be constricted. 'Hello, Roxy. I'm so glad you're here.' I explain about RSVPs and my concerns.

'Ah, don't give it a second thought. The place will be jumping, I promise. It's the island way to keep you guessing.'

I take a deep breath and relax. 'OK. What's next?'

Roxy opens her notebook. 'Catering. Where are we with that?'

'Done, Athena is making meze with *dolmades, souvlakia arnisa* and a range of other delicious finger foods. She'll bring her own waitstaff for the evening. Gran's hired Athena to run that side of things long-term. I've hired mixologists for the evening and one of them has agreed to stay on for the summer.'

'Any chance we can get some arty food pics before the event? I'd love to share those across socials,' Roxy says.

'Great idea. Can you call Athena and ask?'

'Consider it done. She's my second cousin twice removed.'

'Ah.' Pork Chop trots in, steals rubbish from the bin and is out before I can check what it is.

'Who's going to be the librarian for the evening?' The librarian's job is to greet the guests and check memberships, facilitate new signs-ups, and give tours.

'Gran?'

'Has to be, right? After all, she's knows her book collection best and she's charismatic.'

We spend an hour making sure everything is ordered and accounted for, including the issue of where Lucy Strike will be sleeping. 'Your villa?' I ask Georgios, dumbfounded. 'Wouldn't she stay here?'

Roxy gives me the side-eye at this nugget of news.

'You don't have room here,' Georgios says, frowning.

Ooh, I expect Lucy Strike would adore sharing a villa with Georgios. I picture them tipsily zigzagging back to his place, her sex-kitten giggle so obviously a farce to woo the poor fool. No, not on my watch. He's too pure for this world and can't see the manipulation happening right in front of him.

'I'll move out of my villa and into Gran's.'

'And sleep where . . . on Gran's sofa? No, let Lucy stay in my villa. My grandmother is already scrubbing the life out of the bathroom. I'll move in with my grandparents for a few days.'

'Georgios, you could move in with Evie,' Roxy says. 'Her villa has a double bed.'

I gasp, scandalised. It hasn't even been a month and she's expecting I'd let a man sleep over! It breaks every dating rule, including ones I haven't thought of yet.

'It's not a bad idea,' he says. 'I'd be close by for the launch and what I'm guessing will be a hectic few days afterwards when the library is open for business. If you have a sofa in your villa, I'm happy to sleep on that.'

'Erm.' Lucy Strike and her perfect pout spring to mind. That devious diva will probably be knocking on his grandparents' door, asking him for a cup of sugar or some other euphemism that sweet Georgios won't pick up on. 'I do have a small sofa that might suffice.' Just what am I doing here? Breaking all the rules and for what?

'Cool,' Roxy says. 'That's sorted. I'm going to find Floretta and finalise a few things. See you later.' With a toss of her hair, she heads in the direction of Gran's villa.

'You're tense – let me help you unwind.'

I'm expecting he'll pour me a shot of ouzo and I'll slug it back and say keep them coming, but instead he moves behind me, placing his hands on me and kneading the muscles. At his touch, my shoulders do the opposite of relax and fly somewhere up near my ears. The gesture is so intimate I don't know whether to relax or run. He's got magical fingers and despite the awkwardness of the moment, I give in to it.

Eventually, I sink into the rhythm as my body slowly becomes like liquid under his touch.

'That's better,' he says quietly as I feel myself go limp and my eyelids grow heavy.

Time loses all meaning and I only come to when he removes his hands from my shoulders. I'm dazed. So relaxed I'm floppy. 'Where were we?' I say, fighting the urge to fall onto a sun lounger and fall into a deep slumber.

Chapter 21

On Thursday Georgios joins me at Epeolatry to help decorate. We shoo dogs from the bar and get to work setting up so we're free to entertain our celebrity author when she arrives on Saturday. We hang book bunting – not made from real pages *obviously*, there are no crimes against literature happening here – but instead made from photocopies of classical novels printed on old parchment to appear aged.

We stack bundles of leather-bound dictionaries and vintage books on tables. I move a gorgeous antique typewriter to a mahogany slant-front writing desk. The typewriter conjures a grainy image of an author clacking the keys, bringing their characters to life – celebrating their joys, commiserating over their sorrows. We'll never know if a completed manuscript was ever done on this 'office piano' as Gran calls it, and that's what makes it special. The mystery. What might have been.

I place flameless flickering battery-operated candles about. Not quite as classy as my 'old book' scented candles but for safety reasons it's best. There are too many book babies in here to risk a real candle being knocked over.

Georgios is piling copies of Lucy Strike's latest release: *Mafia Love and Lies* on our Book of the Month shelf. Luckily our order for the event arrived in time. We're now drowning in Lucy Strike's oeuvre and I only hope they sell or we'll be stuck with hundreds of them.

As the space comes together I take a moment to reflect. It's really going to happen. We just might save this place or we'll have the party of the century trying. 'We're almost there,' I say. 'I wouldn't have been able to do this without you.'

Georgios turns to me, a soft smile on his face as though he's on the same page as me. 'Sure you would. But planning a party is more fun together.'

'It is.' I get fluttery at the thought. Maybe it's the fact that I'm managing peopling more successfully here in Santorini. Doing things on a whim has had a positive effect on me. Whatever it is, it's quite a radical change and I find myself energised, ready for the next challenge.

I move the heavy velvet drapes to one side and am rewarded with the view of the sea. 'You think you'd ever tire of watching the waves roll in?'

Georgios joins me at the window. 'Not in a million years. When I've had a long workday in New York, and let's face it, that's most days, I yearn for this place, wanting to throw myself into the water and wash the work from my mind.'

'Ever thought about moving here?'

He nods. 'Every day. The longer I stay here, the more I slow down and relax into island life. Don't get me wrong, I love the hustle and bustle of New York. Living in a big city where every-thing is at your fingertips is great, but I'm getting used to the way the days stretch here. It feels like I'm taking a deep breath and my whole body appreciates it. What about you? If Floretta asked you to stay, would you?'

I contemplate it. 'I've got my heart set on being a book scout. For once in my life, I'm determined to achieve it. Probably because no one thinks I can, including me at times. But if Gran did ask, then I'd stay. I love that wild woman and every extra day with her

186

is a blessing. There's part of me that can't imagine not waking up to the sight of the shimmering sea with a dog on my lap and a pile of books on my bedside. If only I could be in two places at once.'

'Santorini has a way of stealing hearts.'

'It's a magical place.'

'I know you'll find the perfect book scout job; it's a matter of time.'

'Thanks.'

He moves close. My body tingles with anticipation. I go to reach for him as the dogs bark, alerting us to a customer, and the spell is broken.

My phone rings while I'm in the middle of comforting an irate customer. Irate because the third book in the series is taller than the first two and she is not impressed by such a difference. I get it; I really do. It can mess up a bookshelf display, but since I don't personally have any control over this I'm not sure what she's expecting me to do.

'Why would they make the book a different size? Now it's going to stand out on my shelf like the unwanted stepsister. Something needs to be *done*.'

'Sorry, I just need to . . .' The phone bleats in time with the pounding in my head. I'm at my limit for peopling today. And honestly, every retail worker in the world should get a pay rise. You almost need a degree as a therapist to deal with customer complaints. Who knew there'd be so many in the book business?

The customer waves me away and continues muttering to herself about sales ploys, marketing gimmicks, the rich getting richer and uneven shelves. Yikes. It strikes me I don't need my anxiety pills as much anymore even with all this retail angst but I do reach for the sugary treats more often. The dopamine boost tends to help, or at least buys me some time when I've had enough, so I put Pee Wee on security patrol and hide under the counter. If only I could do that now!

I shoot my customer an apologetic look as I answer the phone. 'Mom, hi, I'm a little busy right now. Can I—'

Mom brings a beady eye to the screen and cuts me off. 'Too busy for your own mother?'

'And sister!' Posy joins the video chat.

I groan. 'Yes, I'm working in Bibliotherapy. Can I call you back?'

Posy rolls her eyes dramatically. 'I wouldn't exactly call that working, would you? You're surrounded by books. It's a dream come true, not exactly hard work.'

I stifle a sigh. 'Yeah, it's a dream come true, all right.' Little does she know I have a customer mumbling about how her displays are ruined and that this might be the final straw, she might buy a Kindle and be done with physical books forevermore. Go-lly.

Guitar Guy chooses this moment to pop in and ask haltingly for Helena. 'Sorry, I haven't seen her.' He raises his palms as if it's my damn fault Helena up and left him, and he walks into the sunlight. What a day!

My grumpy customer taps her watch and gives me an impatient look. 'Mom was it anything important? Because I really do have to go.'

Mom shakes her head. 'I've had word that Gran is gambling again. Tell me it's not true, Evie.'

How does she always find out? Has she got a network of spies scattered across the world to keep her informed? Or maybe she's planted some kind of listening devices? 'It's not true, Mom.' *Technically* I'm not lying. Konstantine was the one who put it all on red. Not Gran.

Mom's sensitive about gambling due to an issue from Gran's past. It was many moons ago and I'm fairly certain that Gran has full control again, but for a while there she lost her way after she married husband two.

British Florian Fairweather, horse trainer and part-time bookie. It came out later that he was fixing races and diddling punters. Gran never got to the bottom of the scandal because

Florian did a midnight flit, taking with him only the clothes on his back and a suitcase full of stolen cash. The boat he escaped in ran into a spot of bother over the Mariana Trench and the last Gran heard from him was a distress call. She said she wanted to help but since he took all the cash she had limited resources with which to come to his aid and it's not like he was sailing on the river across the road. He'd managed get halfway across the globe, in the Western Pacific for crying out loud.

According to Mom, Gran spiralled for a bit after losing him and finding out he'd stolen from his clients. For reasons unknown Gran tried to gamble her way back to profit, but gambling is a mug's game and she went into further debt.

Eventually, she came out the other side when she met her Japanese soulmate who lived a gentler life. There were no bookies, no racehorses, no gambling. She swapped those vices with tea ceremonies and a spot of karate, in which she earned her black belt and became quite proficient with a katana.

'My sources tell me otherwise, Evie. If I find out you've been covering for her, you're going to hear about it from me.'

Yikes. Mom on the warpath is not fun. 'OK, duly noted. Now I really have to go.'

Once I hang up I turn back to my unhappy customer who is still waiting, head in hands. 'Were you lying to your mom?' she asks, her expression quizzical.

'Yes.'

'Brave.'

'Stupid. Now where were we?'

She shakes the oversized book in my face. Ah. Yes.

Chapter 22

On Friday, I'm at the head-between-the-legs stage, sucking in air so I don't die, when Gran finds me in a corner of the bookshop. 'Darling, what on earth are you doing?'

'Concentrating on staying alive,' I mumble through my legs.

'Is this some kind of New Age thing?'

'No, just your regular inhaling of precious oxygen thing!' I straighten up too fast, and a wave of dizziness hits me. 'Gran, I'm freaking out because Lucy Strike arrives *tomorrow*, and you're prancing around like it's just another day.'

'It is just another day.'

I glare at her.

'Oh you're a pill, Evie. Why are you twisting yourself into a pretzel over her? This is supposed to be fun! She's an author, you adore wordsmiths, so what's the issue?'

'She's . . . a bit over the top for my tastes.'

'You've met her?'

'Well, no.'

'Then how can you say that?' Gran frowns.

'Stop being sensible, Gran! You're supposed to be on my side.'

'Sensible, there's a word that's never usually associated with me.' She rubs my leg. 'I'm always on your side. And all you

190

have to do is give me a sign if Lucy Strike needs to go. I'll make it happen.'

'Go where?' I narrow my eyes at her. The last thing we need is Gran becoming the main suspect in the middle of another investigation. I can see the headlines now: *Celebrity author feared dead. Two American suspects in custody.*

'What do you mean, where? Wherever the hell she comes from! Golly, darling, you act like I'm going to grab her by the ankles and fling her off a cliff or something! Does that sound like the kind of act an eighty-three-year-old would be capable of?'

'Not most eighty-three-year-olds, but you're capable of anything you put your mind to, Gran.'

She kisses the top of my head. 'Thank you, darling girl. With you by my side I feel invincible.'

'So you *will* throw her off the cliff if need be?'

'Just wink and it shall be done.'

We fall about laughing, because obviously committing murder is a step too far but it's nice to know she's on Team Evie. 'What's really the matter? Has she got her sights on Georgios or something? Because if so I will fling her off by her hair, and he will be right behind her.' Gran really can't stand cheaters, but is it cheating when it's fake? There are no instructions for this kind of anguish.

'I guess it's more that I feel out of my depth with this whole thing. There I'll be hiding behind a curtain hoping that no one can see my ballet flats peeking out, and she'll be full of verve and charm and everyone including Georgios will be smitten because who wouldn't prefer a woman who can talk *and* make eye contact at the same time without having a conniption?'

'Well it's only you who thinks like that, my precious Evie. I personally love the way you know your own limits and go invisible when you need a break from people. Simultaneously talking and making eye contact is massively overrated.' She sits beside me. 'You listen more than you talk and there's a lot to be said for a person who takes the time to do that rather than waiting

191

for a break in conversation just to get their point across. Don't you think that maybe you're special because of all these things? That you're more, because you have boundaries, and you stick to them for the sake of your mental health and happiness? If only I could convince you that you're perfect just the way you are.'

I lean my head on her shoulder. 'Aww, Gran thank you. I guess this anxiety is a culmination of all the things that usually terrify me, happening all at once. I'll be OK. Once it's over.' Posy pops into my mind, along with Mom's admission about Posy not being as self-assured as I always presumed. That even she battles with confidence issues every time she gets up on stage. Maybe what I'm feeling is normal? Maybe everyone feels this sort of anxiety to a degree but some people just hide it better? It's food for thought.

She nods. 'Do your best, darling. I don't care a jot about anything else in the world bar you. Maybe we need a code word if you want to escape for a bit.'

'A code word?'

'Yeah why not? Like a safe word. Then I'll know you need some space and I can take the reins.'

'OK, how about banana?'

'Banana? Why banana?'

'Why not?'

She laughs. 'OK banana it is. Any drama and you just say the word.'

'Perfect. Shall I take you through the running sheet?'

'Before we do that I want to thank you, Evie. Thank you for facing your fears and organising all of this for me. Lately, I don't know if it's old age or stress, but I've found the simplest things a chore. I'd worried that for the first time ever, I might have taken too much on but you've stepped up and pulled it all together.'

It pains me to think of Gran suffering in any way and doubting herself like this. 'You've had a lot going on, so you're bound to be a bit over it all. I worry how you'll cope when I'm gone though.

192

Who'll help you in the bookshop? And at Epeolatry if Konstantine continues working?' Or whatever the heck he's really doing . . . ?

She shrugs. 'I'll hire a part-time employee or two. They'll have to love books the way we do. Otherwise nope.'

Where will we find a bookworm who lives and breathes books the same as us? Ah! 'What about Roxy? She's perfect. She's made Santorini home again . . . She's starting her own PR firm but only part-time; maybe she'd like to do some days here too.'

'Yes! She's a riot. Let's ask her.'

Having Roxy work at Bibliotherapy will ease my mind. Not only will she be fabulous in the role of bookseller, she can also keep an eye on Gran, relaying news back in case she does ever need any extra help. Although, I just can't see my formidable Gran ever being reliant on us somehow.

'And what's happening with the Greek god? Any developments? Babies on the way, that kind of thing?'

'Gran!' I gasp. 'You're incorrigible!' Babies on the way! In what realm is she living?

'Thanks.'

I shake my head. 'In all honesty, he's been easy to fake-date. Too easy. I keep getting confused, like I don't know what's real and what I'm faking. What if I've developed some real feelings for the guy? Doesn't that make it super awkward?'

'What? No. Doesn't that make it *easier*?'

'Not really. I get the feeling this is just a holiday fling for him. A way to pass the time. He's commitment-phobic, or relationship-shy.'

There's always that small part of me that thinks this is all too convenient. Like I can't fully trust in him. Perhaps it's because I'm the one being duplicitous?

'Did he say that?'

'Not in so many words, but the understanding was there.'

'Or are you looking for ways to avoid commitment yourself?'

'Wha—'

She bumps her shoulder against mine. 'While I'm all for your boundaries and your rules, and the way you go about self-preservation is great, when it comes to love, you have a tendency to shut down, shut the guy out before he can prove you wrong. Self-sabotage, the cool kids call it. Have you ever noticed you do that?'

I'm a fully paid member of the self-sabotage club but I don't sabotage my relationships. Do I? 'When have I done that?'

'When *haven't* you? You always find a huge glaring fault that cements the reason it won't work and you end it. You don't allow yourself to fall in love.'

I frown. 'That's because they had too many faults to overlook. What's the point in wasting time?'

'So that guy Chase, what was his big downfall?'

Urgh, Chase from Connecticut. 'He said romance novels were formulaic and thus predictable and not of any literary merit.'

'OK, fair call. If he'd have been my boyfriend no doubt he would have come to a stunning end when he tripped and fell into a storm water drain that was strangely infested with yellow-bellied taipans.'

'Wow, not that you're specific or anything.'

She shrugs. 'When you're my age, sleep is hard to come by. These sorts of scenarios play out.'

I narrow my eyes. Could it be possible my gran is some kind of assassin? A spy? Or just a plain cold-blooded killer? I shake the crazy notion away. Of course not! Gran's simply *protective*! It was just a figure of speech!

'OK,' she continues. 'What about that other guy, the accountant? Pasquale . . . ?'

Urgh. Numbers people. I should have known better. 'He continually asked for receipts everywhere we went. We'd split the bill down to the very last dime and he didn't tip! People who treat waitstaff badly are an automatic no. He told me I was flighty. Not ambitious enough.'

'How dare he!'

194

'Gran, aren't you meant to be convincing me that despite their flaws I should have given them a chance?' I laugh.

'Well, yes, but clearly they were meatheads, so there goes that pep talk. All I'm saying is, maybe you're looking for a way out with Georgios when there's nothing actually wrong with him. And jeez, Evie, with that background into the tragic men you have dated, Georgios is a catch, is he not?'

When you compare the men to Georgios he clearly trumps them all. 'There's one small problem. I'm fake-dating him, Gran. None of this is real!'

She raises a brow. 'Is that so?'

When she does the stare-down tactic it can be quite intimidating. 'Uh-huh.'

'Darling, I wasn't born yesterday. In fact, I wasn't even born this century – now there's a depressing thought. When you return after your dates with Georgios you're high on your little love bubble. You can't fake that sort of energy – can you?'

I consider it. He does make every date fun and brings out a playful side to me that I didn't even know I had. 'I get the feeling he's more interested in work than women.'

'That's because he got fired. He's bound to be worried about his job prospects. Just keep an open mind. There's a sparkle in his eyes since you arrived, and that, young lady, can't be faked.'

There's no point arguing about it. Gran's got love on her mind and won't be swayed otherwise. 'OK, let me take you through the order of events and what we expect your role as librarian will entail.'

She claps her hands. 'I've always wanted to be a librarian!'

Chapter 23

The week seems to have sped away and as Saturday dawns, I'm awake before the birds, watching the sunrise outside my window. It's the day we welcome our celebrity author to the island.

While my nerves are jangling, there's also the excitement for tomorrow: launching our wonderous night-time library that will serve Santorini bookworms so well and make Gran's last hurrah everything she's always dreamed it would be. I pull myself from bed, shower, dress and head to Bibliotherapy.

I'm guzzling coffee when Zorba arrives. 'Can you watch the shop while I make more?' I point to the coffee jug.

'I no understand.'

'Yes you do and don't mess up the colours of the books, please. Just for today.'

'What? I no . . .'

'Yeah. Yeah.' Houdini pops his head around the back of Zorba's leg. Does he have a wallet in his mouth? I go to mention it but the dog shoots off before I can comment.

When I return with a fresh pot of coffee, Zorba is gone but he's left his calling card. I sigh as I rearrange the colours once more. Zorba seriously needs to be banned just for the sheer amount of work he creates. If Houdini did steal his wallet, maybe he'll think twice about visiting the bookshop every day.

'Bloody Zorba,' Roxy says from the front door, motioning to the stack of books I'm rehoming.

I smile. 'Right? He's a menace but is so intent about moving the books into a certain order. Have a look.' I point to a row he's reorganised. 'He's moving them into height order – do you think the varying heights bothers him?'

'Ooh, good spotting! Another oddball customer quirk to add to the list. Speaking of oddball customers . . .'

Roxy heads behind the counter and ferrets in her handbag. 'Look what I got.' She brandishes a pen attached to a curly cord with a heavy-duty clip. 'Try stealing this, pen pincher!' She attaches the clip to the counter and winds it on tight.

'Genuis.' I laugh. Roxy really is one of life's problem-solvers. She gives me a triumphant smile, hands on her hips, Wonder Woman pose. 'You're just missing the cape!'

'And a superhero name.'

'The Romance-anator? I'll stop.'

She waggles her eyebrows and pretends to be a swashbuckling book lover. 'We can work on it. Are you all ready for Lucy's arrival? Should we offer champagne? Organic orange juice? What *do* bestselling writers quaff? Probably whisky.'

It's the big day before the big day! Georgios is picking up Lucy at the airport and bringing her here for a tour of Bibliotherapy and Epeolatry before we explore Santorini, finishing with a winery tour.

'Why whisky?'

'You know those moody writer types, up at all hours, bashing away at their typewriters, cigar stuck to a lip, subsisting on a diet of one-hundred-year-old barrel-aged spirits and imported Cuban cigars that sit in a humidifier on the desk.'

'Erm. That's very Henry Miller-esque . . . perhaps Lucy is a little more modern?'

'Yes, yes, you're right. The finest champagne. Only the best for our guest.'

I wring my hands. We've already spent far more than intended for the launch, not including expenditure for the activities we've got planned with Lucy today. Just how much does fancy champagne cost?

I don't want to continually lament our money woes to Roxy so I say, 'Why don't we offer Lucy a literary cocktail? Even better, let's design one around her!'

'Ooh, great idea! I'll email the mixologists and ask them for a spicy cocktail recipe that shall be known as the Lucy Strike!'

I smile. I'm sure Lucy will love the idea and it will save on endless bottles of bubbles that we can't afford right now. Facing myriad micro problems head-on has been a real learning curve for me. While I'd still prefer to hide from any issues that arise, I'm discovering that it only lengthens the whole process.

Roxy shoots off an email and then helps me replace the mixed-up books when Donkey Man arrives. He points to absolutely nothing and orders me about just like normal. Roxy bursts out laughing at his performance. 'What?' I ask. 'What's he saying?'

'He says he comes in every day and asks you on a date, but you give him water for his donkey, coffee, mints, books, once a scarf even though it's summer and never say yes. You're rejecting him because he's too old for you and he understands that, but he's got a lot to offer if you'll only consider him.'

'What! But he did ask for water. I committed the Greek words to memory and have been offering it to customers. So *latrevo*.'

Roxy doubles over with laughter. It takes a full five minutes for her to compose herself, when she does her eyes are bright and her cheeks red. 'You've been saying that to customers?'

'Yes? It's hot out and I thought they'd appreciate some water.'

'It doesn't mean water.'

'What does it mean?'

'I adore you.' She bursts out laughing again.

'Oh. My. God.' No wonder some of them had real worry in their eyes. Here's me thinking I'm simply offering them a refreshing drink and they're wondering if I'm trying to lure in unsuspecting bibliophiles for nefarious purposes.

Soon we're all laughing, mine the more hysterical kind.

I stare at Donkey Man who nods as if he's happy his wishes have finally been translated. 'Dare I ask what he's offering?'

Roxy turns to him and speaks in rapid-fire Greek. They laugh and chat for a bit before she says to me, 'He says he might be old but his donkey is very placid – don't know if that's a euphemism or not – and he will also buy a sheep, since you seem so enamoured with them. He's got a very humble farm that he will gladly redecorate for you.'

The situation is too ludicrous to contend with and I laugh at the thought. 'Can you tell him I'm flattered but I'm in a serious committed relationship although I do appreciate the offer.'

She passes the message on. He takes his fisherman cap from his head and holds it to his chest. He speaks fast to Roxy and she nods wisely before turning back to me to translate. 'If you don't mind, he says, he'd like to keep visiting you as it gives him life.'

Oh golly. 'Sure, sure.'

Soon he's on his way with his very placid donkey.

Roxy turns to me open-mouthed. 'God, look at you go! Not only do you have the hottest man in town kneeling at your feet, you've got Donkey Man all ready to share his life with you. I tell you, this bookshop has magic powers or something. When is it going to be my turn?'

If only she knew one was fake and the other not going to happen in this lifetime. I have a specific dating age range, and one-hundred-year-olds are well out of it.

I laugh at her awed expression. 'Aww, Roxy, I'm just the same as you. Who knows what's around the corner for either of us?'

'What corner? You're on a linear path, one that leads straight down the aisle!'

I scoff. 'The only aisle I'll be walking down soon is the one on the plane. Straight down to my economy seat.'

'At least aim for first class.'

Lucy's arrival time creeps closer. I text Georgios for an ETA but get no reply. Visions of Lucy sprawled across his lap spring to mind. Not helpful, brain. Not in the slightest.

There's not a lot of time to ruminate as the bookshop is bustling with customers as locals come to enquire about the Epeolatry launch and hope to get a glimpse of the famous author. It's all hands on deck as we sign up new library memberships and sell countless copies of Lucy Strike books to be signed at the event.

Roxy's campaigns have proved fruitful as word of mouth has spread. Beachgoers with sandy feet and towels strung over a shoulder wander inside. The dogs are rented and living their best lives. Even Pork Chop doesn't put people off with his trumpeting. For some inexplicable reason customers find it cute. It's his expression of surprise as if he can't believe such a deafening sound could be produced from his own body that seems to win them over.

I dash outside to check on the pooches, to make sure they're being treated well, before heading inside to help Gran who is at her charismatic best, charming the socks off book lovers and selling most of our book bouquets, which she assures customers are a bookworm's dream.

Gran's loving the extra bodies about the place. It's almost like she's energised by the crowd, her own battery charging up that little bit more. The extra sales have put a pep in her step and it gives me hope that this place will be successful, particularly over the summer months.

I'm ringing up books as quickly as I can, while Gran's waxing lyrical about Lucy Strike's romantic suspense series to a customer and telling them about the launch tomorrow night. Sure enough, they pay for membership and RSVP to attend the event. Once they leave with their purchases I motion to Roxy.

'What are the numbers like now? Do you think we might have to cap them?' Who'd have thought we'd get to this stage so late in the game?

Roxy checks the numbers. 'We could, but my concern is we may also have no-shows. It's up to you and your gran, but my advice is to keep it going and if there's a queue on the evening, even better. We'll get some great publicity shots of the long line of people. Epeolatry has plenty of space; we might just have to shuffle guests in and out to meet Lucy.'

'What do you think, Gran?'

'Keep it going. The publicity shots will be great for those who don't come to the launch but visit once the hubbub dies down. Build the intrigue, I say! Isn't this exciting! So many people. Ooh look there's the chief of the Hellenic Police. I better go say hi.'

My heart drops. Could this be a trap! Has Yannis' patience finally snapped because she hasn't paid her rent and sent his buddy to cuff her? 'Wait! Gran, what if he's not here for books?' I hiss.

She frowns. 'Whatever do you mean?'

I whisper into her ear. 'Didn't Yannis say they were old school pals or something? He threatened you, remember!'

'Oh that. I'm not afraid, darling. Let me schmooze him and he'll be putty in my hands.' She pats down her hair and pastes on a megawatt smile.

'Gran! Please do not get arrested the moment Lucy Strike walks in!' My almighty mind with its power of summoning people when I least want to hits again and in walks Lucy Strike herself. There's a hushed awe and the room falls silent as people make space for her like she's a living, breathing goddess.

Lucy blows kisses to customers, pouting and purring like she's a Hollywood starlet and not a scribbler of words. She's the definition of a siren and from the look of the slack-jawed crowd everyone is blinded by her.

Gran barrels past the crowd and introduces herself. 'Welcome

201

to Bibliotherapy, Lucy. We're so grateful to you for agreeing to launch Epeolatry. Would you like a tour of the library bar?'

'Sure, why not? Thanks for having me. I couldn't say no when I heard about this place.' She grabs Georgios' arm and pulls him forward. I didn't even see him behind her big hair. 'And I'd do anything for this guy. *Anything.*'

Cue the eye-roll. She may as well rip her clothes off right now and proposition him – that's how overt she's being.

'Yes, Georgios is a wonderful human. Between us, he's dating my granddaughter and they're very much in love,' she says so loudly I'm fairly sure every inhabitant on the archipelago hears her. 'I'm hoping there'll be a formal announcement soon if you get my drift. MARRIAGE.'

Oh my God. I blush to the roots of my hair and don't dare look at Georgios. He's probably spun on his heel and hunting for a speedboat to get him out of here. I can't help hiding a smile at Gran's ploy though. Not on her watch will Lucy Strike ruin my fake relationship.

'Marriage? Wow. Wonderful. It's an institution I'm not familiar with myself. I prefer my relationships . . . open. Untethered.'

'Uh-huh,' Gran says. 'Back in the Seventies that was all the rage.'

Lucy double blinks. Is Gran age-shaming her? Just how old is Lucy Strike? Hard to tell with the amount of make-up she wears. There's an airbrushed look about her, which makes it hard to gauge. 'I'm an Eighties baby,' she says breathily and the crowd laugh and clap as if she's just announced free books for one and all and not that she's forty-something.

'What a fun decade! Leg warmers, wave fringes and happy pants.'

Lucy smiles. 'I like you.'

'Everyone does, darling. Come and we'll share a cocktail or two and you can tell me all about your love life.'

Lucy waves to her adoring fans as Gran escorts her into Epeolatry. 'Your gran sure made the fact Georgios is off limits clear.' Roxy giggles.

'Yeah she's got a way of making her feelings known.'

Georgios joins us, his complexion a little peaked. Is that because Gran made such a spectacle about our brand-new baby relationship in front of so many locals? He's probably terrified I'm planning our (fake) wedding and (fake) babies already. Would he prefer someone more like our celebrity author who doesn't follow the same dating rules and limits as I do, with her open, *untethered* ideology?

The guy still doesn't speak. I wave a hand in front of his glassy eyes. What the hell happened on that car ride?

'What's up?' I'm not the jealous type so I don't pepper him with questions about the journey from the airport, like for example did she place her hand on his upper thigh? And did they hug? Were her bazookas pressed hard against his chest? That kind of thing. No, I'm above all those petty jealousies so I remain cool, calm and collected.

He snaps back to the present but he still seems distracted. 'Ah. Nothing. Nothing at all.'

She jumped him in the bloody car, didn't she? Poor naïve Georgios!

'I'll leave you guys to it, while I work the counter,' Roxy says.

I face him and whisper. 'Georgios, if we don't have trust we don't have anything. What is it? You're jumpy and skittish, like you've got something to tell me. Spit it out.' Who is this rash person taking charge? This alpha female. This demander of honesty!

He rubs the back of his neck. 'It's nothing to do with you and I, Evie. Or Lucy for that matter. I ran into . . . someone at the airport, is all. It was a bit of a surprise.'

My shoulders drop back to their usual position. 'Is that all? Gosh, you had me worried there for a moment.'

'Why, what did you think?'

I wave him away. 'Oh, nothing.' Just that he might find himself on the watery side of the Santorini cliffs if Gran suspected him of being a big, fat cheater.

The expression in his eyes remained troubled as he says, 'I guess we better go entertain Lucy.'

'You go. Who knows what stories Gran's regaling her with? I'll stay here and help Roxy.' Who did he see at the airport to make him react in such a distracted manner? The question slides away as we rush to serve customers.

Chapter 24

We're inside Epeolatry putting finishing touches on the party prep. 'Squee! It's almost time!' Roxy says, taking her compact from her bag and swiping on lip gloss before turning back to me. 'You look so pretty, Evie. Where did you get that dress?'

I pull it down. It's short and tight and I'm already regretting it. But it's the only black dress I have with me. Black is ideal when it comes to hiding in plain sight. Like a shadow. There are ways and means I deal with events. Top of that list is RSVPing that I'm dead. If that doesn't work and I have to attend, I make preparations to blend in. Become one with the wall. 'Well, I swear it used to be longer. I'm guessing Gran altered it after I showed it to her last night and now I'm left with this micro disaster!'

'Speak of the devil!'

Gran wanders in wearing the most gorgeous sheath dress with a beaded bodice and a sheer caftan over the top, complete with feathered cuffs.

'Iconic,' Roxy says. 'Teach me your ways, Floretta!'

'It's simple, darling. My top fashion tip is: live to be a hundred and never, ever cull your wardrobe. Take it from me, fashion moves in cycles so it's simply a matter of time until each piece is in vogue again. This little number is from the Nineties, but

205

you'd never know. Has served me well too. I got married in this to . . . what was his name?'

'Jimmy?'

'After Jimmy.'

'Ludwig?'

'No, I wore a gold lamé pantsuit to that wedding.'

'Husband seven?'

She clicks her fingers. 'Yes! How could I forget, husband seven Irish Sean. Ruggedly handsome and a fan of the craic. That accent, swoon. I sure do miss him.'

'What happened to him?' Roxy asks.

Gran gives a casual shrug. 'One drizzly night he slipped on a pile of wet shamrock and took a tumble, knocking the sense right out of that noggin of his, breaking a limb or two in the process. *Oh to be sure, to be sure* he would have survived the fall had it not been for an unseasonable drop in overnight temperature. By the time they found my dear old love nugget, he was frozen solid, his mouth stuck open in a perpetual scream. Frightful stuff. Turns out Sean did *not* have the luck of the Irish.'

Roxy's expression is caught between fascination and fear. 'Oh. My. God.'

'Yes,' Gran says, fixing her caftan in place. 'Shocking. But since he was already an ice block I researched a few cryogenic facilities around the world. Sadly the costs were a little too exorbitant. And more importantly would he *be* the same man upon reanimation? No one could assure me of anything, so in the end, he was taken to defrost ahead of burial. Shame, that man was a firecracker in bed.'

Roxy shakes her head, her eyes wide like she's in awe.

'You have had the *coolest* life!'

'Well, Sean's was probably cooler in the end.' Gran bursts out laughing at her own joke.

'*Gran!*' A guy died! Roxy, you're acting as if Gran's telling you the plot to a movie or something.'

'Sorry!' Gran says. 'I can be shameless at times.'

Roxy dips her contrite head. 'I'm sorry too, but to be fair it does seem like a movie plot – that's why it's so fascinating.'

'Wait . . .' I count back in my head. 'Wasn't *Zhang* Chen husband number seven? Zhang who met his untimely death taking a selfie and fell backwards into a crevasse because his belay wasn't clipped in? You gave up ice climbing after that, Gran.'

'Can't get anything past my clever granddaughter. Yes, I had two husband number sevens.' Gran grins. 'Who doesn't love a bit of bigamy, darling? Everyone should try it at least once.'

'Isn't it *illegal*?' I ask, and let's not even start on it from a moralistic standpoint.

'Illegal schmegal. They're both in a better place now, so what does it matter?'

I narrow my eyes. *Two* frozen husband number sevens. What are the chances?

'I need to be more like you, Floretta,' Roxy says, mouth agape. 'After the party is over can we have lunch, and you teach me how to find a husband? I don't need two at once; one would do.'

'Sure, sweetheart, I'd love to.'

'I'm not sure how I feel about this?' Will I lose Roxy to the dark side? Gran will probably suggest all manner of untoward things and my Greek pal has a penchant for the extreme just like her.

'Don't be such a stick in the mud, darling. You should be thanking me too for orchestrating your hook-up.'

'Orchestrating what hook-up?' Roxy asks. 'What have I missed? Is there another man on the go? Gah, you have all the luck, Evie. Georgios, Donkey Man and now this other mystery prospect.'

'There's no other man! I'm a big fan of monogamy I'll have you know. Oh look is that Georgios now?' I shoot Gran a look that conveys she better keep her trap shut. That was a serious lapse from her. Imagine if our cunning plan to get Georgios and his family on-side got out. The little village wouldn't take too kindly to us using manipulation tactics. 'Oops, false alarm it's not him. On that note, shall we begin the festivities? Lucy is expected to make a grand entrance at just after eight so we better be ready.'

'Let's check everything is ready to go,' Gran says and mouths a *sorry* to me when Roxy's back is turned.

We dash off to do our respective jobs. I switch on the battery-operated candles, check Athena has the catering under control, confer with the jazz band who are all set up on the small stage area, and fill up the ice well behind the bar.

Roxy checks over the guest list as Houdini comes bounding in. She ushers him back outside with the promise of a treat, but not before he steals a cushion and what she doesn't see is that he also took her purse. 'Argh, I can't run in these heels. Why is he so fast?!'

'The cushion is a ruse. He's got your purse too. If you're not quick enough the money and your credit cards will be lost forever. We don't know where he's stashing those but he will hide the purse in the drain near the lemon tree.'

'What . . . how many has he stolen already?'

I pull a face. 'Eleven. Twelve if we count yours.'

She blinks rapidly as if in shock. 'What does a dog need money for anyway?'

'Ice cream? The clock is ticking, Roxy.'

I leave her to chase Houdini and only hope she hasn't left her run too late. When she returns, her hair is slightly askew as if she'd had a quick game of tug-of-war with Houdini and lost, but from behind her back, she brandishes the cushion victoriously. 'Winner!'

'That's a different cushion. Where's your purse?'

'Covered in dog slobber and emptied. We'll worry about that later, eh?' She checks her reflection in the mirror. 'Oh my hair's a mess!'

'Go fix yourself up. We can wait a few more minutes.' Roxy dashes to the bathroom while Athena carts out bowls of fruit to the bar for cocktail garnishes. There are slices of lemon, wedges of lime and triangles of pineapple.

'Where *are* the mixologists?' I ask as Roxy returns, hair pristine once more. 'Has anyone seen them?'

'No,' she says as Gran join us.

'Don't panic, darling. They'll be here.'

I twist my hands together. 'Can you call them?'

'Sure, sure.' Gran says distractedly while she makes herself the world's biggest cocktail. 'But let's give it a few more minutes. You know locals around here . . .'

'Island time.' An excuse for everything from arriving late to forgetting about an invitation entirely. Especially if it relates to work. You'll get there when you get there and that's all there is to it.

There's no rush, not even for a cocktail party where the mixologists are crucial for the event. I attempt to channel Gran's level of zen but I quite can't manage it. 'Do we know what ingredients the Lucy Strike cocktail is supposed to contain?'

Gran waves me away. 'We'll wing it. Grenadine fixes everything.'

'It's supposed to be spicy isn't it?' I ask. We've advertised Lucy's eponymous cocktail far and wide and got a lot of traction on social media with the post.

'Tomato juice and Worcestershire sauce then.'

'Isn't that just a bloody Mary?'

'Not today,' Gran says. 'It's a Bloody Lucy.' The joke breaks the tension I'm battling and I relax my shoulders.

'And for those who want a mocktail, we'll make it without alcohol and call it a Bloody Shame,' Roxy says, provoking a gale of laughter.

I've got a lot to learn about the art of letting go. These two are as unruffled as ever, while I'm catastrophising about the Lucy Strike cocktail of all things.

I swing my gaze around one last time. Everything is in order. The goodie bags are lined up near the exit so guests can take one when they leave. The moody lighting is on 'sexy' as Gran calls it.

My heart thrums with excitement. It's a gift to be able to share this special place with people and I only hope they appreciate all the effort Gran's put in. It truly is the most beautiful of spaces to commit to the worship of words, just the way Gran envisioned.

Roxy fires up the laptop ready to sign up new members, and I duck my head into the kitchen. Athena is organised and ready to go. She gives me a thumbs up. 'Just say the word and we'll serve the canapés.'

'Perfect. Thank you.'

Back at the bar one lonely mixologist has arrived. Leo, the guy Gran has employed for the summer. 'Where are the others?' I ask.

Leo shrugs. 'No idea. I'm sure they'll get here eventually.'

I blow out a breath. 'If it gets too hectic for you, shout out and I'll do my best to help.'

'Will do.'

Gran makes herself another cocktail. 'Ready, darlings.' The chatter outside has reached an excited crescendo. We peek through the curtains. There's quite the crowd, dressed to the nines. My excitement ratchets up a notch.

'OK, let's do it. We'll check their memberships and, Gran, you give them the grand tour. Once we've let the bulk of the guests in, we mingle and make sure they're comfortable before Lucy arrives. Gran have you got your speech prepared?'

Roxy is emcee but we thought it would be a nice touch if Gran explained her vision for the place and what they can expect to find here when they visit in future.

She taps her temple. 'All in here.'

I smile. There's a buzz in the air. I give the jazz band a nod and they begin as we swing open the doors.

'Welcome to Epeolatry,' I say in a loud clear voice as the crowd cheers and slowly make their way inside.

Chapter 25

The place is humming with bodies and the smooth sound of jazz. Cocktails are being mixed, shaken and stirred. The mixologist makes it look like an art form. His buddies haven't arrived to help yet, so Gran wanders around doling out glasses of champagne. I catch the back of Zorba, dashing to the kitchen. 'Leo, do you need an extra pair of hands?' I ask across the bar.

He throws a metal canister in the air and catches it behind his back to a gasping crowd. He's wowing them and they seem in no hurry for their own cocktails as they enjoy the performance.

'We're good. Zorba's getting more ice and fruit for me and Floretta is pouring the wine and champagne. I'll yell out if I get overwhelmed.'

'Great.' I remind myself to keep an eye on the bar area so he won't have to leave his position to find me.

I check my watch. Still no sign of Georgios and Lucy. They're over an hour late. I veer between worry that with Georgios' high-speed driving they've been flung off a cliff or worse that they've pulled into a dark alleyway and the vamp is stealing my man. My *fake* man.

I go to the door to help Roxy check in the last remaining guests. 'Where *are* they?' she says, her brow wrinkling. 'People are asking after Lucy and I'm running out of plausible excuses.'

211

'Let me call him again.' I dash into to the quiet of Bibliotherapy and dial Georgios for the fifth time. There's plenty of reasons they might be late. Flood. Fire. Food poisoning.

The phone rings and rings. Why doesn't he answer? I leave a message, in a very calm and reasonable voice. 'WHERE THE BLOODY HELL ARE YOU?' and hang up. Maybe this is how Lucy Strike behaves: arriving fashionably late to make a grand an entrance and be adored by the masses. Always leave them wanting more. What if this anticipation adds to our guests' excitement? I can only hope. The last thing I want is people getting bored and giving up, presuming she's a no-show. What if she is a no-show? Panic swarms and I do my best to tamp it down. She wouldn't do that to her fans.

There's a crunch of tyres on gravel and I peek out the window and see his car. Finally! I open the window and holler, 'Would it be OK for you if we launch tonight, or would tomorrow be better?' I give him a saccharine smile that barely disguises the sarcasm in my voice.

He grins. He actually grins as he exits the car. 'Sorry, Evie. We had a slight issue. The buttons on Lucy's dress were extremely fiddly. I had to call my grandmother to help because she has such delicate little fingers and mine are not quite made for such intricate matters.'

'I see,' I say stiffly. The buttons on her *dress*. The dress that sits on her naked body? That dress?

'Uh-huh.' I fold my arms tight across my chest in the hopes he knows I'm *absolutely* livid. Of all the ploys, can he not see this is 101 of *Seducing your ex-editor*? I mean, the man can't be *that* oblivious surely? 'The library members are getting a tad impatient, so if we could encourage Lucy and her buttons inside, that'd be great.'

'Oh. Of course.' He turns to find Lucy still waiting in her seat.

'She's expecting you to open the door for her, Georgios.' Even though that's clearly our thing, there's no time to debate about

212

morals and what's to be expected of a partner in a relationship. All that will have to wait.

He dashes around to open her door. Gah, he looks hot in a tux. I try my utmost to ignore that and focus on the rest of the evening going without a hitch.

Lucy strides in, all big hair and bigger boobs. No wonder her buttons were difficult to do up; I'm sure the dress is two sizes too small. It highlights her curvaceous figure. I'm all for women's empowerment and if she feels good in that dress I will cheer her from afar while internally boiling about her devious ploy with Georgios.

The old, *I need help with my buttons trick*. How transparent.

'I'll take a glass of champagne,' Lucy says haughtily, not making eye contact. Great, I'm relegated to the land of waitstaff again, even though we spent the better part of a day together yesterday. Am I really that forgettable or is this some kind of power play?

Lucy strides ahead as if she's a runway model and I scuttle after her.

Georgios grabs my hand to halt me. 'Wait, Evie.'

Now there's an edginess to him, as if he has something on his mind. I'm miffed that he doesn't seem to understand we've got a roomful of library members waiting for the guest of honour and for some inexplicable reason he wants to drag this out further.

'We can talk later. We need to get this show started. I appreciate Lucy coming here, we all do, so let's just get this over and done with.' After this, I vow to go back to dodging parties and people. My safe little bubble is a nice quiet place, which is largely drama- and ego-free and I feel most comfortable there. There's no drink-fetching and there's no crowds. There's no . . . whatever this is.

'OK,' he says. 'I'll get Lucy a glass of champagne so you can focus on your guests.'

'That would be great.' Right now, all I care about is getting this party to its culmination so I can escape. Did I mention parties aren't my thing?

Lucy stands by the wrought-iron gate to Epeolatry, her expression downright frosty. Gone is the effusive, flirty persona of the day before. Could this be simply a case of stage fright and, like Posy, she has to steel herself to perform her role under the spotlight? Whatever the issue, *this* Lucy is markedly different from the one who swanned around yesterday, breathlessly laughing and touching everyone's shoulders, posing coquettishly for photos.

There's no way I'm quizzing her on the sudden demeanour change so I say, 'Thanks again, Lucy. If you're ready I'll have Roxy introduce you and then you can make your grand entrance.'

'I'm only staying an hour, tops,' she spits the words like bullets. Whoa.

'Umm, OK.'

Georgios scrubs his face while Lucy glares at me. What the hell is going on here? The friction in the air is palpable. My first instinct is to run, or to allow Lucy to speak to me in such a way – she is the talent after all – but in allowing her to do so, I'm setting a precedent of tolerating this intolerable behaviour when I've been nothing but accommodating to her.

I square my shoulders. 'That wasn't the agreement, Lucy. We've sold boatloads of your books to eager fans in the lead-up to this event; the very least you can do is keep your word. Now if you don't mind, they'd like to meet you . . .'

With that I stride inside and find Roxy and Gran. 'Slight problem. Lucy's here and in a *mood*. She's announced she's only staying an hour at most. I've reminded her of the promises she made but I'm not sure how this will go. Roxy, can you introduce her before she pikes out altogether?'

There's a lot to worry about and, for one moment, I consider using the safe word – banana – until it dawns on me: I don't need to. Why should *I* run away? I'm not the one acting like a diva. I'm not the one going back on my promises. I only hope Lucy doesn't ruin the evening for Gran and our guests, but whatever happens we'll make the best of it, even if I have to get up on the bar and sing 'I Want to Know What Love Is'. Tonight will be a success; I will make sure of it.

'Lucy will only stay an hour, eh? I'll see about that,' Gran says mysteriously.

With great gusto as if the queen herself was visiting, Roxy introduces Lucy and reads out her bio. I see Georgios retreating, glass of champagne in hand. At least he's happy to do her bidding and it saves me from doing it. My confidence has grown here but not enough to deal with a bestselling author whose shapewear must be cutting off the oxygen supply to her brain or something to provoke such sudden hostility. Or maybe it's that I won't *allow* myself to be treated badly anymore – and that's an improvement, right?

'Without any further ado please welcome our guest of honour, Lucy Strike!'

The crowd claps and cheers as Lucy saunters in, her eyes aflame, her hair blowing out behind her like she's a model in some kind of shampoo commercial. How does that even work? When I walked in my hair blew directly into my face and a few strands got caught in my lipstick, so I probably have what looks like little red slash marks all over my cheeks.

Lucy takes the microphone and shares the inspiration behind her latest book. All the while she's batting her lashes and speaking in her husky voice. They're eating it up and I exhale all the tension that's been sitting somewhere around my ribs for the last few hours. Lucy takes them on a journey back to her humble roots; confides that she wasn't able to make rent. Writing was an escape from the humdrum life she never imagined she'd be stuck in.

I take a glass of champagne from a tray and take a long swig. The bubbles burst on my tongue and produce an immediate calming effect. Beguiling Lucy is back, holding the crowd in the palm of her hand. What a relief!

I glance at my watch. Hopefully we'll wrap the party up by eleven at the latest. It's a library bar, not a pulsating nightclub, and patrons are words nerds, not fluoro-dressed ravers. Surely, like me, they'd be happier in bed with a book? Or is that wishful thinking?

The night continues on as I'm pulled away to solve minor dilemmas. We run out of clean martini glasses and have to wash by hand as the dishwashers are already cycling through. We run out of ouzo, so I dash to Gran's villa and steal a couple of bottles from her very healthy stash. Our printer decides to shut itself off, as printers do, so we have to manually take membership details and make promises that the cards will be sent in the mail. All in all, I manage to extinguish most problems as they arise. The only niggle is running around on high heels. My feet protest with every passing step and I rue the fact I didn't wear flats.

When I take a moment to check the time I find it's almost midnight. The crowd hasn't thinned out – if anything it's thickened. Gah! I distribute yet another bowl of feta and olives and plates of *dolmades* for Athena, when I spot Lucy with a small group of people. So much for only staying an hour! Her cheeks are ruddy as if she's put away a fair amount of champagne. My jaw drops when she throws herself into the lap of a twenty-something man who pulls her in for long saucy kiss. What? Who is he?

Gran saunters over. 'Problem solved, eh?'

'You orchestrated – this?' Lucy wraps her arm around the guy's neck possessively as if warning others off.

Gran nods wisely like a sage. 'Sure did. By my great powers of deduction and being somewhat man-mad too, I'm guessing Lucy got rejected by the Greek god. Her feelings were hurt. I introduced her to Stavros, not quite the prize Georgios is, but still, he's a shipping magnate's son with lots of zeros to his name. And voila! We've still got people signing up for memberships, and as for the sales of booze, well, let's just say, we might be able to back pay most of the rent tomorrow.' It takes a moment for me to process what Gran's said. Yay for rent. But . . . Lucy got rejected by Georgios? What!

'Wait – you think Georgios rejected an advance from her?' Where is he? I haven't seen much of him all evening, while I've been dashing here and there. Did she try it on after the button fiasco? Surely not? Perhaps that's what he wanted to come clean with me about outside, but I'd been too concerned about our waiting guests to listen. He has been rather quiet since the airport pick-up, as if he's got something on his mind.

'Why else would she walk in wearing a sucked-lemon face and crow about leaving?' Gran says.

'I'll ask him. How dare she, if she knows he's in a committed – albeit fake – relationship. She spent half of yesterday joking about how sad she was that's he's "off the market" and what – she then took that as a personal challenge?!'

'It comes from a lack of confidence, darling. Things aren't always as they seem. Even the most confident people struggle with feelings of inadequacy. Remember that when you doubt yourself.'

Lucy Strike feels inadequate? Now I've heard it all. But I pause and ponder it for a moment. Like Posy struggles with stage fight, does Lucy Strike suffer as Gran says? It's hard to fathom that this superstar author is anything but a sassy, confident siren. Goes to show we never really know what's happening behind the curtain of a person's heart and soul. With that in mind, I feel differently about her. More understanding.

Have I been living in a world feeling inferior this whole time, alongside so many others who feel exactly the same? Maybe I am perfect just the way I am, like Gran's always telling me.

'Go on and find Georgios, darling,' Gran says. 'We've got everything handled here.'

'OK.' I spot Zorba behind the bar rearranging the bottles. 'Oh, Gran, Leo's not going to be able to find anything if Zorba keeps shifting the bottles around like that.'

'Zorba!' Gran calls. 'They're already in *alphabetical* order.'

'No, understand.'

She turns to me. 'He likes order in a disorderly world. I can't relate but I can empathise.'

I laugh. 'Yes, you're opposites in that respect. Why does he pretend he doesn't understand when he's got a better grasp on the English language than most people?'

'Because then he can get away with murder.' She flashes an innocent smile.

'You told me sixteen pigs can eat a dead man in eight minutes. Zorba owns a pig farm. I'm not one for jumping to conclusions but you can see how I'm joining those dots, right?'

'Darling, you hold a gold medal in jumping to conclusions.'

I give her that. I'm a big fan of figurative jumping rather than the more physical kind. 'Promise me there will be no deaths on the island tonight?'

'This isn't a cosy mystery, Evie. Sometimes I think books have addled your brain.'

'How could feeding a dead person to sixteen pigs ever be classed as a cosy mystery? Sometimes, I think men have addled your brain!'

'Oh that they have!'

I give Gran a peck on the cheek and spin on my heel to search for Georgios. I find him in the history room chatting to a scholarly type. 'Hi,' I say with a smile. It's quieter down this end of Epeolatry. The thick velvet curtains block a lot of the din.

Georgios waves me over and loops an arm around my waist. For some reason it feels natural, as if we do these kinds of lovey gestures all the time. It gives me a little buzz, a sense of belonging. 'Hey, Evie, this is Joe, a local science-fiction author. I've just been telling him about my new publishing company Eros Books, and he's going to submit his manuscript to me.'

I keep my face neutral. At least I try to. He's already named his publishing company? 'You'll be in great hands. Georgios is a wonderful editor.'

'Thank you. I agree. I've been following his career for some time, us being born on the same island and all.'

We chat for a bit about Joe's writing before he takes his leave to replenish his drink.

I turn to Georgios. 'You're definitely going ahead with your very own publishing company then? Did you secure finance? What's the plan? Tell me everything!'

Georgios grins at my sudden burst of questioning. 'I spoke to my financial adviser and drew up a business plan. He suggested I sell off some shares and I take a small loan. Let's hope the gamble is worth it.'

'Of course it will be! And the name: Eros?'

He ducks his head as if he's suddenly shy. 'God of love. Love is at the base of every good book, so it seems fitting.'

Anticipation shines in his eyes. I recognise the look from when I first got the call from Gene about becoming a book scout. There's nothing like that feeling of exhilaration when you're chasing your dreams and they're within touching distance. The goose-bumpy sensation that you've finally hit the jackpot with your career and you can pour your passion into something tangible, something that matters.

'We need to celebrate this milestone! I believe in you, Georgios; now you've got to believe in yourself. You've already got your first submission! Have you read Joe's work?'

'I have and it's brilliant. Groundbreaking for the genre actually. If I can sign him, it'll lead to great things.'

'What do you mean *if*? He trusts you already. He believes in you. Not if, but when!'

'Right. Right. When. It's daunting to have their careers in my hands and my hands only. What if I mess up? What if they don't get the sales they expect? What if no one else submits? What then?'

'Won't happen. You hire a gun marketing person, maybe Roxy, and you have your strategies in place before each book is launched. You take your time with each release so nothing is overlooked and each book has its best chance at success. You know the world of publishing – no book is guaranteed success. Who knows why some fly and some fall? But you'll do your level best to give them every chance to soar up the charts.'

'Wow, Evie, do you want a job? I mean, really, do you?' There's a real happiness in his voice when he speaks of his new venture. It's nice to see that excitement radiate from him again after this spell of him being quiet the last day or two.

'No, I'm good. But thanks for the offer. I'll be cheering you from the sidelines. Speaking of being hands-on with your . . . umm authors, though – is there anything you want to tell me about Lucy? She was shooting daggers playing the ultimate part of celebrity author brat when she arrived.'

He runs a hand through his hair. 'Urgh. Well, we can safely say I'll never sign Lucy to my list.'

'Why is that?'

His cheeks colour at whatever memory he's conjuring. 'Uh, the thing is – she uh . . .'

I laugh and take him by the hand to the leather chesterfield. I have to rest my feet before they explode sideways from being in too-tight stilettos. 'Just say it, Georgios.'

I slip the little torture devices off, and there's that delicious moment of being pain-free. He drops his gaze to my heels, as if worried I might pick one up and brandish it as a weapon.

'What? I'm not going to chase Lucy into the night, high heel at the ready.'

Georgios lets out a strangled laugh. 'She called me and asked me to help her with something, so I went to my villa and there she was standing in her underwear, claiming her buttons wouldn't do up.'

'Oh my God.' I put a hand to my mouth.

He grimaces. 'Yeah, it was *super* awkward. I told her it was best if I got my grandmother to help.'

'Pure sweet boy, you are.' I swoon a little.

220

He laughs. 'That's me. But Lucy was none too happy about it. I ran for my grandmother and explained the situation. We returned together and Lucy was miraculously in the dress and sent my grandmother away.'

'And then she suddenly couldn't do up her buttons?'

'No, like we *really* couldn't do them up. The dress was far too small. Lucy was losing her temper and blaming you for feeding her rich Greek food, as if you'd done it on purpose so her dress wouldn't fit.'

'Me? How do I always get the blame?'

'I made the mistake of laughing and she didn't take too kindly to that.' He shrugs. 'Once again, I got my grandmother back and she managed to get the buttons done up. I was trying to hurry Lucy but she won't be hurried. If anything she went slower, so I was hiding my frustration while she insisted we have a glass of wine, a chat.'

'How *tedious*.' I can't help but shake my head. What was she *thinking*?

'This drags on and I'm worrying about the time, plus I don't want to drink and drive. I'll probably kill us both on those bends.'

'That's true, your driving is atrocious.'

He leans in to me. 'Thanks?'

'Welcome.'

He stares up to the heavens as if wondering why there wasn't divine intervention and continues sharing the sorry saga. 'I finally manage to convince Lucy that her many beloved fans are waiting and get her in the car. As we approach the lookout, she insists we stop for social media photos. Begrudgingly, I do because I know by this stage that disagreeing with her only takes more time. We get out, she throws me her phone and poses this way and that. When I hand the phone back she launches herself at me. I'm so shocked I step to the left. Unfortunately, the dress is too tight for such catapulting, and she stumbles over. Then I have to sort of lift her like a crane because she can't really bend in the dress. She's covered in volcanic earth, like your nose was that very first day.'

'Yikes. She *launched* herself at you?' For some reason this provokes a fit of giggles as I picture the calamity.

'Yes but still I wasn't sure, like was she trying to hug me because the view made her happy – or what? Could have been completely innocent, right? And I didn't want to offend her by presuming. I blurted out that my girlfriend wouldn't appreciate me hugging another woman. In my panic I put the blame directly on you. I should have said, *I* didn't want to hug another woman. But I worried if I handled it badly she might not come to the launch at all.'

He's calling me his girlfriend – already? I take a moment to enjoy the buzz of hearing him say it as if it's the most natural thing in the world. But the buzz is soon replaced by guilt. If he knew the truth about this fake-dating folly, would he still want me in his life? I wish so much I could have a do-over and never agree to this terrible plan. If I'm honest, I'm developing real feelings for him that can't be explained away, even if this did start out simply to help Gran. But you can't build a real relationship on a lie. I have the urge to blurt it all out, confess and hope he forgives me, but at that moment he takes my hand and gives it a squeeze and I lose what little courage I had. As usual, my brain offers an alternate reason – is this a real confirmation of his feelings for me or was it simply a way for him to escape from the clutches of Lucy?

I'm too conflicted by my own deception to ask.

He's staring at me, waiting for a response but I'm still lost inside myself, wondering how to salvage this . . . us. Is it even real? Do girls like me really get their happy ever after with a guy who ticks all the boxes, like he does? Why does the word *girlfriend* suddenly change the status of everything? Is it because he was so aloof about love before and this seems solid, like a big step forward? 'Gosh, what an ordeal,' I eventually manage.

With a nod he says, 'We went back to my villa so Lucy could change. This time I waited in the car. Lucy returned and didn't say another word for the rest of the drive.'

I cover my face in my hands. 'You did the right thing.'

He shrugs as if it's nothing. But he managed to get her here, despite her feathers being a little ruffled.

'Not one part of you was tempted? I mean, she is Lucy Strike.' Men have literally fallen at her feet all the way around the archipelago.

'Not one part. I'm not that kind of guy.'

'What kind is that?'

He gives me a sweet smile. 'I'm with *you*, Evie. That means I'm one hundred per cent with you. I'm not going to look at another woman and wonder what if.'

He's saying all the right things and I want to believe him. I'm impressed that his head isn't turned by Lucy. She's got a certain charisma that turns rational types into molten liquid.

This man really is the whole package. My own lies are on the tip of my tongue and there they stay. 'It's been eye-opening being on the sidelines near a character like Lucy, who is currently sitting on the lap of some shipping magnate's billionaire progeny, so you're safe – maybe?'

With that he visibly relaxes. Playboy he isn't, which I find endlessly fascinating. From our many dates taken around this beautiful island, I've learned that Georgios would rather sit and chat books all day, than be part of a bigger crowd, be seen, be heard, be on display. When we first met I judged him on sight, simply because of the way he looked. He's nothing like I pegged him for; in fact he's the opposite and similar to me in ways I could only dream about. Have I found my perfect match?

He gives a shake of his head. 'Thank God.'

'The library members adore her, so there's that. The place is still pumping and last I checked we were almost sold out of her books.'

He raises a brow. 'You've pulled it off. The party of the century.'

'*We* did! I mean, it's for Gran so it's a given I'll risk peopling, but it hasn't been quite as terrible as I expected. Not saying I'm going to morph into a party girl, but I could possibly attend future events in a purely cameo timeframe: now you see me, now you don't – kind of thing.'

He laughs. 'Parties are overrated.'

'Not for these bookworms. They've almost drunk the bar dry. Luckily Gran's got a stash of booze in her villa.' If Gran manages to pay her rent, and get back in the black with her finances, hire some staff, then it'll be time for me to go home. Leave the island for good and amp up the job hunt. Leave Georgios behind . . .

'Why the sad face?' he asks, tucking a loose tendril of hair behind my ear. It's such an intimate gesture that words freeze on my tongue. Do I want a future with Georgios?

'It's nothing,' I say, smiling. 'Shall we get you that drink?'

'We could – or we could escape? I've got a cracking headache and all I want is a glass of water and absolute silence.'

I step forward and hug him tight. 'How are you so perfect? Let me tell Gran and we'll leave them to it. From the sounds it, these bookworms are going to burn the candle at both ends and I want no part in that.'

Chapter 26

I wake up with a throbbing head from not drinking enough water throughout the launch party. I almost jump outside of my skin when I see a sleeping Georgios curled up in the sheets beside me.

Then it all comes back to me. He'd been twisting and turning on the small sofa, clearly uncomfortable, so I invited him into the bed and made a pillow fort between us like a teenagers do. Not because I don't trust him, but because limbs tend to go akimbo during the witching hour and no one wants to wake up holding a random body part and have to explain that.

Soft shards of sunlight land across his features, highlighting the smooth planes of his face. I have an almost irresistible urge to run a finger over his lips to feel them beneath my fingertip. He's so at peace as he sleeps, his face softer somehow.

He blinks his eyes open and I screech and propel myself backwards, hitting my head against the wall. 'I was—'

'Watching me sleep?' He grins and pulls himself upright.

'No! Trying to work out an escape route so I wouldn't disturb you.'

He does the cool-guy head tilt. 'It's OK, you can tell me the truth.'

I grab the pillow from behind me and hit him with it. 'That's for being presumptuous and also being a happy morning person.'

He takes the pillow and props it behind his shoulders. Urgh, he even smells nice when he wakes up, a mix of his cologne and the sweet scent of sleep.

'You don't wake up happy?'

I lean back on the pillow. 'No, not really. Each night, I tell myself I'll only read one more chapter and before I know it, I'm starting book two of a five-book series. A minute later it's three a.m. and I'm feeling peckish . . . Cake-Lit, gets me every time.'

'Cake-Lit? He pulls the sheet up to his chest, which is adorable considering I've seen him almost naked at the beach.

'Romances set in bakeries, cafés, chocolate shops, pop-up tea vans, that kind of thing. They really should have snack warnings on the cover.'

'Ah. Bookworm problems. Thanks for letting me crash out in your bed. I had the best sleep I've had in a long time.'

I'm almost positive I don't sleep as gracefully as he does: picture-perfect like he's in an ad for pillows or something. Often, I wake myself up sleep-talking, my mouth open in a silent scream.

'Should we go see if the party is still raging?' When we left last night there was talk among revellers about staying to watch the sunrise. I pause and listen for any music. 'You don't think it is – do you?'

Georgios springs out of bed in his tighty-whitey boxer shorts. I avert my gaze out of respect and then remember I'm supposed to be dating him, so eye him up accordingly because it's expected of me. He catches me ogling so I quickly follow him from the bed, allowing him a full view of my lightweight linen two-piece pyjama set that covers almost every square inch of my body. Prim, maybe. Proper, always.

'Let's go see,' he says.

'OK, I'll quickly throw myself in the shower.'

As I open the bathroom door, he says, 'Before we head out . . .' And then stops short. 'Actually don't worry.'

'What is it?' I hover between the bathroom and the bedroom.

He waves me away. 'Nothing. It can wait.'

'OK.' I shower and brush my teeth, exiting the bathroom sheathed in a thin towel. Holding his overnight bag Georgios goes to slip past me, but we don't glide easily; instead we brush against each other. I'm hyper aware there's not a lot covering our sexy bits – just the thought is enough to make my cheeks flush. The moment is charged as I stare into his dark unfathomable eyes. 'You better . . .' My words peter out.

'I better . . .' He bites down on his lip – I've never seen such a thing off the page before, and it's quite intense. How can one little gesture be so alluring? I swallow hard and turn away first. Golly, is it hot in here.

When he shuts the door, I exhale sharply. What was that? He makes my legs weak, literally weak, as if they might not do their job of holding me up.

When I hear the shower go, I drop my towel and dress. There's enough time to apply some light make-up and brush out my hair.

He wanders out in a cloud of steam, towel strung casually around his waist. The vision is almost too much; I'm woozy at the sight of him. Lost imagining the many ways the towel could fall from his body. Ripping it off would be one way. Pretend tripping and using it as leverage for my faux fall would be another. Instead, I cough and clear my throat, mumbling about giving him some space to get changed and leave in a rush, pulse racing.

Outside I gulp fresh air. What is happening to me? I'd been about three seconds away from de-robing the guy! Is that acceptable without some kind of discussion beforehand? While *I* know we're fake-dating, thus the answer would be absolutely not, *he* doesn't know we are. Would he have thought me too forward? Or would he have acted upon his own impulses under the circumstances and asked my consent to throw me on the bed and ravish – stop. *Just stop, Evie.*

This is the product of a late night. A muddled mind and erratic lusty behaviour. But I wanted to remove that towel and damn the consequences. Perhaps I'm low on vitamins. Sugar? *Something.*

Georgios whistles as he wanders into the courtyard. The whistle of an innocent who's not caught up in some strange fantasies and contemplating towel-gate. Yikes.

In the cool of the morning there's only the distant sound of waves rolling in and birds twittering in the olive trees in the courtyard. I still my mind and try and think of anything other than a naked Georgios. But it's no good, the *what could have been* is firmly entrenched in my mind. Maybe this is the by-product of being the lone survivor of a long-term sex drought. I'm so thirsty I want to drink him up.

'Shall we see if there are any stragglers?' he says.

We go through the bookshop and into Epeolatry. The place is spick and span, save a few empty champagne coupes here and there. 'No sign of life.'

'Bet there's some sore heads today,' he says.

'I bet.'

'Evie!' Gran calls out from the entrance of the bookshop, sounding suspiciously sprightly.

We go to join her. 'You look fresh as a daisy,' I say, giving her a hug.

'Of course, darling. I drank plenty of water.'

'This time.'

'We live and learn, many *many* times.'

I laugh. 'What time did it all wind up?'

'Oh a few hours ago now. Lucy went off with Stavros to his yacht. Don't think you'll be seeing her for a bit, Georgios. She asked us to forward her luggage back to Italy. Smitten, she was. For now, anyway.'

Georgios and I exchange a smile.

'After sunrise I had to bid the rest of the bookworms adieu. It's always the readers you have to watch out for. They're the ones who can go all night long with their surprising amounts of stamina. And even better, the stragglers promised they'd return tonight. We'll see – that might have been the cocktails talking.'

I smile at the thought. Yes, the launch might have been a party for some, but for others, it was an introduction to Epeolatry, a place they can now visit and feel a sense of belonging. A place they feel welcomed and among friends, new and old. 'All's well that ends well,' I say.

'And you two, did you have an early night or . . .' Always fishing is my gran. I wait for Georgios to rescue me from answering but he's avoiding Gran's eye. What's that about then?

'We had a relatively early night,' I confirm.

'I better head off.' Georgios paints a smile on his face that doesn't go near his eyes. 'I need to touch base with Joe before he changes his mind and submits his book elsewhere.'

He gives me a chaste kiss on the cheek and takes his overnight bag. 'Thanks for letting me stay, Evie. Goodbye, Floretta.'

'That was weird,' Gran says. 'What's up with him?'

'I don't know. He couldn't look at you. What do you think that's about?' I'm reminded that he wanted to discuss something with me before he showered but changed his mind then too. I'd been too caught up in his presence to dwell on it.

A sinking feeling hits. Is his grandfather going to sell and he doesn't know how to tell us? The loss would be catastrophic, not just of Gran's cash, but her hopes and dreams along with it. Gran doesn't even know this is a possibility. I hadn't wanted to worry her any further but it looks like I may need to be straight with her in case there's magic she can pull out of her hat if the worst does happen.

'Gran, we need to chat.'

Chapter 27

We sit on the love swing and I tell her about Yannis' threats to sell the property.

I expect she's going to rant, and wail and hold her head in her hands, but instead she remains serene. 'Don't let it worry you, Evie. I'll speak to Yannis myself.'

'But—'

She taps my leg. 'It's fine, truly. We made enough money last night to tide us over for a bit. I'll fix the rent arrears today and have a chat with him.'

I'm bamboozled by her reaction. Is she not *listening?* 'Why are you so calm? What if it's too late and he decides to sell anyway?'

'He won't.'

I frown. 'How can you be so sure?'

She closes her eyes and lifts her face to the sun. 'I just am. Now is there anything else, because this night owl needs a nap? This glorious sunshine is making me downright lethargic.'

The dots aren't connecting. 'What about the restraining order – aren't you forbidden to see each other?'

She opens her eyes with a sigh. 'No, I had a good old chinwag with the chief of the Hellenic Police last night. He understands us a lot better now and I told him I'd let bygones be bygones when it comes to Yannis.'

Why is she so relaxed? Is it that she's had a late night and any of her worries are too taxing for the light of day?

'OK.' I can't quite hide the dubiousness from my voice but if Gran's not concerned then I should trust in that. 'If you say so.'

'Why don't you go and do something fun today? The bookshop can wait. Almost everyone in town was here last night so I don't expect we'll have many customers. I'll open later this afternoon.'

'If you're sure?' A day out sounds like just the tonic after the craziness of the launch. Mondays are usually quiet in Bibliotherapy.

We make a promise to meet later for dinner.

I text Roxy and arrange to meet at the beach. As I'm slipping into my swimwear the phone rings.

I check the display and see it's The Precinct. Now what?

'Mom, Posy. How's things?'

'What are you wearing?' Posy says scrunching up her nose.

'My swimming costume. Why?'

'It's grotesque.'

'Posy, we've had this conversation many times. I for one will not wear a skimpy little bikini and practically invite skin cancer to invade my body – I just won't.'

'Is it really that or is it because you're a prude?' She does this infuriating duck-lips thing like she's scored a win. I don't rise to it. OK, I rise to it a little.

'*Excuse* me?'

'You heard.'

I scoff. 'How am I a prude?' I ask, knowing full well I may have prudish sensibilities but don't want to be called on it.

'You're in a baking climate but you're covered head to toe like you're about to trek the Himalayas!'

'And when *I'm* eighty I'm going to have fabulous skin, unlike some people who will wrinkle and wither like a prune.'

231

'Now now, girls. We don't have time for this. I do have a legal firm to run you know, *and* a wayward mother to wrangle; the last thing I need is to referee you two.'

'Mom, surely you need to advise her on the dangerous effects of sunlight on the body? If not you, then who?'

With a sigh worthy of an Oscar, Mom says, 'Posy, wear sun cream and, Evie, your swimming costume looks great. There, satisfied?'

We're not, but we remain silent.

'I'm meeting my friend at the beach, and while it's always illuminating chatting, what's the reason for your call? Let me guess, you want to know if I've found another job?' I'm being facetious – they never ask about my life and I'm not upset about it. I just wish they'd leave Gran alone the way they leave me to my own devices.

'Don't be ridiculous, I know you'll find another job when the time is right. I'm calling because my sources have tracked down Gran's husband, if you can call the yellow-bellied bottom feeder that—'

'—he's in Mexico,' Posy says gleefully.

Mom nods. 'Yes, he's in Acapulco. But get this, two days ago he was in Santorini for twenty-four hours and departed from there to Mexico.'

'Konstantine was *here* in Santorini?' I count back to two days ago. That was the day Lucy Strike arrived.

'Yes, briefly, but we don't know why.'

'Weird! We haven't seen him; at least I haven't and surely Gran would have mentioned it if her husband popped by. Why did he then go to Mexico? Did he get work on another oil rig, do you think?' My mind is spinning with various scenarios, hoping I'll land on one that makes sense.

Posy scoffs. 'If you call a casino an oil rig.'

Another casino? Internally I groan. Is Gran hoping that betting on black this time will get her out of a bind? She promised me she'd lay off the gambling! 'Umm, maybe he was on a break from work?' Perhaps the second oil rig job didn't work out either, but I can't tell them about that.

'With another woman?' Mom says sharply.

'What do you mean?'

Mom sighs. There's a real sadness to her eyes, as if she knows this intel is legitimate. Could it be? 'OK, I'll come clean. The PI from our firm has been following Konstantine, and let's just say he puts the 'con' into his name. The dud of a hub drained Gran's bank account not long after they were married. From the evidence we've gathered it looks as though she managed to pay for most of the interiors for Epeolatry before he took the remainder. There was no oil rig. He escaped to Corfu for a bit and now he's in Acapulco.'

It can't be! Gran said she gave him the money to bet so they'd get out of a spot of financial bother. If Mom knew that she'd hit the roof, so I stay quiet for now. But why is he popping up at another casino?

'And the woman, is she an Uber driver?' Is this Gran's secret weapon? The woman she sent to spy on her husband and make sure he did what she asked with her large sum of money while assuring her husband the woman was merely a mode of transportation.

'An Uber driver? Where do you get this stuff from?' Posy says with a sarcastic laugh. Sometimes I'd really like to shake her but I don't condone violence. Not unless it's absolutely necessary.

She's managed to rile me up and I accidentally blurt, 'From *Gran*, Posy. She's not as uniformed as she'd have you imagine, you know.'

Mom says, 'No, the CCTV footage is quite clear. It shows they met playing roulette at the casino in Corfu and this woman has since hitched herself along for the ride.'

What! Gran lied to me about the Uber woman? Is the gossip from loukoumades Maria true?

233

Gran must have been trying to save face while she figured out what was really going on after he drained her bank account and did a runner. This plot is like an onion: as soon as you peel away a layer, there's another underneath! My poor gran! How could the vile man do such a monstrous thing!

'This . . . is a lot to process,' I say. 'How much did he steal from Gran?'

'Six figures.'

'What!'

'Yep.'

'So there was no oil rig?'

Mom shakes her head 'No. There never was. Gran's not stupid, Evie. She's obviously said that for a reason.'

To buy herself time to figure it out.

'I *know* she's not stupid. I'm the one who trusts in her, unlike you two meddlers. But you're telling me Gran's known all along he's stolen and fled with her life savings and she's OK with that?' I piece all the bits of information I have together. Why didn't she dash off to Corfu to confront him if she knew it was true?

'I'm sure she's *far* from OK with it.'

'Why wouldn't she tell us the truth?' Posy says. 'This is her problem, always making up these grand stories so you can never tell what is fact and what is fiction.'

'She's probably embarrassed.' Mom's face falls.

'I can see why,' Posy says. 'Husband number nine didn't even last a full calendar year.'

'That's not nice, Posy,' I admonish. 'Gran must be heartbroken over this.'

Posy's cheeks turn pink and she ducks her head like a recalcitrant child, which happens almost never. 'Sorry, that was out of line. I get carried away sometimes.'

'This is why we're trying to get her home,' Mom beseeches. 'Look what happens when she's all alone and making spontaneous decisions. Disaster!'

'Forget about bringing her home, Mom. She's happy here.'
I'm still reeling that Konstantine has committed a crime of this
magnitude against my beloved Gran – to steal her money like
that, he may as well have stolen her dreams. My sadness soon
turns to white-hot rage. How dare he! All she wants is to live out
her life in her colourful little cliff-top bookshop, surrounded by
word nerds and rescue dogs and he's tried to snatch that from her.

'We have to get her money back.' My voice is steely with
determination.

'I'm working on it this end,' Mom says.

'Do tell . . . while we don't have the range of skills Gran has,
like a black belt in karate and killer abilities with a katana, I do
know sixteen pigs can eat a dead man in eight minutes.'

'WHAT!' Mom shrieks.

I shrug. 'There's a pig farm here in case it's helpful in any way.'

Concern dashes over Mom's face and I delight a bit when I see
Posy reel back from the camera too. She'd *better* watch her Ps and
Qs, even if she has shown herself to be remorseful today when
she goes too far. 'No one needs to be, uh eaten. Don't you worry
about any of this. Leave it to me; you just make sure Gran's OK.'

'Yeah.' Posy grins. 'Broken hearts can lead to broken hips you
know.'

Chastened Posy didn't last too long! 'Leave her hips out of this.'

'Now, now, Evie, don't get upset,' Posy says grinning. 'Gran will
be OK. Maybe husband number ten will be a keeper?'

I roll my eyes at her attempts to goad me while Gran's sweet
face flashes into my mind. 'What if this ruins her for love?'

'She's a hopeless romantic,' Posy says. 'Emphasis on the *hopeless*. She'll be fine.'

'Urgh, and you're the opposite! You don't have a romantic
bone in your entire body.'

'*Girls.* We'll call again soon when we've done some more digging.'

'OK.'

My head is spinning as I end the call. I sit heavily on my bed as

I process it all. Konstantine came back to Santorini – why? Did he come to visit Gran? Maybe he paid her the money back? Or was he snooping around? Worse, did he threaten her for *more* money?

Then it hits me. Georgios was at the airport picking up Lucy, and ever since then he's behaved strangely in front of Gran. He must've seen Konstantine with his new lady friend!

With a long sigh I open my phone and text him:

Did you see Konstantine at the airport when you picked up Lucy?

Ellipses appear and then the message pops up.

I'm sorry, Evie. I didn't know how to tell Floretta. He was with another woman.

Gah, I knew it. Why wouldn't he have pulled me aside and confided in me? Or given Gran a heads up? Did he plan to simply turn a blind eye?

You should have told me.

There's a longer wait for the next message. My mind goes into overdrive wondering if I'll have to be the one to tell Gran. And something tells me this isn't going to come as a shock for the beloved octogenarian. Gran may not know the full story, but I'm sure she knows pieces and has been puzzling over them since Konstantine left.

I was going to – but I held off because if my family found out Kon had abandoned her I worried that would really put the nail in the coffin for the property and they'd sell, knowing that no salary was coming as promised. We had to focus on the launch and I definitely wasn't going to be the one

*who announced bad news on such a big night for Floretta. I
promised myself I'd tell her this morning but I couldn't do it.
I can't be the one who breaks her heart.*

I relax and text back:

OK that makes sense.

He's not a monster. I put myself in his shoes. He's an empa-
thetic human who struggled to make sense of a hard situation.
I'd have probably made matters much worse by blurting it out or
sending a lengthy email that skirted around the issue for seven
pages before finally adding it at the end in super small font. No
one with a heart wants to be the bearer of such bad news.

My phone rings. It's Georgios.

'I'm sorry, Evie. I feel so bad for Floretta. What can I do to
help?' His velvety voice is thick with concern. He really is one
of the good ones.

'It's OK. Gran will be all right. Mom's working on it from
back home too so it's not a complete shock – I'm fairly sure if
we know by now then Gran's got an idea too.' I don't tell him
about the missing money. It's so huge and not my secret to tell.

'His name is going to be mud around here whenever this
comes to light.'

From what I gather, the locals don't take too kindly to men
running off. If only they knew that he's done more than run off
with another woman, he's drained Gran's bank account in the
process. 'At least that's something.'

'See you later? Dinner?'

I consider it. Now I know the truth I want to stay close to
Gran to make sure she's not hiding her broken heart behind a
fake smile. But first I'll catch up with Roxy so Gran can nap in
the peace and quiet.

I beg off with promises to meet another time.

237

Chapter 28

Summer heat bears down as I make the arduous cycle to the beach, the water like a mirage the closer I get. I'm desperate to plunge myself into the sea to cool down. I chain up my bike and walk down to the shore. Roxy's on her back, book held aloft shading her face.

'Are you reading or using that for sun protection?'

'A bit of both.'

I check the title.

'Is that a personally signed Lucy Strike?'

'It is. The woman sure loves a sex scene. This is more like soft porn than romantic suspense. How does every situation turn into sex, even after the murders, like ew.'

I laugh. 'They sell like hotcakes around the world so it's a winning formula.'

'Blame BookTok. You know she went off with Stavros last night?'

Thanks to Gran pulling the old bait and switch on Lucy so she'd get over her hissy fit about Georgios. 'Yeah I heard.'

Roxy shakes her head. 'He's a heartbreaker, and so is she. I give them a week tops.'

'The flingiest of all holiday flings. And good story fodder, I imagine.' I feel less like tossing Lucy Strike off the Santorini cliffs after my chat with Gran about it all. People are not always as they seem.

'I wonder if we'll make cameos in her next book. She'll probably kill you off in the first chapter.'

'That would be amazing. I'd love to see my name in print!'

Roxy laughs. With the sea breeze blowing against my face, I relax against my towel, willing all the muddy thoughts away for a bit. I can't quite manage it though, with the knowledge that Gran's been shouldering this burden alone.

I throw open my towel and place it on the sand next to Roxy. 'Wasn't last night fun?' The after-party glow is real! I'm not sure if it's because it's over or because it was a success. Maybe a mix of both.

'I had the best time. Everyone's raving about it on socials today. Sadly, I'm no closer to finding a husband but I have faith Floretta will share her wisdom with me and it'll only be a matter of time. You should have seen her antics after you left. That woman is my idol.'

'Oh God.' I cover my face. 'What did she do?' All sorts of visions pop into mind. Gran dragging a hottie atop the bar and doing the mambo with him.

'The jazz band played "The Time of My Life", and in the next breath Floretta and Zorba are doing the dance from *Dirty Dancing* and we're all goggle-eyed waiting to see if they'll do the lift, because surely not, right? But they do it – and it was spectacular. Floretta was so graceful, utterly mesmerising. Her dress sparkled under the light; she looked like a floating angel.'

My eyebrows pull together. 'Zorba the pig farmer and Gran? How would they even know the routine?'

Roxy shrugs. 'They must have been practising. It was flawless. No one could quite believe what they were seeing.'

'Golly. How is she so effortlessly cool?' I'm bummed I missed it. 'Did anyone film it?'

Roxy clucks her tongue. 'I didn't. It was spur of the moment and all eyes were glued to them. I'll check with the official photographer. She might have caught it, and we can look at the Epeolatry hashtag later; hopefully a guest captured some of it. I'm kicking myself about not thinking quick enough to film it. It would have made such a good promotional video. The space is big enough to host dance lessons and last night *everyone* was keen to learn. I'm going to speak to Floretta about it later. How did she learn to move like that?'

My wild and wonderful Gran. So many hidden talents. 'Jimmy from Australia, husband number five, taught her to dance. I didn't know she could do the lift, but they'd do salsa, mambo, all those sensual dances. Gran said Jimmy should have been a choreographer but instead he was an outback tour guide. In retrospect, dancing might have been the safer choice. He was violently killed in a random drop bear attack.'

Roxy gasps. 'What? What the hell is a drop bear?'

I forget this news is shocking the first time people hear it. 'A drop bear is a terrifying Australian marsupial. A carnivorous species of koala. The razor-sharp fang-like teeth were Jimmy's undoing. A wrong place, wrong time situation.'

Roxy shivers. 'How are Australians even alive with the sheer number of predators that can kill them there?'

I shake my head, confused about it too. 'Gran says they're bred tough to withstand the climate and all those poisonous spiders, snakes, jellyfish, and let's not forget the saltwater crocodiles, who kill their prey by means of an underwater death roll.'

'I don't even want to know what that is.'

'Right? It's an efficient way for crocodiles to kill their dinner. Gran loved Australia. She still tells stories of her time there in the outback of the Northern Territory. If Jimmy's injuries hadn't been fatal, Gran would have stayed in Oz.'

We lapse into a comfortable silence and people-watch. My mind drifts to Gran and all the remarkable adventures she'd had. A few beachgoers walking past wave hello. I recognise them from the launch.

'Thank you for all of your help with the launch. You worked miracles to get the word spread so far and wide. We have some money set aside for you, Roxy.'

She waves me away. 'No, we already made a deal about this life-time membership to Epeolatry, remember? It was only one night.'

'It was a lot more than one night. All your PR work and . . .'

She drags her sunglasses onto her head. 'Seriously, Evie, it's been a godsend to get out of the house. Mom is doing really well so we're at that stage where we're getting on each other's last nerves. It's been fun to use my brain again. And the launch has been a helpful experiment to see if there's enough call for PR and marketing on the island, and by the success of last night I believe there is. We're even.'

'That's great, Roxy. But Gran's insisting.'

'I'll tell her myself.'

'Good plan.'

'What about this instead . . . If and when you ditch us for the bright lights of Hollywood, I'd like to be considered for some shifts in Bibliotherapy. PR is my passion but I don't want it to consume my life like it did in Athens. I adore the bookshop and working there a couple of days a week would be a dream come true.'

'Of course, Roxy! Gran was going to ask you last night if you'd consider doing some shifts in the future.'

'Yay!' Roxy puts her hand on her heart. 'I solemnly vow to protect those books and not let anyone buy them for nefarious purposes, like hiding engagement rings or making flowers from their pages. Or God forbid using them purely for display purposes.'

So my bookselling foibles may have come up from time to time? Someone has to watch over those precious tomes.

'Ha. Well make sure you keep an eye out, I'm sure there are so many book-destroying scams about.'

'I'll be a step ahead, don't you worry. One thing – what if Kon quits his oil rig job? They won't need me then will they?

It's mostly that I'm certain I'm going to meet my dream man in a bookshop. It's written in the stars.'

I bite down on my lip to stop the secret spilling out. 'Konstantine won't be back.' *Oops*. 'Don't say anything though.'

She sits up abruptly. 'What? Where is he? This has something to do with you asking me a while back if he was trustworthy, doesn't it?'

It's too late to turn back now so I make her promise it'll stay between us and I tell her the whole sorry story. It feels good to share one of the many secrets I've held so close to my chest. 'I'm not sure why he'd have come back to Santorini though. Why risk being spotted here if he was all set to escape to Mexico?'

Roxy hugs her knees to her chest and considers it. 'Ah! To pick up his passport?'

'*Right*.' How did I not think of that! 'Do you think he snuck into Gran's villa to grab it?' I'm curious to find out if Gran had been aware he'd returned to Santorini, albeit briefly.

'I doubt it. The dogs would have created a ruckus if he did and no way would Zeus let a stranger inside Floretta's villa. Maybe he left it with his mother who lives on the other side of the village?' Roxy's complexion reddens as if she's mad. 'Who does he think he is! Doing that to Floretta! What a vile . . .' she lets out a string of expletives that capture the attention of a mother sitting close by whose child mimics the last F-word.

'Roxy,' I say quietly and tilt my head towards the child.

She mouths *sorry* to the mother and is rewarded with an icy glare. 'Well he is all of those things and more. What does Floretta have to say about it all?'

I make a face. 'I haven't talked to her about it yet. Mom swore me to secrecy and look how well that's going. I'll wait and see what further investigating unearths. My mom sensed there was something fishy going on. I figured they were making a big deal over nothing as usual when it comes to Gran. Turns out this time Mom was right.'

Roxy's forehead furrows. 'Floretta doesn't strike me as the type to let things slide, Evie. You should chat to her about it – maybe she's already planning a way to get the money back. Or revenge. Revenge would be better. I for one would like to see *that*.' She clicks her fingers. 'Better yet, we could go and tell Konstantine's mom what he's done. The family will make good on what he stole, or they'll die of shame.'

I pull my lips to one side. 'It's a lot of money, Roxy. It wouldn't be fair on them.'

'Well it's not fair on Floretta either!'

Roxy has taken a real shine to Gran. 'I'll see how Gran is tonight. I have to broach it carefully because she hasn't opened up to me yet so there must be a good reason for that. And if my mom finds out I've spoken out of turn she'll kill me. Or she'll turn up here when we least expect it. I'm not sure which is worse.'

Roxy waves the worry away. 'Ah who cares. What can she do?'

'You don't know my mother. I'm sure the phrase *if looks could kill* came from someone who made the mistake of crossing her. Solving this muddle of Gran's will be the top of her list and if I mess up her investigations, they'll never let me forget it.'

'You're Floretta's *granddaughter*! Fierce protector of books and words alike. But I get it. Moms can lay on the guilt thick.'

'Yep.'

'So, back to real-life love. What happened with Georgios and Lucy last night? Why were they running so late and what was with Lucy's threat of only staying an hour?'

I blow out a breath, remembering it all. 'Well, the damsel-in-distress act all started with the *I can't do up my buttons* con.' I fill her in on the story as she peppers me with questions as I go. 'No I have no idea what colour the first dress was. Does it matter?'

'Well it matters for *context*.'

I continue relaying what I know.

Roxy gasps. 'She launched herself at him, with *kissy lips* at the ready?'

'He didn't say if she had kissy lips at the ready. He wasn't one hundred per cent sure what she was attempting to do, but what else would you lunge at a guy for? Either to kiss him or kill him – there's no in between.'

'Evie, you are so pedantic about words yet you can't quiz a guy properly about matters such as this? You're missing the *most* important details.'

I hold up a finger. 'There was one. He called me his girlfriend.'

Her eyes light up. 'Ooh, juicy, so things are getting serious?'

I adjust my hat and lie flat on the beach towel. 'I don't know. How can they? He's all set to stay here, and I'll be moving on as soon as I'm sure Gran's OK, or I accept a job offer.' I wish I could confide in Roxy about the fake-dating scam. But I can't bring myself to tell her in case she hates me for it.

'Long distance? Surely he's got to visit New York city for work from time to time and you'll visit Gran here too.'

'Yeah.' I let the conversation die as we squint up at the sun. I can admit now I've developed strong feelings for Georgios, but part of me keeps thinking that this is all too good to be true.

It's a different world here, almost like living in a holiday romcom itself, so I sense this feeling isn't to be trusted. Is this the old version of me speaking? I've grown here, changed, peeled a few superficial layers away and what lies beneath is a shiner more confident person. That's the magic of this island, but I don't know if any of it is long-term. When I'm back home, will all those neuroses creep back in as I'm sucked back into the vortex of big-city living?

Will it all seem like a crazy dream that I'll kick myself for believing in? Will Georgios have his hands full with his publishing company and slowly we'll slide away from each other's orbits? All we'll have left are the memories of these balmy Santorini days . . .

Chapter 29

Gran's behind the counter, tallying the afternoon takings, when I arrive back from the beach.

'Hello, darling. Did you have a nice time with Roxy?' She says over her bright pink spectacles. They're shaped like love hearts and give her a youthful air. I love that she's such a non-conformist, and outrageous with it.

'It was just the ticket after yesterday. Good news, Roxy would love to work here part-time once I leave.' I search Gran's features for any evidence of tears, of heartbreak, but find nothing. In fact, she seems perkier than usual.

'Ooh perfect. Roxy's a gem. But I'll be sad to see you go. Have you heard anything on that front?'

'Val from Olympus Media offered me a job as a PA on location. I'm tempted to accept, as it gets me back in the industry where I might hear about a book scout job on the grapevine. But it's an active role; I'll be dealing with everyone's messes. Is that the sort of thing I want to sign on for?'

'It sounds hectic. I'm not sure you *should* settle, Evie. It hasn't been that long and you've got your heart set on being a book scout.'

There's another option. Gene. 'You're right. Perhaps I can fill that role, but with someone who would love the position. I might

245

have better luck if I head back to LA and "network" even if it kills me. But I hate the thought of leaving you alone.'

'I won't be alone. Kon will be back soon.' Why is she sticking to this story? I understand she might be upset, but Gran's not one to feel shame or worry about what others think of her. Mom will only be kept at bay so long before she collates her intel and presents it all to Gran with an *I told you so* as she drops the thick dossier in front of her.

'Where was the second rig located?'

'Mexico.' She must know exactly where he is!

'Mexico, huh?'

'Uh-huh.'

This is the place Gran wants to stay. She's adopted six dogs, and that's a commitment she wouldn't take lightly; we have to solve the problem of the missing money so she can keep her Santorini dreams alive. I toy with how to push for the truth when Gran says, 'All good things come to those who wait. I don't want you to worry about me.' She gives me a wide smile that certainly appears genuine. If this is Gran assuring me she's got a handle on it then I have no choice but to let it go for now and trust she's got the situation under control.

I change the subject. 'How did it go in here today?' From the pile of euros it seems there's been a busy spell.

'Crazy good. I had my nap and then opened up after lunch. We've had more bookworms sign up for library memberships and we've completely sold out of Lucy Strike books.'

'Wow. We'll have to order more. And line up another guest author.'

'Yes, darling, it'll be such fun.'

I sit beside her. 'Did you get the rent paid?'

'Sure did, and Yannis and I came to an agreement to forget the past and move forward as friends.'

My mouth falls open. They're friends just like that? 'What a relief!' My sweet Gran isn't a grudge holder. You've got to admire that in a person. But it all seems so simple, almost too simple.

With Roxy agreeing to work part-time in Bibliotherapy, and Gran's businesses back in the black there's less need for me to stay. Hollywood calls, loud and clear.

Gran interrupts my train of thought. 'Well, we've agreed to be friends, but you can never tell with cunning old men. They're likely to change their mind on a whim, you know? Darling, if you don't mind, I'd like you to keep fake-dating Georgios.'

Is this her way of asking me to stay a bit longer? Gran turns to face me. 'Unless your relationship has developed organically and you haven't enlightened your dear old gran?' Smirking, she taps her fingertips together while she waits for my response – either that or she's incanting a love spell.

I stay mute. If I give her an inch, she'll be off and running.

'Evie?'

Gah! 'Not sure. He's hard to read.'

She scoffs. 'Hard to read! What is he . . . a book? Ask the damn man and then you'll know.'

'Ask him what exactly?'

'How he feels about you. What the future holds. Whether he wants to make sweet *sweet* love.'

'*Gran!*'

'What?'

'I can't ask those things, especially the sweet, sweet . . . thing.' I can't even say it in front of her.

'Why not?'

I make a moue with my lips before saying primly, 'It's not in my nature to be forward.'

'How is it being forward asking the guy what the future holds?' Gran shakes her head in frustration. 'You two are as a bad as each other.'

'What does that mean?' I suck in a breath, ready for her to tell me all the ways we're suited and a perfect match and how I simply need to express those feelings, as if it's as natural as asking him what the time is.

'You *both* have a hang-up about sharing your feelings, so instead you pretend you don't have any.'

Bingo. But wait . . .

'Are you saying you think he's the same as me?' The idea is so wild it almost makes me laugh. Does he have the same hang-ups? Is it that he's not only focused on work, on words, it's that he doesn't quite know how to express himself in a non-fictional world so he lets it float away – just like me? Or he ends things before they fully develop – just like me? Huh. And how on earth would Gran know all of this?

'*Exactly* like you.' Gran stares at me with wise eyes as if she's known this fact about us both all along. She probably has. She's got a gift when it comes to seeing into the heart of a person and what makes them tick.

'I'll wait and see what happens. If it's meant to be I'll know.' Still, I can't quite be that forthright, take-charge persona. And that's OK. It's not in my make-up.

'But—' Those three tiny letters are full of exasperation. 'How will you know if neither of you speak up? Next minute it'll be the most beautiful relationship that *never* was!'

'I just will.'

'Evie, you're going to let a good man like that slip between your fingers because you're too scared to ask him if he sees anything serious between you both?'

How to explain it in a way that an extrovert over-sharer will understand? 'It's not just that – not *only* that. I feel a heap of guilt that this was all based on a lie. What if he finds out about our little ruse? He might hate me for it and question everything I've said and done. I know *I* would if our roles were reversed.'

She shakes her head and lets out a harrumph. 'Why? It's not like we did it for nefarious purposes. It wasn't done maliciously. And look what it's developed into! If you ask me I've done you one almighty favour because you two knuckleheads would've only stared at each other from afar with love hearts for eyes, never acting on your feelings. You'll be eighty-three in the blink of an eye, Evie Davenport. It's time to act. When it comes to love, there's no other option except to allow yourself to become vulnerable. The payoff is worth it. Trust me, nine husbands later I can tell you that for a fact. I've loved and I've lost and I don't regret a damn moment.'

'That's beautiful. Gran. And I agree. I do. I need to be more vocal, lay my heart on the line. What if he finds out about what we did down the track? It would be a hundred times worse. I'll have to tell him soon.' Gah. I wish I could get past it like Gran so easily has.

'People do it all the time.' Pee Wee runs past pawing a ball.

'What? People fake-date all the time?' I scoff. 'Now you're *really* stretching, Gran.'

Gran drops her gaze back to the money she's put in small piles. 'Trust me, it's a thing. Blind dates are virtually this! Be brave. Be bold and tell him how you're really feeling – forget the fake part. And then you can see what happens.'

Can I broach this with him without mentioning the fact it was all a con – at first? No. God no. It's too soon. It's too much. I'll stumble and mumble and then he'll think I'm in the throes of some kind of panic attack which to be fair I probably will be. Feelings, they're just so *messy*.

'Evie? Earth to Evie. Are you there?'

I don't respond because there's nothing else to say.

After much soul-searching, I turn down Val's offer of a PA job. It's not the position for me; no matter how great an opportunity it is, I feel as though I need to find a book scout role, even if it does take longer than anticipated. I mention to Val that I know of a person with industry experience who'd be perfect for the job and ask if I can pass on his details. Within seconds I get a reply.

Please do. I need an experienced PA urgently as we're about to go on location to the Tetons, Wyoming. Good luck with the job hunt.
Thanks,
Val

Since time is of the essence, I punch in Penelope's number.

'Evie! How's life treating you?' There's a stiffness to Penelope's voice that I haven't heard before.

'Good, good. I'm phoning because I might have found the perfect job. For you.'

There's an audible gasp. 'For me?'

I tell her all about Val and his company and what will be expected of her in this new position, including all the travel perks.

'Oh God, Evie, thank you! It almost sounds too good to be true! Shall I phone him now? Between us, I handed in my notice, so this is great timing.'

My heart hurts for Hollywood Films. Losing Penelope will be a great loss. She has been the cornerstone, holding the place up for so long. 'Yes, call him now. They're off on location soon to the Tetons and ideally he'd like you there ASAP.'

'You don't know what this means to me, Evie, really. I appreciate you.'

I smile. 'You're the best in the biz, Pen. You deserve a good boss.'

There's a little snuffle as if she's crying. 'What about you? Any luck on the job front?'

'Not yet, but it'll happen.'

'Love that attitude.'

'Keep me posted.'

'You too and thanks again, Evie.'

Chapter 30

I avoid catching up with Georgios for a couple of days so I can assess my feelings and the risk-to-reward ratio. We still chat by text and I'm always grateful it doesn't merge into sexting territory, because that's high on my list of NO for the first year or three at least. If ever. OK, I've never done any sexting and I never will because it just seems uncouth. And don't get me started on data breaches and hackers. I totally support others who choose to spice up their love lives however they see fit, but it's not for me. Once you've gone viral on TikTok for all the wrong reasons, you tend to be a little more wary of online content and how quickly it can be shared.

For our relationship to work, the only way forward is to tell him the truth about the fake-dating farce and hope he understands. I'm one of those people who can't build a life together based on an untruth, and even though I had good reasons for doing it, it still doesn't sit well with me.

I'm polishing martini glasses in Epeolatry, getting the place ready for another evening of shenanigans, which thankfully I don't need to be part of. Gran's going to assume her role as librarian and Zorba is going to assist the mixologist behind the bar. Since the launch, the evenings are more sedate – manageable for Gran but still fun for members who enjoy perusing the books and chatting with other bookworms while the jazz band plays.

Tonight we've managed to wangle sci-fi author Joe to do a talk about his writing process and his upcoming novel. Georgios secured worldwide rights and it'll be published by Eros books later this year. I figure the exposure will help them both and give our members another author to admire; even better that Joe is a local and lots of islanders want to help celebrate his book deal.

Once I've finished polishing the glasses, I do a last-minute check to make sure that everything is ready for tonight's event. Fruit is chopped for the cocktail garnishes and is chilling in the fridge. I've stocked up the ice and replenished the bar. Athena is catering so I check the kitchen is tidy, giving the stainless steel benches a wipe-down and tidy the inside of the fridge so there's room for their supplies. That done, I check each room, righting fallen cushions and turning on table lamps, which give the spaces a warm glow and add to the moody ambience.

I get a real pang at the thought of leaving all of this behind. Leaving the island, Gran and Roxy, Georgios. All of it. If I'm honest, I don't want to leave. I'd love to stay forever but I want to chase my dreams and somehow, I don't think Hollywood will come to me.

If I want change then I have to make change. I take my phone and consider my options. One call won't hurt? It rings for an age before he finally answers.

'Evie! How's things in LA?'

He hasn't heard? Gene must really be out of the loop like Betsy promised he'd be. 'I'm at my gran's in Santorini. Hank made me redundant two days after you left.'

He clucks his tongue. 'Ach. I'm sorry to hear that.'

'It's OK, I didn't really love his . . . energy.'

Gene laughs. 'Me either. But I—' He's distracted by someone talking in the background. His words are muffled but I can still make them out. *No, it's not work. It's a work colleague.*

Gene's wife Betsy had high hopes he'd forget about the industry and all those long days that turned into nights. He admitted to me his marriage suffered over the years because he was always working and he regrets not putting Betsy first more often.

OK, OK, I'll be ready in a minute.

'Sorry to cut this short, Evie. We've got lunch plans at the club and God forbid we're five minutes late.'

'That's OK. Just quickly, do you know of any book scout positions going?'

He lets out a sad sigh. 'I'm out of the biz. Betsy – my commandant – makes sure of it. I'm sorry. I wish I could help.' Betsy's voice rings out, something about keeping the Goldbergs waiting.

'No worries, Gene. Enjoy your lunch.'

We say our goodbyes and I feel a rush of sadness for Gene. Maybe it's for the best – for health and relationship reasons – but he lived and breathed the movie biz. You can't say the word Hollywood without conjuring Gene's grandfatherly smiley face. It feels a bit unfair he can't chat properly for five minutes, but perhaps Betsy has to make these boundaries for them both to enjoy their twilight years together.

My last hope is dashed. Gene is a no-go. It's time to return to Hollywood. Pound the pavement. Scary but necessary if I want to achieve my dream.

I won't let myself down by backing out of the one important promise I made myself: to find magical romances and get them onto the silver screen. If I start breaking my own promises, then where does it end? I shake it away for now. There's work to be done here.

I check the bar and replace the library catalogue coasters with new ones that have a picture of Joe and a hook line about his upcoming book. I scatter Epeolatry bookmarks. Life moves slow and yet is whizzing by. I can't help but feel a clock is ticking, reminding me that I've got other challenges to face. Great big fun Hollywood challenges.

I'm standing hands on hips, assessing the room, when Georgios wanders in from the bookshop, Sir Spud trotting just ahead as if leading his charge to me. I lift Sir Spud for a cuddle, nesting my face into his fur.

'Floretta told me where to find you.' For a moment my breath catches at the sight of Georgios, hair mussed by the sea breeze, skin tanned darker by all these long summer days.

I check my watch. 'You're early. Joe isn't starting until seven.'

Lily wanders in and paws his leg, her subtle way of asking to be held. She won't go near any man bar Georgios. She pines for him when he leaves, stands at the gate and howls as if she's heartbroken he's left her behind. There are times I wonder if Georgios should adopt her, she is so taken with him. He bends to her and croons, speaking gently as if she's the most precious thing in the world – gah I can see why she's fallen for him. He gently takes her in his arms and she gazes up adoringly. Even dogs are under his spell!

Once Lily is settled he lifts his gaze to me. 'I'll meet Joe later. I'm here to see you. Are we OK, Evie? I can't help but feel you've been avoiding me.'

I lift a shoulder. 'We've been texting.'

'We went from catching up a few times a day to a few texts . . .'

'Oh.' I toy with a bookmark to look anywhere but directly at him.

Do I tell Georgios the truth now? Get it over and done with fast, like ripping off a plaster. There's a forlorn air about him as if he's expecting the worst. Is he similar to me and can spend days agonising over things?

I blurt out, 'Do you see a future with me?' *God, Evie!* This is what happens when you don't have a plan and Gran's warnings about being eighty-three in the blink of an eye and still single bubble inside your brain. Now I can't go back and we'll have to have the talk.

His lips twitch. Why? Is it funny? Ridiculous. Too presumptuous?

I resist the urge to run. I'm not going to run ever again. I'll stand my ground and shout the loudest if I have to.

He folds his arms. 'Neither of us know what the future holds, but if we can make it work, I'd love to.'

I deflate. The answer is so lacklustre, so vague, I don't know what to make of it. 'Is that – a yes? Can you explain to me where you stand when it comes to us?' This is why deep and meaningfuls are best done over email. That way I can forensically pore over the nuance of every word.

He drops his hands to his sides. 'It's a hell yes.'

I exhale. There are times when Georgios is just as bad at peopling as I am. It makes me like him more. A flawed hero is the best hero. One who doesn't have it all together. A work in progress. It's my turn to speak up but my chest tightens, trapping the truth inside. 'OK, umm then that's one query answered.'

With a grin he says, 'Do you have other queries, Evie?'

Many but they're mainly to do with family conspiracies. 'Ah – not about you.'

He laughs. 'Is there anyone else I should be worried about?'

I pause; now is my chance to tell him about the whole fake-dating scheme Gran signed me up for.

'Your silence isn't exactly making me feel secure . . .'

Oh! He means is there another *man*. A *love interest*. I almost guffaw at the thought. 'No, no nothing to worry about in that respect.'

'Phew.' He gives me a slow smile. 'It struck me yesterday that getting fired led me here, and even though love wasn't on the cards, I found you. It's true things happen for a reason.'

Love? Oh boy. This is the part where I reciprocate, share my feelings for him. 'I've had the best summer of my life . . .' *Tell him, Evie!* '. . . with you. Do you think we'd have dated in the real world?'

'Isn't this real?' He steps closer to me, dogs snoozing peacefully in our arms.

I want to tell him. I swallow a lump in my throat. 'Not really. Nothing is real here. Not even us. This version of us is . . . *fake*. Isn't it?' A look I can't quite decipher flashes across his face, part alarm, part concern maybe?

'Fake?'

I will him to pull the answer from the ether so I don't need to voice it. 'There's a lot you don't know about me. I'm worried if I did tell you it would change your opinion of me.'

He surveys me for the longest time as if debating whether to question me on this. I hope he does. I hope he insists on it. Then I'll have to tell him straight.

'It's still early days, Evie. We've got a lot to learn about each other. There's nothing you can tell me that would make me change my mind about you. Unless you're a serial killer, then I'd have to draw the line there.'

'Do you have secrets?' I ask, wishing his would eclipse mine and then we'd be square.

'Doesn't everyone? We'll get there, Evie. Let's enjoy each other for as long as we've got.'

What does that mean?

Chapter 31

Summer is in full swing. The long languorous days stretch into balmy nights. I'm out with Roxy at the Squashed Olive when my phone rings.

I'm about to set it to silent when she says, 'Answer it. It could be important.'

I shoot her a grateful look and check the display. 'Ooh, it's Gene!'

'Hollywood Gene! Quick, don't let it ring out!'

I accept the call and dash outside past the busy tables of diners, eating under string lights.

'Evie, hi! Sorry I was so abrupt the other day.' I love Gene's voice. It's mellifluous, honeyed like a man from the golden age. He's the type of guy who could sell you any dream because he sounds so *safe*. 'Betsy is really hammering the point home that I'm not to work. She feels that one call will lead to two and next minute I'll be opening a new studio called Florida Films, which isn't a half-bad name.'

I laugh as I find an empty table and plonk myself on a rattan chair. 'She's probably right to be concerned. Are you enjoying your retirement over there in sunny Florida?'

He chortles. 'Couldn't hate anything more. The first few weeks were bliss. Now I'm bored out of my mind. If someone suggests another game of pinochle I'll scream. And don't get me started on the silver sneakers program . . .'

I try to picture Gene being a joiner and just cannot imagine such a thing. He's more of a leader, but in that old-school respectful way. 'What about Betsy, I bet she's loving having you back full-time?'

'The commandant told me I was making the place untidy with all my moping about and then promptly left for a Bahama cruise with her book club gals.' I can almost hear the grin.

'Wow, living the dream.'

'One of us is.' His tone turns wistful. 'You know, I thought I was ready to leave the movie biz, but it becomes part of you. I feel like I've lost a limb. Life is so dull without all that action. But I'll get the hang of this retirement business eventually. Maybe I'll take up golf.'

'*Couples* golf! You could wear matching outfits.'

He scoffs. 'Betsy would love that. Now about your job prospects. I've made some enquiries, and may have a role that interests you. It's not the same as working at the studio itself, with the action that goes on there.'

'I'm listening.' Working on the plot itself had its downfalls. Actors with their big egos and constant demands, producers screaming at the boom guys and lighting team, set design arguing with costumers. The list goes on.

'A pal of mine with an indie studio is searching for romantic comedies to develop for a streamer. Low budget, maybe three mill tops, some even less, so it wouldn't give you a lot to play around with in terms of buying big-name rights, but enough that you could still secure those hidden gems you favour.'

My skin tingles. *This!* This is what I've been searching for. I don't want big-budget blockbusters that come with huge amounts of pressure and A-list celebrities attached to the project. I remain cool. Well I try to. 'Low-budget works for me.' And a cast and crew who really appreciate a chance to work in the industry.

To show off their as-yet undiscovered talent and shine. Together we have a chance to make magic happen.

'You'll be on a retainer, not as much as before. It's not an office position, so you'll work autonomously having the freedom to work wherever you want. Jerry has a base in London and they shoot all over the world, so it might actually be perfect for someone . . .' He leaves the sentence hanging.

'Who doesn't like peopling?'

He laughs. 'I was going to say who works better alone. Like you, Evie who reads double the amount of any book scout I've ever known and makes copious thoughtful notes on each manuscript, giving them all a chance to be considered on their merits. You go above and beyond and that's rare in this industry. Trust me, I've been around for a while.'

'Thank you, Gene. Really.' His praise is just the confidence boost I need. 'It's my dream job. How do I apply? How do I convince Jerry I'm the book scout he's been searching for?' It's hard to keep the desperation from my voice but I feel instinctively this is what I've been waiting for.

'I've told him all about you, Evie and how much I believe in you. You'll be an asset to his company. He's fairly informal and wants to chat with you over video call. If you gel and he thinks you're the right fit, he'll hire you. He's an eccentric sort. I've got a feeling you'll bloom in such an environment.'

'Thank you so much, Gene! I owe you one. How about a game of pinochle when I'm next in Florida?'

'Don't push your luck, kid,' he says with a laugh. 'You can do this, Evie. Remember your worth and be yourself, because that's what he's looking for, OK?'

I take a moment to bite back tears. Gene's always been a fan of mine, telling me I'm more real than anyone in Hollywood and that's a rare trait indeed. He says that my so-called quirks make me the best book scout, because I can relate to a heroine who doesn't have it all figured out and it's those novels that make a compelling story when developed for the big screen. 'Thanks, Gene. I really appreciate it.'

He says he'll email over all the details for a video call with Jerry before we ring off. I almost do a Roxy-style jump-clap before I remember I'm in a public place, so instead do an internal happy dance. I dash back inside with a wide smile that I can't smother and tell Roxy everything.

'Ooh, Evie! What great news! Wait. So does this mean you'll stay on our island?'

I'd been too excited by the job prospect to think that far ahead. 'If all goes well, then I guess it does!'

'Yay!'

If I land this job I can work anywhere in the world. I can make new dreams. Or I could stay here with my beautiful gran. First up, I'll explain to Georgios. Be truthful and show my vulnerable side just as Gran suggested.

'Imagine you two lovebirds! Him reading manuscripts on the beach and you reading romance novels and that's your actual *job*. You are incredibly lucky bibliophiles.'

'*If* I get the job.' Normally I'd twist myself in knots worrying about what might go wrong with the interview, but I don't. From the way Gene described Jerry I know we'll gel. I'd hazard a guess Gene's been putting out feelers and found me the right fit because he's gifted when it comes people, which is why he's been so successful in the movie biz all these years.

'Let's cheers to opportunities then!' Roxy holds up her glass and we clink.

My interview with Jerry looms but there's no sign of Gran, who is a bit like Houdini at times and disappears when she's meant to work a shift. There's no other choice except to take my laptop into Bibliotherapy and hope that it's quiet enough for us to chat.

I set up a table in front of the peacock chair, my belly somersaulting with nerves. But they're the good kind, more anticipation, excitement at what might come of this opportunity if only I sell myself right. There's time for a quick pep talk. *I am smart, strong, capable and this is my dream job. No one deserves this job more than me. No one will work harder than me.*

I fire up my laptop and click the invitation that Jerry has sent. So far so good. There's not a customer about and even the birds outside are quiet.

Jerry joins the chat. He's got a crazy mop of bright red curls that are unkempt, as if he's been out in the wind and bright blue eyes that have a certain intensity to them.

'Hey, Evie, thanks for taking the time to chat. Where are you? That's quite a backdrop, all those colourful spines.'

'Hi, Jerry, thank you for the chance to interview. I'm in Santorini at my grandmother's bookshop, Bibliotherapy.'

He grins. 'Lucky you.'

'Right?' I tell him all about the bookshop and Epeolatry and he seems impressed by the way he jumps in to ask questions.

I'm chatting away about my love of reading when Pee Wee wanders into the screen behind me. 'Who is that little fella?'

I glance behind me. 'That's Pee Wee. Gran started a Rent-A-Dog initiative where we rent the dogs to customers who can loll outside with them and read in the sunshine. We donate that money to the shelter to help care for the other dogs they rescue. It's proven really popular and we've raised a great amount of money for them.'

'Your gran sounds like a great lady.'

Just as I'm about to answer, I see Pee Wee on screen, cocking his leg about to do what he does best and pee on the books. 'Sorry, one sec!' *How mortifying!* 'Pee Wee, no!' I admonish him as I scoop him into my arms and take him outside. What must Jerry think? This is a professional call and I've got a pooch peeing behind me!

When I return, red-faced, I find my laptop turned the other way and a noxious scent that can only mean one thing – oh God

I hope it wasn't audible. I quickly turn the screen back to face me and pretend everything is A-OK. 'Sorry about that, Jerry. Pee Wee is still learning his manners.'

Jerry's laughing, a deep chortle, and I'm guessing that means he heard Pork Chop. 'While you were gone another dog appeared, a brindle fella and let off a sound so loud your laptop did a one-eighty.'

I'm dead. *Kill me.* 'Oh, my apologies. That's, erm, Pork Chop. He's got a few issues with his—' Is this interview etiquette, talking about a dog's digestive upset? '—verbosity.'

It can't get any worse, so I cough and clear my throat, ready to wow him with my brilliance when Zeus appears and jumps into my lap, sending me sprawling backwards. The peacock chair tips over and we go flying. I hate to think of the angle Jerry's got on screen as we tumble backwards arm, legs, paws and tail a tangle.

Jerry is a mess of laughter, which is sweet and all, but the chaos surrounding me doesn't exactly show me in my best light. All I need now is Houdini . . .

I've done it again, summoned him with my mind! I stand, dust myself off and right the peacock chair. Houdini sticks his head up to the camera, his mouth wide with a wallet stuffed with euros.

'Who *is* that?' Jerry sputters, his eyes watering from laughter. I'm not quite sure how to gain control. I right the peacock chair and sit, patting down my hair and act as if this is just another day in paradise. 'Is that a wallet in his mouth?'

'Ah, that's Houdini. He's got a slight issue with stealing wallets, purses, phones and the like. We're working on it but it's proving to be quite difficult. We still haven't found where he stashes the cash.'

Sir Spud doesn't want to be left out and enters the frame, before dramatically rolling over, letting out a bloodcurdling howl and playing dead.

'Is that fluffy fella OK?' Jerry asks.

'That's Sir Spud. He's playing dead for a treat. Ruled by his belly, that one.'

The dogs chase each other and bark up a storm. I can't think straight while they're yapping and dodging and doing circles around my chair. Little Lily enters the fray and yaps once, and they all go quiet. What on earth? Lily stares them down with a beady eye as if warning them to behave. Is she their leader? Well there you go! I'm grateful for the quiet and rush to fix this interview.

'As you can see we've got an eclectic mix of personalities here and . . .'

He cuts me off. 'You've certainly got your hands full there, Evie.' Jerry's screen stutters as if he's picked up his laptop and is moving. Oh no, has he lost interest because of the chaos here?

Jerry walks down a hallway into a large sunroom. 'Meet my unruly bunch.' He slides open a door and a group of canines go berserk, barking and jumping, vying for this attention. 'We've got Sir Mix-A-Lot here, who would take on Pork Chop for breaking the sound barrier. Then there's Jumanji, who rules the jungle. Little Kitty who meows like a cat but is in fact a dog. And Buster, who likes to bust stuff up because he's the biggest. All rescues who have made their way into my heart.'

I laugh as I watch them interact with him. Maybe this hasn't been an unmitigated disaster? 'They're gorgeous.' And just like the gang of six, they go crazy in front of the camera, trying to get my attention.

'They're a handful but I wouldn't have it any other way.' He sits at an outdoor table and Little Kitty, the smallest dog I've ever seen, jumps up on Jerry's lap. 'So, Evie, tell me about what you're looking for?'

Jerry has a realness to him, an open and honest face. Already I feel secure with him. Anyone who adores dogs like we do must be a good person. 'I've loved books since my gran introduced me to fairy tales, and that love has never waned. My passion is finding those hidden gems – books that haven't made all the bestseller lists, that haven't been truly discovered yet – and turning them into films. There's so many beautiful stories that get overlooked for various reasons: lack of marketing, publicity and the likes. I want to share them with the world. There's a lot to be said for those quiet tomes, those forgotten stories that may shine the brightest if given the chance.'

'I agree.'

He does?

'Let me tell you a bit about the way I run things here, and if you like the sound of it, the job is yours.'

It's hard to keep cool but I manage it as Jerry enlightens me on his company and the way in which they work. The best part, my role is mostly autonomous!

'So what do you say, Evie?'

'I say when do I start?'

And it's as easy as that. There's an energy about Jerry when he talks about books that mirrors my own. We're going to get on just fine. Once I end the call I text Gene and thank him for finding me the perfect job.

He replies:

You deserve it. Now go find those beauties so I've got something to watch. G

Chapter 32

That afternoon before Epeolatry opens I find Gran sitting at the bar, solemn expression on her face, which brightens when she sees me. 'Drink, darling?'

'What are you having?' I point to the blood-red cocktail.

'The Stephen King.'

'Why? Feeling a bit murdery?'

She lets out a cackle. 'You could say that.'

Even though it goes against my daytime drinking rules I accept. I could use a little brain-numbing; there's so many secrets and dramas swirling in my mind it causes quite the headache.

'You've got news?'

'I have. Gene connected me with a guy called Jerry who owns an indie studio. He's after a book scout to find romcoms to develop for streamers. Low-budget gems, right up my alley. I had an interview today and he sent me a contract to sign.' I hadn't breathed a word to Gran about the new job prospect. I didn't want to jinx it and get her hopes up about possibly staying, only to snatch that away from her if it didn't pan out.

'Oh, Evie, you superstar. Didn't I tell you it was only a matter of time? Congratulations! We need to celebrate, darling, although you leaving is nothing to cheer about. Better make mine a double so I can drown my sorrows.'

I smother a grin. 'That's the thing, Gran. It's a flexible position. I can work anywhere. We have team meetings via video call. Once a book gets signed for development, I'll have to fly to meet the scriptwriters and do a handover but that's it.'

'You're staying in Santorini?' Hope shines in her eyes. It's so sweet it almost breaks my heart.

'If you'll have me?' I go behind the bar and mix our drinks. Who knew I'd become a dab hand at making cocktails?

'I'd love nothing more and you know it – I hope I get to keep you forever and ever.' I walk back with our drinks and place them down. She takes me into her arms and gives me a life-affirming hug. To be given extended time with Gran is so special it makes me wonder if things happened this very way for this very reason.

'Yeah? What will Konstantine say when he returns home to find me living here?' I'm probing, knowing full well he isn't returning anytime soon, in the hopes she'll finally share the truth with me. Clearing the deck of all the secrets seems like the best plan moving forward, so we can all have a fresh start.

'Oh, I have some bad news, darling. Drink up before I tell you.'

I take a slug, a terrible sense of foreboding washing over me. I search her face for clues; she wears an expression that is a mix of resignation and sorrow.

'There's been a terrible accident. Catastrophic, actually. There was an explosion and the Mexican oil rig became one big great ball of fire. The pressure catapulted a flaming Konstantine into one of the derricks before he fell off the side, unable to be located by the search-and-rescue team. It's presumed he's now shark food at the bottom of the Gulf of Mexico. Dreadful, dreadful stuff. My only hope is that he will live on inside a great white, or perhaps a mako shark.' She dabs a tissue at a suspiciously dry eye.

'What? It exploded! Did *everyone* die?' I get she's mad but would she really kill a boatload of innocents in some kind of rage-fuelled revenge attack? What am I even suggesting here? That my inno-cent, cute-as-a-button grandmother would stoop to murder! *Mass* murder, even! Yes, her trail record of dead husbands isn't ideal but perhaps she's just been especially unlucky. That happens when you live a full and rich life all over the globe like she has.

She plays with her jangly pineapple earring. 'No, luckily not. They were on the tail end of a shutdown, and he was the only one left on board.'

I frown. The cogs in my brain spin before landing on an answer that is obvious in retrospect. 'Gran, he's not *really* dead is he?'

With a sad sigh she contemplates the view outside. After an age she turns back to me, taking a swig of the Stephen King and smacking her lips together. Zeus must sense her unease and pops his chin on her leg, staring up at her with love in his eyes. 'He's as good as dead to me, darling. Now I have to convince Billy the Knuckle to leave him in one piece. Easier said than done.'

What! 'Oh my God. Billy the Knuckle, the mafia thug who threatened to cut your pinkies off?'

'Thug is a bit harsh, darling. He's just misunderstood. But yes, the one and the same. I had to call in the big guns. Don't pretend you don't know what's going on; I know your sneaky mother has had her PI all over this.'

'I uh, well, umm, yeah. OK, she has.'

'Can't leave well enough alone that woman. However, I expect I'll be getting my missing money back any day now. Billy the Knuckle and I made amends years ago. He's helped me out with a few skirmishes over the years, and because I'm a good friend, it's been reciprocated once or twice too. He had that little issue with the Colombians, and I'd bonded with them after the incident hiking through their tomato crop. What goes around, comes around.'

I have no words. I have none. Oh wait. 'Is he going to *kill* Konstantine for real? Like bang, bang, he's dead?' I'm make gun hands and then quickly drop them. I don't want to be an acces-sory to any of this madness!

'Would you mind if he did, darling?'

Umm.

'Joking! Joking. Billy the Knuckle is big on maiming, but me, not so much. I'll be grateful to get my money back and Konstantine can hide out in Mexico for the rest of his days.'

My mind is whirling at the speed of light and I can barely keep up with it. 'Wow, OK. So if Billy the Knuckle did go through with a bit of maiming, how bad are we talking here?'

Gran gives a loose shrug. 'Billy's threatening to cut off a couple of Kon's toes so he can't run away from his responsibilities in future. He suggests it would be doing his next wife a favour. He's more of a finger man usually but he said he'd make allowances because it was for me. Truthfully, Billy's all talk. He's upset that Konstantine stole from a little old lady and he just wants to help get my money back. Kon will be fine.'

What a relief! 'I'm sorry, Gran. I know you loved Konstantine.'

She gives me a bright smile. 'Don't be sorry, darling. As soon as the divorce comes through I'm getting married again. He's already popped the question!'

A divorce and another marriage? This is a lot to take in when my mind is already spinning. 'What! He proposed, already?'

'Yes, in my heartbreak I found comfort in another man's arms and that comfort soon turned to love.'

'Which man?'

'Zorba, darling. Who doesn't love a good pig famer?'

'Zorba?' I'm not sure why I'm so shocked. They've been hanging out for weeks. They even did the *Dirty Dancing* lift together, which suggests they spent a fair amount of time practising. His daily visits to upset the colour of the books now make more sense. He's just the right amount of wacky for her, if I consider him as husband material for Gran. 'Wow, I don't quite know what to say.'

'I've never felt so adored, so alive, as I am with Zorba. And husband ten is a nice round number to finish on don't you think?'

I give her a hug. You've got to love her. Nothing will ever keep her down. 'Ten is a nice round number. It's . . . auspicious, Gran.' If we overlook the two husbands number seven. 'That means we've got a wedding to plan!'

Chapter 33

There hasn't been a spare minute to chat privately with Georgios. Between the bookshop, Epeolatry and getting ready for our new jobs, we've always been surrounded by people in one way or another. I vow today will be the day I confide in him about the fake-dating and hope we can move on together from it.

My book scout job starts in a week, so Roxy's due in today to go over everything with me before she takes over role as bookseller and Gran's right-hand woman.

Roxy knows the ins and outs already but she wants to double-check the ordering process and how to balance the accounts if Gran needs help with bookkeeping when things are hectic at Epeolatry.

Roxy makes a far more sombre entrance than usual. Her face is pale and her eyes full of concern. My heart stops for a moment. I hope it's not bad news about her mom. She's been doing so well to the point that she's been weighing up whether to go back to work part-time with Athena at the Squashed Olive.

'Are you OK?' I ask. 'What's happened?'

Roxy scrapes her hair back and takes her regular stool. 'I'm fine. It's just . . .' Her voice wobbles like she's about to burst into tears.

'Is it your . . . ?'

Before I can rearrange the sentence in my head she blurts out. 'Evie, I overheard something today, and I don't know what to make of it. I – uh. There's no easy way to say this so I'm just going to say it, OK? I mean, I hope I'm wrong. Maybe I am wrong. Maybe I misheard. Or they meant someone else. Or there could be any number of reasons I'm wrong about this so keep that in mind.' Her face is puce as she wrings her hands. Whatever it is, she's afraid to tell me.

'O-K-K.' My first thought is perhaps the Konstantine news has broken. Or Gran and Zorba have been spotted canoodling, and that's confusing to people who don't know what a lying, cheating snake Konstantine is. But Roxy does know all about Konstantine so what else can it be?

'It's about Georgios.'

My stomach clenches. 'What about him?'

'Apparently—' She scrubs her face. I've never seen Roxy this uncomfortable before, as if she's itchy in her own skin and can't scratch. 'I'm really sorry Evie, but he's been fake-dating you under orders from his grandfather. Their ridiculous plan was made to keep tabs on Floretta and make sure she didn't do a runner without paying the rent that was owed.'

'WHAT!' Surely she's got this wrong. *I'm* the one fake-dating him, not the other way around. Have they found out about our plot and she's misunderstood? 'Tell me exactly what you heard.'

She exhales a long breath. 'OK, so I was picking up loukoumades from Maria for Mom, like I do every Friday, but they weren't ready, which is strange as she has a production line going there on account of how popular they are. You know she's famous for—'

'Stay on track, Roxy.'

'OK. OK, sorry. Maria asked me to wait as she was running a bit behind. I said sure, no problem, I'd go visit Georgios in his villa out the back. When I went to the screen door, Georgios and Yannis were having a heated conversation. I froze and then

271

I figured I'd backtrack to the kitchen and leave them to it but your name popped up, so I stopped . . .' she blushes scarlet '. . . and listened.'

'What did they say?'

'Yannis was telling Georgios that Floretta had paid the rent in full so there was no need to carry on fake-dating you now, unless he really wanted to continue with it. Yannis didn't think they'd need any more insider information about your gran since her business seemed to be up and running successfully, and gossip around town is you'd be leaving soon anyway. So he said it would be best if he broke it off with you, so Georgios could start the hunt for a real girlfriend, someone he could settle down with.' Oh God, can it be true? None of it was real?

My heart plummets. 'And what did Georgios have to say about that?'

'He mumbled about it being a stupid ploy to begin with and that he didn't think it had been necessary but at least you'd been fun to hang out with. He mentioned that in future it would be good if *he* could sort his own love life out the way he wants, choosing the woman he wants without their input, because look at what the old man had stooped to. Using him as a pawn for money and him spending his summer having to think before he utters a word to make sure he doesn't slip up.'

I knew it was too good to be true. Why did I ever believe a guy like him would be interested in a girl like me?

'I didn't hear the rest of it because Maria found me and told me the order was ready, and they both turned and saw me standing there. Georgios was so shocked he couldn't speak. He slumped his shoulders and appeared as if his world had just collapsed under him. No doubt he's coming up with some lame excuse but I wanted you to hear it from me first. I'm . . . devastated. You seemed so well suited. Book nerd *soulmates*. I can't imagine how he could do this. It's so cruel, so . . .' Roxy's words fall away as I grapple with what this means.

Dizziness washes over me. I feel sort of seasick, adrift. A feeling I'm very familiar with in my regular life. Stupid me thought this magical island had changed me. Made me brave, bold and beautiful, so much so that the likes of Georgios had been interested. I feel so foolish. So embarrassed.

Sure, I'd been fake-dating him too. But the whole time I believed he really did fancy me, and for that reason I'd opened up to him. I trusted him. And I fell in love with him. To find out it wasn't real on his part sends me into a tailspin, where I doubt everyone and everything. I'm mortified about the words he spoke to his grandfather about me. It seems so out of character, so unlike the Georgios I know, but I guess that was all an act too. I don't know the *real* Georgios.

The old Evie resurfaces, the anxiety-riddled woman so at odds with the world. I should have known this kind of love couldn't happen to me. That this exciting, sunny, vibrant life wasn't real. It was all make-believe. Every single date he took me on was a con. Panic rises and I find it hard to catch my breath. I gasp, as if I'm dying. Another god-awful plot twist in the Chronicles of Evie!

'What are you doing oh – put your head between your legs, Evie! Is it a panic attack? Oh God!' She grabs at her hair. 'I'm so sorry!' She pushes my head down. I close my eyes against the hurt and the pain and try to blank it all out and concentrate on sucking in oxygen.

But he's right there, every time I close my eyes. His words, all those sweet nothings he whispered to me, they were all fake? Eventually my breathing returns to normal and I manage to sit upright again. I remain still until the head rush evaporates. Those passionate kisses – fake too?

I lift my head. Roxy stares at me with rounded eyes, pools of concern. I want to tell her I'll be fine. It's all OK. But I can't get the words out. Maybe I deserve this, for lying to him? None of this feels good. It all feels so very wrong and all I want to do is pack my suitcase and flee. Get off this island and away from them all.

When I catch my breath I say, 'Thanks for telling me, Roxy. I'm glad you did.'

Her face is twisted with sadness. 'What will you do?'

I run a hand through my hair as my mind ticks over. 'I'll go home. I'll make sure Gran's OK and then I'll leave, probably this weekend so I'm ready to start work next week.'

'Nooo. Can't you stay?'

And face him every day? I couldn't. 'I don't think so, Roxy.'

She pours me a glass of water, which I accept gratefully and take small sips from. My heart is still hammering in my chest, so I focus on deep breaths to slow it down. Customers wander in and she greets them and then comes back to keep checking on me.

'I'm going to sit outside for a bit,' I say. 'We can go over everything in an hour or so?'

'Sure, sure take your time.'

I come back inside an hour later, mind made up. I will leave. I'll book a flight for tomorrow and I'll head back to Mom and Dad's apartment until I get on my feet again. Gran will be OK. She's got Zorba, Roxy and the gang of six.

Once I get on my feet, I'll find a place to live. Maybe somewhere a bit quieter than the city. Perhaps a house in Connecticut, so I can rescue a dog of my own and have a canine friend who will love me unconditionally. I'll become one of those reclusive dog ladies who only leave the house for walks and to visit dog-friendly cafés. I can live in a quiet little suburban bubble and read romantic comedies, play with my rescue dog who I'll name Fido, and exist in a safe space away from all the people peopling.

Shored up by the sunshine and the fact that I will get over this heartbreak by going back inside myself, I go to find Roxy.

Behind the counter, she's making up book bouquets. 'OK, shall we go over your list of questions?'

She gives me a nod. 'Yeah.' She says half-heartedly. 'Are you really going to leave?'

'Yes, but I'll visit from time to time, so don't worry, Roxy. And you can visit me too once I find a little place.'

Roxy bites down on her bottom lip and gives me a sad smile. 'Maybe you should talk to him first? Hear his side of it? I mean, what if I misheard or . . . ?'

Before I can answer Gran comes running in, panic in her eyes. 'Is Zeus in here?' While Zeus is one of the most outgoing of all the pooches, he's Gran's shadow and sticks by her side. When she's out he'll trot in and wait to be coddled by customers.

'No, wasn't he with you?' They'd gone for their usual morning walk. The last I saw of him, he'd been sunbaking whilst Gran had coffee in the garden.

'He was, and then I went to visit Zorba. When I left he was asleep on his bed and now I can't find him.'

'OK,' I say. 'Don't panic, maybe he's outside in Muses under the shade of the cypress tree?' After lunch the gang of six seem to head there for the shade and the Rent-A-Dog initiative – knowing there's a possibility of belly rubs and walks.

I run to Muses but only see the other five dogs. Zeus is hard to miss, being the biggest one. Still, I check under the sun loungers, behind the bookshelves and down the sides of the bookshop and call his name.

Roxy meets me, having looped around from the garden on the villa side of the property. 'He's not in her garden or in your villa, but the side gate was open.'

'OK, maybe he's just taken himself off for a walk.' Zeus knows the route; he walks it every single day with Gran.

'Gran, you mind the bookshop and Roxy and I will go down the path and look for him.'

Her face is pale with worry. 'OK, take your phone and call me as soon as you find him. I can't shake the worry someone has taken him.'

I give her a quick squeeze. 'He would have barked, Gran. All the dogs would have alerted us if that was the case.'

275

Gran's worry increases my own. He's a clever dog who knows his way around, but he wouldn't usually stray far from Gran. Maybe it's the thought of the cliffs and the fear that even a smart dog like him might get distracted sniffing away and take a tumble, not sensing the danger. Tears spring to my eyes so I turn away to hide them from Gran.

'We've got our phones. We'll bring him back soon,' Roxy says and we dash out into the bright day calling for him.

'Zeus!'

We shout his name over and again as we make our way down the path to the beach. 'Have you seen a fluffy dog about thigh-height?' I ask walkers as we pass. They shake their heads no. 'If you do see him, he belongs to Floretta at the bookshop on the cliff.'

'We'll keep an eye out.'

Roxy speaks to Greek locals and points to the bookshop.

We search back and forth, to no avail.

'Where can he be?'

She shakes her head. 'I don't know. Do you think someone *might* have taken him?'

It's a distressing thought. 'No, surely not.'

'What about Zorba's place? Maybe he tried to follow Floretta there and got lost.'

Zeus might have tried to follow her on her bike wondering why he wasn't invited along. 'Do you think he'd make it all that way after his big walk with Gran this morning?'

'Let's walk the way she cycles, and we might find him resting along the way.'

'Good plan.' It's a hot day and I'm concerned he's without water if he's trekking from one side of the island to the other.

We head to Zorba's place, my voice going hoarse calling out for Zeus. We go up and down hills. My calves are burning and I wish we'd thought to bring some water for ourselves. Gran's stricken expression springs to mind and I push myself to walk faster.

We get to Zorba's sprawling pig farm but the gate is locked

276

up tight. There are no cars in the driveway and no sign of Zeus.

'Shall we split up on the walk back,' Roxy asks. 'You go the beach route and I'll circle back from the main road?'

'OK, be careful on that road though.' So many cars whizz by at lightning speeds along those perilous bends. I really hope Zeus didn't head out that way, as it could be deadly for him and any car speeding along. While he's street smart he only walks along the quiet paths near the bookshop, not roads.

'Will do. Call me if you find him.'

'You too.' We hug and go our separate ways.

An hour and a half later I arrive back at the bookshop without Zeus. 'Is Roxy back?' I ask Gran whose hugs herself tight as if expecting the worst.

'No, she's not. No sign of him?' she says, her voice catching.

I shake my head. 'Not yet. Roxy took the other way back so maybe she'll have good news.'

'What if we don't find him?' Her eyes well up with tears. Gran's usually so stoic; I can't count on one hand the times I've seen her cry. It's gut-wrenching to witness and there's no way to fix it without producing Zeus for her.

I pull her in for a long hug. 'We'll find him, Gran. He knows his way home so he'll probably totter in when he gets hungry and has had enough adventure for the day. Sit down,' I say releasing her from my arms. 'I'll make you a cold drink.'

She stands there as if frozen. 'Zeus only knows the route from the cliff path. How could I have been so careless to leave the gate unlatched?' Gran folds in on herself and she suddenly looks all of her eighty-three years.

I rub her arms. 'Don't blame yourself. Maybe the breeze blew the gate open. It doesn't matter. We'll get him home, even if we have to search all night.' I grab a bottle of water for Gran. And then lather myself in sunscreen, preparing to retrace my steps in the hopes he has found his way back to the path that's familiar to me. 'What else do you need, Gran?'

'I'm OK, darling.' With teary eyes, she says, 'I'll phone Zorba to keep an eye out in case Zeus is still making his way there.'

'Good plan, and why don't you phone your neighbours too? Maybe one of them has seen him meandering past and we'll know which direction to look.'

'Yes. I'll call everyone now.' She goes behind the counter and gets out her well-thumbed telephone book. Argh. She's so old-school in many ways; it's so sweet it almost breaks my heart all over again. If we don't find Zeus – I hate to think how it will affect her.

While I wait for Roxy to get back I dash up a flyer on the computer. I find a recent picture of Zeus, smiling with a tennis ball firmly in his mouth, his fluffy fur blowing in the breeze. I add contact details. When Gran hangs up from Zorba I ask, 'Should we offer a reward?'

'Yes, darling, great idea. Make it a decent amount so if anyone does have him they'll bring him back. Write: *no questions asked*. I don't care what their motives are, I just want him home.'

I type in a hefty reward, hoping that he's lost not taken, because the thought of anyone having him for unscrupulous reasons is too awful to contemplate.

Roxy returns, face downcast. 'No luck?' I ask, even though it's obvious.

'Nothing.'

'Damn.' I go back to the computer and hit print on the flyers. They shoot out of the printer in a neat pile. 'Want to help me hang these around the place?' I ask Roxy.

'I'll get the staple gun.'

I give Gran a reassuring smile and promise her we'll come back with goofball Zeus. I only hope it's true.

The sun drops as Roxy and I make our way back to the bookshop. We stoop, eyes on the ground as if we're carrying the weight of the world on our shoulders. I swear we spoke to almost everyone who lives in the village and all of the holidaymakers. Not one person even caught sight of Zeus. It's like he up and vanished into thin air.

'I'm not looking forward to telling Gran,' I say, kicking the dirt as I go, annoyed with myself, the world, dog thieves. You hear about these sorts of thefts all the time, and my mind goes to dark places.

'Oh God I don't want to be there when you do.' Roxy checks her phone. 'It's dead. Is yours?'

'Yes, out of batteries too.'

'What if someone tried to call about spotting him?'

'I put the bookshop landline on the flyer too.'

'OK, that's good.'

As the bookshop gets closer our progress becomes slower. Neither of us have the heart to tell Gran her big fluffball is going to be sleeping elsewhere tonight.

We unlatch the gate and head to Gran's villa. I stop short when I hear laughter leach from an open window. Roxy and I exchange a glance and then break into a run. I slide the door open and see Zeus playing with a chew toy, happily munching away, seemingly oblivious to the concern he's caused.

'Zeus!' I bend to rub his fur and kiss to the top of his head. 'Where were you boy? You little escape artist!' Relief floods me that's he back and safe and that my precious Gran won't suffer any more heartache.

When I stand, I come face to face with Georgios.

'He was at Donkey Man's house,' he says. 'Floretta called me and told me he was missing so I went to help search.'

Donkey Man's house! Why didn't I think to start there? He went to play with his donkey pal!

Roxy laughs. 'We should have known.' She smacks her forehead.

'I'm glad he's home, Gran,' I say. 'I'm going to call it a night – it's been a long day.' Roxy gives me an almost imperceptible nod towards Georgios but the last thing I want to do now is talk with him. I'm mentally and physically done.

I spin on my heel and head to my villa. Before long there's a knock the door. I open it a smidge to find Georgios standing there, his brow wrinkled. 'Can we talk?'

'No.'

'I can explain.'

'It was never real, was it?'

'Open up, Evie. I don't want to do this in the dark.'

'No, Georgios, I'm tired. I've walked this entire island twice today and all I want to do is throw myself in the shower and then sleep for week.' Or a decade. Millenia.

'OK, that's fair. Can I come back tomorrow?'

Tomorrow. I'd planned on jetting out of here but with Zeus' disappearance I haven't had a moment to make the booking, tell Gran or explain fully to Roxy about the day-to-day running of the bookshop.

'Goodbye,' I say and shut the door so he doesn't see me cry.

Chapter 34

Over breakfast, I tell Gran my plans about leaving. Her face falls. 'But why? You were all set to stay?'

I explain to her about what Roxy overhead. 'Pish-posh. You did the very same thing for me, Evie, so what does it matter?'

'It matters because I *actually* fell for the guy.'

'And you're telling me he hasn't fallen for you?'

I stare at her.

'Don't give me that look. Have you talked to him, asked him about all of this?'

'No and I won't.'

'Evie, I hate to say this but you'll be making the biggest mistake of your life if you don't. Take it from me, I know a thing or two about love and you can't fake the way that guy looks at you. It's like the sun, stars and moon shine from your very eyes, and he's dazzled by you.'

'Oh please, it was an act.'

'Don't you "oh please" me. When I first met him, he was forlorn, never smiled. You saw him that very first day. He was an empty shell until you came along. He's been here every day, sometimes two or three times a day. That's not a guy pretending to be in love; it's a guy who is *in* love. He didn't have to take it that far, if it was indeed fake. And you'd be a bit of a hypocrite if you didn't give him a chance to explain.'

'Will it get you off my back if I do?'

'It will. But be open to it. Listen to him, darling, promise me that at least?'

'Fine.'

I push my uneaten breakfast plate away and send him a text asking him to stop by for a quick visit.

Ten minutes later he's there, his face pinched, worry in his eyes. He probably doesn't want this getting out around town or his next victim might be more wary of him. Oh yeah, he plays the part of innocent so perfectly. Gran jumps up and takes our plates. 'I'll get out of your hair, lovebirds.' Lovebirds. Hardly. She goes into her villa but doesn't hide the fact she's listening. She'll have a mesh indentation on her nose from how close she's got it pressed on the kitchen window screen.

'Evie—'

I slump against the table. 'Let's get this over with, OK? Gran's insisting I talk to you before I leave. So talk.'

'OK, can we go somewhere private?' Gran's pushed so hard against the mesh I'm sure she's going to fall clean out of the window.

We go to my villa. My suitcase sits on the bed, packed ready to go.

'You're leaving?' There's panic in his voice.

I nod and fold my arms. Try to channel my best glare but I don't have the heart for it.

'OK, let me start at the beginning. When you arrived my grandfather came up with this ridiculous fake-dating idea, which I instantly rejected because I thought it was a cruel thing to do. But you should know, the only reason he even thought of it was because I went home after I met you in the car park, and you had volcanic dirt all over your nose and said I'd met the woman I wanted to marry – but me being me, would have never mentioned a word to you. I'm just that hopeless when it comes to love.'

The woman he wanted to marry? 'That seems a little rushed.'

'Right? Instantly, I tried to snatch the words back but it was too late. I never speak openly like that, never. I'm convinced he came up with the whole fake-dating idea just to spur me on, to make me act on my feelings. And let me tell you something about my grandfather: he can guilt-trip like no other. I said no a hundred times, that it was ridiculous. One minute he was clutching his chest like he was having a heart attack, the next he was head-clutching and lamenting about the possibility of going bankrupt.'

Sounds strangely familiar. *Gran.* 'Go on.'

'He's a bit of a closed book at times, so I didn't know what was fact or fiction. Eventually he wore me down. What if he really did need the rent money as badly as he made out? Then what? He mentioned that my grandmother had to double her loukoumades orders to make ends meet and that concerned me. She had been spending long days in the kitchen and in this heat – were they really having money issues? If they were in trouble it made sense that they needed assurances Floretta would eventually pay up. So against my best judgement I agreed to the whole stupid premise.'

'With no care or concern for me?'

He grimaces. 'I didn't think you'd find out.'

'Would you ever have told me?'

'I told myself I'd do it every day, and then I lost my nerve.'

'Why did you tell him that at least I'd been fun to hang out with but you'd prefer to choose your own person in future?' It hurts, because it suggests he wasn't happy that I'd been the person they chose, as if I wasn't good enough.

'Because who does something like this? I wanted him to feel bad about what he made me do because it didn't sit right with me.'

I fold my arms. 'I'm sorry you had to waste your summer with a person like me . . .' While it would be hypocritical of me to be upset since I've done the same thing to him, I can't help but feel so betrayed having believed he liked me from the very first moment he asked me on a date. I should have known better – I should have kept my guard up because I'm not the sort of girl who gets the guy, the happy ever after; this has been proven time and again in my woeful love life. Yet, I walked straight into this with my heart open because in reality I felt an instant attraction to him that was made more intense when he seemed to feel the same about me. I actually believed it! And none of it was real.

He dashes his hands through his hair. 'No, Evie, you're misunderstanding. I said all of that to him *because* he put me in this predicament. And I've had to watch every word I uttered in case I slipped up. I didn't ever want you to find out what I'd done because I worried you'd turn on your heel and never look back and then I'd lose you for good and that would break my heart. What I hate most is that in going along with this plan you'll always think what we had wasn't real, and I'm telling you with my whole heart that it was; it is.'

Can I believe him or is this simply damage control? I don't know what to think anymore.

'If only I could press rewind, you'd see I'm genuine. I've been on tenterhooks about lying to you, but it was done under duress and because I love my grandparents and I was truly worried about their financial situation. But everything I said or did with you, I meant. I didn't lie and I didn't lead you on.' It's hard to hold on to any negative emotions because I can relate to this exact predicament. We were both stuck between a rock and a hard place, doing what we thought best for our families.

'You did lie.'

He gives me a nod. 'Not about my feelings for you.'

I'm torn because I want to trust in him, and I can't exactly say I don't understand his motivations.

'In the beginning I'd planned to take things very slowly so there wouldn't be any broken hearts along the way.'

'Very slowly? You open-lip kissed on the second date! You call that slow?' I'm outraged.

He gives me a wide smile. 'Well, *technically* you open-lip kissed me on the second date.'

'That's because you took me by surprise!'

'You jumped up onto my hips like some sort of octopus.'

I colour. 'I was trying for a jump-hug, and things got out of hand.'

'It's no one's fault – these things happen.'

'Not when you're me they don't.'

'The point is, I never planned to hurt you, and the only reason I agreed was because the very first moment I laid eyes on you I felt like this goddess had walked into my line of sight. All the while Floretta was showering me with criticisms and I was trying to translate what on earth was happening to me. Then you started threatening me that you have experience with making things disappear ... My dull grey world was suddenly this riot of colour.'

I can't hide my grin. I'm still proud I acted fierce with a capital F on orders from Posy. I really met the brief on that one. 'You can't go around yelling at little old ladies.'

'I wasn't yelling; it just sounds that way in our language. Greek people speak loudly and gesticulate wildly. It's how we express ourselves.'

'Hmm.' I make a mental note to confirm this is true with Roxy.

'It's true. Ask Floretta. She had been calling me some colourful names, but I'm not sure if she meant them or if they'd been lost in translation because her Greek is terrible. At one point she called me an obnoxious floral wheelbarrow, so I'm not sure ...'

'At least she's trying to learn the language.'

'Right, right. I fell for you hard and I spent every moment wishing I hadn't agreed to the plan because it felt all wrong. I wanted to broach it with you early on, but there's been one drama after another ...'

He goes quiet. This is the part where I fess up too. Will it end us for good? I can't say.

'I have something to tell you.'

'OK.' His expression is so sincere I falter.

I drop my gaze. 'I, too, had been convinced to fake-date you. By my beloved Gran who needed my help. I only had her best interests at heart. While it might have been a stupid idea, she figured it was the only solution to keep Yannis at bay until she got things back on an even keel.'

His eyebrows shoot up. 'What! Are you *serious* right now, Evie?'

Yikes. 'Deadly.'

He scrubs his face. 'So wait a minute – you were all prepared to pack up and leave because you found out I'd been ordered to fake-date you, yet the whole time you were fake-dating me? How is *that* fair?'

His eyes cloud.

I take a deep breath. 'It really isn't. But once I found out about you, I doubted everything and that hurt because my feelings are true. I'm sorry about lying to you. I guess we're both in the same boat with this, so we've just got to get past it somehow.'

He lets out a frustrated groan. 'I cannot believe this.'

'It's a little rom-commy. Like the plot of a book.'

His eyes glaze over like he's lost in thought and then he lets out a loud groan. 'Argh! I see it now.'

'What do you mean?'

'There's a whole lot more to this! I'll be back soon.' He dashes out then back in. 'I almost forgot.' He takes me in his arms, and gives me a Hollywood kiss, all the bells and whistles, leaning me back like I'm some sort of screen siren and smooching the life out of me until I'm breathless. 'Just proving this is real.'

'Wow.' That definitely didn't feel like a fake kiss.

'Back soon,' he says with a wink. A wink! What is he playing at!

'Where are you . . .' But he's off and running – to where, I can't even imagine. I find Gran suspiciously close to my villa, pretend-watering her garden.

'That's not even believable, Gran.'

'What ever do you mean?'

'For starters, you haven't turned the hose on, so holding it above the plants isn't doing a heck of a lot.' My mind spins while I wait for Georgios. What did he mean there's a whole lot more to this? I can't handle another plot twist today.

Gran nods. 'With the water on I couldn't hear anything.'

'Did you need to listen in?'

'Of course! Are you staying in Santorini with that perfect specimen of a man?'

I consider it. 'Maybe.' How can I hold on to any doubt after Georgios poured his heart out to me like that? We'd both been forced into the same situation because of our love for our grandparents.

'Maybe?

Gran tries her darndest to get all the scintillating details out of me but I don't share yet. I want to know where Georgios has disappeared to before I say anything. Zeus bounds over, standing excitedly in front of Gran, before giving her a human-like frown, not understanding why Gran's holding the hose but no water is escaping for his usual garden water games. 'Not now, Zeus,' she says. 'I'll take you to the beach soon.'

Georgios reappears, yanking on his grandfather's arm, almost dragging him through the gate. With his downcast expression it seems Yannis isn't exactly a willing visitor.

Georgios says something in Greek and points to me.

'Ooh,' Gran says, eyes twinkling. 'Tell her what exactly?'

Yannis takes his well-worn leather cap from his head and studies the ground, as if hoping it'll swallow him whole. What is going on? Is Georgios going to confront his grandfather in front of me? If so, it seems a little much.

'Georgios, it's OK. I don't need to speak to your grandfather about any of this.'

He gives me a 'just wait and see' smirk. 'OK, good point, Evie. If my grandfather won't speak up, how about you, Floretta? Want to enlighten Evie on your conniving little scheme?'

'What scheme?' I ask with a frown. Are these two allowed to be this close with the restraining order and all? Sure, they may have agreed to a truce but do the rules still stand?

'Go on,' Georgios urges, his eyes bright with a frenetic energy, a smile playing at his lips. 'I *knew* there was more to this; it just seemed too much of a stretch for them to ask us to fake-date for such thin reasons.'

My usually talkative Gran remains mute.

'What's he talking about, Gran?' I'm truly in the dark.

Chapter 35

Gran turns on the hose and mimes not being able to hear. The old doddery lady routine is back. I roll my eyes, and shut the hose tap off.

'Well . . .'

'Spit it out – we don't have all day.'

She makes a show of huffing and puffing before throwing the hose to the ground. 'Fine. Yannis, shall I?'

He gives her a nod and continues fiddling with his hat.

'Yannis and I were lamenting that our favourite grandkids remained resolutely single. And how could that be? They have the beauty, the brains. They're both a catch.'

Yannis smiles. 'They are.'

They share a secret laugh. What the hell is going on?

'We came up with a plan to set you two up. We knew a blind date wouldn't work – you've both railed against them in the past, plus you're both terrible at love, so one date wouldn't be sufficient time for you to see how suited you are. Thus the fake-dating idea was born . . .'

I reel. 'What? But you didn't even *know* I was coming to Santorini?'

She scoffs. 'Of course I did, Evie. You mother called and told

289

me you were on the way to keep an eye on me after she heard about my quickie marriage. She constantly calls and threatens me with all sorts of things but this time it gave me an idea . . .'

'But how? You were almost arrested for disturbing the peace. Unless . . . ?'

She grins. 'Genuis, wasn't it? Yannis is good friends with the Hellenic Chief of Police so we roped him into helping out. We had to make it believable, or it wouldn't have worked. We made sure we argued loudly in a public place with a lot of witnesses so it would travel up and down the grapevine so I'd have to call your mom and tell her and she'd send you straight over. She'd already told me the day before that you'd been made redundant so we had to move fast.'

As soon as I sent Mom the text the morning I was made redundant, she phoned Gran who set this whole crazy plan in place. By the time Mom and Posy called me the next day, Gran had already been fake-arrested and the restraining order was put in place, in the hopes I'd agree to come keep an eye on Gran. Talk about taking a risk I'd be convinced to come!

My eyebrows shoot up. 'When you commit, you really commit.'

'Thank you, darling.'

'Was Mom part of this?'

'God no! She's called the Fun Police for a reason.'

Yannis continues, in halting English, 'Once that took place we had the excuse that I couldn't be on the premises, so I had to send Georgios in my place.'

'We'd spoken to your driver, Evie, so we knew when you'd be arriving. Unfortunately your plane was late so we told him he had to make haste because Yannis had already sorted a time for Georgios to visit me so you'd see him in the flesh, arguing away and being mean to your dear old gran—'

'You . . . ! That driver almost killed me!' Now it makes sense why he drove like a bat out of hell. Golly.

'Oh don't be so dramatic, darling. You're alive aren't you?'

'I guess.'

'We figured we needed to up the stakes, so we made up the lie about me not having paid the rent, thus giving me the excuse you'd need to fake-date him to keep them sweet. Yannis would use the excuse that Georgios had to keep a close eye on us, and make sure the business was viable or he'd have to sell the property. If we both invented money troubles, we knew we could convince you to go along with our plan.'

'Are you saying you don't have money troubles? What about Konstantine?'

'Konstantine did take a chunk of money, darling. Silly me trusting a man with my bank account; I should know better, but I have other accounts. These are the things you come to learn after being married so many times.'

'So the rent – it was paid?'

'Yes, I pride myself on being a fabulous tenant. The rent has always been paid ahead of time. And Yannis owns half the island – he's doing just fine for money too.'

'All those bills with overdue stamps?'

'Fake.'

'The trades?'

'Paid in full.'

It explains why she had money to get her cement path done, all the stock that continued to arrive. 'Lucy? Did you pay her too?'

'Of course. She held out for quite a bit too, the minx. Signed an NDA so legally she couldn't talk about her appearance fee.'

'You crafty little—'

'But were we wrong?' Yannis pipes up. 'You're in love, no?'

How can we be mad at these two conniving grandparents, when their hearts were in the right place? The amount of effort they've put in to make such a scheme happen makes my head spin. 'I'd say – umm.' I can't just go declaring my love in front of everyone, can I?

'I'm in love with Evie,' Georgios says with a wide smile, pulling me into his arms. 'And without you two meddling we probably wouldn't have got every far. You're right, that there's no way I'd have agreed to a blind date. Not after the disasters they've set me up with before. So, I guess what I'm trying to say is – thanks?'

'Yeah, thanks. But can we agree this is the last scheme?' I dread to think what they might resort to if they suddenly see marriage or babies in our future.

Georgios plonks a kiss on the top of my head and our grandparents cheer. We turn when we hear the click of the gate latch.

'What is going on? Why do none of you answer your phone? We've got trouble. Big trouble. Billy the Knuckle is on his way here!'

It's my mom and Posy – they're here in Santorini.

292

Chapter 36

Georgios mouths, *Billy the Knuckle?*

I shrug, clueless how to mime the whole sorry Billy the Knuckle history in a few gestures and lost in the shock of Mom and Posy's sudden appearance. It was bound to happen but I thought they'd at least warn us they were on their way. The Fun Police usually arrive all guns blazing, sirens shrieking, lights flashing, that kind of thing. Unless they wanted the element of surprise? That makes more sense.

'When it rains it pours,' Gran says with a groan. But I know she's secretly happy to see Mom and Posy. She probably knew they were coming. Gran's not averse to hiring a PI either, when it suits.

Mom's face is a picture of concern. 'Did you hear what I said? Billy. The Knuckle. The mafia hood. Coming here. Probably to kill you.'

'Kill who?' Roxy gasps and pushes past Mom, alarm on her face. 'I heard all the commotion from inside the bookshop! What have I missed? You guys have made island life so exciting! Never a dull moment! Who are they?' She jerks a thumb to Mom and Posy.

'The Fun Police,' Gran says.

'The Fun . . . ? OK.' Roxy knows by now to watch and listen when it comes to Gran and whatever gnarly situation she's got herself into this time.

Mom rolls her eyes at Gran's description. 'I'm Adeline, Evie's mom, and this is my Broadway performer daughter Posy.' She can't help herself that woman. 'And we've got ourselves a situation here, so if you wouldn't mind we need some privacy.'

'They can stay,' I say. 'They're our island family.'

Mom harrumphs but lets it slide. 'Fine. I'll repeat myself! Billy is on his way *here*! My PI tracked his flight to Mexico. He had a run-in with Konstantine and now he's on his way to Santorini! He may be on the island already. How he and Kon are connected remains a mystery but the PI is investigating possible links now.'

Gran and I exchange a glance. She knows full well what links there are. I give her a nod to come clean. It's only a matter of time before Mom's PI stumbles on the answers anyway and we may as well put her out of her misery. 'Yes, darling,' Gran says. 'It's true. Billy is on his way here because he's returning something of mine.'

Posy's eyes widen 'What is he returning? Konstantine's fingers? His *heart*? After he broke poor Gran's!' Talk about dramatic!

'Wait – you *hired* Billy the Knuckle?' Mom cries out. 'But you two are sworn enemies! Have you forgotten he wanted to chop off your pinkies and post them to me in the mail?'

Gran rolls her eyes heavenward. 'Oh you do exaggerate. He'd never have posted them, they x-ray mail these days, darling. A couple of displaced fingers would never have gotten through.'

Mom rubs her temples. 'The point is not the fingers; the point is the *threat*! He's a dangerous man! A dangerous man who . . .' she lowers her voice to a hiss '. . . maims people for kicks.'

'Does he though? We don't know that for sure. Besides, it's business, darling, it's not personal.'

The gate opens once more, and we turn to find a very ordinary man with a pale complexion wearing beige *everything* standing there, surveying our group. When he clocks Gran, his face melts into a smile.

'Floretta!' He moves to her and gives her a big hug. 'You never

294

age.' He's familiar but I can't put my finger on it. Ah. Got it. If Elon Musk and Mark Zuckerberg had a love child, this guy would be it.

Wait. This *can't* be wise guy Billy the Knuckle, surely? I turn with a question on my lips but am distracted when my gaze slides to Roxy. Her jaw is practically on the ground and I swear I hear her humming the wedding march. Huh? For this guy?

'Age is a construct. Everyone, this is Billy the Knuckle.'

This guy is the out-of-control mafia hood? He just seems so . . . *un*threatening. Like someone who plays video games all day rather than be a thug for La Casa Nostra. It could be a very clever disguise, a way to hide in plain sight. You always have to be one step ahead in this world so I expect the underworld is even more challenging in that respect.

Billy grunts. 'I've got that little . . . package you requested, Floretta.' I hold my breath, hoping it's not a body part. He hands her a surprisingly big duffel bag. Maybe Gran was right and Greek men do have the biggest—

'My money? You got it all back?' Money! Of course!

'With interest. And let's just say he'll have a little trouble playing those poker machines in future.'

'He lost a finger?'

'It's my calling card, Floretta. You *know* that.' Everyone gasps and hides their own hands.

Ah! That's why he's called Billy the Knuckle! He removes their fingers, I presume up to the knuckle . . . Yikes.

Billy grins. 'Joking, joking, guys! I'd never do that, well not this time anyway. Floretta is a pacifist and I respect that. Kon and I had a little chat about manners and morals, and then I got his mom on the phone. Greek men are the same as Italian men when it comes to their mothers. Let's just say he's more scared of her punishment than any I could dole out.'

Wow, clever.

'Thanks, Billy.' Gran grins. 'I appreciate your restraint.'

Everyone's too wide-eyed to speak. Roxy's making love-heart

eyes at the mafia hood. She can't love a guy who chops fingers off for a living for crying out loud! Some women just love a good bad boy – it can't be helped.

'Well I have no idea what time it is, but I need a drink,' Mom says.

'I concur,' says Gran.

'I could drink,' Posy says.

'Let me show you Epeolatry,' I say.

This motley group of people and our motley gang of dogs follow me inside and we spend the afternoon imbibing way too much alcohol, because sometimes, you've just got to roll with the punches and it's been a helluva few days.

Guitar Guy pops his head in brandishing a book. 'Helena! Helena!' he cries.

'Helena, haven't seen her,' I say by rote.

He points excitedly to the cover of the book and I note the title: *Helena* by Evelyn Waugh. I face-palm. This whole time he was looking for a *book* called Helena! In retrospect, it seems wildly obvious. 'Another mystery solved!' I invite him in for a drink and he readily agrees.

Chapter 37

'I'm sorry things didn't work out with you and Billy the Knuckle,' I say to Roxy, telling yet another porky pie.

'Gah, he had that big . . . tech energy, you know?'

Yeah more like gamer boy than wise guy. 'He did not look the way I expected. Blame the movies.'

'Really? I thought he was dreamy. But after all is said and done I'm not sure I could love a mafia hood. The movies do add a touch of glamour and mystique, but all I can imagine is Billy coming home after a long day with a range of different-sized pinkies in plastic baggies – it's a little stomach-turning. But argh!' Roxy grabs her hair and scrunches it. 'He would have made beautiful babies!'

'Plus his work-life balance is no good.'

'True. I'd be left with the screaming babies while he's off to God knows where to do God knows what. If this were a book do you think there's a chance I'll find love in the sequel?' She gives me a hopeful smile.

'Every chance. You'd be the heroine in book two and I'll be your trusty sidekick.'

'So there's hope?'

'There's always hope, *always*.'

'I'm off to open Bibliotherapy. Meet for lunch?'

'Sure.' Technically, I'm 'working' with a book open on my lap. And this book has real promise. It just might make it all the way to the screen. A fun fake-date trope – what's not to love? I have high hopes it'll be a fan favourite.

The day ticks along and when I look up Georgios is there, manuscript in hand. 'Got room for one more?' He motions to my 'office desk', which is the outdoor table and chairs.

'Pull up a chair.' I grin.

We work quietly together for a few hours and then it's time for my Greek lesson. He's teaching me the language and while I find it difficult, I'm a tenacious student and vow to be fluent as fast as possible.

'I have a special word for you today.'

'Ooh.' I love his special words. I'm learning the basics but each day we have one beautiful word that captures my imagination.

'This word is how I feel about you.'

'OK.' My heart speeds up.

'*Kapsoura*.'

'*Kapsoura*.' I say the word, enjoying the shape and melody of it. 'What does it mean?'

'Well that's just the thing, there's no exact English translation for such a word; nothing comes close to defining the amount of desire and passion it evokes. It's describes a type of love that burns so fiercely it almost consumes itself.'

'It's highly combustible – sounds dangerous.'

He laughs. 'An explosion of love.'

'A supernova.'

We kiss as if our hearts are truly on fire, as if we're stars heavy with heat all set to explode. *Kapsoura*. A love that burns so brightly.

Chapter 38

Gran and I are playing with the dogs, waiting for Zorba and Georgios to arrive for a barbecue dinner. Mom and Posy are inside assembling salads. After two long weeks, they go home tomorrow and I'm already missing them, even though Posy has been getting on my last nerve. Sisters, eh?

I think back to how much has changed since I've been here and how crazy it is that everything has worked out, in one way or another, either with brute force or naturally. Still, there are some questions that remained unanswered.

'Gran, what really happened to all of your husbands?'

Gran shifts her gaze to the heavens. 'They died tragic deaths and no I wasn't involved and if any detectives ask you, you don't know a thing. Call it selective amnesia.'

I scratch Sir Spud's ear. 'Gran.'

She moves to a sun lounger next to me. The breeze blows her long thick hair back. Love gives her a vitality. It's evident in her bright eyes, her happy smile.

'OK, OK, fine. They're all alive and kicking.'

I gasp. *What!* I take a moment to process the men I thought suffered horrible early deaths. 'Why the dramatic demise stories?' They're alive!

Gran stirs her Virginia Woolf cocktail with a swizzle stick shaped like a pineapple. 'Love should be wild and fun. Admitting we broke up because I couldn't stand the fact Vlad insisted the bed be made with hospital corners every damn day doesn't sound exactly thrilling, does it? He'd clean behind me as I made coffee or a sandwich as if any crumb would be his undoing. Jimmy from Australia was fun. We danced those tropical nights away, until the shine wore off, and we stared at each other across a plastic table in a house with no air-conditioning and realised we didn't have a thing left to talk about. Talk about mundane! I loved my husbands with all of my heart – until I didn't. And don't get me wrong, some fell out of love with me first, like Irish Sean who just wasn't the commitment type. For some the spark was there and then it died and I didn't want to waste another minute in their company. It happens. I'm a hopeless romantic, Evie, and I always will be. Maybe I jumped into marriage too soon with some, but I don't regret a single thing. What's love if not a gamble? And that's a risk I'm *always* prepared to take.'

I consider it. It's beautiful, really. That no matter what, she was always willing to give her heart away, even if it had been bruised before. She'd risk it all for the hopes of finding love again. Her *kapsoura* moment. She didn't shy away from it ever.

But wait a minute. 'What about my grandad? If he's alive how come we've never seen him?'

'Oh Gerald? Sorry to tell you this, darling but he really *is* dead. There was that terrible mix-up with the antifreeze.'

'Really?'

She gives me a 'what can you do' shrug. 'Accidents happen.'

Life resumes a slower pace once Mom and Posy leave. Summer is slowly drifting away but the days are still warm and the nights balmy. Georgios texts me about joining him on a hike. Honestly island life is an exercise in itself. There's always a hill, a cliff, or water to traverse.

When he arrives he plays with the pooches who won't let him get near me until they've had a chance to play first. He knows all their quirks and moves his wallet to his shirt pocket so Houdini can't steal it. *Again.* A few days ago, when I was cleaning my villa, I found Houdini's stolen stash of credit cards and cash hidden under my bed. We've done our best to return them to their rightful owners but it's proven hard to track some of them down. You live and learn. Doesn't stop Houdini from his thievery though, so we've had to make signs that read: Beware of the dog – he will steal your wallet. Always a good conversation starter.

Georgios gives Gran a peck on the cheek. 'Would you like to join us on a hike, Floretta?'

She waves him away. 'No, darling man, but thanks for the offer. Zorba is coming over to talk wedding plans. We're thinking Vegas?'

'Vegas, Gran!? Really?'

'Not really. Just wanted to get a rise out of you and look, it worked.'

The minx.

'OK, well we're off,' I say.

'Enjoy, lovebirds.'

Georgios takes my hand and we walk towards the caldera. There's a gorgeous view from a vantage point I haven't seen before and he assures me the arduous climb is worth it. We chat about our lives, how we're living the dream. A dream that seemed just out of reach at the start of summer. As always, he manages to distract me from the burning in my muscles, either that or I'm truly getting fitter and what an achievement that is for this bookworm.

After an age we get to our destination. I'm breathing heavily but the view is worth it. 'It's a heart!' I cry out. Carved by nature into a great big rock is a love heart. Through it you can see the Aegean Sea, the caldera and the volcano.

'It's one of the island's best-kept secrets. *The heart of Santorini.*'

'It's beautiful. I'll even forgive you for bringing me so close to a volcano.'

He laughs and takes me into his arms. 'This is our heart, Evie.'

'Formed by the elements and will last forever?'

'Exactly.'

I turn to him and stare deeply into his eyes, see myself reflected back. See the radiance of someone truly in love for the first time. That love has changed me for the better. It's made me trust in myself, and in others. Opened me like a flower. All my life I felt like I was lacking, I was missing some crucial element, but Georgios has made me realise it wasn't me who had to change, it was the world around me. I'm perfect just the way I am.

We kiss with the Heart of Santorini as a backdrop. It feels like a sign. Like I'm right where I'm meant to be. With Georgios' hand in mine. A man who loves me, quirks and all.

When we pull apart he says, 'Will you marry me one day, Evie?'

I glance at the heart, sure it's pulsing, telling me to say yes, my dating rules be damned. I've always lived in a cloud of doubt, but that part of me is gone. Replaced by this deep abiding romance. The trust that this is true love.

'I'm free next week?'

He throws his head back and laughs.

'I'll take that as a yes?'

'Yes. One day. When the sun sinks into the horizon, turning the water a flame-coloured hue. That'll be our moment. Our *kapsoura*.'

We kiss once more in front of our Grecian blue sea backdrop, framed by a love heart made from solid rock.

A Letter from Rebecca Raisin

Thank you so much for choosing to read *Summer at the Santorini Bookshop*. I hope you enjoyed it! If you did and would like to be the first to know about my new releases, you can sign up to my mailing list.

Sign up here! bit.ly/RebeccaRaisinSignUp

I'm a huge fan of travelling and take inspiration from places I've visited or intend on seeing in this great big world of ours. I love immersing myself and learning about culture, food and history. My greatest wish is that my books take you on a journey so you feel you've had a mini holiday from the comfort of your own home.

I hope you loved *Summer at the Santorini Bookshop* and, if you did, I would be so grateful if you would leave a review. I always love to hear what readers thought, and it helps new readers discover my books too.

Thanks,

Bec xx

http://www.rebeccaraisin.com/

https://twitter.com/jaxandwillsmum

https://www.facebook.com/RebeccaRaisinAuthor

https://wwwtiktok.com/@rebeccaraisinwrites

The Little Venice Bookshop

A bundle of mysterious letters. A trip to Venice. A journey she'll never forget.

When Luna loses her beloved mother, she's bereft: her mother
was her only family, and without her Luna feels rootless. Then
the chance discovery of a collection of letters in her mother's
belongings sends her on an unexpected journey.

Following a clue in the letters, Luna packs her bags
and heads to Venice, to a gorgeous but faded bookshop
overlooking the canals, hoping to uncover the truth
about her mother's mysterious past.

Will Luna find the answers she's looking for –
and finally find the place she belongs?

Elodie's Library of Second Chances

Everyone has a story.
You just have to read between the lines . . .

When Elodie applies for the job of librarian in peaceful Willow
Grove, she's looking forward to a new start. As the daughter of
a media empire, her every move has been watched for years,
and she longs to work with the thing she loves most: books.
It's a chance to make a real difference too, because she soon
realises that there are other people in Willow Grove who
might need a fresh start – like the homeless man everyone
walks past without seeing, or the divorcée who can't
seem to escape her former husband's misdeeds.
Together with local journalist Finn, Elodie decides these people
have stories that need sharing. What if instead of borrowing
books readers could 'borrow' a person, and hear the
life stories of those they've overlooked?
But Elodie isn't quite sharing her whole story either.
As the story of the library's new success grows,
will her own secret be revealed?

An uplifting story about fresh starts, new beginnings and
the power of stories, from the bestselling author of *Rosie's*
***Travelling Tea Shop*!**

Rosie's Travelling Tea Shop

REBECCA RAISIN

The trip of a lifetime!
Rosie Lewis has her life together.

A swanky job as a Michelin-starred sous chef, a loving
husband and future children scheduled for an exact date.
That's until she comes home one day to find her husband's
pre-packed bag and a confession that he's had an affair.
Heartbroken and devastated, Rosie drowns her sorrows in
a glass (or three) of wine, only to discover the following
morning that she has spontaneously invested in a bright pink
campervan to facilitate her grand plans to travel the country.
Now, Rosie is about to embark on the trip of a lifetime, and
the chance to change her life! With Poppy, her new-found travelling tea shop in tow, nothing could go wrong, could it . . . ?

**A laugh-out-loud novel of love, friendship and adventure!
Perfect for fans of Debbie Johnson and Holly Martin.**

Acknowledgements

Dear Reader, as always my greatest thanks go to you. Your support means the world and allows me to continue getting lost inside a story, conjuring characters who I hope touch your heart. It's a gift to be able to work doing what I love and I don't take that lightly. Each sale, review, share is so very appreciated.

Thank you to my family who are always understanding of my work-life and those weekends I'm locked away. You're the best.

Thanks to Abi Fenton and Aud Linton for such exceptional editorial work. I've really enjoyed working on this book with you. Thank you also to Helena Newton who always has such an incredible eye for detail. And to Helen Williams, who somehow picks up the tiniest of errors that we miss. The design team at HQ are incredible and always make the best covers, thank you. Thank you to sales and marketing at HQ – there are so many superstars behind the scenes that help shape and share my work and I'm so very grateful for them all.

Thanks to Helen Boyce from THE Book Club and the review team, you're all gems. Thanks to Rachel Gilbey for hosting the world's most amazing blog tours. Time we met somewhere else in the world, eh? For Frankie and Belinda, who are always there to cheer or cheer up! Love you girls. And to Hilary Steel, thanks for everything, you truly are a keeper!

Thanks,

Bec xx

Dear Reader,

We hope you enjoyed reading this book. If you did, we'd be so appreciative if you left a review. It really helps us and the author to bring more books like this to you.

Here at HQ Digital we are dedicated to publishing fiction that will keep you turning the pages into the early hours. Don't want to miss a thing? To find out more about our books, promotions, discover exclusive content and enter competitions you can keep in touch in the following ways:

JOIN OUR COMMUNITY:

Sign up to our new email newsletter: http://smarturl.it/SignUpHQ

Read our new blog www.hqstories.co.uk

𝕏 https://twitter.com/HQStories

f www.facebook.com/HQStories

BUDDING WRITER?

We're also looking for authors to join the HQ Digital family!

Find out more here:

https://www.hqstories.co.uk/want-to-write-for-us/

Thanks for reading, from the HQ Digital team